OVER THE FENCE

Also by Mary Monroe

The Neighbors Series
One House Over
Over the Fence

The Lonely Heart, Deadly Heart Series
Every Woman's Dream
Never Trust a Stranger
The Devil You Know

The God Series
God Don't Like Ugly
God Still Don't Like Ugly
God Don't Play
God Ain't Blind
God Ain't Through Yet
God Don't Make No Mistakes

The Mama Ruby Series
Mama Ruby
The Upper Room
Lost Daughters

Gonna Lay Down My Burdens
Red Light Wives
In Sheep's Clothing
Deliver Me From Evil
She Had It Coming
The Company We Keep
Family of Lies
Bad Blood

"Nightmare in Paradise" in *Borrow Trouble*

Published by Kensington Publishing Corp.

OVER THE FENCE

MARY MONROE

KENSINGTON BOOKS
www.kensingtonbooks.com

DAFINA BOOKS are published by

Kensington Publishing Corp.
119 West 40th Street
New York, NY 10018

All Kensington titles, imprints, and distributed lines are available at special quantity discounts for bulk purchases for sales promotion, premiums, fund-raising, educational, or institutional use.

Special book excerpts or customized printings can also be created to fit specific needs. For details, write or phone the office of the Kensington Special Sales Manager: Attn. Special Sales Department. Kensington Publishing Corp., 119 West 40th Street, New York, NY 10018. Phone: 1-800-221-2647.

Library of Congress Card Catalogue Number: 2018912548

Dafina and the Dafina logo Reg. U.S. Pat. & TM Off.

ISBN-13: 978-1-4967-1614-9
ISBN-10: 1-4967-1614-0
First Kensington Hardcover Edition: April 2019

ISBN-13: 978-1-4967-1616-3 (e-book)
ISBN-10: 1-4967-1616-7 (e-book)

10 9 8 7 6 5 4 3 2 1

Printed in the United States of America

*This is for Dr. Maya Angelou
and my "other mother," J. California Cooper.
I miss you both!*

Acknowledgments

I am so blessed to be a member of the Kensington Publishing Corporation family. Selena James is an awesome editor and a great friend. Thank you, Selena!

Thanks to Steven Zacharius, Adam Zacharius, Lauren Vassallo, Karen Auerbach, Vida Engstrand, the wonderful crew in the sales department, and everyone else at Kensington for working so hard for me.

Thanks to Lauretta Pierce for maintaining my website and sharing so many wonderful stories with me.

Thanks to the bookstores, libraries, awesome book clubs, my readers, and the magazine and radio interviewers for supporting me for so many years.

A very special thanks to one of the best literary agents on the planet, Andrew Stuart.

Keep the e-mails coming to me at AuthorAuthor5409@aol. com. Visit my website at MaryMonroe.org, and communicate with me on Facebook.com/MaryMonroe, and Twitter @MaryMonroeBooks.

All the best,

Mary Monroe

The Neighbors
Book 2

Hell is empty and all the devils are here.

The Tempest
William Shakespeare

CHAPTER 1
YVONNE

August 1937

*L*ESTER FULLBRIGHT HAD VISITED ME ONCE EVERY OTHER MONTH in the women's prison camp where I had been the state of Alabama's guest for almost two years. He was the man I'd been living with when I got arrested. He'd told me that when they let me out, I could move back in.

But when I arrived at his house that Thursday evening, the day I got released, he looked surprised and a little annoyed when he opened the door. "Yvonne, what the hell you doing here? You ain't supposed to get out until next week!" He looked over my shoulder in both directions as he waved me in.

I felt sure enough frumpy in my drab release outfit: a mud-colored cotton dress, matching paper-thin slippers, and dingy white bobby socks. My hair was in three limp plaits. I had a brown paper bag that contained a few pieces of underwear, the dress I'd been wearing the day they locked me up, my Bible, a comb, and two baloney sandwiches. I'd had a wallet with four dollars and some change in it when they checked me in, but it had mysteriously disappeared. Stuffed way down in my brassiere was ten dollars gate money and a bus ticket back to the county I'd been arrested in. Them two things, and the baloney sandwiches, was what every inmate got on their way out. The bus ticket hadn't done me no good, because the closest depot was even farther than my destination. The sandwiches had such a foul smell, I wouldn't have fed them to a hungry hog.

"Did you escape?"

"Do you think I'd be stupid enough to bust out of jail with only a week to go? They turned me loose early for good behavior." I took a deep breath and set my bag on the floor.

"Whew! Praise God I ain't got to worry about them laws coming after me for harboring a fugitive."

"The same day they told me they was letting me out, I sent you a letter. I told you to find somebody with a truck or a car and come pick me up today."

"Well, I don't know where that letter went, but it sure didn't come to me. You know how bad mail delivery service is in colored neighborhoods. The only things that always make it to me on time is my bills. How did you get here?"

"I walked."

Lester's mouth dropped open so wide, I could see all his back teeth. "Say what? You walked *ten* miles by yourself through dangerous Ku Klux Klan territory?"

"I didn't have no choice. You wouldn't believe how many snakes and lizards I had to dodge. I got so thirsty and hungry, it's a wonder I didn't pass out. If I hadn't come across a spring and a blackberry bush by the side of the road, there ain't no telling what might have happened to me in that hot sun. Anyway, after I'd covered about five miles, a farmer came along on his mule wagon. He gave me a ride the rest of the way."

"Oh. The important thing is you made it home." Lester gave me the once-over and frowned. "You look like a scarecrow in that dowdy frock, but you still a sight for sore eyes," he declared with a great big smile. "Give me some sugar." He puckered up, wrapped me in a bear hug, and gave me a rough kiss on my chapped lips. "We should stop wasting time and get loose so we can celebrate your homecoming. Don't you think so?"

"Yeah, I guess," I muttered. After the wretched day I'd had, the last thing I wanted to do was get loose in bed with a man. But I wasn't in no position to say no. I glanced around the living room. As gloomy as it was, it was paradise compared to where I'd just come from. On top of dirty clothes scattered all over his floor, coal-oil lamps sat on his dusty coffee table and both end tables. There was more clothes and other odds and ends on the saggy couch. "It's good to be free again. We can celebrate, but I need to wash and lotion up first." I slid my tongue across my lips and couldn't believe how dry they felt, even after Lester's sloppy kiss.

"You know where everything is at. Make sure you put some calamine lotion on them ashy lips. And hurry up, so I can show you how much I missed you."

After I took a quick bath and scarfed down two peanut butter sandwiches and a glass of buttermilk, Lester grabbed my elbow and steered me to his bed. We stayed there for the next hour.

Once he was satisfied, he sat up with his back against a stack of pillows, gazing at me with his eyes narrowed. He started laying out the rules in a gruff tone, which was odd for a man that had squealed with pleasure the whole time he was humping me a few minutes ago. "We better get a few things straight right now. You had it easy the last time you stayed with me. You was lazy, spoiled, and came and went as you pleased." I sat up, but I kept my mouth shut, because he was telling the truth. "I ain't going to put up with all that foolishness this time. If you want to stay under my roof, you going to get a job and pay half of the rent. You'll cook all the meals, keep the house clean, wash the clothes, and everything else I tell you to do."

"Is that all?" I sneered.

"Naw! You'll pay half for the utilities, food, and every other household expense. We straight?"

"We straight," I mumbled. I would have agreed to anything because I was too tired to argue. All I wanted to do was relax, organize my thoughts, and figure out what I was going to do with the rest of my life.

"And another thing," Lester continued, wagging his finger in my face. "If I find out you fooling around with other men, you will suffer.

"I ain't going to fool around on you," I assured him, shaking my head. "I ain't never cheated on none of my men."

Lester wasn't the best boyfriend in the world, but the best I could do at the time. He was a little on the bossy side, unpredictable, and self-centered. I'd always overlooked his faults because I liked his light brown skin; cute baby face; hard, trim body; and good hair. He always had a decent job, and he had never beat me. Besides all that, he had been hinting for years that he might make me his wife someday. Since Lester had more of the things I liked than any other man I'd been with, I assumed he'd make a good husband. He was thirty-six now, and I was thirty, so I prayed that he'd be ready to marry me soon.

I could have moved back in with Aunt Nadine and Uncle Sherman. They had raised me after my mama and daddy died in a tractor accident when I was six. My aunt and uncle had moved to Mobile last month, and I wanted to stay on in Branson. It was just another typical segregated small town in Alabama, but I never wanted to relocate because it was the only home I'd ever knowed. And it kept the memory of my parents alive. Most of the residents in our part of town lived on dirt or gravel roads, in ramshackle houses. Lester's place was one of the few on our block that had an inside toilet. The folks that didn't have one had to use the numerous common-area outhouses. Every house had a potbellied stove in the living room, and almost everybody had a garden, a bunch of chickens, and unruly kids running around in their yards. Some folks had backyard pigsties. Unless it was hog-butchering time, they'd let their pigs roam around in the yards, too. Lester was a simple man. He didn't want no livestock or kids, because he believed they would be too much trouble. I didn't agree with him, but I always went along with whatever he wanted to do, anyway.

Katy Harris, my best friend girl since I was ten and she was eleven, lived next door to Lester. She had offered to let me move in with her when I got out, but that would have been an insult to Lester. Besides, cuddling in bed with him was a lot more comfortable and fun than sleeping on a pallet on her hardwood floor.

There was a lot of crime in the neighborhood. Folks that didn't have much to begin with got robbed by folks that had even less. There was armed robberies and assaults on the streets every now and then. But house break-ins happened on a regular basis. Most of the locks was so flimsy, all a burglar needed to pick them was a bobby pin or a butter knife.

Five days after I'd moved back in with Lester, I returned to my old job at one of the biggest sugarcane fields in the county. I'd been doing farm labor from the time I started walking, so I was used to it. Lester worked for a farmer that raised hogs, chickens, and cows, so between the two of us, we made enough money to get by. We worked within walking distance from Lester's house, so we didn't have to depend on the overseers that transported workers on mule wagons and trucks owned by the farmers.

Lester claimed he had a toothache that Friday morning, so he didn't go to work. When I got home at 6:00 p.m., he was gone. I didn't know where he was or when he'd be back. I flipped through magazines, looked out the window every few minutes, and paced the floor for two hours, before I decided to go out and have a drink. I hadn't had one since the day I got arrested, so I was ready for a good buzz. I left a note on the coffee table to let Lester know that I'd be out until around midnight. There was three bootleggers operating less than a mile away. The only reason I went to Delroy Crutchfield's place was that he was the closest.

I spent the first ten minutes in Delroy's crowded living room standing in front of his potbellied stove, watching everybody else get loose. I was counting on some man to buy me a drink so I wouldn't have to spend my money. Somebody suddenly tapped me on the shoulder.

"I been watching you ever since you came through that door," a deep voice told me. I whirled around and seen a grinning man behind me, holding a drink. I had noticed him earlier because he was the only man wearing a white linen suit, and he had had several frisky women all over him at the poker table.

"Who me?" I asked dumbly.

"Yeah, you. I hope you like moonshine." He handed me the drink.

"I do. Thank you." I took a sip and smiled. "What's your name?"

"Milton Hamilton."

"Thanks for the drink." Lester had spies, so I didn't want to do nothing that would draw the kind of attention to myself that made people talk. I attempted to walk away, but Milton grabbed my arm. "Ain't you kind of bold?" I asked, giving him a mild frown.

"Yup," he snickered. "What's your name? I sure would like to get to know you."

"Yvonne Maynard, and I already got a man. We'll be getting married soon. And I noticed you already got a lot of meat on your plate."

Milton waved his hand and scanned the room with his eyes narrowed. The women that had been paying so much attention to him was pestering another man now. "Shoot! Them heifers ain't even clean. I wouldn't touch nary one with a stick. I ain't got no woman right now. I been searching for a long time. I got a feeling my search could end tonight . . ."

I rolled my eyes. "Well, like I just told you, I got a man."

He looked around the room again. "Where is he tonight?"

"Um . . . I don't know. He was gone when I got home from the cane field this evening and—"

Milton didn't waste no time cutting me off. "Why is a pretty little piece like you working in a cane field?"

"Because I can't eat and live nowhere for free," I chuckled.

"A classy woman like you should be able to do a lot better than a cane field. I took you for a rich white family's mammy in one of them big houses on the north side."

"I hope to have a first-rate job like that someday, God willing." I took another sip of my drink. I had to cover my mouth with my hand to hold back the belch threatening to embarrass me. "I been working on farms most of my life."

From the look of pity on Milton's face, I could tell that he felt sorry for me. But a split second later, he eyeballed me like I was something good to eat. It made me feel special and nervous at the same time. "What do you do when the crops is off-season and there ain't no farmwork?"

"I clean houses, take in washing and ironing, and whatever else I can get."

Milton closed his eyes and shook his head. When he returned his attention to me, he looked like he felt even sorrier for me. "I declare, that's a damn shame. Do you live in this neighborhood?"

"All my life."

"Hmmm. That's strange. I been living just down the road a piece from here for almost two years, and I ain't never seen you before tonight."

I didn't care what this man thought about me. But I was reluctant to tell people I barely knew that I was an ex-convict. It was a painful subject that I avoided as much as I could. I finished my drink and set the glass on the coffee table. "I'm a homebody, and so is my man. Other than work, we don't go too many places."

"Your man is lucky. I'd give anything in the world to have a beautiful redbone like you."

"Thank you."

I preferred tall, handsome men with light skin and good hair, and Milton wasn't nowhere near that. His skin tone was chocolate-bar dark, and he was only about three inches taller than me, and I was barely five feet. He had plain features and a dumpy body. His short off-black hair was nappy, but I was pleased to see that he hadn't plastered it down with pomade or lard, like some of the other men in the room. Regardless of how he looked, the other women was still making eyes at him. It had to be because of his charming personality and that white suit. I shook my head to clear out the thoughts I was having about Milton.

"I guess I should be getting back home," I said.

"You just got here a few minutes ago. What's your hurry?"

"Because you getting a little too close, or trying to. And I don't want to say something that'll hurt your feelings," I teased.

"Okay, I get the message," he said with a sigh. "I'm sorry. I ain't going to pester you no more. How far do you live from here?"

"Me and my fiancé live about a quarter of a mile down this road, in that green house at the end of the block. My best friend girl live in the house next door."

"I do declare. We neighbors. I live on the same road, on the other side, a stone's throw away from your place! Come on, I'll walk you."

As soon as we got outside, Milton wrapped his arm around my shoulder, and we started walking.

"Where do you work?" I asked.

"Well, like you, I can't eat and live nowhere for free. You ever been to Cunningham's Grill, that colored roadhouse out by the city dump? I work there Monday through Friday, cooking away all day."

"I know where it is, but I ain't never ate there. I don't have the kind of money you need to be eating out."

"I know what you mean. If you ever want a meal on the house, come by and send somebody into the kitchen to get me. I'll sneak you a plate on the house."

"Thank you. I just might do that."

"I hope you do." His arm got tighter around my shoulder. We didn't say nothing else until we reached my front door.

The lights was still off, so I assumed Lester hadn't come home yet. "I would invite you in, but I'd hate for my fiancé to come in and find me alone with a strange man."

"Don't worry about it, Yvonne. All I wanted to do was make sure you got home safe and sound. You go on in and have a blessed night."

I had locked the door when I left. It was unlocked now. I went in and stood stock-still in front of the door. I didn't turn on one of the lamps, because I knew the shotgun house so well, I could get around in it with my eyes closed. But there was enough dusky light streaming in through the window for me to see that my note wasn't on the coffee table, where I had left it. I assumed Lester had read it and expected me to come home around midnight. His bedroom was next to the living room, and every wall in the house was so thin, you could hear just about everything going on no matter what room you was in. The springs on our bed was so decrepit, they squeaked even if somebody just bumped against the bed. They was squeaking like mad now.

When I eased up to the bedroom door and opened it enough to peep in, I spotted a candle burning on the windowsill. What I seen in the bed took my breath away. The man I thought I was going to marry was on top of a woman, humping like a dog in heat.

CHAPTER 2
YVONNE

I HAD NO IDEA WHO THE WOMAN IN BED WITH MY MAN WAS. THERE was no way I was going to work toward having a future with Lester! Just being under the same roof with him now almost made me puke.

The only place I could think of to go was Katy's house. Her lights was on, but she didn't answer her door when I knocked. She had a lot of men friends and was all the time entertaining one. If that was the case tonight, I didn't want to interrupt her, so I went back to Lester's place.

I was in such a tizzy, I needed something to calm myself down. I decided to go back to that bootlegger's house and get sure enough drunk. But first, I wanted to know who the woman was with Lester.

There was a lot of trees with wide trunks directly across the road. I decided to hide behind one and wait for that nasty female buzzard to come out. I didn't have to wait long. Ten minutes after I'd ducked behind a walnut tree, Lester's lights came on and the door opened. Him and the woman stood in the doorway and kissed and hugged before she turned around. I couldn't believe my eyes. The woman was Katy, my best friend.

I was so shocked, my legs collapsed and I slid to the ground. I had always been a sturdy woman, so I didn't cry easy. I was too mad for something that tame, anyway. I wanted to fight. That didn't seem like the smartest thing to do, though. If I jumped on Lester, not only would he kick my ass, but he'd kick me out of his house, too. If I whupped Katy's ass, she was mean enough to have me arrested. But there was no way I was going to let them backstabbing, two-faced motherfuckers off the hook without chastising them! I couldn't think of nothing mean enough to make up for what they done to me. But I would. . . .

When Lester closed the door and turned off the lights, I wobbled up off the ground and started walking. I had to cool off before I went home. Now I *really* needed a drink. The crowd had got even bigger at Delroy's house. Milton, the nice man who had walked me home, was sitting on the couch with a drink in his hand. His face lit up like a firefly when I plopped down next to him.

"Bless your soul! You can't stay away from me," he teased, grinning as he grabbed my hand and squeezed it. "You don't look very happy, though."

I was so speechless, I couldn't speak right away. When I did, I couldn't control what came out of my mouth. "When I got in my house, my man was in bed with another woman." The words irritated the inside of my mouth like red hot peppers.

Milton gulped and done a neck roll that was so extreme, I was surprised his head didn't spin all the way around. "Hold on now. Is he the same man you told me you was going to marry?"

I nodded and then shook my head. "Yeah, that's him. But we won't be getting married now."

"I should hope not! Shoot. A prize like you don't need to scrape no man up off the bottom of the barrel. You deserve the best." Milton cussed under his breath. "Did you kill him?"

"No, I didn't do or say nothing. They was going at it so hard, they didn't notice when I cracked open the bedroom door."

"Oomph! Oomph! Oomph! Men like him make it so hard for us righteous dudes."

"Well, I'd left a note telling him that I'd be out until midnight. I guess he thought he would have enough time to do his devilment before I got back home."

"Sister, I got a feeling that this ain't the first time your man brung a woman to the house while you was gone. And I doubt if it'll be the last. Now that you know what kind of man you got, maybe the next time he fucks up, it won't be so painful."

"Ha! I ain't going to stick around for no 'next time.'"

Milton squeezed my hand so hard, my flesh tingled halfway up my arm. I believed it was a sign that he was going to be very important in my life. "Yvonne, I know we still strangers, but I only wish the best for you." His voice was filled with emotion.

"Thank you." My flesh was still tingling. If I never seen Milton again after tonight, his words would stay with me forever. "I'm glad you was still here. You say just what I need to hear to make myself feel better."

"You want to talk more about it? I'm a good listener. And, as you can see"—Milton paused and puffed out his chest—"I got some mighty wide shoulders, if you want to cry on one."

"If you don't mind, I don't want to talk about it right now." I was so antsy, I couldn't sit still. I had wanted to get drunk, but now I thought it would be better to have a clear head when I confronted Lester.

"Suit yourself. How about another drink?"

"No thanks. I just came here for a few minutes to cool off. I better get on home and take care of business now."

"Do you think that's a good idea?"

"I don't have no place else to go. I worked almost ten hours today, and I'm tired, so I need to get some sleep," I mumbled.

Milton set his drink on the coffee table, and then he stood up and stretched. "If you going to confront your man, you ain't going to get much sleep tonight."

"I know, but what else can I do?"

"Come on. I'll walk you."

"That's all right! Lester is the jealous type. I don't want you to get in trouble on my account."

"In the first place, you shouldn't be worried about that asshole being jealous, not after what he done. In the second place, I want to walk you to my house. You can cool off some more there and stay as long as you want. Hell, you can even stay the night. My place ain't nothing to write home about, but it's warm, homey, and clean."

"Do you live by yourself?"

"Uh-huh."

"Then let's get up out of here."

Milton's house was warm and homey, like he'd told me it was. I felt like I was in the place where I really belonged. I stood in the middle of his tiny living-room floor, glancing around, while he skittered about, lighting coal-oil lamps and opening windows. I racked my brain to come up with something to talk about. It wasn't easy, because this was the first time I'd ever been alone with a man I had met less than a hour ago. I was a little nervous and scared. I reminded myself that there was more than a few maniacs on the loose these days. Was Milton one that had been waiting on a woman in a weak condition like me? I wondered. My common sense was telling me to leave. But I was curious enough about him, I decided to take a gamble on my safety and stay. I was glad he broke the awkward silence.

"You hungry, Yvonne? I cooked a mess of collard greens that came from my garden. And I baked a possum and smothered it with mushroom gravy. The young lady I cooked supper for this evening stood me up, so I got plenty left."

"That sound real scrumptious, but I don't have no appetite." I sniffed and cleared my throat. "Um, I don't like to bring this up, but is there a chance that the 'young lady' you cooked for might come up in here and jump on me?"

"Nope. That inconsiderate heifer done stood me up one time too many. The only way she'll ever get her tail back in my house will be if she break in." We laughed.

I glanced around some more. There was a framed sign on the wall that was at least a foot high and two feet wide. Printed in big bold black letters on a white background was **HOME SWEET HOME?**

"Why is there a question mark at the end of that sentence?" I asked, pointing at the sign.

"I had the man that made the sign add it. I been living a topsy-turvy life for so many years, no matter where I live, that statement is more like a question in my case."

"Oh. I hope it won't always be a question."

"I hope it won't, neither. My mama and daddy made a very sweet home for our family. Since I been on my own, I done lived in a lot of places. In each one, I never knew if it was going to be a sweet home. When I realized it wasn't, I moved again."

"This is a nice house you got now," I pointed out. Milton's place was almost identical to Lester's but was way more inviting. The windows had crisp white curtains with ruffles on the edges, and there was nothing on the shiny hardwood floor that didn't belong on it. There was a maroon couch facing a matching love seat, and a great big artificial rubber plant in a pot on the floor, in a corner by the door.

"It is as nice as it can be in this run-down neighborhood. I'm tired of folks breaking into my house and taking my stuff! The last crook had the nerve to swipe a pair of my dress shoes and left his run-over boots behind! If things go the way I hope, it's just a matter of time before I move into the kind of home I been praying for. My intuition is so good, when I find my dream home, I'll know it right way. And it'll be my address until the day I die."

"Anyway, the sign adds a nice touch to your living room." There was three framed eight-by-ten-inch pictures on one wall. Two was of people from the Bible. The other one was of Milton and two men that favored him. "Them kinfolks in that picture with you?"

"Uh-huh. My baby brother, Woody, in the middle, and our cousin Freddie on the end. They live in Louisiana, and they both preachers, so they keep a safe distance from me."

"Hmmm. I would think that preachers in the family would try to get you to come to Jesus."

"Oh, they tried for years. But I didn't need nobody to lead me to Jesus. I found Him on my own. My folks don't think I'm close enough, though." Milton waved his hand and chuckled. "It don't matter. I got a blessed life. The only thing missing is a good woman . . ."

"Yeah, you already mentioned something like that," I reminded. "I appreciate you inviting me for a visit. I really like your house."

"I hope this won't be the last time you come here."

I stayed quiet and stared at the floor until he lifted my chin and kissed me on the lips. "That was nice."

"If you don't mind, tell me more about yourself. Where is your people at?"

We finally sat down on the couch.

"My mama and daddy died in a tractor accident when I was six."

"Oh. I'm sorry to hear that," Milton said. "Did your grandmother raise you?"

"Both of my grandmothers had already died by the time my parents got killed, so my aunt and uncle took me in. My two older sisters was raised by some of our other kinfolks. When they got married, they moved up north."

"You got any kids?"

"Three. A girl and two boys. Cherie turned eleven last month, and my boys is both nine, born ten months apart."

Milton's eyebrows raised up. "Girl, you full of surprises. You work in a cane field. That blowed me away. Now you tell me that a itty-bitty woman like you done had three babies? Where they at?"

"I need a drink before I can talk about that."

While I sipped moonshine, I told him how I'd been in and out of trouble since I was a teenager, and that I'd done time in prison. He cringed when he heard that all three of my kids' daddies took off as soon as I told them I was pregnant, and I never heard from them again. "It was hard to work and take care of my children, so I moved back in with my auntie and her husband."

"That's where your kids at now?"

"Uh-huh. My folks decided it would be better for them. And they didn't think it was a good idea for my kids to know I was their mama. They told them their real mama ran off to Chicago with a musician and got killed in a beer garden, and that I'm their cousin."

"Your kids believe that?"

"They was still toddlers when they told them. Years later, when I got locked up, Aunt Nadine and Uncle Sherman came to visit me one day. They made me agree to let them keep my kids permanently, or until they turn eighteen and can fend for themselves."

I couldn't tell from the stunned look on Milton's face if he was surprised, disappointed, or both. "What did you go to prison for?"

I shrugged. "Well, I liked nice, pretty things, but we couldn't afford much. Money was so tight, I dropped out of high school to go to work full-time."

"I dropped out, too, and I regret doing that. People like us need all the education we can get."

"That's true, but sometimes we don't have no choice. Anyway, even with a job, there still wasn't enough money for me to get all the things I wanted. I got frustrated, so I started taking things every time I went in a store. I got caught a few times, but they always let me go. My luck finally ran out. I went in a candy store one day to swipe some peanut brittle to give my man for his birthday. The old woman that ran the place snuck up on me just as I was putting it in my purse. When she tried to look in my purse, we scuffled. She fell and broke her hip. Two other customers, both men, pinned me down on the floor until the police got there. The judge gave me two years, but they let me out a week early. I got out this month." I heaved out a loud sigh and stood up. "I better get going. A nice, upstanding man like you don't need to get involved with a woman like me."

CHAPTER 3
MILTON

*T*HE WOMAN THAT HAD STOOD ME UP WAS GOOCH-EYED, ALMOST bald-headed, and outweighed me by at least sixty pounds. I couldn't believe I'd ended up with a pearl like Yvonne in her place. Her long straight black hair, big brown eyes, smooth light brown skin, with a handful of pecan-colored freckles on her pointy-tipped nose, would look good on a hound dog. She had a petite body, and every pound was in the right place. This was a woman I had to get to know. Knowing what a hard life she'd had made me feel sorry for her. I wanted to make her happy and protect her any way I could.

"Yvonne, me and you got a lot in common. My life ain't been no bowl of cherries, neither. And I don't need no drink to tell you about it."

She held up her hand. "You don't have to tell me nothing else about yourself. It ain't my business. After I leave here tonight, we'll probably never see each other again, anyway."

"I hope that won't be the case."

I couldn't believe how sad her eyes looked. When she stared at me and blinked a few times, I could almost feel her pain. It was a shame a sweet woman like her was engaged to a asshole that didn't respect her enough not to bring another woman to the same bed he slept in with her!

"Milton, my life is a tangled-up mess. I need to straighten it out before I start up something new."

"I see. So, do that mean you might even work things out with what's his face and marry him, anyway?"

Her eyes got bigger, and she looked at me like I was crazy. The next thing I knew, she reared back and screamed, "*Hell no!*"

"Whew! That was the answer I was hoping to hear," I remarked with a sharp laugh.

"As soon as I find another place to stay, I'm moving out."

"What about your best friend girl next door to y'all? Can you move in with her? I know it would be hard living that close to your man now, though."

Yvonne stared off into space for a few seconds. When she turned back to me, she looked mad enough to cuss out the world. With her teeth clenched, she told me in a tone that sounded like a growl, "My best friend girl was the woman he was in bed with." She stopped talking and started breathing through her mouth. I didn't know what to say next, so I decided to wait for her to go on. "Um, where is your toilet?"

"Go straight down the hall to the kitchen. The bathroom is to the left of the stove. I'm out of toilet paper, so you'll have to wipe off with one of them corncobs in that bucket next to the commode."

Yvonne stumbled out of the room and was gone so long, I thought she had slipped out the back door or passed out. I went to check on her. But before I had time to knock on the bathroom door, I heard her inside, puking and crying. Women was so complicated. I decided not to disturb her, and I went back to the living-room couch. Five more minutes went by before she rejoined me. I had set a fresh drink on the coffee table for her.

"Thank you, Milton." She flopped back down and took a drink right away. "Now that you know so much about me, tell me more about you."

I scratched the side of my neck and gave her a thoughtful look. "Well, I ain't been no angel myself. After my mama and daddy died in a house fire when I was thirteen, I had to fend for myself. My folks was never into having a good time like me. My brother was—and still is—so goody-goody, the only things missing on him is a halo and a set of wings."

"How many brothers and sisters you got?"

"Just my brother. Anyway, I do side jobs to get money to keep the good times going."

"On the farms?"

I snickered. "Naw, baby. I don't do farms no more. See, I like easy money. If I come across something that look like a good score, I go for it."

The way Yvonne's lips curled up, I thought she was going to laugh. But in a serious tone she asked, "You a thief, too?"

I bit my bottom lip before I went on. "Well, my daddy used to tell me that if something walk like a chicken, lay eggs like a chicken, and cluck like a chicken, it's probably a chicken. I guess I'm a thief, because the description of one sure enough fits me. But . . ." I paused and held my finger up in the air. "I'm a thief with dignity and morals. I don't take nothing from no-body disabled, elderly, blind, blood related, or that's got mental problems. I mostly break into white folks' houses and grab what-ever I can carry. As hard as times been these past few years, some of them peckerwoods still got money and spend it on shit just screaming for somebody to snatch. Especially jewelry."

"You ever took anything from colored folks?"

"Yup. Them dress shoes somebody stole from me, I had took them from this snooty joker that was always bragging about what he had. I never took advantage of somebody that didn't have it coming."

"I know what you mean." Yvonne let out a loud, drawn-out sigh. "But I don't like being a thief. For one thing, it's tiresome, and the outcome is unpredictable. I can't help myself, so I keep stealing."

"I don't think the rest of us crooks can, neither. It's in our blood, and we can't fight Mother Nature. Shoot! Thieving is the world's oldest profession."

"Uh-uh. The world's oldest profession is prostitution," Yvonne corrected, or so she thought.

"Pffft." I waved my hand. "That's a old wives' tale. Before I took off on my own, I was raised by kinfolks that was Holy Rollers to the bone, so I know my Bible. If you pay close attention to Scripture, you will see that folks was stealing long before women started spreading their thighs for profit."

"I know my Bible, too. I never gave that subject much thought, though. What you just told me make a lot of sense. Oh well. Since thieving is technically just another profession, there ain't nothing wrong with it so long as you don't hurt nobody, like I done. Or get caught."

"I ain't never done neither one. I done slowed down a little bit, though. I'm getting too old to be climbing through folks' windows. And some victims done got downright *dangerous*! I don't know what this world is coming to. In the good old days, jail was the only thing I had to worry about. But the last house I broke into, the old dude—who I thought was at church—came running from a back room with a claw hammer. I jumped back out that window in the nick of time."

"My goodness. You could have got hurt or killed."

"Tell me about it. I went straight home that day and read my Bible. And I asked God to let me live a long life. See, I got big plans for my future. I'm going to be business partners with this white boy I met in prison—"

Yvonne's mouth dropped open. "You been locked up, too? You told me you ain't never got caught."

I nodded. "I ain't never got caught. I went to prison for something I didn't even do!"

"Oh? Did somebody set you up?"

"Not exactly. See, while I was going through a slow spell, one of my buddies invited me out to celebrate my twenty-first birthday. Me and him had pulled a bunch of jobs together, so I read him like a book. Anyway, I didn't know him as good as I thought I did. He didn't tell me he was planning to rob the diner he took me to. Before I realized what he was up to, he pulled out a gun, and so did the man behind the counter cooking up the burgers we'd ordered. Long story short, the cook took my boy out with one shot to the heart. When the laws showed up, nobody believed I wasn't in on the robbery attempt. They slapped me with a eight-year sentence. I been out three. And let me tell you, busting rocks on a chain gang and getting beat up by them racist guards for no reason at all is as close to hell as a colored man can get."

Yvonne shook her head and gave me a pitiful look. "My Lord. That place I done my time in wasn't no paradise, neither. They made me help wash the inmates' clothes, kill and clean chickens, cook, and during crop seasons we all had to work on the farms that supplied some of our food. But you getting locked up for a crime you didn't commit is one of the worst things that can happen to anybody."

"We quite a pair, ain't we?" I reached over and caressed her chin. Her skin was as smooth as a baby's belly. She was such a improvement over all the rest of the women I'd been with. If I got to pester her in the bed only one time, I'd be okay with that. I knew it would be a romp I would never forget. "Um, when can I see you again, Yvonne?"

"I don't know. There ain't no telling how things will play out when I go home and tell Lester I'm moving out."

"You got much to move?"

"Naw. I can fit everything I want to take in one bag."

"Do you need any money?"

She eyed me for a long time. "I got a few dollars to get me through until I get paid. Why?"

I didn't bother to answer her question. I pulled out my wallet and handed it to her. "Take whatever you need." She took five of the fifteen ones I had. "Listen, you welcome to stay with me until you find another place."

"Do you mean that?"

"I wouldn't have said it if I didn't." I laughed. She didn't. "As you can see, my place and what I got in it ain't nothing to brag about. But like I told you, I got big plans for my future. I'm going to start bootlegging as soon as my contact brings me my first order of shine next week."

"What is 'shine'?"

"Oh, that's what the moonshiners call their product. Like Satan, it's got more than one name. I don't know what other folks call it in their neck of the woods, but in ours it's home brew, white lightning, or just plain shine. Most of them highfalutin white bootleggers on the north side just lump it in one category and call it booze. It's all offshoots of whiskey, beer, and everything in between. To get a nice buzz, you drink home brew. If you want to get slaphappy drunk, ask for white lightning. It's the upgraded stuff. If you decide to move in with me, you can drink all you want and help me serve my guests."

"What else would I have to do?"

"That's up to you. If we get real close, that'll be fine with me. If we don't and you'd rather be with somebody else, that'll be fine, too. You can still help me run my business. It wouldn't be backbreaking like that cane-field work. It'd be a heap more fun because we'd make up our own rules, and you'd be making tax-free money."

Yvonne blinked hard a few times, but not enough to hide the tears threatening to roll out of her eyes. "No man has ever been so nice to me without wanting something in return." She sniffled and blinked some more.

"Hell, yeah I want something—*you*. But I ain't the kind of man to put no pressure on a woman."

Before I realized what she was up to, she crawled into my lap and started kissing me from jaw to jaw. We smooched for a few minutes, and then I scooped her up and carried her to my bedroom. We made love until we got so tired, we didn't have no choice but to go to sleep.

When I woke up Saturday morning, a few minutes past 9:00 a.m., she was gone. And she'd took a big piece of my heart with her.

CHAPTER 4
YVONNE

*B*EFORE I COULD MAKE A COMMITMENT TO MILTON, WHICH I WAS itching to do, I had to take care of business with Katy and Lester.

Saturday morning, while Milton was still sleeping, I eased out of his bed. I put my clothes back on and headed back to Lester's house. As soon as I walked up on the porch, I could hear him and Katy inside laughing like somebody was tickling the bottoms of their feet. The door was locked now, so I took my key out of my brassiere and unlocked it. Without giving it much thought, I put the key back in my brassiere and opened the door. Them deceitful devils froze when they seen me.

"B-b-baby, where the hell you been?" Lester stuttered, jumping up off the couch. Him and Katy had been sitting so close together, I'd seen only one shadow on the wall behind the couch.

Katy didn't move. She just stared at me with a blank expression on her face. I wouldn't have felt so insulted if Lester had cheated on me with a woman that looked better than me. Katy was as skinny as a lizard and had a face like a mule's. But according to a couple of her lovers that liked to run their mouths, she really knew her way around the bedroom.

"Um, somebody broke into my house last night, while I was visiting Jeannette Sims, a girl I work with. They took my radio. I came over to ask Lester if he heard or seen anything," Katy said.

I looked at Lester. "Did you hear or see anything?" I asked.

"Naw. Them thieves done got so good, the one that pried

open my door and took my record player last month done it while I was sleeping in my own bed," he griped.

"That's a damn shame," Katy yelled. She gave Lester a pitiful look and shook her head. "The slimy devil that broke in my house while I was at work last Wednesday took them ashtrays and the tablecloth my mama gave me last Christmas."

Nobody spoke for a few seconds, but I didn't take my eyes off Katy's face.

She cleared her throat, scratched her head, and faked a smile, so I could tell she was nervous. "Where was you all night? We was so worried!" The serious tone in her voice was as fake as her smile.

"I went out," I answered in the coolest voice I could manage. "Lester, didn't you see my note?"

"Yeah, I seen it." He marched up to me and folded his arms, scowling like he wanted to punch me in the nose. "What I want to know is who you was out with."

"I went to a bootlegger's house by myself. So what?" I hissed.

"I'll tell you so what," he boomed, wagging his finger in my face. "As long as you my woman, you ain't going to be hanging out at none of them bootleggers' houses or jook joints, unless it's with me. I know how the jokers in them places like to ambush single women!"

I ignored Lester's rant and squinted at Katy. When our eyes met, she turned her head. "What you been up to, girl?" I asked.

"Me?" she asked dumbly, turning back to face me. "Um . . . I ain't been up to nothing much. Just going to work every day and hanging around the house, like I usually do."

"I couldn't find my key when I got home last night. Lester's lights was out the first time I came, so I figured he hadn't come home. Katy, I knocked on your door, and you didn't answer. Was you home?"

"Nope. I guess I was still at Jeannette's house. How did you get in here just now?"

"I used my key."

"You just told us you couldn't find your key last night," Katy pointed out.

"That's right. I was a little drunk and didn't realize I'd put it in my brassiere instead of my purse, like I usually do."

"Where did you sleep?" Lester asked, with his hands on his hips now.

"On a pallet on Delroy's living-room floor. Me and another woman. Her man had left with somebody else."

"Listen here, gal." Lester stopped talking long enough to snort like a bull and tighten up the mean look on his face. "Unless you going to work, don't you never leave this house again without my permission. If I ain't here, send one of them neighborhood kids to come hunt for me! Do you hear me?"

"Or what?"

"Or I'm going to teach you a lesson you won't never forget, and you might have to start looking for another place to live. I ain't going to put up with a hardheaded woman."

"Maybe I should leave," Katy threw in, finally standing up.

I shook my head at her. "You ain't got to leave. I won't be staying. I just came to get my things. I'm moving out."

"Moving out?" Lester and Katy hollered at the same time.

"Y'all heard me." I walked over to the chifforobe on the other side of the room, where I stored some of my clothes and linens in the top drawer. I immediately started snatching out my things. I wanted to haul ass as soon as I could. So instead of looking for a bag to put my stuff in, I grabbed a pillowcase from the same drawer and started stuffing.

"What about your share of next month's rent, which is due in a few days?" Lester whined, walking up so close behind me, I could feel his hot breath on the back of my neck.

I looked at him with the meanest scowl I could come up with. "Why don't you ask Katy to move in? She can help you pay it."

"Me? I got my own place." Her tone was meek and mild, and she seemed nervous. "And why would I want to move in with *your* man?"

"He ain't my man no more. You can have him all to yourself now."

They gasped and stared at me with so much contempt, I thought they was about to wring my neck.

"What the hell you rambling about, woman?" Lester barked. He moved a few steps away from me and went and stood next to Katy, which was where he belonged.

"I didn't lose my key. Y'all was too busy to notice me when I let myself in here last night."

The room got as quiet as a tomb. A split second later, Lester's voice shot through the air like a cannonball. "Well, now you know! And I'm so overjoyed, I could bust open! Me and Katy ain't got to sneak around no more!"

"How long y'all been making a fool out of me?"

"What difference do it make?" Lester boomed, dismissing me with a sharp wave.

"Katy, I thought you was my best friend. How could you do this to me?" If Milton hadn't put me in a better mood, I would have slapped the smug look off her face.

"Humph! Don't you put the blame on me! It ain't my fault you couldn't keep your man satisfied!" she blasted, with her lips quivering.

That was all I needed to hear to lose my cool. I trotted over to her and slapped her face so hard, she screamed and stumbled backward all the way to the wall and slid to the floor.

"Yvonne, you best get out of here while you still can," Lester advised as he helped Katy up.

"Don't worry. I'll be out of here in five minutes."

I zipped to the bedroom and opened the top dresser drawer. I grabbed a few more of my pieces and put them in the same pillowcase. Just as I was about to close the drawer, I spotted one of Lester's gray socks that he had tied into a knot and stuck in the back. That was where he kept his money. He had just got paid the day before, and he never kept more than a dollar and some change in his pocket. He was so stingy, he still had money left from two previous paydays, plus some he'd been saving for years. And he was worried about how he was going to make rent. I was going to give him something else to worry about. If I took his cash, he wouldn't be able to pay rent, buy food, or nothing else until he got paid again. His credit was so bad, nobody I knew would lend him a dime. Without giving it another thought, I dropped the sock in the pillowcase and slammed the drawer shut. I wasn't going to bother with the things I had in the closet, which was only a few blouses and dresses I didn't want. I slung the pillowcase over my shoulder and went back to the living room.

"Once you leave out that door, you better not come back, or you'll be sure enough sorry," Lester warned, with his hands back on his hips. Katy was leaning up against the wall, rubbing the handprint I'd left on her face.

"You can count on that," I hissed, skittering toward the door.

"You stupid bitch! And where you going to go?" Lester screeched.

"Look out the window to the right. I'll be staying in that little brown house with the wraparound porch."

His jaw dropped so low, I could see the base of his tongue. "Wait a minute. That's the house where Milton . . . You leaving me for that *monkey*? A ex-convict?"

"In case you forgot, I'm a ex-convict, too. I'm leaving you for a man that know how to treat a woman." I looked from him to Katy and added with a chuckle, "Y'all have a nice life together. You deserve each other. Toodle-oo!" I left in such a hurry, I didn't realize I still had the key to his house in my brassiere.

Milton must have been expecting me, because he wasn't surprised when I showed back up at his house with my pillowcase. He ushered me in so fast, he almost tripped over his feet. "I declare, I'm glad to see you again." He grinned.

"You told me I could stay here for a while."

"And I meant it."

"I'll be paying my way, so you don't have to worry about me freeloading off you," I assured him. He took my hand and guided me to the couch. We sat down, and I set the pillowcase next to me. "I'll keep your house clean, cook, do all the washing and ironing, and anything else you want."

Milton's response brung it home to me. "Baby, if you want to do all that, it's fine with me. As long as you happy, that's all I care about." And then he kissed me.

* * *

Around 4:00 p.m., somebody stomped up on the porch and pounded on the front door. "Yvonne! Yvonne! Uh, Yvonne! I know you in there!"

It was Lester. My heart almost stopped. Not because I was scared, but because I was mad.

Milton zoomed out of the kitchen, where we'd been fixing supper, and flung open the door. "What the hell do you want, man?" he boomed.

"Where Yvonne at?" Lester yelled.

I shot into the living room like a bullet, still holding the three-legged skillet I had just greased to bake some corn bread. "What do you want, butt breath?" I taunted.

Lester rushed up to me and got so close in my face, his foul breath made me cough. "Give me back my money, bitch!"

"What money?"

"You know what money!"

"I don't know what you talking about."

"You took every dime I had to my name, and I ain't leaving here until I get it back!"

"Lester, I ain't got your money," I said calmly. I sniffed and turned to Milton. "Please make this fool leave."

"All right, fool. You heard the lady." Milton waved him toward the door. His tone was as calm as mine. "Now start stepping."

I could see that Lester was twice as mad now. His nose and both jaws was twitching. So much blood had drained from his face, he looked almost as pale as a ghost. "I ain't going no place!" he screamed.

Before I realized what was happening, his hands was wrapped around my throat. But he didn't have time to do no damage. Milton lunged at him, and in a flash, he was on him like white on rice. He socked him in his face, and that made him turn my neck loose.

"What the hell—" Before Lester could finish his sentence, Milton punched him in the stomach, and he fell flat on his back.

The next thing I knew, Milton dropped down and straddled Lester. Then he pulled a switchblade out of nowhere and held it right above Lester's crotch. "If you don't want to leave here with your balls in your hand, you better get the hell up out of my house," Milton warned. He stood up, with the knife still opened.

Lester was still sprawled on the floor, with his hands up in the air. I had never seen a man look as scared as he did. "All right, man. Let me up," he begged, with snot oozing from his nose and blood trickling from his lips. He stood up, wobbling like a three-legged chair. "Maybe I misplaced my money."

"Or maybe that hussy you dissed Yvonne for took it!" Milton suggested. "I don't want to see your high-yellow punk ass on my property again. Next time I might forget I'm a Christian!"

Lester scrunched up his face and started backing toward the door. "All right! You can have this useless heifer. She can't cook or fuck worth a damn. That's why I had to get myself a real woman. I just kept this raggedy bitch around because I felt sorry for her!"

I went up to Lester and punched him so hard in his crotch with my fist that he howled so loud, he almost busted my eardrums. When he hit the floor this time, I bounced that skillet off the side of his face. It left a gash that looked like a third eye. Me and Milton stood over Lester as he moaned and groaned and wiggled like a worm. He got up again and staggered out the door, holding his crotch and screaming about how sorry I was going to be.

"I guess we showed him." Milton slammed the door shut and locked it. When he looked at me, we busted out laughing at the same time. He closed his knife and put it in his hip pocket. "You ain't got to worry about him or nobody else bothering you so long as you with me."

For the first time in my life, I felt like I meant something special to a man.

Milton reared back on his legs and gave me a curious look. "Tell me this, how did you end up with such a jackass?"

I shifted my weight from one foot to the other. "Well, he ain't always been a jackass. He used to be sweet as pie and as meek as a lamb. He would take me on picnics once or twice a month and

surprise me with gifts whenever I had the blues. When he borrowed a car and took me to Tuscaloosa to meet his mama the
year before I went to jail, I was convinced that he was the man
for me."

"What convinced you?"

"His mama. I liked her right off the bat. She was a lot like my
mama was. I thought if I got close to her, I wouldn't miss my
mama so much. A month later, Lester was in a bad car wreck
that caused a little brain damage. That's the reason he started
being mean to me sometime. I overlooked it because of all the
good times I'd had with him in the past."

"What about your friend girl?"

I had to cough to clear the bile rising in my throat. "Other
than being a two-faced slut, she ain't got no excuse for what she
done," I growled.

"If she got her own place, I wonder why Lester didn't go there
to lay up with her."

"Katy got a lot of men friends knocking on her door all hours
of the day and night. Since Lester thought I'd be gone for a
while, they probably thought it would be more private and safer
to get it on in his place."

"Damn! If he wanted to be with her, why did he have you staying with him in the first place?"

"That's something you'd have to ask him, because I don't
know. Maybe he felt sorry for me because I didn't have no place
else to go when I got out of prison. I don't want no man feeling
sorry for me. I want one that will treat me good, show me some
respect, and never let me down . . ."

"You got one now."

I thought I'd melt into the floor when he kissed my hand. I
felt like one of them girls in the fairy-tale books. "Okay," I giggled.

For supper, we ate the rest of the smothered possum and
greens Milton had cooked the day before with the corn bread
and rice pudding I made. I walked around the rest of the day
with my chest puffed out.

* * *

The anger I felt toward Lester and Katy had eased up. But on Sunday it came back with a vengeance, and I got mad all over again. I had made Lester suffer, but I still had to get back at Katy. She made herself scarce the next few days, so I couldn't catch her on the street and give her the ass whupping she deserved. By now I didn't even care if she called the police on me if I beat her up. No matter what happened, I knew Milton would be there for me.

Katy cleaned rooms at a motel in the next county, seven or eight miles away. The only way she could get to and from work was to ride the bicycle she had made a lot of sacrifices to buy. She treated it like it was the most important thing in her life. There was a yellow ribbon tied to one end of the handlebars, and a gold ribbon on the other. Her name had been printed on the seat in red paint. That cute contraption was mine now, and I had plans for it.

The following Saturday night, around 7:00 p.m., when Milton left the house to go play cards with some of his friends, I decided to make my move against Katy.

I found a cap in Milton's bedroom dresser drawer and tucked my hair up under it. Then I put on a dark blouse and the only pair of britches I'd brung with me. It wasn't too dark outside yet, so I didn't take no flashlight or coal-oil lamp with me.

The lights was on at Lester's house, but not at Katy's. If she wasn't out with another man or her friend girl from work, I assumed she was with him. She'd come to his house around this time almost every night after I got home from prison, to listen to the radio with us. Just to be sure she hadn't changed her routine, I tiptoed up on his porch and put my ear to the door. I was right. They was inside whooping it up and singing along with some honky-tonk singer on the radio like they didn't have a care in the world.

I walked to the end of the road first. Then I went behind the houses on Katy's side of the road and trotted up to her back door. I had brung a butter knife with me to pick her lock, but I didn't need to use it, because she'd left that door unlocked. Just as I was fixing to grab the bike from the corner in her living room, my bowels signaled me that they had a itching to move. Katy had a inside toilet, but I wanted to let nature take its course in a more fitting location. Because of what she had done, I decided her bed was the best place to do my business. What made it so enjoyable was the new white bedspread I had gave her for her birthday three days ago. I wiped myself off with a pink headscarf I found in her dresser drawer, the same one she wore around her neck when she went to church.

I tried to imagine the horrified expression on Katy's face when she seen my stinky calling card smack-dab in the middle of her bed. I wondered how she would feel the next time she wallowed in that bed with another man. Even if she suspected I was the culprit, she couldn't prove it. One thing I liked about the folks in this part of town was that if they seen somebody breaking into a house—unless it was their own—they didn't interfere or blab.

With part of my deed done, I felt better. Now I had to take care of the mission I had come to do in the first place. It took less than a minute to grab the bike and roll it out the same door I had come through.

Once I made it to the end of the block, I got on the bike and pedaled toward Tyler's Swamp, a mile and a half away. When I got there, I stood on the bank and flung that sucker into the snake-infested water.

CHAPTER 5

MILTON

I WAS A CRIMINAL AND HAD NEVER HAD A PROBLEM ADMITTING IT. I had never been married, but I was ready to settle down. As a Christian, I had a right to have a wife. I wanted to tuck her away in a nice house, treat her like a queen, and eventually have enough money so I wouldn't have to bust into other folks' homes and take their property. That was easier said than done, though.

I had been in love and shacked up with a few other women, but nary one had been the kind of woman I wanted to marry. I was very anxious to get to know Yvonne better, and it seemed like she felt the same way about me.

I had asked her if she wanted to go with me to the card game tonight, but she wanted to stay home. "I'd rather iron them clothes of yours in that basket sitting on your bedroom floor," she'd said. Had I stumbled into the kind of woman that was God's gift to men? I wondered. I was so impressed, I doubled the points I'd already gave her.

I wished I had stayed home myself. The card game turned out to be a bust. I didn't know why, but no matter how often I played, I usually lost. But that didn't matter. Gambling was fun, and I enjoyed it.

When I got back to my house a few minutes after 11:00 p.m., minus almost every dime I'd left home with, Yvonne was sitting on my front-porch bannister. August was the hottest month in the whole year. But after the sun went down, it could get right chilly. She was shivering when I walked up.

"How long you been sitting out here?" I asked.

"I decided to take a walk before I did the ironing, and forgot to leave the door unlocked."

"Let's go inside." I put my arm around her shoulder and led her into the house. We plopped down on the couch and hugged until I reared back and looked at her face. Being so light skinned, her nose was red, and so was her eyes. They was also a little puffy. I didn't know if it was because she'd been sitting in the night air so long or because she'd been crying. If she'd been crying because she was missing that asshole she'd left, that could ruin the plans I had in store for her. I was going to do everything I could to make her want to stay with me. "I'm sorry, baby. I don't never want to do nothing to make things harder on you."

"Milton, what I'm going through ain't your fault, so you ain't got nothing to be sorry about."

"I know that, sugar. But I don't like you sitting out there in the dark by yourself. There is a lot of randy men out here just laying for a woman to get their hands on."

"I can take care of myself," she insisted.

"I know you can. I seen you do it. I almost felt sorry for Lester when you batted his face with that skillet." I laughed. I cleared my throat and got serious again. "But you ain't always going to be that lucky. I'll get a key made for you as soon as I can, so you won't never have to sit outside waiting on me again. Want me to get you a blade to keep in your brassiere in case somebody else mess with you?"

"No, don't do that. I don't want nothing to do with no knife. That's a little too extreme for me."

"What about some lye?" The kind of lye I was talking about was a harsh solution that some folks used to unclog pipes and kill pests, like roaches and boll weevils. Women that dabbled in hoodoo or was just plain mean put some in old pill bottles and carried them in their brassieres. They used it to splash on their enemies. Enough could burn a person's skin off down to the bone.

"Thanks, Milton. But I don't want none of that kind of lye. There is enough disfigured colored folks in Branson already. And once you give me a key, you ain't got to worry about me stealing nothing and taking off while you gone."

"Yvonne, anything I got you can have, so you ain't never got to steal nothing from me."

That night in bed, after we'd made love, Yvonne sat up and poked my side. I sat up, too.

"Milton, I hope you never have to use that knife because of me."

"That's a odd thing for you to say at a time like this," I teased.

"If you cut somebody, you'll go to jail. And there would be no telling when I'd see you again."

"Well, as long as nobody bothers me or you, I ain't got no reason to use my knife."

"I'm worried about Lester coming back."

"Why? He ain't got no reason to come over here again unless he want another whupping."

"Well, I don't think he believed me when I said I didn't take his money."

I was sure enough curious now. "You said you didn't . . ."

Yvonne cocked her head to the side and blinked at me. "Milton, don't be naïve. I'm a thief."

"Oh." I waited for her to go on.

"You know I took his money."

I tried to act surprised, but I wasn't. I'd known from the get-go that she had stole Lester's money. That wasn't none of my business. But it was good to know she hadn't come to me empty-handed. "How much money we talking about, sugar?"

"Almost three hundred and fifty dollars. He been saving for years to buy a car. He always kept his cash in a sock in a drawer and was stupid enough to let me know," she said with a smirk. "I got it all, and it's still in that same dingy sock."

I gazed at Yvonne in awe. She had a smug look on her face. "That's big money for such a little bitty woman," I commented.

"I know." She suddenly got as giddy as a fox in a henhouse.

"Guess what else I done?" She didn't give me time to guess. "I got back at Katy while you was at that card game."

"Oh? Did you steal something from her, too?"

She bobbed her head like a rooster. "Yup. While she was whooping it up with Lester in his living room, I broke into her house and took her bike."

I gave Yvonne a concerned look. "How did you get in? Picked the lock?"

"I didn't need to. She'd left her back door unlocked. But I had a butter knife to jimmy it if I had to. See, when I lived with my aunt and uncle, I was all the time losing my key. My uncle taught me how to pick a lock with a bobby pin or a butter knife."

I scratched my chin and gave Yvonne another concerned look. "Taking somebody's property is one thing, but you don't rub it in their face. When Katy see you riding her bike, you going to have a mess on your hands. Where is it now? I know folks over in Lexington I could sell it to or trade it for a different one."

"Pffft! I didn't take it to ride around on. I took it to the swamp and dumped it in. Now she won't be able to get to work, and she'll lose her job."

"Oh well. She and Lester had it coming." I laughed, but only for a few seconds. There was something more serious I needed to bring up. "Um . . . with that much cash, you could move into a nice house on the upper south side, where all the classy colored folks live. Is that what you going to do?" I held my breath and prayed in my head that she'd say what I wanted to hear.

"Yeah, but when I do move, I hope you'll be moving with me." She stared into my eyes and rubbed the side of my arm. "You told me you wanted to move to a better neighborhood when you could afford to. How much do you need to do that?"

What she'd just said had me busting at the seams, but I didn't want to let her know that. I thought that if I seemed too eager, it might spook her and make her think twice about taking me with her if she moved. "I got a few bucks saved up. With that and your stash, we got enough to rent a house on the upper south side. The only thing is, there ain't nothing available over there right now. I been checking every other week for the past four months. Why don't we set the money aside for now? When a house come up for rent, we'll look into it."

"Okay. Now let's get some sleep. Tomorrow night we'll go out and have a few drinks to celebrate our future."

Right away we started spending more time socializing with the local bootleggers so we could pick up some pointers about the business. We learned a lot from Delroy Crutchfield because he had been in the game longer than anybody we knew. By the middle of October, we knew enough to be on our own. It was a struggle to get the drinkers to take us serious. But getting into the swing of things and learning the ropes was fun.

It wasn't long before me and Yvonne was ready to make a permanent commitment to each other. We became man and wife in Delroy's living room the last Saturday night in the month, in front of a dozen drunks. One was the preacher that married us.

CHAPTER 6
YVONNE

I DIDN'T REGRET TAKING LESTER'S MONEY OR KATY'S BIKE. BUT I DID regret emptying my bowels on her bed. I had never done nothing like that before and didn't plan on ever doing it again. Milton was a clean man, so I didn't think he would appreciate me doing something so yucky. I decided not to tell him that part about my latest theft. If Katy or Lester told people about it and it got to Milton, I'd deal with it then.

Things couldn't get no better for me. I was happier than I'd been since I was a little girl. Before I met Milton, I had felt like only part of a woman. He made me whole. But his words described us better: "I'm the grits, and you the butter."

All my other boyfriends had been just dry runs in the bedroom. Sex with Milton was so good, there was times when there'd be so much love juice after we got done, we'd actually slide out of bed the next morning.

When I ran into Lester and Katy in public, they acted like they didn't even see me. She had moved in with him a week after I left. They spent a lot of time peeping out their front window when me and Milton was sitting on our porch. And they did a heap of mean-mouthing about us to some of our neighbors. Their antics didn't even faze me. I thought it was a shame that they didn't have nothing better to do with their time. I had too much going on, so I didn't waste my time keeping tabs on them. But the neighborhood gossips kept me posted. One woman told me that Katy had lost her job because she couldn't get to work after somebody snuck into her house and stole her bicycle, and that was the main reason she had moved in with Lester so fast. The same woman told me that before the bike incident, another thief—or maybe the same one—had broke into Lester's house and took all his money.

The money I'd took had really put him in a bind. And since Katy wasn't bringing in a paycheck no more, she couldn't help pay his rent or none of his other expenses. When he got three months behind, his landlord told him he had to move. The sheriff was scheduled to escort him and Katy out of the house, but they packed up and snuck off in the middle of the night the day before the sheriff's visit. The gossips told me that they had moved to Tuscaloosa, which meant I wouldn't have to worry about Lester coming after me again or about running into him and Katy on the street. She must have been too embarrassed and squeamish to tell folks about the stinky parting gift I'd left on her bed, because nobody never mentioned it to me.

After the way them devils had betrayed me, I wasn't anxious to make no new friends. But I didn't waste no time getting close to Milton's best friend, a hillbilly named Willie Frank Perdue, whom he'd met in prison. Other than the white folks I'd worked for, I avoided them as much as I could. But Willie Frank wasn't no ordinary white man. He had found Jesus while he was locked up, and he had a good heart, so he became one of my best friends, too.

Willie Frank came to our house several times a week to drop off a supply of the alcohol that him and his folks brewed in their still. Sometimes he came over just to visit and eat supper with us. He was a good-looking man, too. His silky blond hair and sky-blue eyes was his best features. The only problem was, several of his front teeth was missing. Every time he smiled, he reminded me of a jack-o'-lantern. But the ladies still loved him—especially the colored prostitutes he frolicked with on a regular basis. And he could afford to pay for his escapades. On top of them side jobs of breaking into houses that him and Milton pulled, which earned a nice profit, he sold alcohol to some of the other boot-leggers and jook-joint owners.

"Do you ever have trouble with the laws and them meddle-some revenuers?" I'd asked him last night, after we'd unloaded several jugs of moonshine off his truck.

"Heck naw," Willie Frank had told me, waving his hand. "I got everything sewed up. Me and my folks been paying them boogers off from day one, so we ain't got to worry about nothing." He paused and took a deep breath and told me in a low tone, "Be-sides, my uncle Lamar is close friends with Sheriff Potts. When-ever somebody in my family get tangled up in a legal situation, he straightens it out."

"Is that right?"

"Uh-huh. When I cut the man that caught me in his bed with his wife, the law wanted to send me to the slammer for ten years. But Uncle Lamar went up to the district attorney, who happens to be his niece's husband, and got me off with only five."

Now that I knew Willie Frank had a connection to the law, I felt better about being a bootlegger. But it wasn't a easy job. For one thing, we had to get the word out so everybody would know we was in the game now. The first few weeks, me, Milton, and Willie Frank buddied up to people in jook joints and houses run by other bootleggers. We let them know how much cheaper our stuff was, and that we offered complimentary snacks. Having me in the mix serving drinks attracted men who liked to be in the company of a pretty woman. But that wasn't all we had going for us. Being in our early thirties and knowing how to have fun had a lot to do with it, too. Our rivals was dull and middle aged or older. Almost every single one had health issues that caused them to shut down business for days at a time, several times a month. If all that wasn't inconvenient enough, some made their own booze, and it was nowhere near the high quality of what we got from Willie Frank. Our stuff got folks drunker faster. The few that did have women helping hired ones with faces and bod-ies that only their preachers and mamas could love. It took us about a year to get our business up to a level that suited us.

Milton taught me a lot during that time. "Girl, no matter what you do, do it good and you'll be very successful. If you going to be a thief, be the best. If you go in a store to swipe a few items, always wear comfortable shoes, in case you have to make a run for it." He had me sew some deep, wide pockets inside one of my jackets, like he'd done with his. That way when I went in a store to lift something, I didn't always need to carry no purse to hide it in. I took what I wanted and slid it into my secret pockets. "If you take something a little at a time, store clerks won't notice. It's when you get greedy that you get caught." I paid attention to Milton's advice. When I got a itching for some new silverware, I went to three stores on different days and took all I wanted. I used the same routine when I seen a three-piece outfit I just had to have.

"Do you ever feel guilty about taking stuff?" I asked Milton the day I came home with a bunch of candy bars and some rouge that I'd slid down the front of a girdle I'd swiped the week before. I wore it when the weather was too hot for me to wear my jacket with the inside pockets.

"That's a odd question coming from you," he snickered, helping me wiggle out of the girdle.

"Well, I felt kind of bad when I took them knives from that new store on Morgan Street," I admitted. "It was the last set they had."

"Girl, *guilty* is a bad word in our line of business. I ain't never felt that way about nothing. If somebody is stupid enough to leave jewelry and other items laying around for folks like me and Willie Frank and you to lift, the least we can do is teach them a lesson to be more careful by taking it. Shoot."

Milton did everything he could to keep me happy. He helped with the cooking and all the other household chores. What more could a woman ask for? Three months after our wedding, he got me hired on as a waitress at Cunningham's Grill, where he was the head cook. It was a full-time day job, so I was able to quit working in the sugarcane field.

In June of '39, Milton told me that there was finally a nice house available on the upper south side and that the owner had told him we could move in right away. I was amazed that my life had improved so much in less than two years. I thought I'd died and gone to heaven.

"Milton, you mean we'll finally get to live around doctors and other high-class colored folks?"

"Uh-huh. And the house is close to the bus lines. People will be glad to come drink at a house in such a nice, quiet location."

Our new residence was just what I'd always wanted. All the rooms was on one floor. And like most of the other houses on our street, it had a big attic, a pantry for me to store canned goods and knickknacks, a large front yard and backyard, and a picket fence. Milton was convinced that this was the home he'd been dreaming about.

The day we moved in, he went back to his sign-painting friend and had him print up a new **HOME SWEET HOME** sign without the question mark. When he got back to the house, he hung it on our bedroom wall facing the bed.

"How come you didn't put it in the living room, where folks can see it?" I asked.

"Because that's where we will be doing most of our business, and drunk folks give out negative energy," he told me. "Nothing can fuck up happiness like bad energy."

I was a little concerned about how our high-class new neighbors would react when they found out bootleggers had moved from the shabbiest part of town to their territory. But on the first day in our new home, the couple that lived one house over dropped in and welcomed us to the neighborhood.

I didn't know what to make of Joyce and Odell Watson at first. She worked at a school as a teacher's assistant. He managed MacPherson's, a moneymaking country store that her mama and daddy owned. They had retired, and now Odell was running the show on his own. Him and Joyce was right snooty. I'd picked up on that ten minutes after they walked through our front door together the first time. They bragged about their jobs, their great marriage, how often they ate at expensive restaurants, and all the nice things they had in their house. For them to be so well off, I was surprised that they didn't waste no time accepting drinks on the house.

The first couple of months flew by fast. We spent a heap of time socializing with Joyce and Odell, mostly at our house. I got the impression right off that they was particular about who they invited to their place. They had fancy, expensive furniture, a telephone, a car, and no telling how much money stashed away, so I could understand why they had such big heads. But that didn't make me feel no better. Me and Milton had agreed from the get-go that they was the type of people that thought they was special and everybody else—meaning folks like us—was in the mix for their benefit. Odell was more uppity than Joyce in some ways. He lived closed enough to MacPherson's so he could walk to work if he wanted to. But he was so highfalutin, he drove to work every day. And even though he had enough time to give Joyce a ride to her job, she rode with one of her coworkers or she walked! That gave us more unpleasant details about them: she was a fool and he was self-centered.

"I can't believe how much nerve Joyce got," I told Milton one evening, after we'd been in the new house two and a half months. She and Odell had just pranced out the door after guzzling down three free drinks apiece.

"What did she do?"

"She refused to drink water from the same dipper me and you and everybody else started using when we ran out of jars and cups. 'The only person I drink after is Odell, because I know where his mouth has been,' she told me. Humph! I offered to pour her some water in a pan, and she didn't waste no time telling me to make sure it was clean."

"Baby, don't let that woman get under your skin. Odell done said worse things to me."

"Like what?"

"Well, one night I complimented him on how dapper he always look, and how much I wish I could get my hair to look as sharp as his. Instead of being humble and thanking me, he told me that with the right clothes and grooming, any man could look good. His eyes roamed over me, and then he said, 'Even you . . .' "

I gasped so hard, I lost my breath and couldn't get the words out fast enough. "He all but called you ugly! What did you say?" I croaked.

"I laughed it off, because it was funny coming from a man married to a plain Jane."

"Baby, from now on, let's feed them with long-handled spoons."

"Pffft! We already doing that. If they keep saying stuff we don't like, we'll just have to start feeding them with longer spoons. If they don't make one of us snap the way Lester did when he came to my house, everything will be hunky-dory. Shoot. With all the resources they got, they might turn out to be the best things that ever happened to us, huh?"

"Yup," I agreed.

CHAPTER 7
MILTON

September 1939

"MILTON, WE GOT A LATE NOTICE FOR LAST MONTH'S WATER bill yesterday. I thought you paid it."

"Huh? I thought I did, too! Hmmm. I guess my memory ain't what it used to be."

"I guess it ain't. In case you thought you paid the electric bill, you didn't. We got a late notice about that one, too. You better stop being so irresponsible with our money, or I'll start handling it."

Yvonne glared at me across the breakfast table. Steam was rising from our coffee cups and the huge piles of grits on our plates. That wasn't what was making me sweat, though. It was her chastising me. I was the man of the house, but she wore pants as often as I did.

"Do you hear me?"

"Yes, baby. But I know I paid the electric bill. That's got to be a mix-up on their end. I'll go down there today, on my lunch break, and straighten out them goofy folks."

"No, I'll go. Now, give me the money I gave you to pay this month's bills."

I lifted my coffee cup and took a swig before I swallowed and said in a raspy tone, "I . . . I ain't got it."

"What did you do with it?" That was one question Yvonne could answer herself, and she did. "You lost it gambling."

I blinked and nodded.

"Milton, what's happening to you? You used to be so respon-sible."

"Sugar, I'm still responsible, but I ain't perfect," I pouted. "I'll try and borrow the money."

"You better try real hard! What do you think our snooty neighbors would say if we got our lights and water cut off—in this nice big house a few doors down from a *doctor*? Now, if you want to gamble again anytime soon, you better borrow enough money for that, too. I'm going to keep a close watch on all our bills for a while."

"It ain't going to be easy borrowing more money. See, I al-ready owe a lot of folks," I admitted. "They been hounding me so much to pay them back, I can hear them in my sleep. That's why I been having them headaches . . ."

It didn't take much to make Yvonne feel sorry for me. She gave me a pitiful look and reached across the table and squeezed my hand. "Well, we can't afford for you to get sick and have to miss work at the grill and cut back on our bootlegging hours. I'll pay the water and electric bills with the money I been saving up to buy some new curtains and a wig hat to send Aunt Nadine for her birthday. But you still better find somebody who'll let you borrow money for your next gambling escapade. And I hope it's somebody that won't badger you to pay them back and cause you to have more headaches. How about going up to Odell next door? His pockets is deep enough to plant a tree. He is so easygoing about lending you money, and too much of a gentleman to ask for it back if you don't repay him on time."

"That's a good idea, sugar. I don't want to wear out my welcome with him, though. I just paid him back a loan three days ago."

"Okay, don't ask him, then. We don't want our new neighbor to think we trying to take advantage of him."

I had to turn my head because I didn't want Yvonne to see the sheepish grin on my face. I was way beyond the point of just "tak-ing advantage" of Odell Watson. I'd been blackmailing him since I'd busted him with another woman a couple of months ago. If I had knowed before I started shaking him down that he was such a pushover, I wouldn't have even paid back none of them previous loans I'd hit him up for. Fool. A man as weak as he was made me suspect he was a sissy, too. If he did have some sugar in his tallywacker, it couldn't be more than a spoonful. I came to that conclusion because him and Joyce had told us how hard they was trying to have a baby. And he had that pretty piece on the side named Betty Jean—the woman I'd busted him with!—whom he kept tucked away over in Hartville and who he had had three babies with.

Well, Odell's secret was mine now. He had no choice but to pay me off if he wanted to keep it that way. I had him right where I wanted him. That high horse he'd been sitting on for so long had shrunk down to the height of the rocking horse I had when I was a little boy.

Of all the things Odell had going for him, brains had to be at the bottom of the list. The stupidest thing a married man could do was tell the outside woman too much of his business. He could have humped Betty Jean and never told her his real name or where he lived. Like me and other smart men done when we creeped on our wives. If he had done that, all he had to do when she got pregnant was disappear. Then he wouldn't be doling out money to her—and now me.

One thing that amazed me was how he'd been smart enough to convince Joyce to marry him five years ago, when the only job he had in her folks' store was stocking shelves. Before that, he had been dragging along as a handyman at a whorehouse. Even though Joyce was educated and worked at a fancy school, she was still naïve as hell. To her, Odell was a blue-ribbon prize. And according to the gossips, she had been so desperate to get married, she would have married a baboon. Landing a handsome joker like Odell was probably rapture to her. He hadn't just pulled the wool over her eyes; he'd swaddled her whole body in it. Lucky for him, and me, Odell had easy access to all kinds of money. Joyce was the only child of one of the few wealthy colored couples in town. They was just as gullible as she was when it came to Odell. Otherwise, he wouldn't be running the store her family had made such a huge success. And he sure wouldn't be living like the Prince Charming he thought he was.

One good thing about my arrangement with Odell was that I could make changes to it whenever I felt like it. Every time I went to him for more money, other than what we had agreed to, he got ugly with me. That didn't rattle me at all. I was used to it by now, so I was prepared to listen to him fuss when I paid him another visit this afternoon.

I had been skunked out of quite a bit of money last week in a Labor Day poker marathon at one of the roadside jook joints, and I had been spending the rest of my money like mad since then. Now all I had was forty-four cents to my name. I could have borrowed from somebody else, but I didn't want to have to pay nobody back. I could have snuck a few bucks out of the funds me and Yvonne had saved up to use in case we had to skip town in a hurry or for some other emergency. But because of Odell, I didn't.

The grill had been super busy since I'd walked in the door this morning. I'd flipped more burgers in one hour than I usually did in three. Since I didn't have no transportation of my own, I had to depend on taking buses, catching rides with other folks, or borrowing somebody's wheels. Instead of walking a quarter of a mile to the nearest bus stop and catching a bus to go into town to take care of my business with Odell, I decided to approach one of our regular patrons and see if they'd let me use their car or truck.

The first one I seen was lanky, freckled-faced Marvin Kelly, a long-term customer at the grill and a frequent guest at my house. He didn't hesitate to let me borrow his wheels. As soon as he gave me the key, I bolted out the front door, jumped into his dusty old truck, and shot off down the road like a bat out of hell.

Black-bottomed clouds blocked out the sun, so I knew we was fixing to have a granddaddy of a storm. A few minutes later, the wind started howling and the windows in the truck was rattling like mad. For the rest of the ride, thunder boomed nonstop, lightning flashed, and it rained so hard, the windshield wipers couldn't wipe fast enough. Because of that, I couldn't drive as fast as I wanted to.

By the time I reached the street MacPherson's was on, my lunch hour was almost half over. But at least it had stopped raining. The closest parking spot was a block away, so when I piled out of the truck, I had to do some trotting. Odell's Ford Model T, which he always kept spit shined, was parked in front of the store. I was going to ignore his two busybody cashiers so I'd save even more time.

I went in the front entrance and walked real fast, with my head down, toward Odell's office. When I got there, the door was open, so I just strolled in. His face froze when he seen mine. I closed the door so we could have some privacy.

"Greetings, old boy," I greeted, giving him a salute.

A frown popped up on his face. "Milton, what you doing here?" he asked in a mean tone. His thick black eyebrows raised up so high, I was surprised they didn't touch his forehead. As usual, he wore a dark suit with a white shirt and a blue tie. In that outfit, with the miserable look on his face and his slicked-back hair, he looked more like a undertaker than a store manager.

"Is that any way to greet one of your best friends?" Even though Odell was acting real cold, I still gave him one of my warmest smiles.

He was at his desk, reared back in his chair like he didn't have nary a care in the world. A pile of pig-feet bones and some hush-puppy crumbs was on a saucer on one side of his desk. An empty Nehi pop bottle was on the other end. I didn't wait for him to ask me to sit down. I flopped down in the chair he always kept in front of his desk.

"Be quick, because I'm busy," he snapped, wiping pig juice and crumbs off his lips with a napkin.

"I can see that," I said with a smirk.

The same clipboard with a scratch pad that he carried around when he was on the main floor was laying on his desk. He'd been playing tic-tac-toe on it again. For Odell to be a grown man, he sure had some childish ways. The last time I visited his office, I seen them tic-tac-toe thingies on his pad. Another time I'd walked in on him licking a Popsicle. Just knowing what a cushy job he had made me sick. I worked my fingers to the bone, cooking away in a stifling hot kitchen five days a week and bootlegging seven days. But I still didn't make nowhere near the kind of money Odell made.

"I need another favor."

He shot me a wild-eyed look. And then he shook his head so hard, I was surprised his neck didn't snap. "So now putting the bite on me is what you call a *favor?*"

I hunched my shoulders. "Yup. What do you call it? And don't say *blackmail*, like you done them other times," I warned, holding up my hand. "That word makes me nervous."

"I'm paying you hush money so you won't blab my business with Betty Jean to my wife. If that ain't blackmail, I don't know what is."

CHAPTER 8
MILTON

ONE THING I HAD PROMISED MYSELF WHEN I DECIDED TO TAKE Odell was that I wasn't going to waste my time arguing with him over details. No matter what he said, it wasn't going to make no difference, because I was the one holding all the cards.

"Odell, you can call it whatever you want, my man." I blinked and scratched the side of my neck. "To me it's still just a business arrangement."

"I been keeping my end of the 'business arrangement,' which is more than I can say for you. I agreed to pay you eight dollars a week," he whined. That tone went right along with the puppy-dog look on his face.

I nodded. "True. And that's still good enough."

Odell rolled his snaky eyes and gawked at me like he wanted to hurt me real bad. "Look, I been paying you off every Wednesday since July, like I agreed. Today is Monday."

I nodded again. "That's true, too. And I expect you to keep on paying me off every Wednesday."

He looked confused. "Then if I give you money today, I don't have to pay you Wednesday, right?"

"Wrong. What I need today ain't part of our arrangement. There is a poker game happening this evening over at Joe Sampson's house, with some pretty high stakes, see. The players is some fools from Lexington. They known for getting so drunk they can't tell one card from another, so they get skunked all the time. Them is the kind of idiots I like to play with. I figured I'd swing by Joe's place on my way home from work and see how good my luck is." The way Odell was staring at me, you would have thought I'd sprouted another head.

"Milton, as much as you lose, don't you think it's time for you to stop gambling or at least slow down?" he snapped.

"Why should I? I ain't hurting nobody. And I don't know why you getting so hot and bothered. All I'm asking for is five dollars. And don't tell me you ain't got it! That's pocket change to a man running a store like this one," I said as I made a sweeping gesture with my hand.

Several nearby businesses had closed because of the Depression the country was still in. But MacPherson's hadn't slowed down at all. They stocked almost everything a person needed: groceries, clothes, meat, and other everyday items. Only a few colored folks had wheels, so they couldn't get to some of the bigger stores. But they could hop on a bus that dropped off and picked up passengers less than half a block from MacPherson's. This place was a gold mine, and all I wanted was a few pieces, so I couldn't understand why that even bothered Odell as much as it did.

He blinked and started breathing through his mouth. "I swear to God, I don't know how much longer I can put up with this. It's been only a few weeks, and I'm already about to lose my mind," he complained.

I could understand how Odell got hisself in such a pickle with another woman. He had the kind of looks women went for. He was more than six feet tall and built like a prizefighter. His skin tone was dark brown and didn't have no wrinkles in sight, even though he was thirty-six. If all that wasn't enough to put him at the top of the heap, he had thick, curly black hair and shiny, cat-like black eyes. Mother Nature had played a prank on me by making me look like a gnome compared to Odell. I was two years younger than him, but I looked older. My looks didn't bother me, because I still had to beat women off with a stick. But it bothered me that "pretty boys" like Odell always got the cream of the crop when it came to women. His wife didn't count. That big-boned plain Jane was all about money—and was going to have a heap more when her mama and daddy kicked the bucket. But Betty Jean, Odell's spare, was one of the most beautiful women I'd ever took a gander at.

"Man, can I ask you something?" Odell's loud tone broke into the thoughts that was doing somersaults in my head.

I hunched my shoulders. "You can ask me anything you want." I smiled again because I wanted him to see that I was still in a good mood.

"What do you tell Yvonne about all the extra money you have these days?"

I rolled my eyes and snickered. "Pffft! She'll believe anything I tell her, so I ain't got to worry about her no more than you have to worry about Joyce. Now, let's finish up this meeting so I can get back to work." I held out my palm, with all five fingers wiggling. From the scowl on his face, you would have thought he was gazing at a cow's hoof. "Well?"

"I don't have no extra money on me right now. The meat vendor will be here in a few minutes, and all I got is enough to pay him."

"I know you don't think I'm fool enough to believe a man like you walk around with just enough money in your pocket to pay a vendor."

"What I mean is, I don't have enough on me now to pay him and you. I'll have to go to the bank first."

"Can't you take it from one of the cash registers?"

"I don't touch that money until I close up. If I start plucking any of it out before then, my nosy cashiers will start asking questions. And the next thing they'll do is put a bug in—"

I didn't want to hear no more excuses, so I cut him off. "You don't need to go into that. I get the picture." I stood up. "I'll tell you what. Mosey on over to your bank when you can and bring me my five dollars this evening. No, make that *six* for making me wait. I'll have to skip getting in that game on my way home from work and get in later. But that's only if you bring me my money before they stop playing."

"Why don't you use some of your own money until I can get some to you?"

"If I wanted to do that, I wouldn't be standing here right now! I don't dip into them funds unless I really have to. Now, you get my money to me this evening, no matter what time. Do you hear me?"

"I hear you, God damn it!"

"Excellent, old boy! Bring Joyce with you this evening and hang around for a little while. If you keep hitting and running like you did last Wednesday and the Wednesday before that, Yvonne will get suspicious sooner or later." I reached out my hand again. "You want to shake on it?" This time Odell looked at my hand like it was a live grenade. Him refusing to touch my hand hurt my feelings! "Okay, I'll see you this evening. Come around six, before we get real crowded." No matter how civil I was being, Odell was still glaring at me, so I was anxious to leave now.

"We finish?" he snarled.

"Just one more thing. Can you at least give me a dollar now?"

With a huffy sigh, he reached in his pocket and pulled out a fistful of change and counted out three quarters, two dimes, and a nickel. It was bad enough he had disappointed me by saying I had to wait until he went to the bank to get more money. Now here he was offering me coins!

"I'll give you the other five dollars this evening," he griped as he handed over the change.

"Six."

"I just gave you a dollar. All you asked for was six, so all I'm going to give you this evening is five!"

I shook my head. "Six. I need this dollar to get some gas for the truck I borrowed to come see you."

"You don't need no whole dollar for gas! You didn't have to use that much to get here!"

"I know that. But being that I'm as broke as a haint now, having a little something extra in my pocket to fall back on sure makes me feel better."

"All right! I'll give you six dollars this evening!"

Just to show that I wasn't too hard-hearted, when I started backing toward the door, I gave him another salute and told him, "Have a blessed day."

Chapter 9
Yvonne

I TRUSTED MILTON AS MUCH AS I COULD TRUST ANY MAN. BUT I wasn't stupid enough to believe everything he told me. If he ever lied to me, I knew it would be because he had a good reason.

I loved making money and having a good time as much as he did. Which was why our business was doing so good already. We brung in decent money, and we spent it as fast as we made it. Usually on things we bought at the spur of the moment. Like our red piano and them new skillets I just had to have. The only way we was going to stay out of the poorhouse was to come up with ways to make even more money, or learn how to control our spending. Meanwhile, I was going to keep enjoying life with Milton, because he was my life.

We usually took our lunch breaks together around noon. Since the grill was so out of the way, we didn't leave the premises unless we had to. Most days, we would find a cozy spot on the side of the building, or if there was a empty table on the main floor, we'd eat there.

When Milton told me five minutes before noon today that he had to go take care of some business in town, I didn't bother to ask him what it was. "Ain't you going to eat nothing before you leave?" I asked, walking him outside to the truck parked by the side of the dirt road that one of our regulars was letting him borrow.

"I been nibbling since I got to work, so I ain't that hungry just now. But if them greedy railroad workers don't eat up all them turnip greens, save me a mess."

At 12:55 p.m., while I was still sitting on the grill's front porch steps, finishing up a bowl of neck bones, Milton returned. He parked on the edge of the parking area, next to a mule wagon that one of our customers had come in. He piled out and ran toward me, swatting at gnats and flies circling his head.

I set my bowl down and stood up. "Baby, you ain't got to be in such a hurry. You still got a few minutes left before you have to relieve Jasper so he can go to lunch." Jasper Hardy was one of the other cooks that helped Mr. Cunningham prepare the meals.

When Milton got close enough, he wrapped his arms around my waist and kissed me on the lips.

"Did you get everything took care of?" I asked, rubbing his arm.

"Uh-huh. It wasn't nothing important," he replied, glancing to the side. Then he started blinking hard and fidgeting, shifting his weight from one foot to the other. These was things he didn't do that often, and when he did, I got nervous.

"Milton, I know you don't like it when I badger you. But I got a feeling you trying to hide something from me. Now, I don't care what business you had in town. I want to know what it was." My heart was beating hard, and I could feel sweat oozing in my armpits.

He gave me a sorry look. "I don't like to keep you in the dark. Um . . . I went to see Dr. Mason."

My head started throbbing right away, and my heart felt like it was going to explode. The thought of my man having a health problem was something I was not prepared to deal with. I had relatives scattered here and there, but I wasn't half as close to them as I was to Milton. Some I hadn't seen in years. If something happened to him, I'd probably stay single for the rest of my life, because nobody could replace him.

"You ain't been sick since I met you. Why did you go see the doctor?" Before he could answer, three customers came out. We moved to the side to let them pass. When they got in their car, I whirled around and stared into Milton's eyes. "You sick?"

He shook his head and grinned. "It would take a bolt of lightning to get me down. And it would have to strike me more than one time."

"If you ain't sick, why did you go see Dr. Mason?"

"See, I been having dizzy spells for the past few days. The kind my granddaddy used to have before he died." Milton gave me a hug and a quick peck on my jaw. "Come to find out, it ain't nothing but high blood pressure."

"Did the doctor give you something to take for it?"

"Naw. He just told me to slow down on eating chitlins and other pig parts."

"I guess you'll have to give up drinking, too, huh?"

Milton rolled his eyes, scrunched his lips to the side, and let out a sharp laugh. "How many bootleggers you know that don't drink? Humph! It'd take more than dizzy spells to make me stop drinking. I will start eating healthier, though."

I was relieved. "I'm glad it ain't nothing you'd have to go into the hospital for and be laid up for a while. But you wouldn't have to worry, because I could run our business by myself."

Milton stared off into space for a moment, and then he gave me a strange look. "What make you think you could bootleg without me?"

"Because you taught me everything I know when it come to making money."

"Yeah, I taught you everything you know." He paused, and a mysterious look I'd never seen before spread across his face. "But I didn't teach you everything *I* know."

I tried to act like that last comment didn't faze me, but it did. A little voice in my head told me I had to keep my eye on Milton, and that was one thing I had learned on my own. Not just where he was concerned, but with everybody else—especially Joyce and Odell Watson next door. They was still nice enough, but now it seemed like they was snootier than ever. We had just started calling them the Queen of Sheba and Prince Charming behind their backs, not to be mean, but because them nicknames fit them. We still enjoyed their company, because they gave us something to talk and laugh about when we was alone.

"Yvonne, let's stop by the Watsons' house on our way home this evening and invite them to come over tonight to hear some of them new records we got. Odell is a fool for that Bobbie Holiday."

"Billie."

"Billie who?"

"That's that new woman singer's first name."

"Oh. Anyway, if they don't make it tonight or tomorrow night, I'm sure they'll come over by Wednesday," Milton said with a sniff. "I swear to God, that couple take the cake and the crumbs. It's a sport just listening to them talk about how good they got it."

"Tell me about it. Well, we better get back to work." I was already heading toward the entrance, with Milton close behind. "There was a mighty big crowd inside when I came out here. A bunch more done arrived since then."

Almost all eight of our tables, four booths, and half of the counter was occupied. Compared to Mosella's, the biggest and most expensive colored-owned restaurant in Branson, Cunningham's Grill was a shack. But it was the only colored roadhouse in town and a lot cheaper than Mosella's. Within walking distance was our rinky-dink train station, our city dump, and several cotton and sugarcane fields. We fed a lot of the folks that worked for them businesses and passengers that had long layovers between trains. We was near the main highway, so a few times a week, folks traveling through stopped to rest and eat at the grill.

Most of our customers was colored, but a lot of white folks came in too. Every single one of the white-owned restaurants in Branson was segregated. If we wanted to eat their food, we was only allowed to get orders to go, and we had to come and go through the back door. We couldn't use their toilets or talk to none of their white customers. White folks waltzed into Cunningham's Grill like they owned the place, and there was nothing we could do about it. A few complained about the service and didn't tip too good, if they tipped at all.

I went to the kitchen to wash my hands. When I got back to the main floor, a couple of stout white women was waddling through the door. They didn't wait for me or one of the other waitresses to seat them. They snatched menus off the counter and plopped down at the biggest table in the middle of the room, which we liked to keep available for the preachers and important white folks that came in.

"You girl. Get a rag and come clean off this table," one of the women grunted, snapping her fingers.

"Yes, ma'am. I'll take care of that right away." I cringed and turned around quick so she wouldn't see my eyeballs rolling and skittered back to the kitchen like a squirrel running from a bobcat. I had learned early in life to be as humble as possible when dealing with white folks. We was not to say or do nothing that would agitate them, especially the females. I avoided looking them in their eyes because I didn't want them to see the contempt in mine. Besides, acting the way they wanted us to got me better tips.

"You look like you seen a ghost," Milton commented as I rushed past him. He was standing over the stove, stirring the oxtail stew, our special every Monday.

I didn't stop or say nothing until I made it to the sink behind him and swirled a rag in a dishpan full of soapy water. "Worse," I said in a low tone. "Two husky white women just pranced in and grabbed the main table. And unless they can't read, they had to see that big sign on the stand by the door telling customers to wait to be seated."

Before I could get another word out, Milton trotted to the door, cracked it open, and peeped out. When he came back over to where I was, he was grinning. "Don't you know who the one with the red hair is?"

I hunched my shoulders. "White women her age all look the same to me."

"That's Lyla Bullard," he laughed. "She's good people and ain't got a mean bone in her body."

I looked at Milton with my mouth hanging open. "Maybe you don't think so. But you should have heard the way she hollered at me to clean off her table," I grumbled.

"Aw, you just too sensitive." Milton waved his hand in my face and gave me a mean look hisself, but I knew he was just playing with me. "Lyla's family used to be real prominent and noble to a fault. Years ago, her granddaddy and grandmama moved to Africa to do missionary work for them natives. When Lyla was a young girl, my aunt Delphine was her and her sisters' mammy. I ain't never seen a white woman love colored folks as much as Lyla do. Her daddy used to own a bunch of cotton fields. But he was one of the first ones to lose almost everything when the Great Depression hit. He took it so hard, he went to Mobile and jumped off a bridge. She had already moved to Michigan and got married when that happened. When her husband took off with another woman, she moved back here. Her divorce settlement was so sweet, she had enough money to buy that hat store on Franklin Street."

"Oh yeah! I remember her. She used to have brown hair and was a lot skinnier. A few weeks before my mama died, Lyla gave us a ride to town in her daddy's brand-new Model T. I wondered what had happened to her. How do you know so much about what she been up to?"

"I used to pick cotton for her daddy, and I got along good with her whole family. And after she moved north, I would bump into some of her kinfolks every now and then, and they would update me on her. I seen Lyla and her cousin Emmalou at a jook joint last Thursday. They told me they going to start coming to the house to drink with us."

I scrunched my lips to the side while I tried to think of what to say next. I usually went along with whatever Milton wanted to do when it came to our business. But us socializing with a *white* woman—especially one from a used-to-be prominent family— was a awkward and scary subject.

"How come you looking so distressed?" he wanted to know.

I took my time answering. "Baby, Willie Frank and his family is one thing, but I don't know if it's a good idea to start letting other white folks come to the house."

"Pffft. Don't be no worrywart. The only color we need to be concerned about is dollar-bill green. That's the only color the Jim Crow laws don't care nothing about."

CHAPTER 10
YVONNE

I WENT BACK OUT TO THE DINING AREA AND WIPED OFF THE TABLE where the white women was sitting. They stopped talking until I finished. Then Lyla looked at me and wagged her plump finger in my face.

"Wasn't Maybelle and Roscoe your mama and daddy?" she asked, gazing at me with her eyes narrowed. People rarely asked about my dead parents. Whenever they did, it made me sad. I had to blink hard to hold back my tears.

"Uh-huh," I muttered.

"That was my uncle's tractor they was on when they got squashed. Uncle Lucas never got over what happened. He died in the same hospital that was just half a mile from the accident and had refused to admit your folks because they was colored. If they had got medical attention in time, they would have made it." Lyla gave me a sympathetic look and let out a loud sigh. "I hope I live long enough to see the end of segregation."

"Me too," I said firmly.

"Bless your heart. Lean down so I can give you a hug," she ordered.

I held my breath and leaned toward her. After the quick hug, she gave me a pat on the shoulder. I straightened up, still holding my breath, because being hugged by a white woman was a first for me. Lyla was in her forties and looked it. She had a few strands of gray hair, her eyes was puffy and had dark circles and wrinkles around the rims, but she wasn't a bad-looking woman. Rumors had been floating around for years that she'd spread her legs for a snake. When I was a teenager, people used to talk about how she'd hang out at the colored jook joints and fool around with some of the men. But she was smart enough not to let no white folks hear about her loose behavior with colored men. I was glad she interrupted my thoughts, because my mind was wandering way off course.

"I liked your mama and daddy so much, I still think about them."

"Thank you, ma'am."

"Don't 'ma'am' me!" she scolded. "I ain't that much older than you. I was just telling my cousin here, me and Milton go way back." The other woman looked up at me and smiled. "Emmalou, Yvonne here is Milton's wife."

"Howdy do, Yvonne." Emmalou's voice was as deep as a man's. She eyeballed me with a lopsided smile on her moon face. "Bless your heart. I knew your parents, too. It's a crying shame they died so young. Your daddy didn't look too hot, but your mama was a beauty. I'm pleased as punch to see you took after her."

"Thank you." I didn't think I could stand to hear another comment about my mama and daddy, or my good looks, so I changed the subject. "Lyla, Milton told me he seen you at a colored jook joint last week."

"Sure enough. I was just at the same one two nights ago. During Prohibition, the jook joints was the only places me and my family and friends would drink at. The white bootleggers wasn't much fun. And even when the law made drinking legal again a few years ago, we still went to the places run by colored folks. The bars and stores was too expensive, and they served weak drinks. But in the future, I won't be drinking at none of the same jook joints I used to go. The jokers running them places nowadays serve the nastiest-tasting shine I ever drunk. I hear tell you and Milton is at the top of the game, so I got a itching to pay y'all a visit real soon. Me and Emmalou both," she said, looking at the other woman. "Right, cuz?"

"Yessiree," the Emmalou woman chirped. Looking at her closer now, I could see that she was not bad looking, either. She had thick brown hair hanging halfway down her back, pretty blue eyes, and dimples in both cheeks.

"I'm pleased to hear that. Can't nobody say we serve nasty-tasting drinks. Our guests always go home happy. That's why they keep coming back."

"Ooh-wee," Lyla squealed. "I hear tell y'all live over there in that well-to-do neighborhood, among them highfalutin colored folks."

"That's right." I grinned.

"I can't wait to pay you nice folks a visit," Emmalou tossed in. "I'm pleased to hear that your house is in a much safer and cleaner neighborhood. The colored bootleggers on the lower south side can be so inhospitable. A few are downright savage."

I was so happy when they finally placed their orders—chicken feet and corn on the cob—so I could leave before I said something I'd regret. I never bad-mouthed people in my own race when I conversated with white folks. But there was things about some of our new colored neighbors that I didn't like, which me and Milton discussed when we was alone. Most of the folks had been kind of standoffish when they found out we had moved from a shack on the lower south side. But they had gradually got friendlier when they found out we was bootleggers. They was happy that they didn't have to go to the rough areas and rowdy jook joints to drink now.

And Joyce and Odell was the happiest ones. One of the things I regretted now was us offering them two oddballs drinks on the house the first night they came over. That had been a stupid move on our part. Now they was so used to us serving them drinks and not asking for no money, they never offered to pay. And we didn't ask them to. But we made up for it by serving them recycled booze. When guests didn't finish their drinks, we poured every drop back into the original containers when they went home. After all the bragging Joyce and Odell had already done about drinking high-quality booze at some of the uppity restaurants they went to, I felt right justified giving them second- or thirdhand drinks.

I didn't expect Odell and Joyce to show up tonight, but they showed up around nine. They hugged and greeted a few folks before they sat down on the couch. I occupied the footstool across the room, facing the couch. Milton was in the kitchen with Willie Frank.

It wasn't long before Joyce started bragging about the expensive whiskey they had recently started buying from a liquor store. "We only serve it to our special guests, and everybody else gets elder-berry wine," she admitted with a sheepish grin. Since elderberry wine was all they ever offered us when we went to their house, she was also letting me know that their "special guests" didn't in-clude me and Milton. And she had the nerve to say it right in front of me! That heifer had no shame. But, since I was trying to be more of a "lady," I let that go . . . for now.

"This sure is some good home brew," Odell commented. He had swallowed almost half of what I'd poured into his jar in one gulp, and they'd been in the house only ten minutes. When Mil-ton came into the living room and sat down on the couch next to Odell, he started drinking even faster. A few minutes later, him and Milton got up and left the room.

Right away, Joyce started her "my life is so blessed" routine. Tonight most of her bragging was about Odell. If I'd had a muz-zle, I would have strapped it on her face to shut her up. I wasn't the only one getting fed up with her out-of-control chattering. She was too blind to see the exasperated looks on other people's faces and all the eyeballs rolling. A married couple that had been standing close by abruptly moved across the room. I fig-ured they was just as tired of hearing about the wonderful Odell as I was.

"I'm happy to see Milton and Odell getting closer," Joyce said, rambling on. "Milton can learn a lot from Odell."

"My husband is okay just the way he is," I insisted. I felt

slighted because she was implying that my man needed improvement.

"Is having somebody that is just 'okay' all you want, Yvonne?"

I smiled, but I didn't answer her question. I knew that no matter what came out of my mouth, it wouldn't make us look no better in Joyce's and Odell's eyes. If we stood on a rooftop, they'd still find a way to look down on us. "Excuse me. I need to go tend to them folks waving their empty jars at me."

It was a profitable night. If anybody had ever doubted that we was the best bootleggers in Branson, they couldn't say that now. Compliments was flying at my ears left and right. I was pleased to see everybody having such a good time. We couldn't change the records fast enough. Middle-aged folks that hadn't been on a dance floor since they was teenagers was dancing up a storm. I was also pleased to see people I hadn't seen in months. There was the lady who used to do my hair before she retired, and a man that lived next door to us in our old neighborhood. I roamed around with a jug, refilling jars and thanking folks for their business.

"Yvonne, I'm going to spread the word about how much fun I had over here tonight. This is where me and my man will be coming to party from now on. Most of the other bootleggers and jook joints don't offer free snacks. The ones that do never have nothing but stale cookies and peanuts. The only music they got is somebody blowing on a harmonica or strumming a guitar. Who can dance to something that lame? Thank God y'all got a record player and some of the latest records." Talking to me as I poured her another drink was a woman I'd gone to school with. She worked as a live-in maid for our mayor's daughter.

"Thank you, Della. Please tell all your friends and neighbors about us. Make sure you let them know we don't put up with no rowdy mess like they do in them other places, so they ain't got to worry about getting shot or cut up." I excused myself so I could go pour another drink for myself.

CHAPTER 11
MILTON

*A*FTER ME AND WILLIE FRANK HAD DISCUSSED A BUSINESS DETAIL in the kitchen, I went back to the living room and chatted with folks. A few minutes later, I took Odell to the kitchen so I could discuss a business detail with him.

"I need a extra five dollars tonight," I told him, speaking in a low tone.

Just like I'd expected, he got hot and bothered. The way he screwed up his face, you would have thought he'd just bit into a sour apple. "What? I'm already giving you a extra six dollars tonight," he snapped, handing me some crumpled-up one-dollar bills.

"I mean extra to this."

"Look, Milton. You getting way out of hand. When you came to the store today, you told me you needed five dollars so you could get in a card game tonight. That turned into six, not counting the one I gave you before you left the store. And that's all I'd planned on giving you until Wednesday."

"Shoot! You didn't get here in time for me to get in the game," I complained.

"So? That ain't my fault!"

"But I told you to be here by six o'clock. You dragged your tail up in here almost three hours later."

"Well, something came up. Anyway, you got the money. Use it in your next game."

"Let's get something straight, Prince Charming." He didn't even bat a eye when I accidentally called him by the nickname me and Yvonne used behind his back. "When you don't do like I tell you, you make it harder on me, and on yourself. If you want us to stay friends and keep everything going smooth, when I tell you to do something, you do exactly that."

"Milton, I couldn't get here no sooner than I did. My in-laws was at the house, and we couldn't leave until they did. Man, be reasonable. There is going to be other times when I can't follow all your rules. Give me a break!"

"I'm giving you a break already. Do you think anybody else would let you off with only eight dollars a week with all the stuff I got on you?"

"You right. I'm sorry for flying off the handle." Odell swallowed hard and rubbed the back of his neck. I still had a hard time believing he was such a pushover. I couldn't have stumbled upon a weaker person on a deathbed! He pulled out his wallet and handed me five more one-dollar bills.

"See there. Now, that wasn't so hard." I clapped him on his back. "Now let's get back outside and have some fun."

I was in a very good mood the rest of the night. Even though Odell was grinning and chitchatting with folks, I knew he was faking. I had to admire him for being able to act so normal. Who would have thought that he was leading a double life? Or that he was being blackmailed? Because of my allegiance to the Lord, I still had a conscience. Every now and then, I felt a teeny-weeny bit of guilt about what I was doing. But I needed the money more than I needed a good conscience.

I thought that if my early life hadn't been so hard, I might have turned out better than I did. But now I had so much going for me, I didn't want to change.

I should have never hitched a ride after work over to that Brewster Road jook joint Tuesday evening. Within ten minutes after I walked into that shack behind a cornfield, I lost all the money Odell had gave me last night. It was a good thing my next payment from him was due tomorrow. And if I wasn't in a crappy mood by then, I'd be nice and not ask for more than the eight dollars he owed me.

Willie Frank was at the house when I got home a few minutes past 8:00 p.m. He immediately pulled me into my bedroom and locked the door, so we could conversate in private. I couldn't remember the last time I seen him looking so hyped up. His eyes was sparkling like diamonds, and he couldn't stop wringing his hands.

He leaned up against the dresser facing my bed and started talking fast, but in a low tone. "Listen, Milton, old buddy, I'm hatching a good scheme that might make us some big money." I couldn't wait to hear what he had up his sleeve.

"What is this scheme? Easy money, I hope." I eased down on the side of the bed.

"Pffft!" Willie Frank waved his hands in the air. "It's better than that, and I ain't talking about no chicken feed. The only thing bigger and easier would be if we woke up one morning and found dollar bills growing on one of our trees." We laughed. "Anyway, you know me and my kinfolks supply most of the booze to almost every bootlegger in our county, right? And we do business with a few that live in some of the dry counties."

"I know that because I seen you do it."

"And you know how lamebrained and careless they can be. It's high time we start using their faults to our advantage."

"I'm listening."

"Once we deliver a order, we'll sneak back during the night, when the bootlegger is alone. We'll go in through a window or unlocked door and take back as much of the shine as we can carry."

"How do you know which ones don't keep track of what we deliver to them? Some of them jokers been in business for twenty, thirty years. If they was too dumb to keep some kind of records, they wouldn't still be in business." I let out a loud breath and stood up. "Hmmm. On top of that, we could be taking some risks."

"So what? There is always risks involved when it comes to making money. If we don't pull off a successful deal but one time, we'll still make a nice piece of change."

"Hmmm. I guess that's worth taking a risk for," I agreed.

"Damn straight. We can resell the same supply two or three times to either the same customers or new ones."

"Willie Frank, for somebody that ain't never set foot in a schoolhouse, you one of the smartest men I know. Hell's bells. Why didn't I think of that?" I laughed and slapped the side of my head.

"You ain't no dummy yourself. You came up with the idea to recycle your guests' unfinished drinks," Willie Frank reminded. "They say great minds think alike. I could sure use some extra money."

"Lord knows I could, too."

As long as I'd been hustling, I ain't never had enough money to do nothing real nice for myself and my woman. It made me sad when Yvonne complained about how Joyce bragged about them glad rags she got from the catalog, which was way out of our price range. Yeah, we made good money bootlegging, but as unpredictable as the law was, there was no telling how long we'd be able to stay in the business.

"When things get real busy tonight, let's go visit Cleotis Bates," I said. "We can start by taking back that double order we delivered to him Sunday night. I know for a fact he don't lock his doors. And he go to Aunt Mattie's place every Tuesday night, right after his Bible study and choir practice at his church down the street from her."

We waited until we had a standing-room-only crowd before I hid a couple of jugs of shine. Then I told Yvonne that we was almost out and that me and Willie Frank had to make a run to his house to get more.

"Milton, how did you let our supply get low?" she hissed in a low tone so none of the guests in the living room could hear her. "From now on, I'll be keeping track of our supply. Y'all go now and hurry up and get back here. There ain't no telling what might happen if we run out completely while I'm up in this house with all these thirsty people."

"Baby, we'll be back in less than a hour," I assured her.

Our plan didn't go well. When we got to Cleotis's neighborhood, we parked behind some trees and walked to his house. We peeped in his front window and seen that one of Aunt Mattie's girls was with him.

"I don't believe this shit! Every Tuesday for the past five years, that horny pig been going to Aunt Mattie's house to do his business with one of the girls. That double-crossing sneak! I swear to God, you just can't depend on nobody no more! Maybe this ain't going to be such a good plan, after all," I griped. Me and Willie Frank had already started trotting back to his truck.

"You could be right. Don't worry, though. We'll come up with another moneymaking scheme real soon."

Each day, I got a little more anxious to get more money. But I lost interest in stealing back liquor we'd already sold and delivered. In the meantime, I had to depend on the paycheck I got from the grill and on Odell's deep pockets. I kept myself occupied so I wouldn't spend too much time thinking about it.

When I didn't feel like doing none of the things I normally did to keep myself busy when I wasn't working, like fishing, taking Yvonne on picnics, or visiting folks in our old neighborhood, I relied on Willie Frank. He would pick up me and Yvonne and drive us to the hills so we could socialize with him and some of his relatives.

"Milton, you as close as family," his mama had told me during a recent visit. "Maybe one of these days, you and Yvonne can talk Willie Frank into finding hisself a wife so he won't grow old alone."

"Aw, Mama Perdue"—that was what she'd told me and Yvonne to call her, and we called her husband Papa Perdue—"Willie Frank ain't going to grow old alone. Me and Yvonne will move him in with us before we let that happen."

That conversation had took place earlier this month, the Saturday before Labor Day. We had all just come from fishing in the creek behind the three-bedroom, tin-roof shack Willie Frank lived in with his mama and daddy and eight other kinfolks. He shared a bed in the living room with his paraplegic grandfather and two of his teenage nephews. He slept at the head of the bed with the old man, and the kids slept at the foot. The family made a good living manufacturing and selling homemade alcohol. But their money was tight because they had to pay off them greedy revenuers and corrupt lawmen so they wouldn't shut down their still. On top of all that, they had to support a bunch of unemployed relatives that was too lazy and/or slow witted to work. It was a miserable environment, which was the main reason Willie Frank spent so much time at our house.

I was worried about my buddy not having a main woman in his life. Every time I mentioned that subject, he shut me up by telling me how much fun he was having with the women that worked for Aunt Mattie. "If they wasn't colored, whore or not, I would have married one by now," he confessed, with his eyes twinkling.

I didn't know what I'd do without a good friend like Willie Frank. He was loyal, honest, dependable, and a heap of fun. Me and him smoked a lot of the rabbit tobacco he grew in his backyard. It made us feel right mellow. Yvonne had smoked it a few times, but it didn't relax her the way it did us. She didn't like the way it stunk up the house. When I wanted to roll a few cigarettes and indulge myself, she made me do it outside. As important as Willie Frank was to me and Yvonne, I had to keep in mind that he was still white. My daddy used to tell me that no matter how good you treated a snake, it would always be a snake, and biting folks was their nature. But so far, Willie Frank was the only man, colored or white, that had never let me down, especially when it came to business. And, as hard as it was to believe, neither had Odell.

CHAPTER 12
YVONNE

ABOUT A HOUR AFTER OUR GUESTS LEFT TONIGHT, ME AND MILTON cleaned up and went to bed. I wasn't the least bit sleepy, though. It was a few minutes before midnight. Right after my head hit one of the flat pillows on the saggy bed we had picked up at a secondhand store, I started tossing and turning like a flea-bitten hound. I leaned over and lit the kerosene lamp we kept on the wooden crate we used as a nightstand by my side of the bed.

"What's wrong, sugar? You seem kind of jumpy tonight," Milton noticed, turning on his side to face me.

"I am kind of jumpy."

"Why come? You seemed like you was having as much fun as everybody else tonight."

"That Joyce is one of the most complicated women I ever came across!" I hissed.

"Aw shit. Here we go again. What's wrong now? Did she say something you didn't like tonight? And while we on the subject, I bet she talks to Odell about some of the things *you* say that she don't like."

"I'm sure she do."

"Well, in that case, y'all in the same boat."

"And if we keep loading bad blood in it, it's going to sink," I said.

"All right, now. Let's talk about this and get it over with so we can get some sleep. Or do something else more fun." Milton liked to sleep buck naked, but I always slept in a gown. He slid his hand inside my panties and started poking between my thighs as he talked. "Since we already on the subject, I'll mention how I didn't like the way she screwed up her face when I handed that last drink to her in a jelly jar. Like she ain't never drunk out a jelly jar before. With the crowd we had tonight, I couldn't wash the good jars and cups fast enough to keep up, so I had to start serving drinks in whatever was available. She lucky she didn't have to drink out of a soup can, like Willie Frank. That woman ought to know by now that we ain't got none of them fancy glasses like her and Odell. What all did she say to you?"

"She bragged about her teacher's aide work at that uppity Mahoney Street School *again*. In the next breath she told me I should go back to school so I could get a real job."

"You already got one. If waiting tables ain't real, I don't know what is."

"Milton, she got white folks' attitude. She don't even know what being a regular down-home colored woman is all about. She even try to talk all proper like a white woman. She ain't even got that down pat. When she was running off at the mouth about her job, she used 'ain't' twice in the same sentence."

"That just go to show, she ain't as smart as she make herself out to be. And working at a school with college-educated teachers probably ain't the fairy-tale job she try to make us think it is. Them folks might have her cleaning toilets and scrubbing floors for all we know." We laughed.

"I doubt if that's true. And I doubt if her job is half as hard as mine is at the grill. The bottom line is, her cheesy black ass grew up on easy street, so she wouldn't know hard work if it bit off a piece of her butt."

I stopped talking and thought about what I'd just said. I suddenly realized that some of Joyce's remarks hadn't been *that* bad. A few had even been kind of nice. She'd gave me a good compliment about the new flowered curtains I had put up at every window in the living room. And when a clumsy ox dropped his jar of moonshine on the floor and it broke into a million little pieces, she squatted down with me and helped clean it up.

"She can ruffle my feathers real easy, but I will admit that that was a good point she made about me going back to school. It wouldn't hurt for me and you both to get more education. Maybe I'm being too hard on her. I guess she thought she was just being nice and helpful by suggesting that. And then again, I don't call making fun of folks being nice and helpful." Some of the issues I had with Joyce was too bothersome to dismiss, though I didn't like to stir up a mess. But this was one I couldn't overlook, because it involved Milton. I was the only person who could make a sport of my man and get away with it.

"Huh? Who did Joyce make fun of, Yvonne? Bowlegged Sally Rhine?"

"You."

Milton's body froze like a block of ice. He stopped poking me, but his fingers was still between my thighs. "Me? What did you say?"

"When you took so long to count out the change when you broke that dollar bill for Willie Frank, she shook her head. She didn't know I could hear her on account of she was whispering. She told Odell that them fourth grade kids at her school can count better than you."

"Say what?"

"Uh-huh. Like you some kind of idiot or something."

"That bitch! That heifer! She ain't the Queen of Sheba she think she is!"

"That wasn't all. A few minutes after they got here tonight, she pulled out a handkerchief and started dabbing at my lipstick."

Milton snickered. "Excuse me for laughing, but that's funny. That was her way of telling you that you had on too much lipstick, huh?"

"Thank you!"

"Oomph, oomph, oomph! I declare, Joyce and Odell sound like the kind of folks that could be your best friends and worst enemies at the same time. I can tell that Joyce is really starting to get under your skin. She is almost twice as big as you, but you could probably whup her ass with one hand behind your back."

"Lord almighty, sugar! I hope it never get to that. I don't want to start beating up on the neighbors. I don't want to go back to jail."

"I feel the same way. As long as we careful, we won't never have to worry about doing time again." Milton frowned at the scar in the palm of his right hand, which a guard had sliced open during a jailhouse riot. He never complained about it, but it was a sensitive subject with him. Then his voice got sad. "If the laws ever convict me again, they'll have to kill me, because I'll never do another day in no prison camp. Shit."

"Let's move on to something else. Like concentrating on having a closer relationship with Joyce and Odell, and what's in it for us. If you know what I mean."

"Sugar, I know exactly what you mean. I been thinking about going up to Odell and asking him to let me open a line of credit at the store. With all them free drinks him and Joyce gulped down tonight, it's the least he can do," Milton snarled.

"I been meaning to talk to you about that. If we don't start asking them to pay for their drinks, like we do everybody else, I don't think they ever will. I wish we hadn't started off like that in the first place. I don't know what we was thinking!"

"Don't even worry about that. All the stuff we steal from MacPherson's evens things out." Milton pulled his finger away from my crotch and licked it. I liked to see him taste my juice before we made love. From the dreamy-eyed look on his face, I knew he liked the way I tasted. I knew he was ready to get it on, and so was I. But I had a few more things to get off my chest first, so I gently pushed him to the side.

"I swear, sometimes Joyce sound like a broke record. She told me for the umpteenth time tonight that she and Odell still trying to make a baby."

"Maybe they ain't trying hard enough, or maybe they don't do it often enough."

"Oh, they do it often enough. I also overheard her say that they fuck almost every night. Except she didn't say 'fuck.' She said 'make love.' That proper-talking bitch. She just as white as she can be."

"Something is wrong," Milton suggested.

"That's what I was thinking. Maybe her eggs done dried up. Or his jism is too weak to swim up far enough to reach her baby-making section." I laughed.

"Odell told me he loves kids so much, he would like to have at least three or four. I don't care about having none, one way or the other, but I feel for the people that do and can't."

"I feel for them, too. Anyway, Joyce is coming over again to-morrow evening so I can show her how to knit."

"Yvonne, we can't afford to do everything for them for free. We done gave them enough free alcohol to fill a bathtub. Now you going to give Joyce free knitting lessons? I don't want to be friends with them that bad. We didn't get this far being too generous with none of our resources."

"I know, baby, and I know when to quit. But I'm thinking ahead. She love them pot holders I knitted, and asked me to show her how to make them. I told her I'd love to so long as she supplies all the material and include enough for me to make us a few more. I got a lot of material already, but I ain't about to use it up on the woman whose folks own the store I stole it from," I chuckled. "Speaking of the store, if Odell don't give us a line of credit when you ask him, try to get him to give us a big discount every time we buy something. That would be just as good. Maybe even better. We need to take advantage of every opportunity that come our way. Such as they got a car *and* a telephone. We could get a lot of mileage out of them things. Think of the bucks we could save by not having to take that damn bus or pay somebody to haul us around."

"That's been on my mind quite a bit lately." Milton paused and gave me a pensive look.

"What's the matter?"

"And they got the nerve to serve us elderberry wine when we go to their house. Next time Joyce and Odell come over, give them the cheapest alcohol in the house."

"Milton, what could be cheaper than the recycled stuff we give them now?" We laughed.

"Just always make sure it's part of the *cheapest* recycled batch. Meanwhile, let's stick to our original plan and keep on trying to be good friends with them, too. They could be the best meal ticket we ever get."

"You got a point there. And one more thing, maybe Joyce and Odell ain't as uppity as we think. Some people just naturally crude and rude and say a lot of stupid shit that they don't mean. But we can overlook that so long as they don't say nothing too bad to or about us. Besides, I don't think they got much street smarts. If we do some sensible plotting, even if it mean kissing every inch of their butts and licking their cracks, we'll have them eating out of our hands. By the time we get through milking them, we'll be better off than they is."

CHAPTER 13
MILTON

I SPENT A LOT OF TIME THINKING ABOUT SOME OF THE THINGS bouncing around in my head. The one I thought about the most was my sweet arrangement with Odell. If he ever decided to stop paying me, I'd go up to Joyce lickety-split and blow the whistle like a diesel train. I'd tell her everything. Even about all the money he was stealing from her parents to give to his other family and me. Being the lovestruck fool Joyce was, she just might be crazy enough to forgive him! The thought of that chilled me to the bone, so I pushed it to the back of my mind.

It didn't matter what was going on between me and Odell. I still considered him and Joyce good people. The biggest complaint I had—even before Odell put me on his payroll, so to speak—was how fickle they behaved from time to time. I couldn't decide if they was friends or foes. They would cruise by in that shiny black car, see me and Yvonne dragging along down the street, and wouldn't even acknowledge us, let alone offer us a ride. Other times we'd bump into them in public, and they would grin and fawn over us like we was long-lost kinfolks.

At the end of the day, they was getting benefits from us, too! We had a few things they wanted, other than free alcohol and us being a low-ranking couple for them to look down on. Last Saturday, Joyce had a wedding to go to and needed to get her hair done. Her mama had promised she'd do it. When Joyce went to her mama's house that morning, come to find out, Sister Millie was fixing to go to a church bake sale and was on her way out the door. Joyce was fit to be tied. The next thing me and Yvonne knew, she was at our door, with a jar of hair grease, her straightening comb, and her marcel curling iron. She begged Yvonne to do her hair, and my baby didn't even hesitate. She'd been busy washing clothes at the time. But she put that chore aside and started straightening that briar patch on Joyce's head right away. That was the kind of friend girl Yvonne was to Joyce. Joyce didn't offer her a plugged nickel, but she promised to go by Mac-Pherson's and pick up three or four jars of pickled pig feet and bring them to the house the next time she came over.

When Joyce got home from that wedding, she came straight to the house with three jars of pig feet and a big batch of tea cakes for us to serve our guests. I was real impressed. It seemed like she and Odell was trying to be nice to us, after all, but only when it was convenient for them.

Even though Joyce and Odell had been drinking at our house for "free" from day one, they wasn't as stingy as we thought. One of our other neighbors had told me the same day we moved in that he'd been borrowing money from Odell and Joyce ever since they moved to the neighborhood. He had a system going that I'd never heard of. He'd borrow a dollar from one or the other and pay it back when he said he would. A few days later, the same neighbor would borrow another dollar and pay it back on time, too. He had been doing that at least twice a month for the past year. I wondered if it was the same dollar bill that got passed back and forth. Another neighbor gloated about all the merchandise he stole from MacPherson's every time he went in and how easy it was. I wasn't stupid enough to admit to nobody that me and Yvonne had been helping ourselves to merchandise from there, too. I didn't want to ruin the good thing we had going, not to mention my arrangement with Odell. Stealing from that place was like taking candy from a blind baby, and we wanted it to stay that way.

When Odell came over to bring me my money on Wednesday night, he told me that he was going to let us have a line of credit at the store. *After* I'd asked him three times.

With today being Friday, me and Yvonne expected the usual wall-to-wall crowd to come to our house after everybody got off work, so we needed a heap of stuff for snacks. Mr. Cunningham had closed the grill two hours early because his sister had called and told him his wife wasn't feeling good. We caught a ride with one of our regular customers and had him drop us off at Mac-Pherson's. We didn't want to spend the money we had on something we could get on credit now or steal. That was why we went from aisle to aisle, grabbing things without even looking at the prices. There was too many other customers roaming around, so we decided not to steal nothing. In our case, credit was as good as us stealing merchandise, because we would never pay for it. Odell would be paying that tab when it came due. He didn't know it yet, though.

We didn't think he'd mind giving us a ride home when he got off at five, so after we got our stuff checked out and bagged, we went up to him on the opposite side of the store.

"Y'all find everything?" he asked as he adjusted his tie. Before we could say anything, that happy devil started whistling. That was how blasé he was.

"We found everything we was looking for," I told him. "Now we need to go home and start getting things ready for tonight. Can we get a ride home with you?"

He stopped whistling and gave me a dry look. "I can't do that today. After I close up, I got to do inventory, and that could take quite a while. When I finish that, I got somewhere to go."

"Hmmm. If you don't mind our company, we wouldn't mind riding along with you," I tossed in with a sheepish grin. I knew that the "somewhere to go" was Betty Jean's house. And, from the tight look on his face, I could tell that he knew what I was thinking. If Joyce was gullible enough to believe that he spent so much of his free time fishing and visiting his sick daddy, she deserved whatever she got in the end.

Odell cleared his throat and glared at me. "Um, I need to go out and check up on my daddy. I'll probably be out there the whole weekend," he claimed.

"Can you take a few minutes off now and take us home?" Yvonne asked in a weary tone.

"I can't do that. I'm too busy right now," he claimed.

Busy? I had to force myself not to laugh. The busiest thing Odell had going on was humping two women and making babies! He claimed he spent a lot of time on his job, doing paperwork, ordering stuff, meeting with vendors, and whatnot. But the gossipy elderly cashiers—Buddy Armstrong and Sadie Mae Glutz—and the random teenage boys that stocked the shelves done all the real work. Odell probably had the most laid-back job in town. Almost every time I went in the store, he'd be holed up in his office, reading magazines or whistling, strutting around, and scribbling on a notepad. The bottom line was, him and Joyce had it made in the shade. I didn't have no problem with people having it easy, but I had a problem when they looked down their noses at their friends and got stingy with their favors, the way Odell was doing now.

"We got a bunch of heavy canned goods, so it'll be hard to tote these bags. Can you at least leave for a few minutes and give us a ride as far as Liberty Street? We sure would appreciate it. From there, we'll walk the rest of the way home or catch the bus. It's been a long, sad day for us," I whined.

"No, I can't give y'all a ride, period!"

Odell's outburst stupefied Yvonne so much, she whimpered and stumbled a few feet to the side. I scrunched my lips off to one side and stared at him so hard, he cringed. I thought that by now he'd go out of his way not to get *me* riled up. He had to know that it wouldn't do our friendship no good.

"Leave them bags here and go out on the street and find somebody with a car that can take y'all home. But y'all better get back here before I close up. Otherwise, them bags will sit here until I open up on Monday." Odell glanced at the clock above the door. "Excuse me, but I have to get back to work. And if y'all ain't buying nothing else today, y'all have to leave. That's our new policy since we been having so much trouble with shoplifters lately. We can't keep a eye on everybody."

I didn't appreciate being lumped in with the run-of-the-mill shoplifters—especially by a deceitful sucker like Odell. It was a good thing I had smoked me some rabbit tobacco before I left the grill. I was feeling pretty mellow, and that helped me keep my cool. But I could hear Yvonne breathing hard and mumbling cusswords under her breath.

"Okay, we'll let you get back to work. We'll take our bags with us. Maybe we'll run into somebody we know with transportation, and they can give us a ride," I grumbled.

He glanced at the clock again. "It's just four o'clock. How come y'all ain't still at the grill? Done got fired, huh?" he said with a sneer.

Odell was pushing his luck. His shoplifting comments had hurt my feelings bad enough. Now he was accusing us of losing our jobs.

"No, we didn't get fired," Yvonne blurted out. "Mr. Cunningham's wife had some kind of fit, and he had to rush home and tend to her, so he closed up early today."

"Good God. I'm sorry to hear that. I hope Sister Cunningham is going to be okay. She is one of our best customers." I was pleased to see Odell show some compassion for somebody other than hisself. He actually sounded sympathetic. "No wonder y'all looking so down in the dumps. Um . . . what's going on Sunday evening? If it ain't too late when I get home from visiting my daddy, me and Joyce might come over and have a few drinks."

"I hope you do come, Odell," I said. "I put in a double order with Willie Frank this week, so we'll have plenty to drink."

He surprised me with a wall-to-wall smile. "Your hillbilly friends sure know how to operate a still. They brew some of the best spirits I ever drunk. I'm surprised they ain't ran the real liquor stores out of business by now."

"Well, there's too many stores for something like that to happen. But Willie Frank and his family have to stay on top of the game, so they just started using a more sophisticated still that brews better and bigger batches. It set them back a pretty penny, so they had to go up on their prices again. They charge us al-

most twice as much as they used to." I stopped talking when
Yvonne snuck a kick to my foot.

"We can't afford to let *nobody* drink on the house no more,"
she lied. It was one lie that needed to be told, though. It was
time for Odell and Joyce to start paying for their drinks like
everybody else.

"Pffft!" He waved his hand and snickered. "Me and Joyce
don't mind paying for our drinks next time we come. We don't
need to mooch off nobody." He turned around and strutted off
without saying another word. Not even bye.

My face felt like it was on fire. "Well, I'll be doggone. Odell
seem to get snootier by the day," I complained.

"Sure enough. I would hate to see how he'd treat us if we wasn't
his friends and neighbors," Yvonne hissed. "Maybe the reason he
get so flustrated sometime is that he ain't getting enough nooky."

"Uh-uh. He getting more than enough of that."

CHAPTER 14
YVONNE

*J*OYCE CAME TO THE HOUSE FRIDAY NIGHT, A FEW MINUTES AFTER 7:00 p.m. "Odell wanted to come with me tonight, but he had to go straight from the store to his daddy's house," she announced right after she came through the door.

I was pleased to know that a man as high and mighty as Odell was so devoted to his daddy. "Well, he'll be blessed for being so caring. I'd give anything in the world to have a daddy I could spend time with," I said. I didn't plan on dwelling on this subject, because I could already feel tears flooding my eyes. "Come on in, Joyce, and make yourself at home."

She dropped down on the couch. It was already occupied by two nurses that worked at the colored clinic. They was the chatty type, and it was hard for anybody else to get a word in edgewise. I was happy that Joyce wasn't behaving like the Queen of Sheba right off the bat for a change. She was as quiet as a mouse. When the nurses got up and started dancing, I sat on the couch next to Joyce. She didn't waste no time loosening up her lips, and it was the same old tired subjects she always harped on. And then she said something that made me want to slap her.

"Yvonne, let me know when you have some free time on a Saturday. I need to take you to see the lady that does my hair sometime—and quick!" She gawked at my hair and shook her head in a slow "I feel so sorry for you" way, which made my temperature rise.

"Um, beauticians charge too much for me. I always do my own hair," I replied, wondering where she was going with this.

"Well, please stop doing that," she requested, giving me a pitiful look.

Her comment felt like somebody had bounced a brick off my head. I had a good comeback for her, though. "I'm lucky I got good hair, so I don't need no grease and hot combs like you," I fired back. I wasn't going to let her off too easy. "By the way, I noticed you been using a different shade of face powder."

There was a tight look on her face now. "Yeah, we can't keep my nut-brown shade in stock. I don't like using a lighter shade, because it makes my skin look like sandpaper."

"Well, make-up can only do so much. At least it covers up them lines on your forehead."

That shut her up and brung her down a peg. And then she suddenly "remembered" that a friend from work was coming to pick her up so they could go out tonight, and she had to leave. I didn't know if she was telling the truth or not, because she'd used the same excuse to leave early before.

After Joyce left, the crowd got even bigger and the place really started jumping. A group of men squatted down on the floor in a corner of the living room and started rolling dice. There was a pile of dollar bills laid out in front of them. There was another pile of money on the kitchen table, where four other men was playing poker. As much as Milton liked to gamble, he didn't do it at home too often. The main reason was that he had to stay focused on helping me and Willie Frank serve the drinks and collect the money.

Since we'd moved to the neighborhood, the class of the people we entertained had gradually climbed up the ladder. The majority of them was no longer just the low-level types we'd been dealing with since we got in the bootlegging business. Now all three of the doctors that lived in the vicinity came over at least once a week. In addition to them nurses, tonight's crowd included a retired teacher who had taught at Grove High when

I was still there, and one of the only two colored barbers in Branson.

A few people who used to go to the jook joints and other bootleggers' houses had dropped by because some of their friends had told them what a good time they'd had during their drinking frolics at our place.

Aunt Mattie, a fish-eyed, tough old madam with a good heart that ran the most popular colored whorehouse in town, showed up at 8:30 p.m. A hour later, Dee Dee, a great big, fat, but attractive woman in her middle thirties that took care of business with the men for Aunt Mattie, waddled through the front door, huffing and puffing. She had just made a house call to one of her regular tricks that lived four doors down from us. As soon as she got close enough, Aunt Mattie got on her case.

"It took you long enough to do your business! Ain't no telling how many other tricks you lost out on all the time you was gone!" she blasted. Then she snatched Dee Dee's purse and rooted around in it until she got her hands on the money. She slid it into her brassiere and folded her arms like she was scared somebody was fixing to reach down in there and snatch it.

Dee Dee didn't say nothing, because she knew Aunt Mattie would fire somebody at the drop of a hat. Times was too hard for a colored woman to risk her job, no matter what it was.

Howard Cunningham, the kindhearted elderly man that owned the grill me and Milton worked at, and three of our coworkers eventually showed up.

"None of y'all better take off Monday with a hangover, or you'll be unemployed," Mr. Cunningham warned, wagging his finger at us and raking another finger through his white hair. He was glad his wife was doing better, so he could come out and have some fun.

Me and my coworkers laughed, because our boss wasn't as strict as Aunt Mattie was. He was determined to help as many colored people survive the Depression as he could. Other than killing somebody on the job or setting the place on fire, I couldn't think of nothing bad enough that would make that sweet old man fire one of us.

By 10:00 p.m. we had a full house. Lenny, the albino musician we'd wooed away from another bootlegger, was playing the old red piano we kept in a corner in the back of the room. The music was so good, almost everybody in the room was dancing.

Willie Frank was in such a party mood, he was twirling around the floor with Aunt Mattie and Dee Dee at the same time. "Milton, every night is like Christmas at your house!" he yelled without taking his eyes off Dee Dee's face or his hand off her double-wide butt.

"And you Santa Claus. The stuff you brung me tonight is some of the best liquor I ever tasted!" Milton yelled back, nodding toward half a dozen gallon-size jugs of fresh liquor sitting on the floor.

Me and Milton used to visit a lot of local bootleggers before we got in the business. Now the ones that wasn't too jealous visited us. One of the reasons was that they had heard about the high-grade stuff Willie Frank and his family brewed, and wanted to get in on the deal. Milton had made Willie Frank promise that if he did start supplying more bootleggers, other than the ones he'd been doing business with for years, he would charge them twice as much as he charged us so it wouldn't interfere with our profits. So far, Willie Frank had kept his word. One thing I could say about him was that he was a true friend. He had never done or said nothing to offend me or Milton. Which was more than I could say about Joyce and Odell . . .

I was still pissed off about the way Odell had treated us when we visited him at the store on our way home this afternoon. And I was just as pissed off about that hair comment Joyce had made tonight. I wondered if they really did think they was better than us. I knew the answer to that question. They did.

All our guests' jars was full, and they could help themselves to the snacks, so me and Milton had a few minutes to ourselves. A slow song came on that he liked. He grabbed my hand and pulled me up off the couch.

"Will you dance with me, baby?"

"I guess," I muttered.

As soon as we got on the floor, he started grinding against me. But I was dragging my feet like they was blocks of ice.

"What's the matter with you tonight, Yvonne? You act like your mind is a thousand miles away."

"I was just thinking about something."

"Well, whatever that something is, you need to push it off your mind and get loose like the rest of us. I seen you turn down Willie Frank when he asked you to dance a little while ago."

"Don't make me laugh. That man hops around on a dance floor—and on a woman's feet—like a jackrabbit. My toes still trying to come back to life from the last time I danced with him."

Milton laughed. "Well, he barefooted now. He stepped out of his boots a hour ago."

"I'll dance with him later. He look like he was having too much fun with Dee Dee, anyway. Besides, I'd much rather be in your arms."

"I don't know why. You feel stiff as a plank," he complained. "If something or somebody is bothering you, you need to let me know. I'll straighten things out."

"I know you would, baby. But it ain't that simple. What's bothering me is how Joyce and Odell treat us sometime. It seem like every time me and her conversate, she say things that hurt my feelings."

"Ain't we gone over this before—more than once?"

"Yes, and we'll keep going over it."

"Whatever," he tossed in with a shrug. "Joyce ain't got no reason to want to say nothing that'll make you feel bad, especially now that y'all done got closer."

"I know. But like I told you before, I don't think she even realize she doing it. I don't like feeling bad about myself."

"What I'd like to know is, How can a tough cookie like you let a prissy woman like Joyce keep getting under your skin?"

"What you getting at?"

"Before we got married, when somebody disrespected you, you didn't let them get away with it. Remember the night at Delroy's when a woman throwed a drink in your face because she thought you was flirting with her man? You knocked her out with one punch. And I bet Lester's balls is still throbbing after the hurting you put on his crotch."

"Aw, Milton, I ain't about to do nothing physical to Joyce. I don't settle things with violence no more. I just wish . . . wish she would stop making me feel so bad."

Milton looked so exasperated, I was sorry I had brung up the subject. "You need to tell me what you want me to do about the way Joyce be talking to you. If I can stop her, I will so you won't keep harping on this issue. I'll even set her uppity Queen of Sheba ass down and tell her to stop low-rating you."

My body stiffened even more. "No. That would make things worse. But it's nice to know you'd be willing to do it." I laughed. "Whenever she provoke me, I do a little low-rating on her to her face, too. That's a step in the right direction, I guess."

"Good. Keep going in that direction. Just remember we still looking at them as our cash cows, so don't go too far off the rails and run them out of our lives completely." Milton stopped talking and gave me one of the most loving looks he'd ever gave me. "Yvonne, no matter what nobody say about you, you my Queen of Sheba."

"And you my Prince Charming."

CHAPTER 15
MILTON

*I*T DIDN'T MAKE NO DIFFERENCE TO YVONNE THAT I WOULDN'T WIN no blue-ribbon prizes for my looks. Right after she got to know me, she said it was the beauty of my soul she'd fell in love with. And that this was more important to her than a handsome face and a world-beating body. That was why she'd married me. I was everything she'd been looking for in a man. When she needed to get something off her chest, my ears was always open. I just wished she hadn't done it tonight, while we was dancing.

"Don't pay no mind to what Joyce says about you," I suggested.

"It ain't just that. Another thing that's been bothering me lately is the fact that they've only invited us to their place *one* time. And the whole time we was there, they kept looking at the clock, like they couldn't wait for us to leave. You should have seen the way Odell's eyebrows shot up when you put your feet on their coffee table. After I used the bathroom, Joyce rushed in and fanned the air with a magazine. And I hadn't even left no stink!"

"She done the same thing when I used the toilet that evening."

"And they supposed to be Christians! Do you think they behave the same way with their other friends when they visit?"

"Maybe they do. If that's the case, we shouldn't take nothing personal. Anyway, I try not to let petty bullshit like that get to me too often. But if it really bothers you, we need to do something about it."

Yvonne leaned her head back and rolled her eyes. "And just how would you fix something like them not wanting to invite us into their house?"

"Easy. We'll invite ourselves."

"I don't know about that. When I dropped in uninvited one Saturday afternoon, she had company. Some white woman and her husband. The way Joyce was sucking up to them turned my stomach inside out. I can't stand to watch colored people act as giddy as trained monkeys when they get around white folks. I thought Joyce was smart enough to know that it don't do no good to try to impress crackers."

"That's the way the so-called 'good' white folks expect us to act."

Yvonne glanced around for a few seconds. Willie Frank was dancing with Dee Dee only a few feet away, so she whispered, "Our hillbilly and his family don't expect us to act like that."

"The Perdue family is just as righteous as they can be. Like us, they take their religion serious. Folks that really got the spirit don't look down on nobody. And don't use that word around them. Especially Willie Frank. He is the last person in the world I'd want to upset. We need him, and I really like having him in our lives."

"What word?"

"*Hillbilly.* That's a low rating to a redneck." I stopped talking and gave Yvonne a curious look. "I wonder if the folks you seen with Joyce was the same elderly pair I seen Odell grinning at and fawning all over last week, when I popped into the store?"

"No, it couldn't have been them. The folks I seen was in their thirties. The woman's family own a café in Mobile, and the husband work in the sheriff's office. He must be a deputy or something like that."

"Sheriff's department, huh? That's ominous news any way you look at it. Nothing good never came to me when it involved somebody connected to the law."

"Me neither."

"Well, if we go next door again and that couple is visiting, we won't stay long. We won't get too friendly with none of their white friends, period. Now that I know Joyce and Odell a little better, I can tell that they the kind of Goody Two-shoes white folks like to buddy up with so they can make it look like they care about colored people. I figured that out a long time ago. Peckerwoods will do all kinds of good deeds for colored folks to help ease their conscience and make them feel less guilty about slavery and segregation. But they'll turn on a dime and cause all kinds of problems if they take a notion. Shoot! That's their nature. And I especially avoid white women."

"What about Lyla Bullard and Emmalou? You going to 'avoid' them, too?"

"Pffft!" I snickered and waved my hand. "They cut from the same cloth as Willie Frank's female kinfolks, so they ain't nothing to worry about."

"Make one mad enough and see."

"Stop talking crazy. You know what I mean. I wouldn't give none of them white women we friends with no reason to turn on me. It's them other ones I'm talking about. Like the ones we pass on the street. I don't even look at them pale-faced heifers. I ain't going to give nary one a chance to accuse me of rape. When I was nine, the Ku Klux Klan stormed my uncle Roland's house while I was spending the night. They lynched him in his own front yard, with me, his wife, and his four kids watching. And all because a white woman claimed he had *looked* at her like he wanted to rape her."

"Milton, I know all about the Klux's handiwork, so we don't need to go there. I'm more interested in talking about Joyce and Odell. She claimed she was going out with a friend this evening. That's why she left so early. But she didn't go nowhere."

"How do you know that? We been pretty busy tonight, so you ain't had time to be keeping tabs on her."

"I ain't too busy to peep out the window every now and then.

That lying wench was on her porch, beating a rug, a little while ago. If a car had pulled up over there, I would have heard it."

"She must have changed her mind. Or maybe her friend had to cancel."

The music was still going, but I stopped dancing and steered Yvonne to a corner. We started talking in a low and more serious tone.

"Baby, stop wasting time fretting over things we can't change," I said. "Think about all the money we saving by swiping stuff from the store. Next time I go up in there, I'm going to take so much snuff and chewing tobacco and sell to them hillbillies, we'll have enough to pay our light bill for the next few months. And as bad as we want a telephone, as long as we can use theirs, we ain't got to spend no money getting one put in our house for a while."

"Hmmm. That is a good point."

"And they got that car, so when we need a ride, we can go to them."

"Oh yeah? Odell wouldn't give us no ride home today, so we can't always count on them for transportation."

"Maybe not all the time. Anytime we can get a free ride is better than nothing. Listen up, Yvonne. Let's be cool for now. We'll milk them cows next door while the milking is good. They could turn out to be good friends in the long run. And even teach us how to be more polished citizens like them. I would love to see what it's like to be looked up to and respected by folks that's been looking down on us all our lives."

"I would like that, too."

"Odell used to be lowly—doing handyman work in a whorehouse and farm labor. Look where he at now."

"I realize that." Yvonne let out a long, heavy sigh. "I see some jars that need to be refilled. Let's stop yakking and get back to serving drinks."

We had never had a relationship with people that confused us as much as Joyce and Odell. We never knew when they was going to be fun to be around or say or do something to make us feel bad about who we was. I had to admit to myself that they was probably as confused and skeptical about us.

"Even if we don't never get no respect from respectable folks, once we have all the things we want, we might not even want to associate with Joyce and Odell at all."

"And that's a fact, baby," Yvonne agreed.

CHAPTER 16
YVONNE

*F*ALL WAS MY FAVORITE SEASON, SO I WAS GLAD IT WAS OCTOBER now. I enjoyed the cooler weather and how all the brown and orange leaves fell off the trees and covered the ground. Every yard on our street looked like somebody had covered it with a patchwork quilt. This fall would be a big deal because Willie Frank would be celebrating his thirty-fifth birthday next month. Since it was a milestone for him, we had already started planning a big party. Me and Milton's birthdays was in February, three days apart. We always threw a big shindig that week.

We decided to pay Joyce and Odell a visit when we got home from work the first Monday in October. We knew they had company, because there was a strange truck parked in front of their house, right behind their car. When we got up on their front porch, we could hear people inside laughing and talking. I had to knock twice and hard before Joyce came to the door.

"Where y'all going?" she asked, looking annoyed. For a woman smart enough to be working with schoolkids, I couldn't believe she'd asked such a dumb question. She must have realized how ridiculous it was, because a split second later she tossed in, "I mean, we weren't expecting y'all this evening. Is everything all right?"

She was looking at me, but Milton answered. "Yup. Everything is fine on our end. We ain't seen or heard a peep out of y'all the past couple of days. We wanted to make sure everything was all right. That's what good neighbors do, right?"

Joyce cleared her throat and gave us a testy look. "Thanks for the concern, but y'all don't need to worry about us. Everything is fine on our end, too," she claimed with a fake smile.

She had on a navy-blue, mammy-made dress; shiny, black, round-toed pumps, like the ones old ladies liked to wear; and make-up. She was still as plain as white rice, though. Poor Joyce. A fairy godmother couldn't make her look cute. She always wore the wrong shade of face powder and rouge, but her maroon lipstick looked nice on her liver-colored lips. I was about to pay her a compliment, something I suspected she didn't get too often. Before I could, she gazed at my hair and shook her head.

"Were you in a fight?"

"No. Why do you ask?" Her odd question threw me for a loop. I suspected she was about to say something else that would get a rise out of me. I was right.

"Because your hair is all over the place again." She didn't say it in a mean tone, but it hurt my feelings just the same.

I took such a deep breath, I could feel the air going all through me. "It's windy, and I couldn't find my scarf when I left the house this morning," I muttered. I had no idea why she had to make a comment about my hair *again*. I thought it looked way better than them cockleburs on her head.

"I'll get some scarves for you the next time I go to the store," she went on, shaking her head again. Then she offered up another fake smile. "So, what's up with y'all this evening?"

"Nothing much. We had some free time, so we thought we'd come see you and Odell for a little while," I replied.

"We can't stay long," Milton threw in. "Willie Frank let us borrow his truck, because we got other places to go tonight. We stuck a note on the door, telling all the drinkers not to come back until after nine."

"Well, we have company right now. But since y'all already here, y'all welcome to join us," Joyce said with enough hesitation for me to notice.

Welcome? It was plain as day she didn't mean it. I would have had more respect for her if she had been woman enough to tell us to come back when they didn't have company. She waved us into the living room, where Odell and a homely middle-aged white couple in drab clothes sat on the couch. There was four empty glasses on the coffee table, some dominoes, and a huge, half-empty bottle of Calvert Extra whiskey, the most expensive store-bought brand available in Branson.

Odell looked at Joyce, then at us. From the corner of my eye, I seen her give him a shrug. "Yvonne, you and Milton come on in and meet Mamie and Jeb Wagoner," he suggested with a smile as fake as Joyce's. "They own a feedstore on the north side, right next door to their lovely home on Willow Street."

Just like I'd always suspected, any white folks that Joyce and Odell invited into their home had to have money and prestige and had to live in the most expensive part of town, on the same street as our mayor. Odell moved from the couch to the easy chair facing it. The Wagoners looked dazed, but they nodded as me and Milton plopped down on the couch next to them. Joyce shuffled over to Odell and sat down on the arm of his seat. I was happy she didn't look so annoyed now.

It didn't take long for me to figure out that the Wagoners was just as snooty as Joyce and Odell. Mamie looked like she was going to pass out when Milton said we was bootleggers and lived one house over.

"I bet the politicians are kicking themselves in the butt for ending Prohibition. The bars, liquor stores, and restaurants are losing money left and right. The same folks that were drinking illegally are still going to the bootleggers, because it's cheaper," Mamie sneered. Then she sucked on her teeth and squinted her dull brown eyes. "Y'all ain't afraid to let strange people come into your house to drink?"

"No, because we don't serve no thugs," Milton said, beaming like a lightbulb. I was glad he added, "Besides, the nice bars and restaurants don't serve colored folks . . ."

"And that's a fact. Anyway, I apologize for our ignorance, because we thought all the colored bootleggers lived on the lower south side with all those brutish types," Jeb eased in. He had big, dingy teeth that clicked when he talked.

"Most of them do." I couldn't get the rest of the words out fast enough. "We used to live over there, until we saved up enough to move to this neighborhood back in June. With the low crime rate over here, we get more business and a better class of people. Besides that, we love our new location so much, we might even try to buy our house."

"I see. I know bootlegging is a lucrative business. We have several houses in our vicinity. One arrogant, brazen scoundrel lives three doors down from us. He always wears a suit and hat—even when he takes out the trash! My Lord!" Mamie hissed, looking from me to Milton with one eyebrow raised.

Colored bootleggers didn't make nowhere near the kind of money the white ones on the north side made. The white ones got all the rich white folks' business, so them bootleggers always dressed to the nines, carried guns, drove fancy cars, and lived in houses that looked like palaces compared to ours. Willie Frank had told me some of the ones he supplied booze to hired cabaret dancers on the weekends and holidays to entertain their guests.

Mamie sniffed and went on, with both eyebrows raised now. "Y'all must be doing good to be looking so prosperous."

"We doing all right for colored folks," I replied, smoothing down the sides of my new green cotton dress. Milton was as sharp as a tack in his beige seersucker suit. We didn't get dressed up just to visit Joyce and Odell. We had other plans for later today. Mr. Cunningham's wife was still recovering, so we wanted to pay her a short visit. After that, we planned to go to Mosella's for supper.

The Mamie woman exhaled and gawked at Odell, probably wondering what kind of relationship him and Joyce had with us. I decided to take care of her curiosity myself.

"Joyce, I hope you and Odell come over again later tonight. We got our piano tuned up yesterday, and Willie Frank dropped off some new spirits that I know both of y'all will like," I said with a smirk. "Aunt Mattie's coming with a couple of her girls."

The Wagoners looked horrified. Everybody in town knew who Aunt Mattie was.

"Um, I don't know if we can make it tonight," Joyce mumbled.

"Well, since y'all regulars, drop by anytime, day or night." Milton grinned.

Mamie and Jeb gasped at the same time and shifted in their seats. They left five minutes later.

It turned out to be a fun evening, after all. For us at least. We stayed another half an hour. Being around Joyce and Odell had become a sport, and me and Milton was big sports fans. They was the only people we knew who could make us jealous, mad, and amused all at the same time.

I almost busted out laughing when Odell complained about how bad the shoplifters had got at the store. "I'm fixing to hire a security man to help watchdog the aisles," he said in a stern tone. "It's a damn shame folks can't run a business without having to worry about the customers robbing them blind! I would love to get my hands on some of them crooks! I'd whup their asses until they shitted, and then I'd whup them for shitting!"

I gave Odell the biggest smile I could turn up my lips to form. I was thankful to pieces that he had alerted us about his plan to hire a "watchdog" security man to crack down on the shoplifting. That didn't scare me, and I knew it didn't scare Milton. He'd busted into houses and businesses that had security guards and *real* dogs and never got caught. The bottom line was, nothing could keep competent crooks like us from taking care of business. All we had to do was keep being careful.

We decided to drop in on Joyce and Odell again the very next evening. The door was cracked, so we walked in without knocking. We didn't expect them to be entertaining company two days in a row, so we was surprised to see a mule-faced cracker and his frizzy-haired, pointy-nosed wife sitting on the couch. It was the same pair Joyce had been entertaining when I'd paid her a unexpected visit a few weeks ago: the café woman and her sheriff's deputy husband. I didn't like them the first time, but this time they really spooked me, because the husband had on his uniform, his badge, and a holster with a gun in it. Milton must have felt the same way, because he suddenly "remembered" that we had company coming in a little while, so we stayed only five minutes. We decided that day that we wouldn't visit Joyce and Odell again for a few weeks, unless they invited us over.

Friday night, when Joyce and Odell was about to leave our house after gulping down three drinks apiece, I walked them to the door. They was the last to leave.

"Joyce, I might come over tomorrow so you can show me how to make hush puppies." A few hours earlier, Odell had mentioned that he would be spending most of the weekend with his daddy. Milton had plans to meet up with Willie Frank in the morning and maybe go fishing and drop off some deliveries. And I didn't want to spend all that time by myself.

"That'll be just fine. I like to lie in bed after I wake up on weekends, and read for a while. If you decide to come, don't come before eight," she told me. I was stunned when she hugged me. "Good night, y'all."

After I shut the door behind them, I stood in front of it as silent as a mute, gazing at Milton sprawled on the couch.

"Why you so quiet now? What's going on in that busy brain of yours?" he asked.

"I was just wondering if she'll feel like hugging me when I get over there tomorrow morning."

Milton shrugged and then yawned. "I hope she will. It's a blessing to see you and Joyce making progress."

"The only thing is, I don't know what we progressing to."

CHAPTER 17
YVONNE

I ARRIVED NEXT DOOR AT FIVE MINUTES PAST EIGHT ON SATURDAY morning. By nine, Joyce had finished showing me how to make hush puppies. After we ate a few, we cleaned up the kitchen and sat down at the table to chat. She hadn't said nothing to offend me yet. All we'd talked about so far was her great life, recipes, shoe sales, what the news was reporting, and a few other mundane subjects. I was getting bored, so I was happy when she said something that sounded interesting.

"I don't care for Saturdays the way I used to." She let out such a long, deep sigh, you would have thought she was in pain. On top of that, she gave me a weary look.

"Why come? At least you don't have to go to work. You can spend the day doing all kinds of other things."

"Yeah, but when Odell is gone, the day seems so much longer. I don't expect him, or want him, to stop spending so much time with his daddy. These could be Lonnie's last days. I'm just thankful Odell and me still got our daddies." She paused and patted my arm. "I know you miss your parents, and I pray they are at peace."

"I appreciate you saying that." Like always, when that subject came up, I had to blink hard to hold back my tears.

"I can see that that's an uncomfortable subject for you. Let's talk about something that's not so gloomy." Before I could say anything, she popped her fingers and abruptly stood up. "Come in the bedroom so I can show you a couple of new dresses I ordered from Sears and Roebuck."

Her bedroom was just what I'd expected. There was a four-poster bed with matching nightstands and a huge chifforobe. The bedspread matched the frilly yellow and green curtains. But when it came to fashion, all of Joyce's taste was in her mouth. So I was not surprised by what she had in her closet. There wasn't a piece in it that I would wear even to a Halloween party. One of her newest dresses was plaid and had sleeves that looked like bat wings. Another one could have been mistook for a tent with a green bow tie that looked like a two-leafed clover. I couldn't believe how organized everything was. Odell's clothes was at one end of the closet; hers was at the other. The dresses was first, the blouses was next, and her shawls and sweaters was at the tail end. Shoes so long they looked like little boats was lined up in a row on the floor. If some hadn't had high heels, I wouldn't have been able to tell hers from Odell's. The whole room was so neat, it didn't look lived in. On top of the dresser, there was a large picture of Joyce and Odell on their wedding day, cheesing it up with the preacher and some of their guests.

"Y'all looked so nice," I commented.

"I know. To this day, some folks are still telling us that. Girl, it was such an amazing ceremony." Joyce's eyes got glassy, and tears pooled in them. She pulled a handkerchief out of her brassiere and blew her nose. "Speaking of wedding pictures, do you have any?" She laid her handkerchief on the dresser, so I figured she'd probably do some more swooning and have to blow her nose some more.

"Uh, no. There was a date mix-up with the man that was supposed to come with his Kodak. He didn't show up until the next day."

Joyce gave me a puzzled look. "Where did y'all get married?"

"At Delroy Crutchfield's place. Since that was where me and Milton met for the first time, he wanted to marry me there."

Joyce stared at me for a few seconds with her mouth hanging open. "My Lord. Y'all got married in a bootlegger's house?"

"Uh-huh."

"Delroy's place is one step above a *shanty*! I'm so sorry to hear that that's where you spent your special day. Odell would never have asked me to do such a lowly thing."

"It's a blessing to hear that. I guess them few years he spent living and working in Aunt Mattie's whorehouse before he met you was lowly enough for him . . ." To keep her from going on again about Odell, I rushed into another subject. "You read all them books?" I pointed at a stack on the dresser, next to the wedding picture.

"Yup. I've read my favorites more than once. Reading is a good way to ingrain better grammar than that ignorant gibberish most colored folks speak." I couldn't believe how proud Joyce was of herself. She puffed her chest out so far, it almost looked like she had strapped on a pillow. "If you ever want to borrow a few, just let me know. And you better borrow my dictionary, too. Otherwise, you'd have to skip over a lot of the words, and you might not enjoy the books as much as I do."

"No thanks. Even when I was in school, I didn't like to crack open a book. And when I had to read one, I didn't learn much."

"I can tell."

That comment wouldn't have stung so sharp if she hadn't shook her head and gave me such a pitiful look to go with it. She was so happy being Joyce Watson.

"Joyce, thanks for showing me your new dresses. Someday I hope to have some stuff that sharp and a bedroom as nice as yours."

"I hope you do, too. By the way, how can you stand to sleep in your bedroom the way it is now? Nothing matches, and it's so bleak." Joyce twisted her mouth into a grimace and shuddered.

"Because Milton is in there with me."

I guessed she didn't know how to respond to my answer, because all she did was gaze at me for about five seconds. "Come on, Yvonne. Let's go to the living room."

When we sat down on the couch, she gave me one of the strangest squinty-eyed looks I ever seen. It seemed like she was trying to look inside my head. Her silence was making me nervous, so I said the next thing that came to my mind.

"Maybe I will borrow some of your books. It might help me sharpen my mind, like I should have done in school. But I didn't like school, and money was so tight, it didn't take long for me to make up my mind to drop out and go to work full-time. I doubt if them teachers at Grove High missed me."

Joyce's jaw dropped so low, I was surprised it didn't reach her neck. "You went to Grove High? So did I!"

"Yeah . . . Wait a minute. Sweet Jesus!" I raised my finger in the air and waved it at her. "Girl, the first time I seen you, I told myself I'd seen you before. I was three grades behind you when I was at Grove High, but we had a study hall together. I missed a lot of days before I dropped out, but I remember you now. You and two other girls used to hang out together. Their folks was well off, too, so y'all wore pretty clothes every day. Me and the other girls that lived on the lower south side wore the same drab things, sometimes two or three days in a row."

Joyce looked like she was about to laugh. I was glad she didn't. "I'll never forget the girls from your neighborhood. Especially the ones that came to school stinking up a storm, like they didn't know what soap and water was. But I don't remember you at all. That's a mystery, because there's only one high school for colored kids in this town, and everybody knew everybody."

"That is a mystery." I'd been expelled for cussing at my teachers, fighting, and causing other ruckuses. With all of that, how could Joyce not remember me? I wondered. Especially if everybody knew everybody. And another thing, I had never come to school "stinking up a storm." Her comments sliced through my feelings like a knife. She was making me feel smaller than I really was. I felt like I was shrinking with each word that spewed out of her mouth.

"Most of the kids from the lower south side came to class only a few days each month. There was this one girl named Bonnette Pittman. I could never forget a piece of work like her! She only came to school on the first day of each new semester and when we had holiday parties. She didn't show up again until the last day of school, to attend the end-of-the-semester party and get her report card." Joyce threw her head back and laughed like a hyena. "The teachers always passed Bonnette on to the next grade, even though she could barely read and write. I guess it didn't matter one way or the other. Even with a high school diploma, some colored people still don't do a damn thing with their lives. She was from a family of fools, so it was no wonder she was so trifling. The last time I saw her was on the first day of our senior year. I wonder what happened to her."

"The reason she didn't return was that she got in some trouble."

"Oh? What did she do?"

"The weekend after school had started, Bonnette went to Florida with her bootlegger boyfriend to visit his folks. She got in some trouble in a jook joint one night, when she bumped against a white woman and made her spill her drink. The woman called her a clumsy nigger and punched her. Bonnette stabbed her to death. She been in prison ever since and still got thirteen more years to go."

"Prison!" Joyce screamed. "Oomph, oomph, oomph! That Bonnette. She was such a jook-joint jezebel, I'm not the least bit surprised. If she had the nerve to kill a white woman, she had to be crazy, and they should have put her in a nuthouse, not a prison. Oh well. I'm sure one place is as bad as the other, so in the long run, it doesn't matter. What matters is that they got her off the street." Joyce sniffed and leaned closer to me. "I don't know why some colored people won't behave. Me and Odell have never had any trouble with the law or white folks. And that's only because we know our place and stay in it." Joyce sighed and gave me a weary look. "As much as I hate to admit it, this is a white man's world."

On top of everything else, she was a Uncle Tom, too. Just like I'd suspected when I seen how meek she was with that white feedstore couple that day me and Milton paid her a visit. She'd just confirmed it.

"Grove High had so many busybodies. Which blabbermouth

told you what happened to that sleazy Bonnette? I still feel so sorry for her," she said.

Joyce had really struck a nerve with the comments about Bonnette. "Her mama was my mama's baby sister. Bonnette was the only true friend I had the whole time I was in school."

"Oh. I guess I don't feel as sorry for her now that I know she had at least *one* friend." Joyce squinted and gazed at me so hard, I squirmed. "Now that I look at you closer, I can see the resemblance between you and her. I guess good hair and high cheekbones run in your family, huh?"

"Yeah. We got Indian blood."

"Pffft! You and everybody else—or so they say. There ain't enough Indians in America for all the colored people that claim to have Indian blood to be telling the truth."

"I ain't got no reason to lie. My mama's mama was a full-blooded Apache. Before Mama died, she used to take me and my sisters to visit her kinfolks on the reservation in Oklahoma where she grew up."

"Well, at least you look it. I guess every colored person in this country got some mixed blood, including me. My grandmothers on both sides had babies by the white slave masters they belonged to. But with my complexion and nappy hair, folks can't see my mixed blood as easy as they can yours."

"I know what you mean," I agreed, with the smuggest look I could come up with.

Joyce was like a lot of other colored women when it came to skin tone and hair texture. Skin darker than tobacco was a real sensitive subject, with nappy hair close behind. But she was not that dark. And even though her hair looked like barbed wire when she didn't use her hot comb, it was fairly long and thick, so she had something to work with. She still couldn't hold a nub of a candle to me. The biggest thing wrong with her was her height. She was almost as tall as Odell, and he was six feet four. She was probably self-conscious about it, and I was about to find out.

"If you don't mind me asking, where do you get your clothes from?"

Joyce puffed out her chest again, crossed her legs, and brushed off her sleeve. From the self-satisfied expression on her face, she must have thought I was complimenting her good taste. That wasn't the case, because the floor-length brown dress she had on looked like a horse blanket with sleeves.

"Like I already told you, I get a lot of my clothes from the Sears and Roebuck catalog." She grinned. "That's how I keep up with what's in style."

"You lucky you got catalogs to turn to. Because most of the stores I shop in don't carry nothing that would fit a stout, strapping woman like you. And that's a damn shame."

Her confidence disappeared. "Yeah . . . it is a damn shame." As big as Joyce was, her voice suddenly sounded small enough for a woman my size. "My mama makes a few outfits for me, too." She gave me a sorry look and bit her bottom lip. "Um . . . I guess I should get up and start doing some of my chores. I have a basket of laundry to wash, and I need to scrub my kitchen floor today. When I finish, I might go visit my parents." We stood up at the same time.

"I have a heap of stuff to do at home myself. The men that work at the sawmill get paid today, so we expect some of them to drop in on us later. You coming back to the house tonight?"

"If I get everything done and don't stay at my parents' house too long, I might." Joyce glanced at the wall clock above the stove. "Goodness gracious. I didn't realize how late it was." Next thing I knew, she pranced to the door and opened it for me. She was that anxious to get rid of me. And I was just as anxious to get away from her.

"Thanks for showing me how to make hush puppies. And I really enjoyed conversating with you."

She scrunched up her face like I had just cussed at her. "Yvonne, 'conversating' is not a real word."

"It ain't? I been using it all my life."

"I don't think it is, but it doesn't matter. I know what you meant. My daddy and Odell use that word all the time."

"Anyway, I enjoyed your company. We should get together more often. Just me and you."

She took her time responding. When she did, she sounded like I'd just offered her a dose of castor oil. "Yeah. We'll do that." Joyce suddenly looked uneasy. She cleared her throat and scratched the back of her neck. "Um, before you go, I'd like to apologize for what I said about your cousin and the rest of your family being fools. I didn't mean it. I'm not a mean person. It's just that I've never been able to control my tongue. I got that from my daddy."

Her apology and excuse for her behavior surprised me, and it made me feel a little better. "Joyce, don't worry about it. It didn't bother me." What surprised me even more was when she hauled off and hugged me before I left.

Maybe there was still a chance that she and I could become real good friends, after all. But I was not about to get my hopes up too high.

CHAPTER 18
MILTON

*O*NE OF THE MANY THINGS I LOVED ABOUT YVONNE WAS THAT SHE wasn't no wimp. She wasn't even scared of bugs and rats, like every other woman I knew. But she hated being alone, because it reminded her how sad and lonely her childhood had been. Her aunt and uncle would leave her in the house by herself for hours at a time while they went shopping or fishing or to visit folks. Every Sunday she had to sit in church for hours on end, and she had to read the Bible every night—after she had done whatever housework needed to be done at the time. I didn't like to leave her by herself too often. But I had things to attend to today that I couldn't do with her breathing down my neck. Me and Willie Frank wanted to go fishing and then drop off some liquor orders to a few of his customers.

The fish wasn't biting, so we gave up on that after only half a hour and headed out to do our deliveries. The first customer was a fifty-year-old widowed farmer named Oscar Lewis. He lived by hisself on the outskirts of town, not far from Cunningham's Grill. He gave poker parties several times a month, so he led a busy life. He was fat and slouchy, but he had a decent-looking face, so he didn't have no trouble getting women. When he was between girlfriends, he called up Aunt Mattie and had her send one of her girls on a house call.

Oscar was doing pretty good for a man who had dropped out of school in the second grade. His field hands, Jerome Fisher and Amos Cobb, had been helping him run his farm as far back as I could remember. He grew corn, watermelons, and other produce. And since most white folks didn't like to see us doing too good, he sold his crops only to colored folks.

Me and Willie Frank dropped off three gallons of moonshine that Oscar had ordered to serve at his next poker party. We hadn't planned on staying long, but he kept bugging us to have a drink with him, so we did. Sometimes he was so cranky, folks didn't like to visit him. Whenever they did, he went out of his way to get them to stay as long as possible. He loved to talk, and he always had something interesting to blab.

"I recently lucked up on me some sweet goodies," he let out with a smug grin. Oscar was kicked back in a rocking chair, facing us, with a flyswatter in his hand and a toothpick dangling from his lip.

"You must have come into some mighty big money," Willie Frank said, nudging me with his elbow. Me and him was sitting on Oscar's living-room couch.

"Nope. I ain't had to pay nothing for it, and it's some of the best. See, that siddity geechee that live down the road came here last week and talked me into a game of poker. Well, I fixed his tail. When I got him good and drunk, I switched his cards with one of my special decks, the kind that guarantees I win," Oscar gloated, winking one of his ratty eyes.

A little voice in my head told me that before I got in another poker game, I needed to mark me a deck of cards.

"Good for you," Willie Frank said, with a thumbs-up. "How much did you take him for?"

"He didn't have no money, but he had something just as good." Oscar paused and looked from me to Willie Frank, grinning like a clown. "I got me some new tires for my tractor, three hoes, a shovel, a pickax, and the top-of-the line plow I been wanting for years. Oomph!"

"Ooh-wee. You did do all right." I grinned, rubbing my hands together. "You better keep that stuff hid real good. Branson got a heap of folks always looking for something to swipe."

Oscar waved his hand. "Pffft! I ain't worried about nobody taking nothing from me. I had Jerome help me put them new tires on my tractor yesterday. The rest of the stuff is in my barn, up under a pile of hay and some old horse blankets, until I get ready to use it. Jerome and Amos is the only ones that know about it." Oscar let out a mighty burp and stood up. "Y'all excuse me for a minute. I need to go see a man about a horse. My bladder is about to bust wide open."

As soon as Oscar was out of earshot, Willie Frank tapped my shoulder. "If this ain't a opportunity for us, I don't know what is," he whispered. "Anybody fool enough to blab about the stuff he got by cheating and where he got it hid don't deserve to keep it."

"You right. Especially after things didn't work out when we tried to pull that scam on Cleotis. Stealing back liquor that we done already sold don't sound like nothing I want to try again. But Oscar just answered our prayers to find another good score to make up for Cleotis."

We heard Oscar's heavy feet walking back toward the living room and him huffing and puffing, like his trip to the toilet had wore him out. He flopped back into his chair with a groan. "Where was we?" he panted.

"I was about to say, you shouldn't have told your field hands where you put them things at. They might up and decide to run off with it," I warned.

"I had to tell them. I couldn't tote that stuff by myself, so I needed them to help me get it home and hid! I ain't worried about Jerome running his mouth. Amos is a slow wit and a alcoholic, though, and I done told him twice to keep his mouth closed if he want to keep his job. They been working for me going on ten years and ain't stole nothing from me yet, so I trust them." Oscar coughed and then hawked into a dingy handkerchief. "Y'all want another drink?" he asked, looking at my empty cup.

"Um, no. We have to haul ass. We got other orders to drop off," Willie Frank explained, nodding at me.

"Yup, that's right. And we expect a big crowd tonight, so I need to get home and help Yvonne get the house ready," I added, already moving toward the door. "We'll stay longer the next time."

"Good. Willie Frank, you sure put your foot in this batch of moonshine. My head is spinning, and I can't hardly keep my eyes open," Oscar chuckled and then yawned.

"You go on and take a nap, then. We'll let ourselves out," Willie Frank advised. "But before we go, can I go get a glass of water?"

"Go on. You know where the kitchen is at." Oscar belched and waved Willie Frank toward the back of the room. "Y'all drive careful, and don't run over none of my chickens. Next time I won't drink much, so I can stay woke and chitchat with y'all a little longer. Bye, y'all." He stood up and starting shuffling down a short, dim hallway, already taking off his stiff plaid shirt and yawning and stretching his arms above his head.

We drove just a few yards down the road and parked. We waited about fifteen minutes before we walked back to Oscar's property. We went straight into his barn. The plow and all them other goodies was right where he said he'd hid them. I was amazed. I knew a lot of other farmers who would put out some sweet money to own such nice equipment.

"Before we do anything, let's creep back into the house and make sure he ain't playing possum," Willie Frank suggested in a low tone.

I followed him to the back door, which he had made sure was unlocked when he went to get a glass of water. Once we got in the kitchen, we tiptoed toward the living room. Oscar had three bedrooms, so we didn't know which one to look in. His loud snoring led us to the right one. I cracked open the door and seen him belly-up in his bed.

"That fool is dead to the world," I whispered.

"Yeah, but for how long? We need to do our business lickety-split," Willie Frank whispered back.

"You go get the truck, and I'll keep a eye on him," I said.

"What if he wake up before I get back?"

"I'll tell him we seen a couple of suspicious-acting characters heading this way when we was leaving, and we just came back to make sure he was all right. Now, you hurry up and go get the truck."

It didn't take but a few minutes for Willie Frank to get back. He parked behind the barn, and we loaded up the equipment. It was one of the easiest jobs we'd ever pulled. It gave us a good rush, but we still smoked some rabbit tobacco during the ride back down the road. We was feeling so good, we didn't want it to end. So, we stopped off at Aunt Mattie's house. Her girls was glad to see us. But since we didn't have a lot of time or money to spare, all we got was blow jobs.

CHAPTER 19
YVONNE

I DIDN'T BELIEVE JOYCE AND ODELL'S MARRIAGE WAS AS PICTURE-perfect as she made it out to be. Maybe the real reason she worked during the summer every year was to have something to do to keep her mind off all the time he spent with his ailing daddy. And that had started to sound mighty suspicious to me.

According to the story they had told us, a few weeks after they got married, Odell started spending a lot of his free time with the old man. Odell's stepmother didn't like Joyce, so she went with him only every now and then. His daddy's brain was going to mush real fast, so Odell had gradually started spending more time with him. If he was as bad off as Odell had people thinking he was, he should have been dead by now.

Thirty minutes after I got back home from making hush puppies and visiting with Joyce, I started feeling kind of lonesome. I didn't know none of the other neighbors well enough yet to drop in on them, so I ended up going back to Joyce's house. The chores she had mentioned must not have been too important, because she was reading a book when I walked in. She seemed happy to see me again so soon.

"I'm as pleased as I can be that you came back. After you left, I got so bored, I wanted to scream," she admitted, setting the book on the coffee table. I would have felt better if she had told me she was pleased I'd come back because she was lonely. I didn't like to think of myself as something people turned to when they was bored. I hoped I wouldn't regret coming back.

"What about your chores and visiting your parents?"

"Huh? Oh, I'll do chores tomorrow, and I don't really feel like dealing with Mama and Daddy, after all."

I dropped down on the couch, and Joyce rushed into the kitchen to get us some elderberry wine. Before I had time to swallow my first sip, she got on the subject of her great life. She focused on her work the first few minutes. She had already told me so much about her job, I could probably do it myself with my eyes closed. Every time I steered the conversation toward me, she steered it back to her.

"Sometimes I still can't believe I've been married for more than five years now. Lord knows what I would be doing if I was still single. My life had been so miserable and empty before I met Odell." She smiled from ear to ear. Then, all of a sudden, she got a sad look on her face. "I don't tell too many folks, but several of the men I dated before I got married treated me real bad."

I was surprised to hear that, and just as surprised to hear that she'd had "several" other men before Odell. "Did any of your used-to-be boyfriends ever beat you up?"

"Good gracious, no. But they hurt me in other ways that were painful. They would make love to me, and then I wouldn't see them again until they wanted to do it again. One had the nerve to tell me that he wasn't the marrying kind. A few weeks later, he married a woman from my church." Joyce gave me a sorry look and asked, "Has any man ever beat you?"

"Girl, my daughter's daddy used to beat me for sport. After him, almost every man I got involved with was violent."

"Milton too?"

"Oh no. When I told him how the others had treated me, he promised he would never lay a hand on me. And he ain't."

"It's good to know that Milton's got at least *one* good quality."

Joyce's last comment made me cringe. I decided to say something that I thought would distract her so she wouldn't go off on a rant about my man. "You are such a lucky woman. You got a dream job, a dream house, and a dream husband." The moment them words left my mouth, I realized that the last thing I needed to be talking about was wonderful Odell. She ran with it.

"I know how lucky I am. I suspect that *every* woman I know would trade places with me in a heartbeat if they could," she practically swooned. "And I'm so grateful for all my blessings. Especially Odell."

It ruffled my feathers when I had to listen to Joyce heap praises on Odell over and over and over. She made him sound like such a prize, I wondered what my life would be like if I had a man like him.

"Odell is so much more thoughtful than other men. That's why I don't have a problem turning over most of my paycheck to him every payday. If I had to take care of our finances, we'd be in a lot of trouble." Joyce laughed and clapped her hands together. "Running all over town to pay utility bills and keep track of how much we have in the bank would be too much of a hassle for me. I need to focus on my job, keep an eye on my parents, and give Odell the attention he deserves." She suddenly steered the conversation in a totally different direction: my children. I had already told her why they wasn't with me. "I sure would like to meet your kids someday."

That brung a smile to my face. "I got a letter from my aunt last week. She wrote that they might bring them to visit me in the next week or so. If they don't come on a weekend, they'll come during the week."

"Aren't your kids in school? Or have they dropped out already, like you and Milton?"

I could feel my insides knotting up. I should have knowed she would say something like that. "Aunt Nadine and Uncle Sherman would never let them kids drop out of school."

"I'm glad to hear that *somebody* in your family has enough sense to go in the right direction."

"The school my kids go to is going to be having some repairs done on their water pipes, so they'll be shutting down for a few days soon."

"Do you ever go visit them?"

"It's too hard to get somebody to take me to Mobile and back. If I take the bus, I'd have to transfer four times coming and going, so it could take five or six hours each way."

"Well, whenever the kids do come, I'll help you entertain them. If it's during the week, I'll even take off from work."

I gasped. "Joyce, that would be so nice. If I have a little extra money, we'll take them to Mosella's for lunch—"

Joyce cut me off so fast, it made my head spin. "Don't you worry about that!" she gushed. "You won't have to spend a plugged nickel. Everything will be on me. We can swing by the store and let the kids pick out whatever they want. Odell is a fool for the young kids that drop in, and he always has a lot of play-pretties in stock." She abruptly stopped talking, and within seconds, her giddy demeanor shifted to gloom. "Now, I hope you don't take what I'm about to say the wrong way."

Whenever somebody told me that, I did, anyway.

She went on. "I know you love your babies. I hope they won't resent you when they finally find out you are their mother, after being lied to for so many years. I know I've mentioned it to you before, but I can't say it enough. I still think they are better off with caring, settled-down people, like your aunt and uncle, instead of being with you or tucked away in the orphans' asylum."

"I agree with that. That's why I didn't make a fuss when they decided to keep them," I mumbled. At the same time, my heart felt like it was breaking into a million little pieces.

"Good! God has His reasons for not allowing some women to raise children."

There was no need for her to add that last hurtful remark. And I didn't waste no time turning the tables on her. "I'm sure He got a good reason for not blessing *you* with no kids . . ."

"I'm going to keep praying for some, anyway," she said in a feeble tone, with a miserable expression on her face.

Because of the comment Joyce had made about my children being better off with my aunt and uncle, her offer to help me show them a good time threw me for a loop. That was the only reason I didn't feel too offended. But the next subject I picked to discuss was as far away from our relationships with men and children as I could get: the weather.

"I think it's fixing to rain."

Joyce glanced out the window and nodded. "It sure looks that way."

"I'd better get home and make sure my windows is closed. I'll see you later, Joyce."

The sky had looked like a gray blanket when me and Milton got up this morning at a few minutes before eight. After I got home from Joyce's house a little while ago the sun came out and it looked like it was going to be a nice warm day, after all.

Willie Frank dropped Milton off a few minutes after one o'clock. I was disappointed that he hadn't caught no fish, because I had planned to fry some for our lunch today. A few minutes after we had gobbled up one double-decker hog-headcheese sandwich apiece, he went out to mow our lawn. A couple of times when I looked out the window, he was at the front edge of our yard, leaning over the fence, laughing and chatting it up with neighbors passing by.

We'd been at our new address about four months now, and each day was better than the last. Moving to such a nice area had really lifted our spirits, especially Milton's. In our old location, he used to get moody on a regular basis. It bothered him that other folks had more than us. Having a friend like Odell had done a lot for his self-esteem. It seemed like they got closer by the day. I believed that if Milton continued to spend time with Odell, he would eventually be just as well turned out and refined.

By 5:00 p.m., I had fried ten pounds of green tomatoes, broiled three dozen chicken feet, and baked four dozen hush puppies. On top of all them goodies for our guests to eat, we had several gallon jars of pickled pig feet.

People started knocking on our door at 6:00 p.m. sharp, and it wasn't long before our house was packed to the gills. We had more guests than we had expected. One reason was that it was Aunt Mattie's birthday. She refused to tell anybody her age and would admit only to being a teenager when Lincoln freed the slaves. Instead of celebrating her big day in her own place, the way she usually did every year, this time she decided to pay us a visit. She brung all five of the women that worked for her.

Aunt Mattie had on a long pink dress with a matching shawl. The thick black hairnet covering her head could have been mistook for a spider's web. But her workers was dressed to kill in tight, low-cut blouses and skimpy skirts with designs that included big loud colored flowers, stripes, and polka dots.

The men that had come without their own women couldn't stop pestering the prostitutes. Every time I turned around, somebody was grabbing a titty or squeezing a butt. When Aunt Mattie started giving them men the fish eye, they calmed down. But that wasn't the only thing that scared them off. Almost everybody in Branson had heard the rumor about the hatchet job folks claimed she'd done on her husband and about how she'd buried him in her backyard. That didn't discourage Willie Frank at all. He was all over the place, hugging, kissing, and groping the prostitutes, and some of the regular women, too. He visited Aunt Mattie's poon palace at least once a week, and so did a whole lot of other white men, mainly the businessmen and the bootleggers. But the only other place Willie Frank paid attention to colored women was at our house.

"Don't touch the merchandise, fool!" Aunt Mattie barked, slapping Willie Frank's hand when he attempted to grab another titty. She was so drunk, every time she tried to get up off the couch, she fell back down. "My girls don't give out no free samples. You can look all you want, but you can't touch. If you want to have some fun tonight, you got to pay your two dollars like everybody else. Shoot!"

"All . . . right," Willie Frank mumbled before he slunk to the other side of the room with a hangdog look on his face.

I walked over and stood next to Annie Pearl, one of Aunt Mattie's most popular "employees" for the past ten years.

"I'm surprised Joyce and Odell ain't here tonight," Annie Pearl commented, standing in the middle of the floor, with a drink in one hand and a plate in the other. Even though she was forty, she was so good at whatever she did, tricks had to make appointments to be with her several days in advance. With her thick dark brown hair in a French roll, just a smidgen of make-up, and her simple brown corduroy jumper, she looked more like a preacher's wife than a prostitute.

But the one that really stood out was Tiny: a cute, baby-faced, four-foot-tall midget with enough attitude for a woman three times her height. All the men she serviced raved about the mean blow jobs she gave.

"I seen Joyce peeping out her window when we rolled up. I still can't figure out what a man like Odell see in her," Tiny snickered, flopping down on the arm of the couch. "I wonder what she would say if she knew what a frisky dog he was before he married her. When he worked as our handyman and lived in the house with us, he'd lick—"

Aunt Mattie cut her off real quick. "Hush your mouth, you little heifer! I done told y'all not to be putting my customers' business in the street."

"Pffft! Aunt Mattie, when was Odell ever a 'customer'?" Tiny hollered. "He never paid to do the hoochie coochie with us. I guess he thought that because he was working for you at the time, he didn't have to."

"Humph! Speak for yourself. He paid *me* two dollars up front every time, like all my other tricks," Annie Pearl gloated. "But he is so damn good looking, I did let him hit it for free on his birthday and Christmas."

"Yvonne, the next time you see Odell, tell him I said if Joyce ever slack up on her bedroom job, to let me know," Aunt Mattie piped in. She snorted and looked dead at Annie Pearl. "And make sure you tell him I don't care how good looking he is, so he won't be getting nothing else free at my house."

The folks close enough to hear Aunt Mattie's comments laughed long and loud. Even with the ruckus going on around me, all I could think about was how overjoyed I was that I'd be showing my babies a good time real soon. And that Joyce would be paying for it.

CHAPTER 20
MILTON

I WAS PLEASED TO SEE EVERYBODY HAVING SUCH A GOOD TIME. DR.
Patterson, the sharp-featured general practitioner that lived four
houses down the block from us, shuffled up to me as I opened
the front window to let in some fresh air.

"I declare, Milton. I have to hand it to you and Yvonne. I
haven't had so much fun since I was in college. If y'all don't
have any plans for Thanksgiving, I'd like to invite y'all to eat supper at my house. Eloise is going to bake a turkey, a rump roast,
and a coon, so there'll be plenty to eat. She told me to make
sure I asked you before we leave here tonight." No doctor had
ever gave me so much respect. I had never even dreamed I'd be
socializing with a man like Dr. Patterson, let alone having supper with him and his family in his house. I wished my mama and
daddy had lived long enough to see how far up the ladder I had
climbed.

"We would love to eat Thanksgiving supper with you and your
family next month. I'll even make some sweet potato pies to
bring!" I damn near swooned. "Yvonne will be tickled to death
when I tell her."

When Dr. Patterson went off to conversate with somebody
else, I rushed across the room to where Yvonne was standing.
"Baby, Dr. Patterson invited us to have Thanksgiving supper with
him and his family."

She reacted the way I thought she would. "Sure enough? Well,
I hope you told him we'd be there!" She grinned.

"I did."

We was beaming like glowworms. Nobody could have told me that we wasn't on our way to the kind of respectability we had always wanted. The last holiday invitation we got had come from Joyce and Odell back in July. They'd wanted us to join them for a cookout in their backyard to celebrate the Fourth. That had got canceled because of a storm. But Joyce had cooked some ribs in the oven, and we'd had a good supper, anyway. The main reason I didn't hesitate to accept the good doctor's invitation was that I didn't think we'd get one from nobody else, not even Joyce and Odell. With the way things was going between me and him now, I knew he didn't enjoy my company no more. Sometimes when I took a gander at him from the corner of my eye, he'd be looking at me like he wanted to beat me into a spasm. I hoped that after enough time had passed, he'd be as comfortable with our financial arrangement as I was.

When our last guest left a few minutes before 1:00 a.m., we recycled the leftover alcohol right away so it wouldn't have time to go flat. We laughed every time we did that, because in some cases, we resold part of the same drink so many times, we lost count. After we finished tidying up, we sat on the couch and cuddled.

Suddenly, Yvonne huffed out a loud breath. "Baby, I just thought of something. What if Joyce and Odell invite us to eat with them on Thanksgiving?"

"We'll have to tell them we already made plans. Maybe we can skip bootlegging on Christmas Day and invite Joyce and Odell to eat supper at our house."

"You know we can't do that. We make more money on that holiday than any other day in the year, and I ain't giving that up for nobody." Yvonne's voice sounded tired, but she sure wasn't acting tired. She was a little more affectionate than usual. She kissed the side of my neck and rubbed between my thighs at the same time.

It never took much to get me fired up. My pecker felt as hard as a rock. I started humping and moaning, and she stroked harder. "Take it easy, sugar. I ain't as young as I used to be. I can't keep pleasuring you almost every night, like I been doing since we met."

Yvonne had been giving me sexy looks all evening. She was hotter than a six-shooter now. But for some reason, she decided to let me off the hook tonight. She stopped rubbing me and pulled her hand away. "Just hold on tight to me, then. I'm feeling down in the dumps tonight and kind of lonely."

"You ain't got no reason to be feeling lonely. I'm here, and we just had a houseful of company. We made a pretty penny tonight, so that ought to have you jumping for joy. I'll put tonight's profits with the rest of our funds first thing in the morning."

Like a lot of folks, we didn't deal with banks. We kept our cash in a cigar box up under a pile of old clothes in the attic. The way banks was treating folks these days, I wouldn't trust them to hold a plugged nickel for me. Years ago, my parents had stashed away a couple hundred bucks in Branson First National. When they died, them crooks refused to give that money to my other relatives because the beneficiary my parents had listed was my uncle Jadoo. He had disappeared a week after my parents died. Every colored person in town was convinced that the Klan had done away with him. He hadn't picked up his last paycheck, took none of his clothes or his old car with him, so we knowed he was dead. Because there was no proof, the bank refused to release the money. Nobody in my family could afford to hire a lawyer, so that was the end of that—unless Uncle Jadoo turned up to claim it someday. I was tickled to death when I heard that Branson First National was one of the first banks to crash when the Great Depression hit.

Yvonne cut into my thoughts with a sharp tone. "Make sure you cover up that money good."

"You know I will. Now, what's this about you feeling down in the dumps and lonely?"

"Joyce said some things that hurt my feelings."

"Again?"

"Yes, again." She went on to tell me everything that Joyce had said to her yesterday and everything she had said to Joyce.

"Well, at least you gave her a taste of her own medicine," I chuckled. "I wish I could have seen the expression on her face when you asked where a woman her size bought her clothes. But I wish you wouldn't keep getting upset about some of the stupid comments that come out of her mouth. You know by now she ain't as sharp as we thought she was."

"Joyce ain't a slow wit. She wouldn't have a job working in a school with kids and teachers if she didn't have all her marbles."

Yvonne laid her head on my shoulder, and I raked my fingers through her hair as I spoke. "That don't mean nothing, sugar. The dumbest dog can be trained to do just about anything a person can do. Joyce ain't no exception. I suspect she got that job because she always had the right people in her corner and she was easy to train. You ever thought about that? If that is the case, you ought to feel sorry for her. That poor woman might be mentally off kilter. A condition like that could cause her to be snooty, thoughtless, gullible, and God knows what else."

"Could be, could be. Especially when it come to Odell."

"Damn right. I bet he could tell her black is white and she'd believe him."

"I bet she would, too. But she'd never have to worry about nothing like that. Odell ain't the type."

"What do you mean by that, Yvonne?"

"For one thing, he would never do nothing that he'd have to lie about. I wish—"

I didn't waste no time interrupting Yvonne. "You wish what?"

"Sometimes I wish you was more like Odell."

My body stiffened, and I stopped raking Yvonne's hair. Not only was I hurt, but I was mad, too. "I ain't never going to be no Prince Charming, like he think he is. You stuck with a frog prince . . ."

"No, you ain't no frog! Don't low-rate yourself like that!" she hollered.

"Well, the way you keep rubbing Odell's glory in my face, you make me feel like one."

"I'm sorry," she claimed, speaking in a baby voice. "Even if you was a frog, I'd still love you. And I mean that from the bottom of my heart."

Hearing that made me feel better. I wanted to stop conversating before she backtracked and let out something else I didn't like. "We better get some sleep. It's been a long day, and me and Willie Frank got more orders to drop off in the morning."

CHAPTER 21

MILTON

WHEN WE GOT IN THE BED, YVONNE WENT TO SLEEP RIGHT AWAY. I had so much on my mind, I was wide awake for at least another hour. Me and Willie Frank figured Oscar had found out by now he'd been robbed, so we was going to wait a few days to give him time to cool off. Then we would sell his property to a colored farmer named Eugene Scruggs. He lived in a little town called Schenly, a few miles from Branson. I had never met him, but Willie Frank had run into him during one of his recent visits to Aunt Mattie's house. They'd hit it off right away. That wasn't the only thing on my mind, though, and it wasn't bothering me as much as what Yvonne had said about wishing I was more like Odell. Sometimes *I* wished I was more like Odell. But she had stomped on my ego enough already, so I would never admit that to her.

When I got up at 8:00 a.m. on Sunday morning, Yvonne was already in the kitchen, boiling grits and frying a mess of cow brains, my favorite breakfast. She cooked these mouthwatering treats only when she was trying to butter me up.

"Good morning, sugar," she cooed when I went up to her and wrapped my arms around her waist. Her sweet tone told me she was up to something. I didn't hold her too tight, because I didn't want to get a hard-on and have to tote her back to the bedroom. "You sleep good?"

"Yup." I moved a few steps away and nodded toward the food

cooking on the stove. "What is it you want me to do this time?" I teased.

"Huh? Why you asking me that?"

"Because that's the main reason you would be cooking such a scrumptious breakfast without me asking you to. I thought we ate the last of them cow brains last Tuesday."

"Oh, didn't I tell you?"

"Tell me what?" I narrowed my eyes and moved a few more steps away from her.

"Odell dropped off some the other evening, while you and Willie Frank was making deliveries to them white bootleggers on the north side."

"That was mighty neighborly of him." I tried not to sound sarcastic, but I did. "I wonder why he didn't mention that to me. How many other times has he 'dropped off' stuff that I don't know about?"

Yvonne pursed her lips and gave me a thoughtful look. "Let me see . . . oh!" She snapped her fingers. "Last week he brung over some buttermilk and a bucket of lard. Something about him having to unload surplus stuff he didn't have enough room for." There was suddenly a dreamy-eyed look on her face. "You know, I used to get pissed off with Odell when he was bragging or acting snooty. But that don't bother me so much now."

"Oh? And why is that?" I folded my arms and gaped at her from the corner of my eye.

"Well, he still brags about everything he got and is as uppity as ever. And he usually show up in a dark suit, looking like a undertaker, when most of our other men guests have on overalls. Even them doctors and the real undertaker that was here the other night. But at the same time, lately, he seems more mellow. I'm sure he's just itching to help polish you up. You want some gravy on your grits?"

"I don't want no gravy!" I snapped, with my hands on my hips and my chest getting tight. "I want to hear why you think I need to be 'polished up' in the first place. You make me sound like a rusty nail!"

Yvonne wagged in my face the long-handled spoon that she'd been stirring the grits with. "Why, Milton Hamilton, if I didn't know no better, I'd swear you was jealous of Odell. And that's a damn shame. He almost as good a friend to you now as Willie Frank."

To be as hot as I was, I managed to keep my cool. "Ain't nobody as good a friend to me as Willie Frank! And I ain't jealous of nobody!" I boomed. "Especially a sissified, mealymouthed sucker like Odell."

Yvonne glared at me like I'd stole her purse. "If I had some lye soap, I'd use it to wash out your mouth. You need to give Odell a little more credit for being a friend and a good neighbor. I thought we agreed that we'd be real nice to them—at least to their faces—so we could get more out of them. More stuff from the store and loans when we run short."

"Um, you right, baby. I was just blowing off steam. But when you high-rate other men, I feel lower than a snake's belly."

Yvonne laid the spoon on the stove. Next thing I knew, she grabbed my hand, led me to the table, and pulled out a chair. She pushed me down in it and stood in front of me, with one hand on her hip, the other one wagging a finger in my face. "Milton, you want us to have a nice car, a telephone, and a few other things that we can't afford. We can't get all that unless we rob a bank, which I wouldn't even consider doing after what happened to that Bonnie and Clyde a few years ago. Remember how gruesome they looked in that newspaper clipping your cousin sent you from Louisiana a few days after they got shot up?"

I still had that newspaper clipping. I carried it around in my wallet and took it out to gaze at every time I thought about doing something as crazy as robbing a bank. "Yeah," I sighed, rubbing the pocket where I kept my wallet. "I don't want nothing bad enough to do something that stupid."

"The only way we might get all the things we want is with help from somebody. Now, if Dr. Patterson was to take us under his wing, he might be a good prospect to set up. But his four grown kids and that wife would be a problem, so I ain't going to hold my breath. Meanwhile, Joyce and Odell is still our best shot at the good life."

I dipped my head and gave Yvonne a sorry look. "You right, but I wish you wouldn't keep reminding me what Odell is and what I ain't."

"Baby, it ain't no big deal. I'm sure there is a bunch of other colored men that wish they could be more like Odell. After all, he is damn near perfect."

Yvonne's recent "fascination" with Odell had caught me off guard. I hoped it was just a short-term phase she was going through, because I didn't like it one bit. I knew that if I didn't change the subject, I'd say something I'd regret. "You cooking up something else besides them grits and brains? Why don't you tell me what it is?"

She giggled before she answered. "I want you to be in a good mood today."

"Why?"

"I didn't want to tell you before now, but Aunt Nadine sent a letter last week. She said she and Uncle Sherman might drop off my kids one day soon so they can spend some time with me."

"So? Why do you think I need to be in a good mood to see your babies? I know how much you miss them."

"Because I know most men don't want to be bothered with another man's children. In my case, three other men."

"Sugar, I knew before we got married that you had them kids. It didn't bother me then, and it don't bother me now." I exhaled and scratched the side of my neck. "If they spend the night, we can borrow Willie Frank's truck and take them back home."

Yvonne nodded. "I'm glad to hear you say that. The only thing is, if they come on a weekday, I'll have to take off from work and give up a whole day's pay. That's money we'd have to make up for some other way. I don't want our guests to start paying more for their drinks, since we ain't been in business that long." Yvonne chuckled. "Especially since we already scamming so many folks with recycled drinks. But my daughter's birthday was back in July, and I didn't get to spend it with her. I might even bake a cake if they come so I could make up for that. And in the meantime, maybe you could borrow a few more dollars from Odell to have to fall back on in case some unexpected expense come up while the kids here."

"I don't know about borrowing from Odell too often. He might say no." Whatever money me and Willie Frank got when we sold the stuff we took from Oscar's barn, my share was already spent. I still owed Aunt Mattie a couple more dollars for the poontang and blow jobs I'd added to my tab last month. And in the past three weeks I'd lost quite a bit in every card game I got in. So, I was a little behind with everything.

"As long as you pay Odell back, he ain't got no reason to start saying no," Yvonne assured me.

"That's right, baby."

"I doubt if he'd ever turn you down. A man like him—"

I held up my hand and cut Yvonne off. "Um, keep my food warm. I need to go sit on the commode for a while." I didn't have to use the toilet, but I couldn't stand to hear Yvonne go off on another tangent about the magnificent Odell no more this morning.

CHAPTER 22
MILTON

*T*HE FOLLOWING SATURDAY, ANOTHER LETTER CAME FROM AUNT Nadine to let Yvonne know she'd be dropping the kids off on the coming Monday. I was grateful that Joyce had volunteered to take off the day and help show them a good time. I sure didn't want to do it, because them little devils gave me a run for my money. I never complained, because Yvonne felt bad enough not having her kids with her.

Whenever a letter came saying that the kids was coming for a visit, we never knew what time of day they would be dropped off. The last time, Uncle Sherman had dropped them off at 7:30 a.m. the day after one of our most hectic nights. I had had a few drinks too many the night before and had woke up with one of the worst hangovers I ever had. Not knowing what time they was coming today, and me not being in the mood to deal with them, I made plans to make myself scarce. I decided to leave for work a hour and a half earlier. If I was lucky, I'd be gone by the time they arrived. When I told Yvonne, she wasn't too happy about it.

"Milton, why did Mr. Cunningham ask you to come in early to help him get the chicken feet ready when he usually do it by his-self?"

"I don't know, baby. When the boss man ask me to do something, I don't ask him why. And don't you bring this up to him."

"I won't. But it's a shame that he asked you to come in early the last times the kids came, too."

"That wouldn't happen if the kids came on a weekend."

"I hope the next time they come, it will be a weekend, so you can spend time with them, too."

What Yvonne didn't know was that whenever she told me the kids was coming on a weekday, I went in early to help Mr. Cunningham prepare a mess of chicken feet, our lunch special every day. I'd cut the toenails, scrape off calluses, and then they had to be boiled up to two hours. I didn't mind helping do that ungodly chore—and not because my boss asked me to. The reason was so I could leave the house early so I wouldn't have to deal with them kids.

I liked Yvonne's babies and treated them as good as I would have my own. But they hated my guts. Aunt Nadine and Uncle Sherman had spoiled them rotten, so they was as wild as jackrabbits. They didn't have a lick of respect for me and had even called me a thug to my face one time. They came only two or three times a year, but that was too many times for me. No matter what I told them to do, they always told me, "Aw, hush up! You ain't my daddy!" It didn't help for me to be nice and generous to them. I'd borrow Willie Frank's truck and take them on long rides, give them candy and toys and other stuff. But they never thanked me or showed no appreciation at all, so I stopped.

Ten minutes after I got to the grill, I told Mr. Cunningham I had to take a longer lunch so I could go see a man in town about some new furniture. I asked him not to mention it to Yvonne in case I decided to buy it, because I wanted to surprise her. I had been looking for some new furniture, but I couldn't get that until I had more money. I was actually going with Willie Frank to unload the stuff we'd stole from Oscar.

"How much do you think Eugene will pay us?" Willie Frank asked as we cruised along in his truck. He had met me behind the train station fifteen minutes after 12:00 p.m. so nobody would see me with him, or the swiped equipment in the bed of his truck, which was covered up with a tarp.

"I don't know," I replied, scratching my head. "I know we won't get whatever it's really worth. But some money is better than none. I sure do need it."

"Buddy, you know you can always bum a few bucks from me—if I got it. It seem like the more I give them lazy kinfolks of mine, the more they want. But if you need it more, I'll hold them off. You always pay me back when you say you will. They don't."

"I hope I don't have to ask you for a loan no time soon."

I borrowed from Willie Frank every now and then. I didn't like to, because once I paid him back, I was back in the same hole he'd pulled me out of. I didn't know what I'd do without the money I was getting from Odell and from other scams me and Willie Frank pulled off. But until I stashed enough cash away or learned how to manage it better, hustling was the only way I was going to keep me and Yvonne out of the poorhouse.

I didn't know how long the kids would be at our house, so I planned on getting in a few card or crap games this evening. I hoped that by the time I got home, they'd be gone or too tired to give me a hard time. Another problem I had was that we couldn't entertain guests with children in the house. We had promised Aunt Nadine and Uncle Sherman from the get-go that we never would. Every thirsty soul we didn't let in the house meant more money we'd be out! I hadn't planned on putting the squeeze on Odell again too soon, but I would if I had to.

"That's the place," Willie Frank blurted out, cutting into my thoughts. He turned onto a narrow dirt road and drove toward a big house with red paint peeling, a tin roof, and tar paper covering one of the front windows. There was a wraparound porch with a silver glider on it. A shiny black truck was parked in the front yard.

"Well, do say," I commented, staring in awe. "From the look of things, this Eugene ought to be good for some sweet money."

Before we could park and get out, the front door swung open. A stocky man in his sixties shuffled out. He was so fair skinned, I thought he was white. But when he got close enough for me to see how nappy his hair was, I realized he was just another colored person with a cracker on the family tree.

"It's about time y'all got here," he boomed, walking toward us. His dusty bare feet looked like uncooked chickens.

After we piled out, Willie Frank introduced me to Eugene Scruggs.

"Nice to know you. I hope we can make a right good deal today." I greeted him with one of my most businesslike smiles and shook his hand.

"I hope so, too," Eugene replied in a gruff tone. I didn't like the skeptical look on his face. "Let me see what y'all got."

We unloaded everything and laid it on the ground at his feet. That skeptical look was still on his face as he looked from one item to another.

"Hmmm. I don't know how much y'all want, but I ain't got but four dollars."

I couldn't believe my ears. "Now, look here, Eugene. I don't know what this much stuff sell for in a store. But I got a feeling it's more than four dollars," I said in my sternest tone. "We can do a whole lot better than that."

"Then why don't y'all? It ain't no skin off my nose," he snickered.

"Look, buddy, we took a big risk getting this stuff. And you said you needed it. Can't you be a little more generous than that?" Willie Frank piped in.

"All right. I'll throw in a bushel of potatoes," Eugene added.

"Potatoes? Man, do we look hungry to you!" I snapped, talking so fast I almost choked on my words. "There's so many fields around here, we could swipe enough potatoes to last us from now on. We need money. If you don't want to give us nothing fair, we'll find somebody that will."

Eugene lifted his hands in the air like we'd just pulled a gun on him. "All right then. I'll throw in another fifty cents, and that's only because y'all seem like nice young men," he snapped.

Me and Willie Frank looked at each other at the same time and hunched our shoulders.

"Well, at least it's four and a half bucks more than we got

now," he said with a heavy sigh. "Besides, I have to get this stuff off my truck before some nosy snoop sees it."

"You right about that," I agreed.

After Eugene handed us two dollars and a quarter apiece, we started to get back in the truck.

"Wait a minute!" he hollered. "I got a bad back. I can't tote that stuff by myself. My field hand ain't coming again until tomorrow, and I ain't about to let this stuff lay on the ground until then."

"So?" I said.

"So, y'all need to load it back on that truck and haul it around to my barn," he whined, like he was the one that had just got gypped.

"That'll cost you another fifty cent," Willie Frank said.

If I had said the same thing, it wouldn't have got the same results it got coming from a white man. Eugene smiled at Willie Frank and gave me the stink eye before he rooted around in his pocket and pulled out a couple more quarters.

CHAPTER 23

YVONNE

*T*HE OLD TRUCK MY UNCLE OWNED WAS ALMOST AS LOUD AS A train. I could hear it coming up our street Monday morning, a few minutes after 10:00 a.m., while I was in the kitchen, cutting up some collard greens. I wiped my hands on my apron and ran to the front door.

Uncle Sherman parked in front of our house with one front tire up on the curb. But him and Aunt Nadine didn't get out. They never did. It wasn't because they was too lazy; it was because that old truck was so rickety, once the motor was turned off, it could take up to a hour or longer to crank it up again. If that wasn't bad enough, that truck couldn't go no faster than thirty miles a hour, so the forty-five- to fifty-minute drive from Mobile always took them quite a while.

My aunt and uncle had enough money to buy a better vehicle, but they refused to do so. They was both retired but still did a few jobs on the side for extra money. Uncle Sherman did handyman work for various wealthy families. Aunt Nadine took in washing and ironing, and she done a lot of daywork for rich white women while the kids was in school. As much as I missed my babies, I was still glad that they was in a more wholesome environment. They had nice clothes and more toys than they needed, and they never complained about spending several hours in church every Sunday. They was living by the golden rules. But I didn't get my hopes up too high that they would grow up to be upstanding, law-abiding citizens. I'd been raised by them same rules, and look how I'd ended up.

The kids piled out of the truck bed and whooped and grinned as they ran toward me as I stood on the sidewalk. "Cousin Yvonne," they yelled at the same time. Just hearing the word *cousin* made my heart skip a beat. I couldn't wait for the day they would call me Mama.

Cherie, who had turned thirteen back in July, got to me first.

"Happy belated birthday, sugar! I'm tickled to death y'all came!" I was crying and laughing. I wrapped my arms around her and kissed her forehead. "Girl, you almost as big as me. Did you enjoy your birthday?"

"Yes, ma'am. I got two new dresses!" Cherie gushed, twirling around for me to gaze at the dark brown smock frock she wore over a beige cotton dress.

"You look so pretty!" I complimented, fluffing her long silky ponytail.

"You should have seen me yesterday!" She twirled around again. "I wore my other new dress to church!"

I kissed her forehead again, and then I hugged my eleven-year-old sons, Jimmy James and Ishmael.

"You smell like lard," Ishmael noted, fanning his face and wiggling his nose. Both boys had on overalls and plaid shirts.

"Watch your mouth, boy. You know you ain't allowed to disrespect grown folks," Uncle Sherman scolded, raising his thick gray eyebrows.

"I do smell like lard," I acknowledged with a laugh. "Milton bought me some new smell goods last week. I'll splash some on as soon as we get in the house."

The only things my kids had inherited from me was light skin and good hair. Everything else had came from their good-looking, no-good daddies.

"They done ate breakfast already," Aunt Nadine yelled. This was the first time they had visited since we'd moved. She eyed my house with a pinched look on her face. "That's a right smart house. Bigger than I expected. And I just love that picket fence.

Me and Sherman had one around our first home after we got married. I spent a lot of my time leaning over it to chat with my neighbors."

"I love our fence, too. But we have company so often, somebody always forget to close the gate."

"How many bedrooms y'all got?" Aunt Nadine asked.

"Three. All the rooms is on one floor. Every house on this street got a nice big attic. The landlord had every room painted before we moved in. I wish y'all could come in and see how nice it is inside."

The pinched look was still on my aunt's jowly, tobacco-colored face. "I wish we could, too. But you know if Sherman turn off this motor, there ain't no telling when we'd get back home," she snapped, glancing toward the house again. "Where Milton at? Still in the bed?"

"He went to work. He wanted to take off today, too. But until we save up some money, we can't afford for us both to take off the same day without pay."

"Both of y'all working at that roadhouse grill and bootlegging, and y'all *still* got money troubles?" Uncle Sherman asked in a gruff tone.

"Uh-huh. Our rent is a lot more over here," I explained. "We been saving up as much as we can so we can get a car, new furniture, and a few other things."

"Do you mean to tell us y'all moved into this lovely house with all that same old broke-down furniture?" Uncle Sherman grunted. "Girl, with your good looks, you could have got a man that had way more to offer you than that broke-ass mud puppy you settled for."

I couldn't figure out why some folks felt they had to remind me that Milton wasn't drop-dead handsome and rolling in dough. If I had married a man like the one my folks thought I deserved, I doubted if I would have been able to hold on to him. Handsome men with money usually didn't stay with the same women for too long. I didn't care how much Odell loved Joyce. He would have been singing a different tune if she hadn't been born to well-to-do parents. He probably wouldn't have married her in the first place.

"I love my 'mud puppy,' and he is good to me," I declared. I didn't want to hear no more comments about Milton, so I ended the conversation as fast as I could. "I don't mean to rush off, but I'm going to take the kids inside so we can plan our day." I turned to the kids. "Didn't y'all bring no changing clothes?"

Uncle Sherman answered for them. "Naw. They can't stay long. Have them ready for us to pick up by seven o'clock this evening. We'll go visit some of our old neighbors here and do a little fishing until it's time for us to come back."

"I thought they was going to spend the night!" I wailed.

"We said they could spend the day with you, not the night. We need to get back home in time for these kids to finish the chores they should have finished yesterday. So you better have them ready when we get back here. Do you hear me, girl?" Aunt Nadine growled.

"Yes, ma'am," I muttered with my head hanging low.

"Kids, if y'all don't behave, there'll be some whuppings coming," Uncle Sherman warned.

They said their good-byes and took off, and me and the kids headed toward the house. I looked over at Joyce's window. Sure enough, she was peeping from it, something she and Odell did on a regular basis. I waved at her. She waved back and suddenly disappeared. Before I could get the kids inside, she popped out her gate and skittered through mine.

"Come on over and meet my little cousins," I told her.

She was grinning like a fool as she followed us into my living room. "My goodness! These kids are so precious and cute! Just look at all that pretty hair and white teeth. Who's who?" she asked, wringing her hands and looking from one face to the other.

"I'm Cherie." My daughter introduced herself with a wide smile and a gleam in her eye. Joyce was at least a head and a half taller than she was, so Cherie had to crane her neck to look up at her. So did the boys.

"I'm Jimmy James, but they call me JJ."

"My name is Ishmael, just like in the Bible."

"I'm Joyce, from right next door." I knew she loved kids, but this was the first time I'd seen her so giddy. I couldn't imagine how much she fawned over them students she worked with.

The kids didn't seem that impressed with her, so I jumped in and told them something I thought they'd like to hear. "Miss Joyce is going to treat us to lunch today."

"Is that all?" Ishmael mumbled, looking disappointed.

I laughed, but then I went on in a stern tone, "Boy, let me give you some advice that I hope you'll remember the rest of your life. Don't never look a gift horse in the mouth. Times is still hard, so if you can get something for free, give thanks to the Lord. Miss Joyce's folks own a big store a few blocks from here. They got all kind of nice things for kids."

Joyce was still grinning and eyeballing my babies like she wanted to kiss their feet. "We even got candy and toys," she added. The kids started grinning just as hard as Joyce.

"When can we go to that store?" Cherie asked.

"Well, that's up to your cousin. My husband drove our car to work, so we'll have to walk down the street apiece to the bus stop." Joyce turned to me with a anxious look on her face. "Yvonne, I'm ready to leave whenever you want. I just need to run back home and get my purse and lock up."

We left a few minutes before 10:30 a.m. Since we had to walk to the bus stop and wait for the bus—which was fifteen minutes late—it was 11:30 a.m. when we got to Mosella's. Me and Joyce got the oxtail plate, and the kids wanted burgers and fries, a treat Aunt Nadine hardly ever cooked. She was more into serving pig body parts, corn bread, and greens four or five times a week.

"This is a real nice restaurant for colored folks," Cherie said, looking around. "Nice tablecloths, clean floor, plates that ain't got no cracks, a record player—and I ain't seen no flies or roaches yet."

We all laughed.

"If you think this place is nice, wait until you see my family's store. It's the only one in Branson that is owned by colored folks," Joyce gloated.

I had hoped we'd get through the day without her tooting her horn about her blessed life. I knew she'd eventually tune up her mouth to ease in a bunch of comments about Odell. She started up on him as soon as we walked through MacPherson's front door.

"My husband manages the store, and he is so sharp, everybody in town looks up to him. Even white folks."

"You look up to him, too, Cousin Yvonne?" JJ asked.

"Uh-huh," I admitted.

CHAPTER 24
YVONNE

I WAS SO HAPPY THAT ODELL'S TWO NOSY CASHIERS HAD A BUNCH OF customers to check out, so they couldn't slow us down. A couple of stock boys was shuffling around with boxes and whatnot, but we ignored them all and marched in single file behind Joyce toward the back of the store. All the way, the kids was oohing and aahing at all the nice things on the shelves. We stood off to the side as Joyce pushed open the door to Odell's office.

"Odell, there is some children here itching to see you!" she hollered.

Even from where I was, I could hear Odell gasp. Something crashed to the floor, and he rushed over to Joyce. "Huh? W-what children?" I couldn't understand why he was acting and sounding so nervous. He loved kids as much as Joyce.

She ushered us into the office. On the floor there was a lamp in pieces, which had to be what I heard crash. Odell glanced from me to my children and blinked. "Yvonne, these your cousins I done heard so much about?" he asked, sounding and looking relieved, which confused me. I couldn't understand why he had reacted in such a odd way when Joyce told him some children had come to see him.

"Yup." I introduced each one. To my surprise, they took to Odell like ducks to water.

He shook hands with my boys and patted Cherie on top of her head. "You taller than Joyce! And look at them wide shoulders!" she commented with a frisky grin, which was too much like flirting in my book.

"Mr. Odell, can we have some candy?" JJ asked.

"Sure enough! Let's go out to the main floor, and y'all can pick out anything you want."

The kids squealed like pigs and followed him to the aisle where the candy and toys was located.

"I didn't know Odell would be this excited to spend time with kids he just met," Joyce commented. Me and her walked a few feet behind him and the kids. "I just wish . . ." She stopped talking and turned to me with a sad expression on her face. "I just wish I could give him a few so he wouldn't feel so left out as a man."

"Why do you think not having kids of his own make him feel left out?"

"Yvonne, I knew from the get-go how often he dreamed about being a daddy. I hope I can make his dream come true before my baby-making equipment shuts down."

For the next hour, Odell let the kids pick out all the toys, candy, and clothes they wanted. We had too many bags to carry on the bus, so he insisted on driving us home. During the ride, with the kids squeezed together on the front seat with him, he conversated with them about school and what they wanted to be when they grew up. Then they started asking him all kinds of questions and heaping praises on him, too.

"How come you ain't got no kids, Mr. Odell?" Cherie wanted to know, squirming like a maggot on Ishmael's lap. "You don't want none?"

Them questions must have really caught him off guard, because he almost ran up on the sidewalk. "Huh? I love kids. Me and Joyce plan on having a bunch someday," he mumbled.

"How did y'all get so old and not have none by now?" Ishmael asked.

"Well, it takes a while for some folks," Odell answered with a nervous cough.

"Mr. Odell, I wish you was my daddy!" JJ zoomed in. "You the best man in the world."

"Sure enough!" Ishmael agreed.

"And the best-looking one I ever seen," Cherie swooned. "Ain't he, Cousin Yvonne?"

"Um . . . yes, he is," I agreed.

"I'm going to marry a man just like you, Mr. Odell," Cherie added.

"Now, y'all calm down. I ain't that special," he chuckled.

"Yes you are, baby," Joyce cooed. She leaned forward and reached up and squeezed his shoulder. He turned around for a second and winked at her. I thought that if me and the kids hadn't been in that car, they would have pulled to the side of the road and pleasured each other in the backseat.

When she turned back to me, her tone was dry. "Too bad Milton didn't take today off. I'm sure Odell would have let him pick out a few complimentary items. Lord knows he could sure use some better-looking shoes and aftershave that doesn't smell like kerosene. The next time, make him take off so he can come with us, okay?"

"Okay."

It was a blessing Milton hadn't come. Listening to the kids praise Odell would have been torture for him. I suddenly missed my man and couldn't wait for him to come home so I could show him some love.

When we got to my house, Odell helped us carry everything inside. Before he went back to work, Cherie hugged his neck, and the boys shook his hand. Odell grinned and carried on like these was the first kids he'd ever been around. Right after he left, Joyce gave me the most desperate look I'd ever seen on her face.

"See what I'm talking about? Odell has so much love for children, he deserves to be a daddy more than any man I ever knew." Her tone sounded so hopeless. But a few seconds later, she perked back up. "Let's take the kids to my house so I can give them some tea cakes. You and I can have a drink."

While the kids was at Joyce's kitchen table, eating tea cakes, me and Joyce sat down on the living-room couch and started drinking some of her weak elderberry wine. I wanted a shot of the good whiskey Joyce and Odell served their special guests, but I was too proud to ask for some. Besides that, I couldn't drink nothing too strong while my babies was still with me, because it would stay on my breath for hours. It was already after four o'clock. If my aunt and uncle returned at seven or sooner, they would smell it, and there was no telling when they'd bring the kids to see me again.

"I had so much fun with y'all today," Joyce told me with a woeful look in her eyes. "Kids are such a blessing. I fell in love with your sweet angels."

Her comments made me feel warm all over. "I can't wait to have them back all to myself."

I wondered if I had misjudged her and if she was not as mean spirited as I had thought. That thought had crossed my mind before. But almost every time, she had said something that made me reconsider. This time was no different.

"No offense, Yvonne, but when I become a mother, we'll probably move. And we won't be visiting this neighborhood too often."

I tensed up, because I had no idea what she was leading up to this time. "Huh? Why? I thought y'all liked this location."

"We do. But things have changed a lot since we moved here. Things that are giving the neighborhood a bad name . . ."

"You talking about Janey Hemphill, that bug-eyed old lady across the street, with them eight cats that run wild all over the block? And the fat man next door to her, who waters his grass in his pajamas, with the crack of his butt showing? I agree with you. Their antics is giving the whole block a bad name." I groaned and shook my head.

Joyce went on with a deadpan expression on her face. "Those things were happening before y'all moved over here. I'm talking about something a little more personal." She got quiet and scanned my face for at least five seconds.

"Don't go mute on me now. Tell me what that 'personal' thing is."

"Well, I've already mentioned to you that Odell is particular, especially when it comes to family. He is devoted to his daddy and never complains about all the sacrifices he has to make to spend so much time with him. And you saw how he behaved with your kids today. He has told me more than once that nothing is more precious than children and that it's our responsibility to keep them away from bad influences. Especially bootleggers and other riffraff . . ."

"But you and Odell spend a lot of time around bootleggers and other riffraff."

"That's different. We're grown and know how to handle things like that. Kids don't."

Mine was still in the kitchen and couldn't hear us, but I lowered my voice, anyway. "How do you know you'll ever have any if you ain't had none by now?" That put a woeful look on her face.

"I'll have some eventually, God willing."

"We ain't never had no trouble at our house with our guests. Me and Milton is quiet, mature, God-fearing people. We don't do nothing that would make us look half as bad as some of the heathens in this town."

"Not yet," Joyce eased in, wagging her finger in my face. She was lucky I didn't bite it off. I held my breath as she continued. "On top of y'all being bootleggers and best friends with a snaggle-toothed hillbilly who makes his living operating a still, you and Milton are ex-convicts. All that could be a recipe for disaster if there were young kids in the mix. If you could put yourself in my shoes—and Odell's—I'm sure you'd feel the same way."

I was so stunned, it felt like my brain had froze up. I didn't care how nice a day we had had and how much free merchandise Odell had let us take, I wanted to slap Joyce. I had to keep reminding myself that no matter what spewed out of her mouth or what she did—so long as it wasn't too extreme—I couldn't end our relationship until me and Milton had got all we could from them. "I'm sorry to hear that you don't want the kids you *might* have someday to get close to me and Milton." It was hard, but I managed to keep my voice firm. I didn't want her to know how weak she made me feel. "I was eager to introduce my kids to you and Odell because I wanted them to see the kind of high-class folks me and Milton associate with."

Joyce held up her hand and tried to backpedal. It was too late, though. She'd already slid into the hole she'd just dug with her mouth. "And I really appreciate that. The next time they come, we'll do something else they'll enjoy. If I ever get up enough nerve to learn how to drive, I'll take the car from Odell and drive you to Mobile to visit with them. I'll even pay for all the gas and whatever it costs for us to have a good time."

Her gentle tone, fake smile, and generous offer helped a little. But I was still upset, and I wanted her to feel a little pain, too. I knew that not being a mother was a sensitive issue with Joyce. I decided to run with that. "I'm glad to hear that you have so much love for the kids you might *never* have. I feel so sorry for you . . ."

She started off talking again in a tone so low I could barely hear her. "If I never have any children, only God knows how I'll be able to go on. And poor Odell. He'd never admit it, but I know he'd be truly disappointed in me if I never give him some children."

I rubbed her shoulder. I was angry and sad for her at the same time. "You need to stop harping on this subject. I'm sorry we got on it in the first place. I can see how hard it is on you. Just be thankful that at least you got Odell."

"I am, praise the Lord." She took a sip from her wineglass, and her eyes got glassy. "I still can't believe I'm married to such an incredible man. He gets better each day, bless his heart."

I'd drunk enough to have a mild buzz, which was all you could expect from something as spiritless as elderberry wine. It helped keep me from saying something sarcastic. I stayed quiet and just stared upside Joyce's head, wondering what stupid thing she was brewing up to say next.

With a smug look on her face, she started talking again. "I know I've told you this before, but I'll tell you again. You'd be so much better off if you'd married a man like Odell."

"And I'll tell you again. Milton is the only man I ever really loved."

"Oh well." She hunched her shoulders and paused before adding with a sneer, "I'll pray for you. Have some more wine. It'll make you feel better about your situation."

"That's all right. I done drunk enough. And, anyway, I don't need to feel better about my situation. It's just the way I want it to be." I gave her the most contented look I could come up with. "Me and the kids better be on our way. I need to have supper ready when Milton come home." I couldn't collect my children and leave fast enough.

CHAPTER 25
MILTON

*A*LL DAY LONG I HAD BEEN PRAYING THAT I'D FIND SOMEBODY willing to give me a ride to a house where some high-rolling gamblers was supposed to be playing at this evening. At quitting time, I hung around the grill, shooting the breeze with the cleanup crew, still praying somebody with a car would mosey along. God must have been listening, because as I was walking to the bus stop, Willie Frank's truck came barreling down the road toward me, kicking up more dust than a sandstorm. He pulled to the side and stopped on a dime next to me, with his brakes squealing like a woman making mad love. From the frantic look on his face and the way his cap was sitting sideways on his head when he leaned out the window, I knew something bad was up.

"Great balls of fire! Thank God I found you!" he hollered. "We got a mess on our hands."

"Oh shit! What's wrong?"

"Anybody come at you?"

I did a double take. "Come at me? Who . . . What in the world is going on, Willie Frank? You act like Satan chasing you."

"That could be the case." He wiped sweat and dust off his face and peered up and down the road. When his eyes shifted back to me, he looked even more distressed. "Get in so we can talk."

I snatched open the passenger door and scrambled in. He made a U-turn and shot off back down the road before I could even shut the door all the way.

"Man, you scaring me. What's the problem?"

"That Eugene we sold the stuff to is the problem. Guess who he's related to?"

I hunched my shoulders. "I don't know. I just met him for the first time when you took me to his house to unload them goods we stole from Oscar. Why?"

"Oscar's sister is his common-law wife. Him and Eugene got a lot of bad blood between them and is always trying to outdo each other. Eugene didn't waste no time going out to Oscar's farm to show off his equipment. Well, you can guess where I'm going with this."

"And Oscar recognized his own stuff, huh?"

"Sure enough. Eugene told him right off who he bought it from."

"Shit!" My heart started thumping like mad, and I was having trouble breathing. "Who told you?"

"Sweet Sue, that new gal Aunt Mattie hired last week. I had a little fun with her a little while ago. Oscar had paid her a visit before I got there, and he told her."

"Hmmm. Let me think." I scratched the side of my head, and a idea suddenly came to me. "I got it!"

"Well, I'm all ears, so give it to me," Willie Frank advised.

"We can say we bought that stuff from somebody and didn't know it was hot."

"We can say that, but it sounds pretty flimsy, even to me."

"Not if we tell it right. Oscar mentioned that only his field hands knew where he hid his stuff, remember? Jerome and Amos?"

"So?"

"So they could have stole it and sold it to us. We can say that. And if Oscar told them and us, there ain't no telling who else he told."

"I never thought about that, but you got a good point there."

"No, wait! We'll leave Jerome's name out. We'll lay the blame all on Amos, the slow-witted alcoholic. From what folks say about him, he is a good worker, but his mind is a hodgepodge when it come to anything else. He wouldn't remember if he stole the stuff or not. We'll spread the news around that Amos traded it to us for some white lightning and refused to tell us where he got it from. Remember now, Oscar never showed us nothing, so for all he know, we ain't got no idea what it look like. How was we supposed to know Amos had double-crossed his own boss? Anyway, as fast as news travel in this town, it's bound to get to Oscar before he get to us. It'll be our word against Amos's. Who do you think he'll believe? Well-respected, bona fide businessmen like us or a man with mush for a brain?"

"Well, Milton, that plan sounds as good as anything else we could come up with." I was happy to see that Willie Frank didn't look so rattled now.

"Sure enough. Pull over and let me out for a minute. You had me so riled up, my bladder went crazy."

"Don't you want to wait until we get to a cornfield, so you can have some privacy? There is one coming up in a few minutes."

"I can't wait that long," I insisted, squeezing my thighs together.

Willie Frank stopped and left the motor running while I got out to go pee. Before I could finish, another truck rolled down the road behind us. I recognized it right off. It was Oscar's, and Eugene was riding shotgun! I let out a yelp and crouched down until they passed. I finished peeing and jumped back in the truck. Willie Frank was slumped sideways in his seat. He seemed more stressed now than he'd been when he picked me up. And so was I.

"Woo-wee! Did you see who that was?"

"Sure enough," Willie Frank croaked, sitting back up. "They didn't recognize my truck, praise the Lord. As soon as I spotted them, I ducked. We need to lay low until we get that rumor up on its feet that we did business with Amos. If we lucky, by the time we see Oscar or Eugene again, they'll have chastised that slow wit and we'll be in the clear."

"Good."

I looked down the road and was glad to see that Oscar's truck had reached the crossroads and turned off. I was surprised to see so much more sweat on Willie Frank's face. He seemed as scared as I was, and he didn't need to be. Even if Oscar could prove Willie Frank had something to do with the theft, he knew that confronting a white man—especially one in Willie Frank's position—could get him lynched. For that reason, my butt was the one on the line. But being my sidekick, I knew Willie Frank was going to help me get through this mess alive.

"Humph! I can't believe Oscar had the nerve to make a fuss over some stuff he got by cheating in a card game. Some people ain't got no shame," I remarked.

"I feel the same way." Willie Frank chuckled. "You going home, or do you want me to drop you off someplace else? Sweet Sue sure gave my pecker a good workout. Oomph! You want to let her fix you up before you go home?"

"My pussycat tab is past due again. Aunt Mattie told me I can't have no more fun with her girls until I bring my account up to date. That greedy old bitch!"

"Don't worry about that. It'll be my treat."

That got my attention right away. "Oh yeah? What do Sweet Sue look like?"

"Well, she could stand to put on a few pounds, and I got more hair on my chest than she got on her head. But her tail is damn sure worth two dollars."

"Hmmm. Then I guess I'll have to check her out soon. I got me a piece of tail from Tiny last week, so I'm in good shape for a few more days. So for today I'll settle for the tail I got at home. I don't like to spread myself too thin, like some men."

I immediately thought about Odell. Poking two women full-time for more than five years, he had probably wore his pecker down to a nub by now. Willie Frank was looking straight ahead, so he didn't see the grin on my face.

"Drop me off at that jook joint on Brewster Road," I said. "I guess I should try my luck at a poker game while I got the urge and a few dollars."

It was a fifteen-minute ride to the jook joint. Since we had

come up with a plan on how to deal with Oscar, we didn't discuss
him no more during the ride. I was still concerned about how
this theft thing was going to play out, but I didn't see no sense in
dwelling on it. Besides, I was anxious to get in on a game. That
was what I needed to focus on. By the time Willie Frank let me
out, we was laughing and joking like we didn't have nary a care
in the world.

It was a good thing I had put a deck of marked cards in my
pocket before I left home. If I hadn't, I would have lost every
dime in my pocket.

"Milton, you sure is lucky this evening." Talking to me was
Casper "Cap" Griffin, the man who ran the jook joint I was at.
He was only ten years older than me, but because he was a great
big fat man who was usually jolly and easygoing, he seemed a lot
older. One of the reasons I had chose to cheat at his place was
that he was known to be the meek and gentle type. I'd never
heard him raise his voice when people pushed his buttons. And
because he didn't seem threatening, it made more sense to me
to start cheating at his place instead of one that had a history of
violence.

The other four men I had skunked had already left the kitchen,
where we always played on a table with mismatched legs. Me and
Cap was still sitting across from one another. He didn't look too
happy. I was feeling so good, I thought I was going to bust open
from all the joy in my heart. Why hadn't I thought about mark-
ing a deck of cards before? For all I knew, them suckers that had
skunked my tail so many times had probably used marked cards!
With that thought in mind, I didn't feel the least bit guilty. I did
feel a little guilty about stealing Oscar's stuff, though. I almost
wished we hadn't done it. But if we hadn't, I wouldn't have had
enough spare money to get in the game tonight.

"Well, as long as I been coming over here—and losing most of
the time—my luck was bound to change sooner or later, my man,"
I said.

"Luck changing a little is one thing. You won almost every

game tonight, and that's mighty suspicious." Cap folded his arms across his barrel-shaped bosom. "Let me check out them cards you insisted on using. I don't know why I didn't think to do it after you won them first three games in a row."

"Now, wait a minute. I won fair and square. You ain't never been a spoilsport before." I scooped up my cards and slid them back into my pocket.

Me and Cap had been friends since before I went to prison. This was the first time I seen a frown on his face, and the first time I heard him raise his voice. "I ain't never lost so much money to you before! You can't be *that* lucky without some kind of scheme!"

"Now . . . now, you hold on there! I don't like it when people drop hints about me that ain't true. Shoot! You just hurt my feelings." I thought a little sulking would make my case stronger.

"If you ain't playing with marked cards, you ain't got nothing to worry about. But I want to see that for myself!"

"Shame on you, Cap! I thought you was one of my best friends, and that you trust me as much as I trust you. I see I was wrong."

"If you want me to stay one of your best friends, you'll let me take a look-see at them cards!"

"I . . . I can't take no . . . no more of this abuse," I stuttered, with my bottom lip poked out like a second tongue. I eased up out of my chair and started backing toward the door, shaking my head. "Your behavior is unspeakable! And you just got baptized last month! I'll come back tomorrow, when you sober. But for now, I'm going to get on down the road. Everybody with wheels done already left, and it's a long walk to the bus stop."

"You know damn well them buses done stopped going to the colored part of town this time of day."

"Then I'll have to walk, like I done the last time I stayed out here too late."

"You ain't going no place until I check them cards!" Cap slammed his fist down so hard on the table, it almost fell over.

I didn't waste no more time. He weighed almost four hundred pounds, and his hands was so humongous, he could have laid me out with one tied behind his back. With him being so fat, he couldn't stand up fast enough, let alone chase somebody as fleet footed as me. While he was struggling to wobble up out of his chair, I bolted out the back door. Before he even made it outside, I was in the wind. When I got about half a mile away, I took the money I'd won out of my pocket and hid it in my shoe. That was where I planned to hide my money until I felt safe again.

CHAPTER 26
MILTON

*I*SPRINTED DOWN THE ROAD UNTIL MY LEGS COULDN'T TAKE IT NO
more. Then I started walking. My feet was aching so bad, a
minute later I slowed down even more. It was a miserable route
to be on any time of day. There was trees on both sides, which
anything or anybody could be hiding behind. A small flock of
crows was flying above my head, cawing like crazy. When one
dipped down so low its foot brushed the top of my head, I
started flopping and waving my arms so they'd leave me be.
Getting pecked by enough of them black devils could get me
more injuries than a beating from Cap.

"God, get me home safe and sound," I prayed out loud. I hadn't
read my Bible in a while, but I was definitely going to read a few
pages before I went to bed tonight.

A few trucks and cars whizzed by, going both ways, but nobody paid no attention to me. But ten minutes after I'd started
walking, a truck slowed down and stopped. I stopped, too, but I
didn't recognize the long-faced colored man behind the wheel.
I could see the barrel of a shotgun propped up on the passenger
seat.

"Where you headed?" he asked with a friendly smile. A lot of
motorists driving on country roads offered rides to strangers, so
it wasn't nothing out of the ordinary.

"I'm going into town."

"You want to get in? At the rate you dragging along, it'll be dark by the time you get there. I can take you as far as Willow Street."

"No, I'm all right. I don't mind walking. I need the exercise," I laughed, patting my potbelly.

He shrugged and drove off. As bad as I needed to take the load off my feet, I didn't accept a ride with this stranger, because for all I knew, he could have been one of Cap's friends. If Cap had told him that he thought I'd cheated him and some of his friends out of their money, there was no telling what he might have done to me with that shotgun.

I'd also refused the ride because I didn't feel like chitchatting with nobody. The long walk would give me enough time to clear my head and figure out my next move. If somebody asked me why I took so many chances on getting my butt whupped by some of them mean rascals I'd conned, I couldn't tell them. I'd been deceiving folks for so long, it seemed like second nature to me. That was one thing me and Odell had in common.

It was at least five miles from Cap's place to my house, but it seemed more like ten. Before I turned onto my street, I seen Uncle Sherman's truck coming in my direction. I stopped and squatted down and made out like I was tying my shoes. I kept my head bent low enough so he couldn't see my face. After he passed me, I stood up and watched until he turned the corner. I could see Yvonne's kids in the bed of the truck. I was glad they was not spending the night, because I was not in the mood to deal with them after what I'd been through with Cap. A man could take only so much.

The second I let myself in the front door, Yvonne lit into me. "Where you been all this time, Milton?"

"Huh? Oh, well, after I got off work, I had Willie Frank pick me up and take me to Cap's place so I could play a few games of poker. Um, I thought the kids was going to stay all night. I just seen Uncle Sherman's old truck creeping down the street." I brushed past Yvonne and plopped down on the couch. She stood in front of me, giving me the stink eye.

"I thought they was going to spend the night, too. But Aunt

Nadine and Uncle Sherman wanted to get them out of the house before we started entertaining this evening. I got a feeling they ain't never going to let my kids stay with me more than a few hours as long as we bootlegging."

"You probably right. Well, we'll just have to deal with it for now. We need the money if we want to stay on in this neighborhood, so we have to do our business as often as we can." I patted the spot next to me, and Yvonne sat down. She flinched when I tried to get me some sugar.

"I ain't through with you!" she hollered, scooting a few inches away.

"Baby, please do me a favor and don't be like that. Show me some love. I been thinking about you all day."

"Never mind about that. What I want to know is why you was playing poker all this time. You ain't never stayed at no game this long."

"I wasn't. The game ended over a hour ago. See, I lost all my money, and nobody wanted to give me a ride home, because I couldn't give them no money for gas. I had to walk all the way."

Yvonne's voice got soft, and she gave me a pitiful look. "You walked all the way from Cap's place? That's at least three or four miles from here."

"Five."

"It's dangerous walking along them backwoods roads."

"Baby, you worry too much. Tell me how the day went with the kids."

Yvonne took a deep breath, and her face looked more relaxed. "Well, it was a real nice day, Milton. Joyce treated us to lunch at Mosella's, and then we went to MacPherson's. Odell let the kids pick out all kinds of nice stuff."

"Oh?"

"I ain't never seen a man, colored or white, treat kids as nice as Odell treated mine today." Now she was speaking in the kissypoo tone she'd started using when the subject was Odell.

"Humph! He can afford to do as much treating as he wants!" I growled. Every time she mentioned that sucker's name these days, my chest tightened. It didn't matter if she was praising him or bad-mouthing him.

"The kids was all over him. Cherie even told him she wanted to marry a man just like him. It was so cute. Odell was tickled to pieces."

I rolled my eyes. I couldn't stand the glassy-eyed look on Yvonne's face now. "What you cook for supper? We'd better eat before company start coming."

She kept talking like she hadn't even heard me. "On top of all the stuff Odell let the kids take, he drove us all the way home. And I don't have to tell you how Joyce was beaming and acting like Odell really is Prince Charming. She is so lucky and love to rub it in my face. If I had a man like Odell, I would be a lot more humble than she is."

"Tell me this, how do you know Odell is as perfect as you think he is?"

Yvonne gasped so hard, she hiccuped. "Hold on now! I ain't never said he was perfect. But he is *almost* perfect. That's what I said. I know the man is a braggart. But if you had as much going for you as he—"

I had to cut Yvonne off before I lost my mind. "Baby, let's end this conversation. I'm tired and hungry." I gave her the most hopeless look I could manage.

"All right, all right. I'll go warm up everything." She stood up and skittered into the kitchen.

A little while ago, I had been worried about what Cap was going to do to me. Now that I'd had time to think about it, it didn't seem like such a big deal. I was sure that I wasn't the first person to cheat at his house. And I wasn't too worried about Oscar coming after me, neither.

The thing that was bothering me the most now was Yvonne and her preoccupation with Odell—that seemed to get more serious and bothersome to me by the day. I knew now that so long as he was doing his Prince Charming act, she would never let up. Well, I was tired of it! If I didn't do something about it, she was going to drive me crazy. I had a notion to go by his office on

Wednesday to collect my payment, because I knew that if he came to the house this close after being so nice to her babies, I'd have to listen to more of her giddy bullshit.

There was just one thing I could do to make her see him in a different light: tell her about Betty Jean and them kids. The next time she made a fuss about him, I was going to do just that.

CHAPTER 27
MILTON

I DIDN'T HAVE TO WAIT UNTIL WEDNESDAY TO SEE ODELL. A HOUR after I got home from Cap's place, him and Joyce showed up. Yvonne let them in, and the first thing out of Joyce's big mouth when she flopped down on the couch was, "Milton, did Yvonne tell you about the good time the kids had with Odell today?"

"She told me," I said in a dry tone. "What you want to drink tonight, Joyce?" I got up off the couch, and Yvonne flopped down on the footstool.

"Today was sure enough hectic, so I need something a little stronger than what I usually get. How about some white lightning? And make sure it's from a fresh batch. The last time I drank some that had been sitting for a while, it made my stomach churn after I got home." Of all the people that came to our house, Joyce was the only one to say something so offensive. But by now, I didn't expect no less from the Queen of Sheba. Then she jumped back on the subject of the kids. "Yvonne, it's a shame your aunt and uncle got those sweet children believing you're their cousin. Milton, how do you feel about that?" She suddenly stopped talking, and a wild-eyed look crossed her face. "Oops! Did I just let the cat out the bag? I didn't mean to say that! It just slipped out!"

"Joyce, you ain't got to fret none. I know the whole story about Yvonne's kids. Someday we hope to have them come live with us."

Joyce sighed with relief, gave me and Yvonne a sheepish look, and went on. "Oh. I think Yvonne did tell me you knew they were her children. I always have so much on my mind, sometimes I can't remember things. Anyway, if y'all ever do get the kids, Milton, I'm sure you'll make a good stepdaddy if you try hard enough," she added as she scooted closer to Odell at the other end of the couch. He had been as quiet as a mouse since they walked in. "Odell is going to make a wonderful father when we have some cherubs." She practically sung her last sentence.

"I'm sure Odell will be a wonderful daddy." I let them words hang in the air for a few seconds and enjoyed watching his jittery reaction. He was blinking and biting his bottom lip like a man on the way to his own execution.

Joyce's eyes got real big, and she started running her motor-mouth again. "Guess what, y'all? Daddy gave Odell a raise today."

"Oh? Is that a fact?" I said, with my eyebrows raised up as high as they could go. From the corner of my eye, I seen Odell scowling at Joyce like he wanted to wring her neck. I knew he didn't want me to know about his raise.

"Congratulations, Odell," Yvonne piped in. "I hope it was a nice raise. I'm sure you deserve it."

"Girl, my daddy is not stingy when it comes to rewarding people for doing a good job. We don't need the extra money—which will be fifteen percent more each month—but it's always good to have extra in case a financial emergency comes up." Joyce was glowing like a bonfire, while Odell was still acting like a mute. I was going to get a reaction out of him if I had to stand on my head.

"A financial emergency always seem to come up when you least expect it, right, Odell?" I couldn't wait to hear what he had to say to my taunt.

"Right," he replied, barely moving his lips.

I could have hauled off and kissed Joyce for letting the cat out of the bag about Odell's raise. I was going to throw it in his face the next time he made a fuss about giving me extra money.

"Odell, you want white lightning, too? You look like you could use a good strong drink." I gave him a sly wink, and he gave me a frown that would have scared a ghost.

"Yeah. And make sure it's a big one," he added in a gruff tone.

"Um, Odell, if you don't mind, before I pour you a drink, can you come in the kitchen with me for a few minutes? I want to show you my hot new fishing reel."

"Oh . . . okay," he mumbled.

He wobbled up off the couch and followed me into the kitchen. I clicked on the back-porch light and beckoned him to follow me outside. Before I could even open my mouth again, he got up on me and stabbed at my chest with his finger. "Look, Milton. I didn't appreciate that little jab you made about me being a good daddy. I hope you don't plan on playing them silly games with me too often, especially in front of Joyce. She don't like to be reminded that she ain't gave me no kids yet."

"In case you ain't noticed, she is the one that usually bring up that subject," I pointed out, stabbing him back in his chest with my finger.

"You don't need to encourage her!" he blasted.

I dipped my head and gave him a apologetic look. "You right. I won't do it no more." I tried to look and sound sorry. But I wasn't. I had enjoyed watching him squirm. The news about his raise was too hot for me to hold off on. "So you got a big raise, huh?"

"It ain't that big."

"Fifteen percent might not be big to you, but it is to me. It's a good thing you and Joyce don't need no extra money . . ."

"Milton, where you going with this?"

"I'm just making a comment." I sniffed, and then I got serious. "What I need to know is, When was you going to tell me you got a raise? Was you even going to tell me at all?"

"It ain't none of your business how much more money I make!"

"Oh yes it is! But I ain't going to get too greedy."

Odell gave me a dismissive wave and practically spit out his next words. "Greedy? You crossed that line a long time ago! Will you stop pussyfooting around and tell me why you brung me out here?"

"*Pussy*? That's a good choice of words. Especially since you getting so much of it these days." I laughed and rubbed my hands together.

"Where is your new fishing reel?"

"Fishing reel?"

"The one you claim you wanted to show me!"

"It's up in the attic, but that ain't the reason I need to talk to you in private."

"Then what is the reason?"

"You got my money?"

He rolled his eyes and folded his arms. "I figured that's what you really wanted. Look, I done already set aside your money for this week, which I was planning to give you on Wednesday, like always."

"I can't wait that long. I got a financial emergency that I might need to take care of before then," I explained.

Odell gazed into my eyes as he squinted. "Milton, if you want this thing to keep going, you got to work with me. Every time you need extra money, I have to make a bunch of adjustments."

"Pffft! Like what? I heard about all them free goodies you let Yvonne's kids take today. That don't sound like you had to make 'a bunch of adjustments' to me. And with that big raise you just got, you can't use that excuse no more. We all heard Joyce admit that y'all don't need the extra money."

"Milton, merchandise and money is two different things. It didn't cost me a dime to let them kids take a few play-pretties. And my raise won't kick in until next month. If you don't mind telling me, what is your financial emergency?"

I glanced toward the door to make sure nobody was peeping or eavesdropping. "Now, don't get mad, but it's really *two* financial emergencies."

CHAPTER 28
MILTON

"WHAT IS THEM EMERGENCIES?" ODELL WANTED TO KNOW, glaring at me like some kind of wild animal.

That didn't even faze me, because a man that was a possible sissy was probably not the violent type. I knew I was putting the screws to him real tight, but I didn't have no choice. If he hadn't been so uppity in the first place, I probably would have been easier on him. He was lucky I still wanted to be friends with him. Otherwise, I would have picked him clean to the bone by now.

I moved closer and even wrapped my arm around his shoulder. "One is it ain't fitting for a bootlegger on my level not to have a few extra bucks to fall back on. The other one is I had a little card game trouble this evening."

"Humph! I figured gambling was involved. For you to have such limited income, I can't believe you continue to get in them games when you almost always lose."

"Ta-da! I didn't lose this time," I gloated, twirling my finger in the air. "I was on fire this evening, and I skunked everybody."

Odell reared back on his legs and let out a snarky grunt. "That's something I never expected to hear from you. Where at?"

"Cap Griffin's house. Me and him and some of his regulars. The cards I insisted we play with was marked. Dummied them up myself. I put a itty-bitty dot with black ink on half the cards in the deck."

"You cheated?"

I nodded.

"Why you telling me?"

"Well, I didn't think it would hurt for me to let you know how far I'm willing to go when I need money," I explained.

"Humph! I already figured that out on my own! Did you get caught?"

"Well, Cap accused me of cheating. But I wouldn't admit it, and I took off before he could check my cards."

"Lord have mercy, Milton. Cap is one of the nicest men I know. When I was down on my luck before I met Joyce, he let me sleep on his couch, eat his food, and he didn't ask for nothing in return. He is the last person you should be taking advantage of. If you needed money bad enough to cheat, I bet he would have gave it to you and not asked you to pay it back."

"I don't know about that. He was pretty pissed off when I wouldn't let him check my cards. If I hadn't ran out the door when he started getting aggressive, he might have beat my brains out. I guess my guardian angel was looking out for me."

Odell got this glazed-over look on his face. For about five seconds, he just stared at me, shaking his head. "W-well, if you won, what did you do with that money?"

"I still got it. But to keep the peace, I might give it back."

"What in the hell is wrong with you, man? You know gamblers ain't nobody to mess with. You could get killed!"

"Pffft! I know all that. It's just that when money is involved, I get so slaphappy, I make bad decisions. But if I give the money back, I won't have to worry about Cap and his friends."

"Give the money back." Odell blinked and ran his fingers through his hair. Then he pressed his lips together and shook his head some more. "I think I get the picture now. If you give that money back, you'll be broke again. That's why you dragged me out here, right?"

"Right. Not only that, but something tells me them suckers might take not only the money I skunked from them, but also the money I went out there with."

I could see that Odell was exasperated, but it wasn't my fault he was so sensitive. "Today is Monday. You'll have them eight dollars I owe you on Wednesday."

"True. But I still need to have a few dollars to fall back on for the time being. Especially if I have to give them assholes their money back before Wednesday."

"Milton, if you don't straighten up and fly right, you might end up in a world of trouble. I heard about you and Willie Frank taking Oscar's equipment."

I gulped. "Who told you that *lie?*"

"Oscar came in the store just before I closed up this evening and told me hisself. He was mad as hell."

"Me and Willie Frank ain't stole nothing! Honest to God!"

"Then tell me this. Where did y'all get the stuff y'all sold to Oscar's brother-in-law?"

"Huh? Oh! Um, we bought it off Amos, one of Oscar's field hands."

"Amos stole it?"

"I guess he did. All I know is, Oscar told me and Willie Frank about the stuff he had, and he admitted that he had told Amos and his other field hand, too. He got some nerve accusing me of stealing!"

"You better straighten out this mess, and be quick about it. Oscar got three shotguns in his house, and he ain't scared to use one."

I gave Odell a thoughtful look. At the same time, I was thinking about Oscar's shotguns. "When you see him, tell him what I said about Amos."

He shook his head. "Man, that cock-and-bull story ain't going to fly. Amos's mama checked him into the hospital for foot surgery the day *before* Oscar's property went missing. He had some complications and just got released today. She told me that herself this afternoon, when she came to the store to get more bandages for him."

I had to swallow hard to loosen up the lump that suddenly got stuck in my throat. "All right. I'll come clean. Um . . . I don't like to tattle on my friends, but Willie Frank stole it. I was just along for the ride."

"It don't matter which one of y'all stole it. You and him in it together. You done already riled up them gamblers, and people been talking about how some of them other bootleggers and jook-joint owners got axes to grind with you and Yvonne for taking some of their long-standing customers."

"Hmmm. I was only going to ask you for money so I could get Cap and them other gamblers off my back. But now I might as well get enough to calm Oscar down."

"You done spent the money you got for selling the stuff you stole from him?"

"The stuff *Willie Frank* stole."

"Whatever you say, Milton. If that's the case, I'm sure Willie Frank gave you part of that money."

"Uh-huh. But since my name is already in the boiling pot, I might get beat down whether I give the money back or not. So, I think I should keep it. Besides, Oscar can't prove nothing."

"Didn't you just admit that Willie Frank stole it and that you was with him? Milton, you ain't got a leg to stand on. Don't you know that?"

I sighed in exasperation. "You know something, buddy? You could be right." I sighed again and massaged my temples. "Oh well. I guess I'll send Willie Frank to visit Oscar and give him the money we got from Eugene. But I got a good mind to keep what I won at Cap's place for all the aggravation it done caused me. Shoot!"

"If you plan on doing that, why do you need extra money from me now?"

"I disappointed Yvonne today by not coming home in time to help entertain her kids. I want to make it up to her by buying her some new glad rags."

"That's fine. We got some nice new stuff in stock. You can pick out something for her and not worry about charging it to your account. Now, if you don't mind, I'll keep the few dollars I got on me, and I'm going to go finish my drink. Then I'm getting the hell up out of here. I knew I shouldn't have let Joyce drag me over here tonight!"

Odell turned to leave, but I grabbed his arm. "You ain't going no place until you give me some money."

"Milton, I see now I can't reason with you." He cussed under his breath and reached in his pocket and pulled out his wallet. There was a wad of bills in that damn thing big enough to choke a mule. "How much?" he barked.

I didn't even answer. I grabbed his wallet and reached in and took it *all*. And then I told him, "I'll see you on Wednesday for my regular pay."

"You finished with me? Is there anything else you got to say before I go back to the living room?"

"Since you asked, I got just one more thing to conversate about." I pursed my lips and looked at him with my eyes narrowed. That made him more uncomfortable than he already was, and he let me know that by tapping his foot and rolling his eyes. "How is Betty Jean doing these days? With that juicy butt she got behind her, I bet frolicking in bed with her is like riding on the back of a horse." I had to stop talking long enough to laugh. Odell's face looked like it had turned to stone. I stopped laughing, and in a serious tone I asked, "And what about the boys? I hope them cute little *cherubs* is doing all right, too."

His reaction made me shudder. He gave me the evil eye and shook his head so hard, he caused a light breeze. "Don't worry about my boys! They doing just fine," he snarled. "What do you care?"

"I just wanted to make sure you was being a real man and is taking good care of them. It's a shame you can't bring your boys to Branson and let them run loose in the store, the way you let Yvonne's kids do today. It must be real hard on you keeping them cut off from the world."

CHAPTER 29
YVONNE

"MILTON, WHAT WAS YOU AND ODELL TALKING ABOUT OUT on the back porch?" I asked. It was a few minutes past midnight. Everybody had left, and we was cleaning up.

"Huh?" he asked, almost dropping a jar. "Was you roaming around this house, spying on me?" Milton had been guzzling some of Willie Frank's strongest brew all night. He was so drunk now, he could barely stand up straight. I'd had only one and a half drinks, so I was still fairly sober.

I stopped sweeping and let the broom fall to the floor. "This is my house, too. I can roam around in it as much as I want to. I just happened to go in the kitchen to get a glass of water, and I heard y'all talking out on the porch."

"Oh? If you heard us, why you asking me what we was talking about?"

"With all the noise coming from the rest of the house, I couldn't make out nothing y'all was saying."

"Well, I just wanted to get Odell alone so I could thank him for being so nice to you and the kids today."

Just him mentioning my children made my eyes water. "Joyce practically promised that when and if she ever learn to drive, she'll drive me over to Mobile to visit them. I'm going to tell her tomorrow that I can do the driving, if Odell don't mind."

"Humph. You know how possessive Prince Charming is when it come to his car."

"I might ask him, anyway."

Milton gave me a dry look. "Go ahead, then. He might be generous about letting folks take stuff from the store and lending money, but I don't think he'll be generous enough to let you, me, or nobody else drive that damn car. So, I wouldn't count on that if I was you."

"If you was more responsible, you'd stop gambling so much and start putting money aside so we can get a car! Why can't you be more like Odell?"

Milton flinched, and his face scrunched up like I had slapped him. I assumed that to some men, being compared to one that had so much more going for him was a slap in the face. But I did wish Milton was more like Odell. "That did it!" He kicked over the coffee table, and jars and ashtrays went flying every which way. With his eyes bugged out and his lips turned down like a horseshoe, he swayed from side to side and then crumbled to the floor like a stale tea cake.

"Get your black ass up off that floor and talk to me!" I demanded, pulling him up by his arm.

As soon as he was on his feet, he belched and farted loud enough for everybody on our block to hear. He dropped to the floor again, with me on top of him. "Arghhh!" he howled as we teetered back up on our feet. I was still holding his arm, and he was still wobbling. Next thing I knew, he pinched my hand so hard, I didn't have no choice but to turn him loose. And I moved back a few steps. He stiffened, stood ramrod straight, and folded his arms.

"I done had enough of your sweet talk about Odell—in my face and in my own house at that! Ain't it bad enough we have to listen to Joyce spew that same shit?" Milton did a good imitation of Joyce. He bucked his eyes out, licked his lips, and chanted, "Odell this, Odell that. I'm so lucky I got me such a sweet man for a husband! Hallelujah. Thank you, Jesus!" Then his voice got downright mean. "If me and Odell emptied our bladders in different buckets ain't a woman in the world would be able to tell his pee from mine. And another thing, I bet a dollar to a doughnut you wouldn't be nowhere near as happy as you is now if I was more like Odell!"

That last comment threw me for a loop. "How do you know I wouldn't?"

"Because . . . because Odell ain't what you think he is."

"Pffft! I know he's snooty and probably two-faced. But who ain't? Me and you bad-mouth him and Joyce as much as they probably do us. So what?"

"You ain't listening." Milton's grouchy tone annoyed me. "You don't know the Odell I know. I been wanting to tell you the truth about him for a long time. What I know about him is so hot, it would put blisters on your ears. But . . . um . . . I swore to him I wouldn't snitch."

I walked up to him and looked straight in his eyes. "What do you mean by that? What do you know about Odell to snitch?"

He held up his hands. His lips was moving, but no words was coming out. Then he put his hands down and mumbled in a baby-like voice, "Nothing."

"Nothing, my ass! You ain't getting off that easy. You going to tell me what you getting at!"

"I ain't getting at nothing," he insisted, dismissing me with a wave. "I'm drunk and . . . and I'm talking out of my head! I'm fixing to go to bed. I'll finish cleaning up tomorrow—"

I stomped my foot and shook my fist in his face, which was so twisted up by now, it looked like he had put on a mask. "Oh hell no! You ain't leaving this room until you tell me 'the truth' about Odell!"

He kept quiet and just blinked.

"Milton, you scaring me. I can't imagine what it is about Odell that has got you acting like a fool. What is it?" I gave him a few seconds to answer, but all he done was blink some more. "Look, if you don't tell me right here and now, I'll go up to him tomorrow and ask him what you swore you wouldn't snitch about him!"

"Please don't do that! It would ruin everything!" he yelled, wringing his hands.

"It's up to you. Now, shit or get off the toilet!"

Milton was not the crying type, even in the worst situations. Six months ago, a thief broke into our old house while we was visiting Willie Frank. That sucker stole a ham, a clock I had just bought, and a jug of white lightning. None of them items mattered much. But he—or she—also took a medal that Milton's grandfather on his mama's side had got when he was a soldier for the Yankees during the war between the North and South. It had been in his family since then, passed from one generation to the next. Aside from me, that medal had always been Milton's most cherished possession. I cried like a baby, but he didn't shed a single tear. He was the only person I knew that could peel a dozen onions in one setting and not get teary eyed. He told me that he'd cried so much when he lost his mama and daddy, his body had mysteriously programmed itself so that the death of somebody he cared about was the only thing that could make him cry now.

But he must have thought I was going to kill him, because he looked like he was about to bust out crying now. He didn't, though. I held my breath and moved a few steps away from him.

"All right," he whimpered, wringing his hands some more. "I'll tell you."

"And you better not leave nothing out, or you'll be sorry," I warned. I didn't care what I had to do. I wasn't letting Milton leave the room until he told me what I needed to know.

His next words flew out of his mouth. "Odell got another woman over in Hartville."

Chapter 30
Milton

YVONNE THREW HER HEAD BACK AND LAUGHED LONG AND LOUD. "You think Odell is fooling around? Is that all he is supposed to be doing?"

"You don't think that's a big deal?"

"Maybe it is to you, but it ain't to me. Shoot. I thought you was going to tell me something I could sink my teeth into. Like him being a sissy, pretending to be a normal man, and that Joyce is just a front. Something that juicy could keep us conversating all night. Now that I think about it, for all we know, Odell and Joyce might not even be having sex. That could be the reason they ain't had no kids."

"I don't know if Odell is a sissy or not. But I do know they trying to make a baby, because they won't stop talking about it."

Yvonne gave me a puzzled look. I didn't give her time to say nothing about my last comment.

I said, "And I know for sure that he is having sex with somebody else . . ."

"What if he is? I still don't think that's so juicy. Heck! A lot of married men have a few flings somewhere along the line. Odell ain't no saint. If Reverend Hayes can't keep his pecker in his pants, we can't expect regular men to do it." Yvonne's lips curled up at both ends, like she was about to laugh some more. "I guess I shouldn't be surprised to hear that Odell done stepped out on Joyce. When women get around a man as handsome as he is, they ain't responsible for their actions. I'm sure them young girls that shop at the store make goo-goo eyes and shake their tail feathers at him all the time."

Me and Yvonne had never been violent with one another, but this was one time I wanted to beat the dog shit out of her. Somehow, I managed to keep my hands to myself. "He ain't that good looking!"

"You might not think that, but I do. And so do every other woman I know. If Odell got a side woman, Joyce must not be keeping him as satisfied as she think she is! Humph!" Yvonne shook her fist in my face and kept talking. "If *you* ever get crazy enough to fool around with another woman, you better make damn sure I never find out. Because if I do, you'll have to start peeing from a different body part!"

"I ain't never cheated on you, and I swear to God I never will. But when a married man have a short fling or a one-night, hit-and-run type of episode with another woman, that's one thing. Even God can excuse that. That ain't the case with Odell." We was still standing in the middle of the floor. I didn't like the way this conversation was going. I had already blabbed too much.

"My Lord. I never would have guessed . . . Can't you talk some sense into him?"

"Baby, Odell's private life with another woman is his business, not ours."

"When he dragged you into his mess, he made it your business. And anything that involve you involve me. I ain't about to stand by and let us get caught up in a cheating mess that could scandalize our names."

"All right. I'll tell you everything I know. I'm a little drunk, and you done pestered me into distress. I need to sit down before I go on." We dropped down on the couch. I gazed at the floor for a few moments. When I looked back at Yvonne, her face was scrunched up so tight, I knew I had to finish what I had started, or I'd be sorry. The inside of my mouth was so dry by now, I had to jiggle my tongue a few times before I could keep talking. After I took a deep breath, the words rolled out like marbles. "Odell is crazy in love with this other woman. What do you think about him now?"

Yvonne looked at me like I'd just sprouted another nose. "Did he tell you this?"

"Naw. I caught him with her myself."

Her mouth dropped open, and her eyes got as big as pot holders. "When?"

"Back in July."

"I—I can't believe my ears."

"Well, you better believe them ears! And that ain't all. He got three little boys with her. I seen them, too."

"Come on, Milton. You ain't that drunk, and if you trying to be funny, it ain't working. I know you get jealous of Odell, and I can understand why. I get jealous of Joyce sometimes, too. But I wouldn't stoop low enough to tell such a tall tale like the one you telling me now."

"I ain't never lied to you!" I hollered, slapping the side of my thigh.

"Calm down, sugar," she said, rubbing my arm. "I know you ain't never lied to me on purpose about nothing serious. But there is a first time for everything. Maybe you can't help your-self. But this is a mighty big whopper for you to start with. If it's true, you ought to be able to prove it."

I snorted and waved my hand. "You damn right I can prove it. When we get off work tomorrow, I'm going to borrow Willie Frank's truck and take you to Hartville so you can see I ain't lying."

Yvonne gasped. "You taking me to the woman's house?"

"Naw. I don't know her address. But I know somebody that know all about her and Odell. One of them waitresses at the restaurant where him and her was eating at."

"How do you know that waitress ain't lying?"

"I seen him all over his other woman with my own eyes, and I heard them little boys call him Daddy."

"Good God!" I had never seen Yvonne looking so spooked. "Do Joyce know?"

"What's wrong with you? If she knew he was playing her for a fool, do you think she'd still be with him? And do you think he'd still have that sweet job?"

"Well, she'd be a *damn* fool if she knew about that woman and stayed with Odell, anyway." A angry look crossed Yvonne's face, and she shuddered so hard, her eyes crossed. "When did you tell him you knew what he was up to?"

"That Monday after I found out, I paid him a visit at the store. You should have seen how wimpy he got. He whined and blubbered and begged me not to tell nobody. I was surprised he didn't shit his pants."

Yvonne got quiet and looked deep in thought. "Him being a next-door neighbor and such a close friend, with beaucoup money, did he offer to make it worth your while to keep quiet?"

"Something like that."

"Something like what?"

"Um . . . he said that if we fell behind on our credit account, he'd overlook it and give us extra time to catch it up. Odell being such a good buddy of ours, I told him that what he was doing wasn't no business of mine. But I didn't want the guilt of carrying his shame to burden me too much. So, for my own peace of mind, I let him have a piece of my mind! I told him that his behavior was giving the rest of us married Christian men a bad name. He got so overwhelmed, he almost got the heebie-jeebies, and he begged me not to tattle. I swore I wouldn't. He was so grateful, he gave me a hug."

"A *hug*? Is that all? A man in a pickle like he is should have at least gave you a few bucks. He didn't offer none?"

I shook my head. "Even if he had, I wouldn't have took it. I would never take advantage of a close friend. Now can we end this conversation?"

Yvonne gazed at me for a long time before she said, "Yeah . . . for now."

CHAPTER 31
YVONNE

WHEN WE FINALLY WENT TO BED, IT TOOK A WHILE FOR ME TO GO to sleep. I couldn't stop thinking about what Milton had told me about Odell. If everything he said was true, I would never be able to look at Odell the same way again. I didn't know how I was going to listen without screaming the next time Joyce bragged about him. Even though I had always thought Odell was a snob, I'd still had some respect for him. Just knowing that a colored man was managing the most prominent colored-owned business in town had made me realize nothing was impossible. It had gave me hope that Milton might be as successful as Odell someday. I should have realized Odell was too good to be true. I was as mad as I was shocked. It was like finding out Santa Claus was a member of the Ku Klux Klan!

I woke up before daylight Tuesday morning. The first thing I did was nudge Milton until he started wiggling. "Did you tell me last night that Odell had a woman on the side and three kids with her?"

"Why?" he asked, without opening his eyes.

"I just want to make sure that my mind wasn't playing tricks on me and that I hadn't dreamed it all."

"You ain't dreamed nothing. Now, I ain't going to talk about this no more until we get Willie Frank's truck and go to Hartville when we get off work this evening."

"How do you expect me to get through today with this on my mind and not talk about it?"

"You ain't got no choice. Now, get up and go fix me some grits so we can get our tails to work."

I was glad we was so busy at the grill, I didn't have much time to think about what Odell was up to. Halfway into our shift, Milton called up Willie Frank from the telephone in Mr. Cunningham's office. Milton asked him if he could come to the house this evening and let us borrow his truck so we could go check on Milton's sick cousin in Lexington, one town over. When we got home, Willie Frank's truck was parked in front of our house. We had gave him a key to our house, so he was stretched out on the couch when we walked through the door.

"I'm so happy to see you, I could wrap it in eggshells," Milton told him, sitting down on the arm of the couch. "And we sure do appreciate you letting us borrow your truck."

Willie Frank sat up and wiped his eyes. "Anytime. Which cousin you going to check up on?"

"Columbus. Last week that numskull tried to take a shortcut home from his job through a pasture and got trampled by some cows that went on a rampage. He was doing all right until yesterday, when he started having headaches and stuff. His wife called me at the grill this morning and told me," Milton explained.

We didn't like to lie to Willie Frank, but sometimes we didn't have no choice. We couldn't tell him the real reason we needed to use his truck. Milton's cousin that "got trampled by some cows" was actually in jail for stealing a cow.

"Hmmm. I hope Columbus ain't too bad off. Y'all want me to go, too?" Willie Frank said.

"No, we need you to stay here and hold down the fort. I'm sure some folks will drop in before we get back," I told him. "Just make sure they wipe their feet before they come in, and don't give out nothing on credit."

Me and Milton didn't waste no time. We changed out of our work clothes and rushed out the door. When we got outside,

Odell was strutting up on his porch. He gazed at us with a curious look on his face as we hurried toward Willie Frank's
truck.

"How y'all folks doing this evening?" he hollered. Before one
of us could answer, Joyce peeped out the front window and
waved.

"We doing fine," Milton replied. "Um . . . we on our way to visit
my sick cousin over in Lexington. Crossed-eyed Columbus, with
the bald head. He got trampled by some cows."

"Lord almighty! Them narrow, bumpy dirt roads going into
Lexington is dangerous, so drive careful. I'll pray for your
cousin, and y'all, too," Odell said.

I was tempted to tell him to pray for hisself, because he was
going to need it. "We'll see you later!" I yelled.

Milton cranked up the truck, and we eased on down the
street.

"By the way, you never told me why you was in Hartville that
day you seen Odell. We don't know nobody over there," I said
before we even made it to the corner.

"Cecil Braxton asked me to drive him over there in his truck.
He don't drive too much since he had his stroke. Anyway, we
went to this restaurant that he wanted to go to. Odell was already there with that woman."

I gasped. "Cecil seen them, too?"

"Naw. The place was too crowded. He don't know nothing.
Why don't you rear back and take a nap? You look tired, and it's
hard for me to drive and talk to you at the same time."

"I ain't sleepy. It never bothered you before to drive and talk
at the same time. And don't change the subject. What I want to
know is, If you and Cecil was together in that restaurant at the
same time, how did you talk to that waitress and he didn't
hear?"

"He was using the toilet while me and her was conversating."

"And you didn't mention it to him?"

"Hell no. He ain't broad minded like me. He would have

gone up to Odell and busted him right then and there. I wasn't
about to let Cecil embarrass Odell in public."

"Oh. Well, if we ain't going to the woman's house, exactly
where in Hartville you taking me to?"

"You'll find out soon enough. Now, be still and hush up until
we get there. You making me nervous."

Hartville was about a hour away, so it was hard for me to be
still and stay hushed up for that long. But I did.

When we finally got there, Milton parked across the street
from a restaurant with a sign outside, on the wall next to the
door, that said PO' SISTER'S KITCHEN. There was at least twenty
folks lined up waiting to get inside.

"This place must serve some damn good food to draw such a
big crowd," I commented.

"Baby, it's so good, it'll make you want to slap your mama for
what she fed you. You should have seen how many folks was here
the day me and Cecil came."

"I hope you don't expect me to stand in that long-ass line. I
done been on my feet enough today."

"Don't worry about that. We didn't come here to eat. I'm
going to go straight up to the counter and ask for that waitress I
told you about."

When we got to the doorway, I followed behind Milton as he
plowed his way through the crowd. People started grumbling
right away. We kept walking until we got to the counter, where a
cute dark-skinned waitress was plucking deviled eggs off one
tray and loading them onto a plate.

"What the . . . ? Look, y'all have to wait in line like everybody
else!" she barked.

"You just the person I'm looking for. Do you remember me?"
Milton eased in.

She set her tray down and squinted. "Nope. Should I?"

"I ate here one day back in July. There was another customer
eating at the same time, and I thought it was somebody I knew. I
asked you about him, remember?"

"Pffft! I don't remember most of what happened last week, let alone last July. Now, if y'all plan on eating or ordering something to go, get in that line, like I said."

"We ain't ordering nothing, ma'am. And we'll be out of here in a minute or two. But if you don't mind, I need to talk to you about something." Milton didn't wait for her to respond. "When I was here in July, I asked you about that tall dark-skinned gentleman with his pretty redbone wife and their three little boys. They was at a table not far from where I was sitting."

The waitress smiled, and a goo-goo-eyed look crossed her face. I suspected she was another foolish woman that had been dazzled by Odell's good looks and charm. She didn't waste no time getting chatty. "Oh yeah. You mean Odell Watson. Him and his wife, Betty Jean, and their kids come here almost every weekend. Odell always leave me a good tip. A whole quarter." I almost gagged when I heard how generous he was when it came to food. But when it came to drinks at our house, him and Joyce never tipped more than a nickel. The waitress glanced at me, then back at Milton. "What about him?"

"Um, nothing. I told my wife that I had seen somebody in here that day that looked just like somebody we know . . . her long-lost cousin we been hunting for, for three years. She didn't believe me, so I brung her here to see for herself. I thought maybe he'd be here this evening."

I'd had no idea Milton could come up with lies so good so fast.

"Well, this is his favorite restaurant, so he might show up later this evening."

"You know him good, huh?" he went on.

Once the waitress's mouth started running, she couldn't stop it. "Yup. I been knowing Odell for over five years. We belong to the same church. Last Easter, Pastor Bradshaw let him make a speech about the importance of family. Poor Odell leaned on that pulpit and boo-hooed like a baby because his wife and kids is the only kin he got left. So he can't be nobody's long-lost cousin. Thank God his wife got a bunch of kinfolks to help nurture him. His sister-in-law been working here for years. I feel sorry for that sweet man, having to spend so much time alone on the road. See, his job as a traveling salesman keep him away from home quite a bit. What's your names? I can let him know somebody asked about him."

"That's all right," Milton threw in. "With a wife and three kids, and him having to travel so much for his work, he got enough on his plate. He don't need to know that a stranger was asking about him."

"Okay. I won't say nothing to him about it. He is such a wonderful man, I wouldn't want to do or say nothing to rattle him." The waitress sighed and kept talking, with her eyes looking even more goo-goo. "I wish I had a man like Odell. He is the best-looking one I ever seen. And he is so devoted to his family. Betty Jean struck gold when she latched onto him. Woo-hoo!"

I realized now that there was no end to women swooning over Odell. Poor Milton. Up until I found out what Odell was up to, I had been one of them women.

"Thank you, ma'am. That's all," Milton said. "Now we'll let you get back to work."

He grabbed my arm and led me back outside. "See there? You believe me now?" There was a satisfied expression on his face.

I shook my head and followed him back to the truck. "Odell got these folks believing he is a traveling salesman—and he done joined a church over here. He is so busy visiting with his 'sick daddy' two or three days a week, he rarely got time to go to church with Joyce. But he got time to join one with his other woman? Sheesh! If Joyce had even a slight inkling that she got a bona fide fake for a husband, she would have a foaming-at-the-mouth fit! When the shit hit the fan, I hope he get everything he got coming! That—that phony-baloney devil! When I think about how he talked down to us that day we tried to get a ride home from work, my blood sizzles. We might not be sophisticated and well to do like him and Joyce, but other than us doing a little shoplifting and serving recycled drinks, we stay smack-dab on the straight and narrow!"

Milton patted my shoulder. "Calm down now, sugar. I know you upset about Odell hoodwinking us in such a unholy way. But this is our secret. If it get out, a heap of lives could be ruined—including ours. We can't even let Willie Frank in on it. Promise me you won't spill the beans."

"I promise."

Chapter 32
Milton

*T*HE RIDE BACK TO BRANSON WAS UNCOMFORTABLE, TO SAY THE least. For the first five miles, we didn't say nary a word.

I didn't want to discuss Odell too much more, because I was scared I'd slip and say something Yvonne didn't need to know. Not telling her I was blackmailing him meant more money for me. But I wasn't selfish. I did spend some of that hush money on her. I bought her gum, smell goods, and hair knickknacks.

When we did start talking, it was about what Yvonne was going to cook for Willie Frank's birthday party next month and a few other random things. Odell's name didn't come up again until we turned onto our street, and I was the one to bring it up. I figured it wouldn't hurt to let Yvonne know what was on my mind about how I wanted us to handle what we knew.

"Now that you know what a low-down, funky black dog of a cheater Odell is, I want you to go on about your business like you don't know nothing. When you see him, treat him the way you been treating him. Except . . ."

"Except what?"

"Now that you know he ain't nothing but a wolf in sheep's clothing, I hope you won't rub it in my face about how wonderful he is no more. Especially them comments about wanting me to be more like him."

"I won't. Now that I done seen the light, I realize he could never be as honorable as you," Yvonne said with a heavy sigh.

"Baby, don't never change." She squeezed my hand and gave me a peck on my jaw.

There was several cars and a truck parked directly in front of our house. I had to park behind Odell's car. The lights wasn't on in his house. Either him and Joyce had gone out for the evening and was riding with somebody else, or they was socializing with our guests. I prayed that they wasn't in our house. After the mess of a day I had had with Yvonne because of Odell, I was agitated. He was the last person I wanted to see while I was in such a state.

I was happy to see at least a dozen folks in our living room, drinking and frolicking like they didn't have a care in the world. Before I could greet any of our guests, Lyla Bullard teetered up off Willie Frank's lap on the couch and staggered up to me. I couldn't imagine what she'd been thinking when she squeezed her pear-shaped body into the tight red dress she had on. There was a hat on her head that reminded me of a crow's nest. She hugged me like she hadn't seen me in years, and started talking loud and fast.

"Milton, I couldn't wait to get over here so I can start having some of the good times I hear y'all got going on. I was hoping you'd get back before I left. I didn't know y'all lived in the same neck of the woods as all three of Branson's colored doctors. Y'all done climbed way up the ladder, and I'm sure enough impressed." Lyla's cousin Emmalou was in a corner, chatting it up with one of our coworkers from the grill.

"Yes, we done climbed up the ladder," I agreed, gazing at Lyla with a proud expression on my face. I had my arm around Yvonne's waist, and I hadn't hugged Lyla back.

I wanted to show my wife as much affection as possible tonight and not even act like I wanted to get too friendly with another woman—especially a white one. I was going to work even harder to keep Yvonne happy, because the news about Odell had really busted her bubble about men. And I had to watch my step, so she wouldn't have no reason to get suspicious of me. I'd make love to her like she was the only woman left on the planet, and I'd spend more money on her, too. But first, I needed to get *more* money. . . .

Money. Next to *God,* that word was the most important one in the English language. It seemed to be the one subject I couldn't put on a back burner. Every time I looked up, I had another reason to need more of it.

"How was your cousin?" Willie Frank cut into my thoughts just as Lyla sank her humongous rump back down in his lap. I could tell from the grimace on his face that all that meat put a strain on his thighs. But he was too much of a gentleman to protest.

His question caught me completely off guard. But it didn't take me long to get my bearings back. "Huh? Oh yeah! Um, Columbus is doing just fine. Thanks for asking."

"Good, good. I'll pray for him. I hope you gassed up my truck. It's a long drive back to the hills. I don't want to get stuck out in the middle of nowhere, with no gas stations within miles, not that none are open this late, nohow," Willie Frank added.

"I filled up your tank. Thanks for letting me use your truck, and thanks for taking care of our guests."

Around 11:00 p.m. Lyla teetered up off the couch again. She stretched her arms and yawned. "Well now! I truly enjoyed myself tonight. But me and Emmalou can't keep our peepers open, and we got to open up the store on time tomorrow, so we best skedaddle." Lyla had so much liquor in her potbelly, she could barely stand. I would have offered to drive her and her cousin home, but I didn't want the wrong crackers to see me driving a truck with two drunk white women in it.

"Give me that key," Emmalou demanded, snatching Lyla's key out of her hand. "With the shape you in, you'll drive us into a tree." Emmalou wasn't that drunk, so I felt better knowing she was going to drive. They was good customers, and I liked them, so I didn't want nothing to happen to them. "I sure enjoyed myself, Milton. Now that we know where you live, we'll slide through here quite often."

"Emmalou, me and Yvonne enjoyed your company, so you and Lyla please come back again soon."

After they left, Yvonne motioned me to the kitchen. I groaned, but I followed her. We didn't stop walking until we reached the farthest corner in the room.

"What's wrong, sugar? You been acting mighty strange since we got home. I hope it ain't because of Odell."

"Milton, it ain't that." She let out a moan and folded her arms. "I really like Lyla and Emmalou. But do you think we should start entertaining white women?"

"What do you mean, 'start' entertaining white women? What about Willie Frank's womenfolk? His cousins Peggy Louise and Molly been here several times. And so have his mama and sisters."

"That's different. White women on that level don't count. Willie Frank's come only once or twice a month, and they always come and leave with him."

"Hush up! Don't be making something out of nothing. We got more important things to worry about."

"You got a point there, I guess." Yvonne sighed and threw up her hands. "Oh, well, let's get back to our company."

When we got to the living room, Willie Frank beckoned for me to join him in the kitchen. I steered him to the same corner Yvonne had steered me to a few minutes ago.

"You was too busy, and I couldn't tell you before now that you ain't in the clear yet," he began with a agitated look on his face. My chest tightened right away. "Johnny Ray, one of them stock boys that work for Odell, came here tonight, about fifteen minutes before you and Yvonne got back. He told me he'd stopped off at Cap's place on his way over here. Cap told him about you winning all that money with them marked cards and that he didn't like being made a fool of. I couldn't get you somewhere in private to tell you until now."

"Hmmm," I said, caressing my chin. "News sure do travel fast in this town! I hope Cap don't stay mad too long." I gave Willie Frank a dry look and went on. "Odell told me that Oscar stopped by the store and told him about the stuff that got stole out of his barn. Oscar think I had something to do with it, so I guess he mad at me, too. And we can't scapegoat Amos and get nobody to believe he done it. He was having foot surgery at the time." I shrugged. "The thing is, the damage already been done. And I . . . Wait!" It seemed like a bright light suddenly went on in my head. "I got a idea. Maybe we should buy that stuff back from Eugene and return it to Oscar. That should calm him down."

"Buddy, I could feel trouble brewing, so that same idea already came to me last night. I went back to Eugene this afternoon and tried to buy that stuff back, but he wanted to keep it. I left there and went to Oscar's. I swore to him that I didn't know nothing about his stuff getting stole. I didn't want to lose a long-term customer like him, so I played the Good Samaritan and done the Christian thing. I gave him what Eugene paid us—plus two extra bucks. He was glad to get the money, but I think he still might hold a grudge for a while."

"That was a good move, Willie Frank. Remind me to pay you my part. As far as Cap is concerned, he can't prove I cheated. But I won't go back to his place until that bee get out of his bonnet."

"Um . . . Oscar did tell me to warn you to watch your back."

"Pffft!" I chuckled. "I been doing that all my life."

CHAPTER 33
MILTON

"**Y**OU SURE IS IN A GOOD MOOD," YVONNE COMMENTED WHEN I walked into the kitchen, whistling, on Wednesday morning. It was five minutes before 8:00 a.m. She had already made coffee and set the table, and she was at the counter, buttering a slice of toast. I noticed a pan of grits and a platter of home fries already on the table. Even as hectic as yesterday had been, I'd made love to Yvonne last night, and we'd fizzled out like dead lightbulbs and slept like babies the whole night through.

"Why shouldn't I be? I got a lot to be in a good mood about." I went up to her and kissed her long and hard. I couldn't believe she hadn't brung up the Odell thing again, but I knew it was just a matter of time before she did. "I'm married to the most beautiful woman in the world, and I'm the best bootlegger Branson ever had. Except for not having enough money to suit me, I got everything a man need to be happy."

"What about your health?"

"My health?" I reared back on my legs, waved my hand, and looked at Yvonne like she had just asked the stupidest question I ever heard. "You ain't blind. Can't you see I'm as fit as a fiddle? I ain't had no ailments since I had chicken pox when I was eleven." I flexed my arms and pounded my chest a couple of times with my fists. "Pour me some coffee."

"You don't want no grits and toast?"

"Naw. Sometime when I eat breakfast too early, I get cramps.

Especially after all the alcohol I drunk up last night." She filled my coffee cup and set it on the table. I sat down and started guzzling.

"I'm glad you grateful to be in good health. I'm grateful you is, too." Her words made me curious.

"Yvonne, do you know something I don't know? Why you all of a sudden worried about my health?"

"Milton, last night Johnny Ray told me about you cheating them gamblers at Cap's place. Cheating ain't nothing but glorified stealing."

"Pffft!" I waved my hand and laughed. "You ain't got no room to be talking about me stealing! That's what got *you* convicted! Shoot!"

"Don't change the subject. We ain't talking about me. You can't go around cheating the people you gamble with."

"You know how it is with gamblers when they lose. Some get real disgruntled."

Yvonne nodded. "I know that, too. My cousin DeBow got shot to death by some disgruntled gambler he'd cheated."

"DeBow was a lowlife and had it coming. I'm surprised it took so long for somebody to put his lights out."

"Baby, I just don't want nothing bad to happen to you over a few dollars."

"It ain't going to happen. Me and Cap been good friends for years. I done did favors for him. Remember when that tornado blew the roof off his house? I helped him repair it and refused to take his money when he tried to pay me. And don't forget about that time he was so broke up about his lady friend dumping him, and we brung him to the house and nursed him out of his depression. Do that sound like a man I need to be worried about messing with my health?"

"I guess not." Yvonne finally gave me a smile. "Please be careful, anyway. Everybody got a breaking point. Even good friends you done favors for."

*   *   *

A few minutes before noon, I got one of the railroad workers who had just come to the grill for lunch to let me borrow his car to drive to MacPherson's. I told him I needed to go repay a loan to Odell, and I made him promise not to tell Yvonne, because she'd get on my case about borrowing. She had agreed to help Mr. Cunningham shell crowder peas out in the back, and that always took quite a while. She wouldn't even know I'd left the premises.

"Hello, Milton! Good timing! We just put out some fresh pig feet," Sadie gushed when I walked into the store. Buddy was busy with a customer, but as soon as he heard her say my name, he whirled around and gave me the fish eye.

"Thanks, Sadie. But I'll pass today. I got just enough time to talk to Odell, and then I have to get back to work. I might come back on my way home to get some of them world-beating pig feet, though."

I didn't want to say nothing else to her, so I picked up speed. Within a few seconds, I was in Odell's office. He was sitting behind his desk, with his feet propped up on top of it, next to a empty Dr. Pepper bottle. I strolled over and stopped by the side of his desk.

"What you doing here, Milton?" He stood up and put his hands on his hips. The scowl on his face would make a bulldog look like a baby cat.

"It's Wednesday," I smirked. "Payday."

"You didn't have to come here. I was going to drop by your house this evening."

"Well, today I preferred to drop by here instead."

"I hope you don't make a habit of coming here too often to get your money. Buddy and Sadie will get suspicious sooner or later and will start asking questions," he hissed like the snake he was.

"So what if they do? You the boss," I chuckled. "Now, give me my money and I'll be on my way."

Without saying another word, he pulled out his wallet.

"Add a couple extra bucks this time, please."

"Look, this 'extra' shit is going to have to stop! You been suck-ing the life out of me since you started this mess!"

"I ain't the one that started this 'mess,' as you call it. You the one that couldn't keep your pants zipped up!"

Odell's jaw was twitching, and the mean look on his face looked even meaner now. I was more than ready to leave. The ten one-dollar bills he had just took out of his wallet was still in his hand. "Milton, one of these days, you going to mess with the wrong person. And from what I keep hearing, you getting closer and closer to that person."

I snatched the money and put it in my pocket. "If you mean Oscar or Cap, they ain't nobody for me to worry about. Oscar is just as big a con man as I am, and Cap probably is, too. Did you know that before Cap got religion a few years ago, he done time in the penitentiary for robbing a fruit stand?"

"So?"

"So, he ain't got no room to be having too much of a attitude with me over a few dollars. Besides, with all the money I done lost playing cards with him and his crew, I was just getting back what they owed me! And how do I know they didn't use marked cards all them times when they skunked me?"

"Milton, you got your money, so please leave." Odell flopped back into his chair and waved me to the door.

"Keep your shirt on. I'm going, I'm going." I started moving away, and then I stopped. "You and Joyce coming to the house tonight?"

Odell did a double take. "I don't want to see you again too soon!" he snapped.

"That's a shame. I'm sure Yvonne will be disappointed. You made a damn good impression on her kids. She can't stop prais-ing you . . ."

"That's real nice of Yvonne."

"She want to show her appreciation this evening and cook some hush puppies with butter, the way you like them. She said you put them kids in the best mood they been in since Christmas."

"Oh yeah?"

"Yeah."

I could see this pantywaist turning as soft as jelly right before my eyes. Now I was sorry I hadn't asked for more than a couple extra dollars.

"I'll talk to Joyce and see if she is in the mood to come over tonight. Just because me and you got a few kinks in our friendship, I don't want Yvonne to be disappointed. Let her know I'll try to make it over tonight."

"Good. I'm sure she'll be overjoyed to see you again."

CHAPTER 34
YVONNE

"*H*ELLO, YVONNE. MILTON TOLD ME YOU WAS COOKING HUSH puppies with butter instead of lard this evening."

I was in the kitchen, at the counter, about to dump a huge batch of hush puppies into a skillet. Just hearing Odell's voice spooked me so bad, I whirled around and almost dropped everything. "Odell, I—I didn't know you w-was already in the house," I stuttered, but I composed myself right away. "You get first dibs on these hush puppies for treating my kids so good."

I was still grateful that he had been so nice and generous. But knowing what I knew now, I had a hard time being alone with him and not telling him what was really on my mind. If he was a womanizer and a Goody Two-shoes that wore his shoes on the wrong feet, what else could he be? I wondered. Now I didn't think all them goodies he'd let my children take was really "complimentary," as he had called them. For all I knew, he could have made up for that by juggling the books! Maybe he'd used me to put on a good show in front of Joyce to keep her sewed up in the web he'd spun. And he'd dragged my babies into it, too!

"Did Joyce come with you?"

"Yeah, she out there, on her second drink. I'm on my third." They had finally started paying for their drinks. But because they'd mooched off us for so long and gave lousy tips, we was still serving them recycled alcohol.

"I'll bring the hush puppies out directly."

"Good. They sure do smell scrumptious. Well, I better get back to the living room before Willie Frank bore Joyce to tears with all his bragging about how well his business is doing."

I couldn't let his last comment go without saying something. "I hate it when folks brag," I tossed in, rolling my eyes.

My ears had a hard time listening to what he said next. "Me too. I hate it with a passion. That's why I never do it. As much as me and Joyce got going for us, can't nobody accuse us of not being humble."

Even with all the things I had on my mind, it turned out to be a fun night. I went out of my way to avoid talking to Odell again, though. But I couldn't get away from Joyce. About a hour after my conversation with him in the kitchen, I went back to get more hush puppies. Right after I dumped a fresh batch into a bowl, she barged in. She looked distressed.

"Yvonne, I know it's none of my business, but do you and Milton plan on letting white women come here often? That Lyla and Emmalou don't seem like the kind of people you and Milton would want to be friends with."

Lyla and Emmalou had come back to our house again tonight and was the life of the party. They was telling jokes that had everybody laughing up a storm, and they was sharing stories about how hard it was to please some of the fussy women that bought hats in Lyla's store.

I leaned up against the stove, still holding the bowl. "What's wrong with them?"

"Nothing, I guess. But you and I both know that it's not a good idea to socialize with white women in a place like yours."

"I know what you mean, and I done brung that up with Milton. But he reminded me that we ain't never had no trouble by socializing with Willie Frank's female kinfolks. Besides, Lyla and Emmalou buy a lot of drinks, and they tip good. That's more than I can say for some of our guests . . ." I threw out that last remark, hoping she'd take the hint and start tipping more than a nickel for her drinks. "And it's a sport to watch them dance."

"I agree with that. Some folks have two left feet. Lyla's and

Emmalou's are on backward." Joyce giggled, and then her voice got serious again. "I'm sure they are nice people, too. My mama buys all her hats at Lyla's store, and she thinks Lyla and Emmalou are as sweet as pie. She claim they treat her the same way they treat their white customers. But Odell told me he got skittish as soon as he saw them up in here tonight."

"What about them white women you and Odell have coming to your house? Do they make him skittish?"

Joyce sucked on her teeth and folded her arms before she answered. "That's different. They have spotless reputations and always come with their husbands. On top of that, they spend a whole lot of money at the store." Joyce leaned closer and lowered her voice. "Buddy and Sadie told me they heard Lyla and Emmalou have been known to crawl into bed with colored men. Nary one of our white female friends would consider going against the Jim Crow laws."

"Me and Milton can worry about our white women friends. You and Odell can worry about something else. Like him spending so much time away from you . . ."

Joyce suddenly perked up and got downright giddy. Her eyes got wide, and she started grinning. "I'm glad you brought that up." I didn't know if I'd struck a nerve or if she was about to go into her usual swooning act whenever Odell's name was mentioned. "Pffft! That doesn't bother me. God couldn't have sent me a better husband. Odell is so sweet and considerate, and more concerned about his loved ones than himself. I don't know any other man that spends whole weekends at a time taking care of his daddy."

"Uh-huh. Whole weekends *and* a few days during the week," I reminded. Keeping another woman and three kids happy had to take up a lot of Odell's time. There was no way he could be spending even half the time he claimed with his daddy. I wondered just how often he actually did visit his daddy. That old man could have already died, for all anybody knew.

"Well, he told me that he might start spending a little more of his spare time with Lonnie. Bless him." She unfolded her arms and patted her chest. "Just thinking about my husband and how caring he is makes my heart go pitty-pat."

My mouth dropped open. "How is he going to find more 'spare' time? He got a full-time job and already spend a lot of time with his daddy. Then he go fishing and to meetings with vendors and whatnot. Plus, he spend hours at a time drinking at my house."

"I do, too!" Joyce protested.

"Let me finish." I took a deep breath before I went on. "If he was my man, I'd make him spend more time with me. You ought to make him cut his weekend visits to his daddy short, so he can come home early enough on Sunday and go to church with you and take you on some weekend picnics. After all, Lonnie got a wife that used to be a nurse. Ellamae must be lazy as hell or done forgot how to take care of a sick person if Odell have to spend every Sunday out there instead of with you."

Joyce snapped her fingers and gave me a smug look. "For your information, his daddy and stepmama are going to visit some of her folks in Huntsville the weekend after next. Odell is going to church with me that Sunday. After the service is over, he is taking me to Mosella's for a nice, quiet, romantic lunch."

"That's nice, Joyce. I wish I was going with y'all."

"If you and Milton don't have plans for that day, y'all can come to church with us. I wish I could invite y'all to go to Mosella's with us, too. But Odell wants to spend some quality time alone with me. You know what kind of man he is."

"I sure do. He likes to show his love . . ."

"You must be talking about how he took such a shine to your kids."

"Yeah. That's what I'm talking about."

Joyce gave me a look words couldn't describe. "I don't know if you've noticed, but I can tell that Milton has already changed for the better. He is so lucky Odell was willing to take him under his wing. But he still needs a little more work to smooth out his rough edges. Lord knows he needs all the help he can get. And, since you and I have been spending so much time together, I can see that you're a little more sophisticated than you were when I first met you."

"I can't tell you how much that means coming from a woman like you."

"Excuse me?"

"I'm tickled pink to hear that you have a higher opinion of me now. I don't care how hard I try, I don't think I'll ever be on your level."

"I know. God loves all of us equally. But He's got his reasons for not blessing us equally. Me and Odell are so fortunate."

"I feel the same way," I agreed, with my stomach churning. I had never heard anybody say such a boastful thing before in my life. But it wasn't a surprise coming from Joyce. Somehow, I managed not to bust out laughing. I didn't know how much more of her and Odell's foolishness I could stand before I let them have a big piece of my mind. "I better get these hush puppies out there before they get cold. I know Odell is anxious to dig in."

Before I could take a step toward the door, Joyce leaned her head over the bowl and sniffed. Then she frowned and rubbed her nose. "They smell and look overcooked. Maybe the next time I come over, I'll cook a batch for you to serve. Mine always turn out perfect."

CHAPTER 35
YVONNE

*T*HE STUFF MILTON HAD TOLD ME ABOUT ODELL EARLIER THIS week was the heaviest burden I'd ever had to carry in my life.

Just as I was about to start cooking some dumplings for supper Thursday evening, I heard a car door slam. Like always, I rushed to the living-room window and peeped out. It was Odell. I shook my head when he got out and trotted around to Joyce's side to open her door. She was holding a huge bouquet of roses. I cracked the window open enough so I could hear what they was saying.

"Watch your step, sugar. I don't want you to break none of my bedroom toys," he teased in his most *charming* tone. He grabbed ahold of her arm and helped her out. She giggled like a hyena.

No man had ever held open a car door for me or gave me flowers. It amazed me how Odell could be so attentive and thoughtful to his wife when he had another woman he probably loved just as much, if not more. Joyce was still jealous of the attention I got from men, though. I realized that back in July when we'd gone shopping and to lunch. Almost every man we'd run into had tried to pick me up, and one even paid for my lunch. I could tell it bothered her by them sly narrowed-eyed looks she gave me when it happened. But if I had one doing all the things for me that Odell was doing for her—and probably for his other woman, too—I wouldn't care if another man never whistled at me or tried to pick me up again.

Milton had left the house with Willie Frank ten minutes ago to deliver orders that some other bootleggers had put in. I'd be by myself for a while. I couldn't understand why I suddenly got so jumpy. Even after I drunk a shot of moonshine, I couldn't sit or stand still. I would have gave anything in the world for some-body to knock on the door, just so I'd have somebody to talk to. I knew we'd have a nice crowd later on, but I needed somebody to talk to now. Before I could stop myself, I headed next door. Joyce must have seen me coming, because she opened the door before I'd even made it to her porch.

"Joyce, I hate to bother you, but I was wondering if you had a few chicken necks I could borrow? I'm making Milton some dumplings for supper and just realized I didn't have no meat to season them with."

"Come on in. I'll go check." She motioned me into the living room, and she skittered toward the kitchen. Odell was already kicked back on the couch, reading the newspaper. A big ceramic vase sat on one of the end tables, with the flowers I'd seen Joyce with.

"Hi, Odell. I know y'all just got home a little while ago, so I won't stay but a minute." It was hard for me to sound so gracious in the presence of a devil.

"You ain't got to be in no hurry." He laid his newspaper on the coffee table and waved me to the love seat facing him. I didn't plan on staying long, but I sat down, anyway. "You want a bottle of pop while you waiting?"

"No, that's all right." I fidgeted in my seat and stared at the floor. I could feel his eyes on me, so I looked up to face him. "How was work today?"

"Girl, each day is better than the last. Even after all these years, I still have to pinch myself to make sure I ain't dreaming. I'm so blessed."

"I know." I gave him a sharp look, which he didn't even no-tice. Just then Joyce returned, holding a plastic bowl covered with wax paper.

"I threw in a few gizzards and thighs, too," she said, handing the bowl to me.

"Thanks, Joyce. Oh, I love your flowers." I nodded toward the vase. "I wish somebody would give me some one of these days." I didn't like to whine, but this time I couldn't help myself.

"Well, we can't all get everything we want. If you get in faith and stay in it, God will bless you, too." She gave me a sympathetic look. It didn't take a mind reader to know what she was thinking. I knew she was feeling sorry for me *again* for being married to a limited man. "Did you and Milton decide whether or not to go to church with us Sunday after next?"

"I'm pretty sure we'll make it. But since we belong to New Hope Baptist, I feel funny about it, though. If our preacher was to hear about us going to a different church, since we ain't been to his since last Easter, he might feel slighted."

"Pffft! I wouldn't worry about Reverend Hayes! Almost everybody in this town knows he's fooling around with one of his wife's best friends. Odell and I agree that an unfaithful man does not deserve any respect!" Joyce snapped.

Odell had a hangdog look on his face. When he seen me gazing at him, he suddenly perked up and started nodding in agreement with her. I wondered what went through his mind when Joyce said that a unfaithful man didn't deserve no respect.

"I don't know why you and Milton joined that run-down church in the first place," Joyce added.

"Well, there ain't but three for colored folks in Branson. The other one is too close to the swamps to suit us. When we went to one of our coworker's funeral at that church a few weeks ago, a lizard crawled across the floor in the middle of the eulogy. We joined New Hope on account of it's the same one we went to for school studies during the week when we was kids. And at the time we joined, we lived just a block from it, so we could walk. I feel kind of attached to it."

"I still want y'all to go with us at least this one time. It's Reverend Jessup's thirtieth anniversary at Tabernacle Baptist. Folks who haven't been to church in years will be there. It would mean a lot to him to see a full house. I've been trying to talk Odell into getting up and giving a speech that day about how God has blessed us, and how much the reverend's spiritual guidance helps us keep our marriage thriving." She chuckled. "If Odell does speak, I hope that busybody Aunt Mattie and some of her minions are there to hear it. Maybe then they'll stop wondering about how secure our relationship is." Joyce eyeballed Odell like he'd just been served to her on a platter.

I swallowed hard and looked at him with my head cocked to the side and my eyes narrowed. "Odell, I sure would love to hear what you have to say about marriage . . ."

He shifted in his seat and started scratching his neck. I wondered what lie he'd tell Betty Jean about why he wouldn't be coming to see her that day.

"I bet you could give other men a lot of pointers on how to be a good husband," I blurted out.

"I believe I could. I take a lot of pride in being a good role model," he replied, bobbing his head. "But I'm only human, so I do have a few minor faults."

"Sure enough," Joyce giggled. "Like leaving dirty clothes on the floor and forgetting to refill the water pitcher."

If that was what she called Odell's "faults," what would she call his bedroom shenanigans with Betty Jean? This couple was beyond my range of belief.

"You and Milton can ride to church with us. But since we made plans for lunch, y'all will have to hitch a ride home with somebody else, take the bus, or walk," she told me.

"That's all right. We don't mind. We used to taking the bus and walking. I just pray that someday we'll be able to afford a car."

"Yvonne, keep praying. It's the most honorable way to achieve success, prosperity, and a happy home. Odell and I are living proof of that. You know, you have a really good attitude for somebody that grew up in the slums. It's a shame the rest of the people over there aren't as humble and optimistic as you. Anyway, having such a bleak background and being an ex-convict is nothing to be ashamed about. Your being honest is a virtue. It builds character. Keep that in mind. Right, Odell?" Joyce said with a smug look on her face.

"Sure enough. I can't stand liars," he said sharply.

I couldn't believe he could say such a thing with a straight face. As deceitful as he was, it was a wonder he hadn't turned into a pillar of salt by now.

CHAPTER 36
YVONNE

W HEN I GOT HOME, I THOUGHT ABOUT HOW ODELL HAD BOASTED this time, and especially about his comment about having to pinch hisself to make sure he wasn't dreaming. It made me feel lowly and sad, because it was a reminder that me and Milton was still struggling to get to his and Joyce's level. The more I thought about what he'd said, the worse I felt.

I was slumped on the couch, guzzling some home brew, trying to cheer myself up, when Milton came home a few minutes before 7:00 p.m.

"Baby, you look like you done lost your best friend," he noticed. He dropped down next to me, wrapped his arm around my neck, and gave me a few hungry little kisses on my jaw.

"I got cramps," I lied. Female body issues gave Milton the heebie-jeebies. I let out a moan and rubbed my belly to be more convincing. Whenever I didn't want him to badger me about nothing, that was the route I took to get him off my back.

He shuddered and stood back up. "Cramps, huh? You want me to brew you some tea and get them pills out the bathroom?"

"No. I'll be fine. I took some already. I'm glad you finally home." I cleared my throat and managed a weak smile. "Baby, Odell and Joyce invited us to go to church with them the last Sunday in the month."

"No shit?" He laughed and sat back down.

"Be nice now. It's Reverend Jessup's thirtieth anniversary.

Let's go. Odell might give a speech about how wonderful their marriage is."

We busted out howling at the same time. We laughed nonstop for a whole minute. Milton got so carried away, he started choking, and I had to slap him on his back.

"I wouldn't want to miss a dog and pony show like that. I'd even *pay* to hear it," he said.

Then we laughed some more.

The last Sunday in October had finally arrived. I couldn't wait to go to church and hear Odell's speech. Milton and I had agreed that it would give us enough comedy to laugh for weeks to come.

There was no telling what Joyce was going to wear to church today for Reverend Jessup's anniversary sermon. I decided to wear my V-necked lime-green blouse and a navy-blue skirt. It was one of the few outfits I had that was suitable for church. I had a ribbon with red, yellow, and green stripes holding my ponytail in place; and a pair of green earbobs, which I had stole last month from Branson's only jewelry store, dangled from my ears. Milton had just got his blue pin-striped suit dry cleaned, so the leg creases looked almost as sharp as a knife blade. His black-and-white spats made his feet look so much better than the round-toed, high-topped brogan shoes he usually wore.

Around 9:00 a.m. we headed next door.

"We better sit in the back of the church, because I won't be able to stop myself from laughing when Odell go up to that podium," I whispered as we walked up on the porch.

"I was thinking that same thing," Milton whispered back.

When Odell opened the door, dressed in one of his undertaker-looking black suits, I could barely look in his eyes without laughing already. "Where y'all going this time of morning dressed up like peacocks?" he asked, looking amused as his eyes roamed over us. "Halloween ain't until Tuesday."

Me and Milton gave each other puzzled looks, and then we turned back to Odell.

"We going to church with y'all this morning," I answered. "Did you forget already?"

"I guess I did. Y'all look . . . uh . . . interesting." He scratched the side of his head and beckoned us into the house.

A few seconds later, Joyce came into the room, wearing black pumps and a flouncy yellow dress with black dots and ruffles at the end of the sleeves. There was a great big yellow and black bow fastened to the side of her head. She looked like a giant bumblebee. I guessed she didn't realize Halloween wasn't until Tuesday, either. She stopped smack-dab in front of me and stared at my blouse. Without saying a word, she whirled around and dashed toward her bedroom. She came back about a minute later with a black knitted shawl and waved it in my face.

"It's going to get mighty warm today. Yvonne don't need no cover-up," Milton said with a confused look on his face.

"Um, that blouse she got on is cut a little too low. Those old setting hens at church might get offended, and we don't want y'all to embarrass us," Joyce explained. She wrapped the shawl around my shoulders and then had the nerve to clamp it shut with one of her fancy ivory brooches! I had hoped that I'd get through the day without her saying or doing something I didn't like. I was sorry I had got us in this mess.

The church was only a little over a mile away, but Odell drove so fast, we got there in less than a minute. It didn't do no good for me to hide my bosom. The moment I stepped inside, them women looked at me like they wanted to stone me. There was no room on the back pews, so me and Milton had to go up front and sit on the first one with Joyce and Odell. If sitting that close to them wasn't bad enough, Joyce's elderly parents occupied the same pew. They gazed at me and Milton like they was seeing us for the first time.

"Evening, Brother Mac, Sister Millie," Milton greeted with a big smile. "Me and Yvonne sure is happy to be here today."

"Sure enough," I agreed.

"It's nice to see y'all again," Mac muttered, glancing from me to Milton and back. "I never would have guessed it'd be in a church, though," he added in a snippy tone, with a guarded look on his beefy brown face.

Like Joyce, her parents wasn't nothing much to look at. Mac and Millie was both overweight, had blunt features, and was covered in liver spots. He was real tall and sturdy for a man his age. But he walked with two canes. His wife was just as wide at the top as she was at the bottom. They was big shots in Branson and sweet as sugarcane in public, but I had a feeling them old goats was just as la-di-da as Joyce and Odell. They lived on our street, only a few blocks from us, but had never set foot in our house— even though we had invited them more than once. And they had never invited us to visit them. Since I knew how holy they was and how they felt about bootleggers, them being so stand-offish didn't bother me at all. But whenever we bumped into Joyce's parents on the street, or if they happened to be in the store when we was there, they always treated us with respect.

"Daddy, be nice," Joyce advised, giving the old man a stern look.

Like that cranky whorehouse-running Aunt Mattie, Mac and Millie had also been born into slavery. They'd done well since Lincoln set the slaves free. They liked to gloat about how successful MacPherson's was, so every colored person in town knew they had money. I wondered how long it would take Odell to feather his nest when his in-laws died and left everything to Joyce. As big a trickster as he was, he would probably sell the store behind her back. If he done that, he wouldn't need her no more. He'd be in hog heaven then, because he could be with the Betty Jean woman all the time.

"Odell, I wouldn't miss your speech for the world," Milton said with a self-satisfied smirk on his face. "I can't wait to hear what advice you got to share with the rest of us menfolk about having a good marriage."

I had to hold my breath to keep from laughing.

"I hate to disappoint you, but I decided not to make no speech. I didn't know so many folks would turn out. I'm shy, so I get nervous and tongue tied speaking in front of big crowds.

And I ain't about to embarrass Joyce and my in-laws," Odell prat-
tled. He was about as shy as a rabid dog.

"That's a shame, son. We understand, though," Millie told
him, patting his arm. Then she turned to Milton. "Y'all must be
doing real good for you to afford that snazzy suit."

"Yes, ma'am. I got this one at your store." Milton cleared his
throat and looked at Odell again. "I'm going to get me a few
more, and a lot of other stuff from y'all."

"Good. I'm happy to hear that you giving us your money, and
not that place on Pike Street run by white folks that don't give
their colored customers no respect. Putting Odell in charge was
the smartest move I ever made—since I married Miss Millie. He
done turned our business into a bonanza I never expected."
Mac was beaming like a flashlight as he clapped Odell on the
back. "Boy, thank you for being such a flawless businessman,
and a heavenly son-in-law."

"I appreciate hearing that, Mac. I work hard at both. But I
couldn't do it without God's help," Odell said.

I couldn't believe my own ears! It was hard to listen to a devil
like him say something so noble with a straight face. Milton
must have felt the same way, because he looked like he wanted
to puke. This time, the level of ecstasy on Joyce's face was as
high as it could go. Me, I was straight-up amused—and angry!
Odell's deceit was so out of control, I couldn't go too much
longer without taking him down.

For the next half hour, emotional people paraded up to the
podium and praised Reverend Jessup; some even cried. Then
the sorry-sounding choir sang three hymns in a row. After that,
we had to listen to the preacher talk for an hour. When the collection plate came around, it got to me and Milton first. I tried
to act like I didn't notice the horrified looks on Odell's and
Joyce's faces, and her parents', when we dropped in a nickel
apiece. They each put in a whole dollar! When the service was finally over, we seen that collection plate coming around again.
Well, we wasn't about to make another donation to a church we
didn't even belong to. We stood up and started inching toward

the door. A few people stopped us along the way to shake our hands and hug us.

Joyce and Odell was roaming around, shaking hands and hugging folks, too. They finally rejoined us a few steps from the door.

"I hope y'all enjoy your lunch at Mosella's," I told them.

"We will. Pig ears is the lunch special on Saturdays, so I wish we could have gone yesterday," Joyce whined. "But since Odell spends most of his Saturdays with his daddy, it's been months since we got to enjoy that dish. No matter how I season mine when I cook them, they never turn out the way I want."

"Well, y'all ain't tasted no scrumptious pig ears until you taste Yvonne's," Milton boasted.

"I cook mine with a pinch of vinegar, gingerroot, and cayenne pepper," I said. "Then I drop them into a pot of collard greens and let them simmer for a while. That's what I'm cooking for supper tomorrow. Why don't y'all join us?"

"Ooh-wee! We would love to." Joyce grinned and elbowed Odell. "Right, baby?"

"Um, right. I love pig ears," he replied in a dry tone.

"Then we'll see y'all around six tomorrow evening," I said.

The next thing I knew, Odell said something that made my head spin.

"Yvonne, several ladies made some unflattering comments about your blouse." His tone was gentle, but he was giving me a peeved look. "I hope the next time you come to church with us, you dress more respectable, like Joyce."

I couldn't believe this motherfucker could say something like that to me after I'd just invited his cheesy black ass to supper! I shouldn't have been surprised. No matter how neighborly me and Milton was to them, they still treated us like country bumpkins that didn't have no feelings.

Odell went on. "Why don't you come to the store and let me help you pick out some decent blouses? I want to make sure you don't come back to my church and embarrass me and my family like you done today."

Joyce didn't waste no time putting in her two cents. "I guess that shawl I wrapped around you didn't help much. You can keep it, though. It still might do you some good someday."

"Thanks, Joyce," I muttered. "I'll put it to good use." I wondered what she would say if I told her I was going to use it to hand scrub my floors. "Odell, can I come pick out something tomorrow, when I go on my lunch break? I'll ask Mr. Cunningham if I can use his truck to come into town." My head was still spinning so bad, I could barely stand it. Before Odell could answer, I turned to Milton. "Baby, you don't mind having lunch tomorrow without me, do you?"

"Naw," he grunted. "I'd like to see you in some better glad rags myself."

"Odell, I'll be there anytime after twelve," I chirped. "I hope you have some acceptable blouses I can choose from."

"Every blouse I got in stock is more acceptable than the one you got on now," he declared, gawking at my blouse like it was a fig leaf. "A married woman like you don't need to go around dressing like a floozy."

"Okay," I mumbled.

His last comment was the straw that broke the camel's back! If I went one more day without letting him know that I knew what a fraud he was, I'd go crazy.

CHAPTER 37

MILTON

*B*EFORE I COULD GET MY BEARINGS BACK AFTER JOYCE'S AND Odell's crude comments about Yvonne's blouse, that long-winded, mulish Reverend Jessup started walking toward us.

Joyce gasped and took hold of Odell's arm. "Oh-oh. If we don't escape now, he'll hem us up until the afternoon service, and we'll miss our reservation at Mosella's," she mumbled. She and Odell didn't wait long enough for us to say nothing. They eased toward the back door and bolted. The preacher was too close for us to make our getaway without looking too obvious.

"Well, now, Brother Milton and Sister Yvonne! It's good to see y'all today! I must say I'm as surprised as everybody else must be!" Reverend Jessup boomed in his deep, throaty voice. I didn't care how holy he was or claimed to be, I seen his eyes roaming all over Yvonne, focusing mainly on her bosom.

"We glad to be here for your anniversary celebration," she replied, pulling the shawl tighter around her shoulders.

"I declare, Reverend Jessup, you preached a foot-stomping sermon!" I whooped. "I don't remember the last time I seen so many sisters jump up and shout right out of their shoes."

Instead of thanking me and being humble, Reverend Jessup scratched the side of his long face and damn near growled, "Humph! Y'all ain't heard nothing yet. With so many high-ranking backsliders on the premises this morning, I could smell the brimstone as soon as I took to the podium. I'll have to preach up a storm this afternoon to get the dust and cobwebs off some of these souls up in here today." His eyes darted from me to Yvonne and back, so it was obvious he thought of us as "high-ranking backsliders."

"Um, we won't be able to stay for that. We made plans to attend the afternoon service at our own church. Right, Milton?" Yvonne snuck a jab to my side with her elbow.

"That's right! And since we have to take the bus, if we don't leave soon, we'll be late," I blurted out. "But we sure enjoyed being here today!"

"Well, everybody is welcome to come worship at my church, even bootleggers." Reverend Jessup stopped talking and stood up straighter, running his crooked fingers though his thin gray hair. "In spite of the fiery road y'all stumbling down, we belong to the same flock. So, I'm going to pray for y'all . . ."

I had to force myself to keep a straight face. "That's nice. We'll pray for you, too." I cleared my throat and grinned.

The way Reverend Jessup was gazing at us, shaking his head, and muttering under his breath, you would have thought we was buck naked. After a loud snort, he went on. "A bootlegging environment is akin to Babylon. Selling alcohol without authorization is a dirty business and could lead to destruction and more profound crimes. If you ask me, I'd say y'all been in the storm too long. Now, I know plenty of farmers in this county and several others. I'm sure that if I went up to them on y'all's behalf, they'd be happy to have y'all come work for them."

"No offense, Reverend, but the last place we want to work again is on somebody's farm. I done picked enough cotton to make glad rags for a whole army. When I worked in the cane fields, swinging them machetes, I came close to losing fingers more times than I can count. Thank you, anyway, though. Now, you have a blessed rest of the day," I said.

We laughed off and on about our church experience all the way to the bus stop.

Sunday night was slow. Only a dozen guests showed up. But since Lyla and Emmalou was among them, we made pretty good money. I was happy when the day ended, though. We slept like babies and didn't wake up until 8:00 a.m. Monday morning.

I was glad Yvonne didn't ask me to go to MacPherson's with her today on our lunch break. She was just going to pick out some blouses and didn't need my help no how. But I had to give her a little piece of advice on the subject, anyway.

"Don't let Odell give you none of them drab blouses, like the ones his dowdy wife be wearing."

"Pffft! Milton, you know better. I wouldn't be found dead in nothing like any of them mammy-made pieces Joyce wear."

We laughed.

A few minutes after Yvonne left, I used the telephone in Mr. Cunningham's office and called up Willie Frank.

"What's up?" he asked when he picked up on the second ring.

"Same old, same old. I just called to conversate for a few minutes. See, I got a itching to try my hand at poker again."

"You got to be kidding," he said with a chuckle.

"What you mean by that? I been gambling since I was fourteen. I ain't about to quit now."

"I didn't mean you should quit. But don't you think you need to lay low a little longer? You done riled up a lot of folks. And from the talk over at Aunt Mattie's, what folks been saying ain't in your favor."

"Such as?"

"The word is, Oscar still got a bug up his ass about his property that got stole. He is convinced that *you* was the ringleader. He's telling folks he ain't going to stand for a colored man making a monkey out of him, and he is going to learn you a lesson you won't never forget."

"You tell whoever told you that, that I said for them to tell Oscar I done already learned my lesson. He ain't got to worry about me no more. When you deliver his next order, I won't go."

"I doubt if he'll order anything else from me. Yesterday one of the Dawson brothers gloated that Oscar just set up a deal to buy his liquor from them."

"Pffft! The Dawson brothers make some of the weakest shine in the county. I heard they can barely pay off them revenuers and the laws so they won't pester them with arrest warrants. I don't think they'll be in business much longer," I pointed out.

"I heard the same thing, so I ain't worried about them slowing down my business. When that crybaby Oscar gets tired of the Dawsons' weak stuff, or when they get shut down, I'm sure he'll come crawling back to me. I added two new white bootleggers to my roster this week. They'll make up for Oscar, and then some."

"Hmmm. That's good news, Willie Frank. Anyway, I ain't going to let Oscar or Cap get me down no more. I'll find me some new poker buddies. Four of them train-station workers came in for breakfast today. They play at different places once or twice a week. I'll join them. And I can always get a game going at my own house."

"I just hope Cap ain't already spreaded word around that you cheat. I'd hate for you to have to go all the way to another town where nobody knows you when you want to gamble."

"I doubt if it'll come to that. I'll see you at the house tonight?"

"Yup. I'll be there around nine, after I swing by Aunt Mattie's to go at it with Sweet Sue again. But please watch your step, buddy."

I couldn't understand why Willie Frank was so worried about me. He was beginning to sound like Yvonne. I wasn't about to slow down my gambling, and I was not about to go out of town when I wanted to gamble again. I was going to join them railroad workers tonight.

CHAPTER 38
YVONNE

Mr. CUNNINGHAM DIDN'T HESITATE WHEN I ASKED HIM TO LET me borrow his truck so I could go into town.

"Don't run over nobody, and look out for them possums, deers, and squirrels jumping out the bushes. I just got new tires, and I don't want no blood and guts on them," he told me, peering at me over his silver-rimmed glasses.

"You ain't got to worry about none of that. I been driving for years, and I ain't never hit nothing yet."

I took my time driving down the bumpy dirt road and still ran over a snake. "Shit!" I stopped and got out, was glad to see there wasn't enough blood and guts for Mr. Cunningham to notice. I was a little shook up and had to sit in the truck for a few minutes and pull myself together. I drove even slower after that, so it took almost twice as long to get into town as it usually did.

When I got to the store, there was no other customers there. On one hand, I was glad. It had been a while since I'd conversated with Odell's two busybody cashiers. I wanted to keep them happy so that the next time I came to swipe a few items, they wouldn't pay too much attention to me. But I was also disappointed that I'd have to waste good gossip and part of my lunch break on them. I had already wasted time because of that damn snake incident.

I stopped between the two checkout counters and showed off my biggest smile. "How y'all doing? Buddy, you look like a film star in that flowered shirt. Sadie, you look younger and younger each day." I stopped talking just long enough for them to grin and preen. Buddy stood up straighter and ran his fingers through his hair; Sadie licked her lips and brushed off her smock. I didn't give them time to say nothing. I wanted to stay in control of the conversation, so I could end it when I wanted to. "Did y'all hear about Reverend Hayes fooling around with one of his wife's best friends?"

"Pffft!" Buddy threw up his hands and batted his ratty eyes. Sweat was all over his homely face. "Girl, where you been? That news is as old as Methuselah. Him and that loose-bootied heifer been involved for months."

"On top of that, I heard Sister Hayes know all about it. But I suspect she don't care. After twelve kids, I'm sure she done had enough of that old frog mounting her," Sadie threw in. She was just as homely and miserable as Buddy. Other than church and work, neither one had much of a life, so gossiping and meddling was like a happy-making potion to them. "And guess what else, Yvonne?"

"What?"

"He just started lusting after his choir director, too. The way he eyeballs that sister would make Jesus weep."

"Honest to God?" I hollered.

"Yup!" Sadie and Buddy thundered at the same time.

I shook my head and let out one of them sighs of disbelief. "Well, shut my mouth. I don't understand why his wife put up with his mess. I sure wouldn't."

"Me neither. Some men is so trifling. If they ain't chasing women, they doing every other kind of devilment," Sadie snarled. Without missing a beat, she asked, "By the way, how is you and Milton these days?"

"Blessed. Things couldn't be better for us. We went to church with Joyce and Odell yesterday. Reverend Jessup brung the house down with his preaching."

Buddy and Sadie gazed at each other, then back at me.

"I was there. I would have come up and hugged y'all, but by

the time folks stopped hugging me, y'all was gone," Sadie said.

"I was there, too. But I took off in a hurry so I wouldn't get hugged by none of them juicy women, with my jealous lady friend so close by." Buddy shook his head and raised his eyebrows. "By the way, you and Milton and Joyce and Odell done got real chummy, huh?"

"Uh-huh, praise the Lord. We spend a lot of time together." I stopped and nodded toward the back of the store. "I hate to run, but Odell is expecting me."

"For what?" Sadie wanted to know.

"Um, I didn't get nothing but lye soap and witch hazel for myself that day me and Joyce came in with my little cousins. He told me I could come back anytime I was ready and pick out some blouses."

"How come you didn't get none when you was here the last time? You was here long enough," Buddy said with a smirk.

"Odell didn't have what I wanted in my size," I explained. "Now I'll let y'all get back to work. I'm on my lunch break, so I can't stay long."

I didn't wait for them to say nothing else. I whirled around and rushed toward Odell's office. When I got to the door, I stopped and held my breath. I was nervous and was tempted to change my mind, but I'd come too far. I knew that if I didn't confront him now, I might not get up the nerve to do it again.

"Odell, you in there?" I asked, knocking at the same time.

"Come on in, Yvonne."

I opened the door and hurried in. "You told me to come by today to get some blouses," I reminded.

"Indeed I did!" He grinned. I was glad to see him in a cheerful mood, but I knew that wouldn't be the case by the time I left. He stood up from his desk, still grinning. "Some sharp tops came in last Thursday. I hope you like ruffles and stripes. Most of all, they all got high necklines, so you ain't got to worry about exposing your bosom the way you been doing. Now, as you know, we never get more than four or five of the same clothing items in the same sizes at the same time. It's a good thing you got here before other small-boned women came in and picked out the good stuff. Come on and pick out what you want." I followed him outside, to the women's clothing section. "Help yourself," he said, pointing toward a bunch of blouses on a rack.

"Okay. I really appreciate this, Odell."

I didn't care which ones I took, so I grabbed two from the middle. They was loud and so unlike anything else in my wardrobe, but they wasn't low cut or skimpy enough to offend nobody. I didn't know when I'd go back to church, but they was the kind of blouses I wouldn't wear no other place.

"These will do."

"You made a good choice. Them the same two Joyce liked the most. It's a shame they don't come in her size. Now, you hold tight and let me run and get you a bag." Odell rushed over to Sadie's counter and grabbed a bag. He was whistling when he trotted back to where I was. "I hope we still on for supper this evening. Joyce couldn't stop talking about them pig ears last night," he chuckled as he folded the blouses and slid them into the bag.

"Um, yeah. I marinated them pig ears overnight in butter. They'll be nice and tender when we eat them this evening," I muttered.

"Good! Now, do you need anything else today?"

I held up my hand to shut him up. "No. But I need to talk to you about something before I leave."

He gave me a blank stare and then broke into a grin. "If it's about you paying for the blouses today or putting them on that credit account I opened for y'all, don't worry. Since I'm the one that suggested you improve your wardrobe, the cost is on me."

"I'm glad to hear that. But that ain't what I need to talk to you about. It's something a lot more important."

"*You* got something important to discuss with *me*? What in the world could that be?"

"Take me somewhere more private," I advised.

Odell glanced over at Buddy and Sadie before he ushered me into his office. I shut the door behind me, because I wasn't about to take a chance on Buddy and Sadie eavesdropping. He went behind his desk, sat down, and motioned for me to sit down in the chair facing him, but I didn't. I wanted to be on my feet in case he got ugly enough for me to run.

"What is this important thing we need to be conversating about behind closed doors?" he asked in a gruff tone. I couldn't believe the change in his demeanor. He was looking at me like I'd stole his wallet.

"Hold your horses. I'll get to it." I didn't want to be too abrupt. I figured it would be more pleasant for us both if I eased into the situation. If I stayed calm, maybe he would, too.

"I ain't got time for games, Yvonne." He blew out some air and narrowed his eyes. "What is it?"

I leaned over his desk and whispered, "I know something about you."

He squinted so hard, his eyes looked like they was almost closed. "Listen here, if you got something to talk to me about, do it and stop acting like a child!" His sudden mean tone and name-calling made me mad.

"Who you calling a child? I'm thirty-two years old!"

"Then quit acting like a ignorant *pickaninny*—"

I didn't give him a chance to insult me more. I realized I was going to have to get tough with him. "I know what you been up to, you nasty buzzard."

Odell did a double take. "Excuse me? Who in the world you talking to?"

"Do you see anybody else up in here besides me and your happy-dick self?"

He gasped so hard, I was surprised he didn't swallow his tongue. "Yvonne, you drunk?"

"I ain't had no alcohol since last night!"

"Then you must have lost your mind! I declare, I ain't never heard you say nothing so crazy!"

"And I declare, I know all about you and Betty Jean."

He didn't move or say nothing for the longest time. He just sat there staring at me, with his mouth hanging open. He didn't even blink.

"Did you hear me, Odell?"

"I heard you." His voice was as raspy as that of a sick old man. He fidgeted in his seat and blinked a bunch of times. "I guess Milton told you, huh?"

"Yup. But he didn't mean to."

"If he told you something he swore to me he wouldn't tell, he meant to tell."

"Now, don't get mad at Milton. He was drunk, and I pestered him until he broke down and told me."

"So, you know everything?"

"Everything he know."

Odell reminded me of a rat I'd backed into a corner one day, before I clobbered him with a whisk broom. And just like that rat, he glanced around like he was looking for someplace he could hide. After a loud, painful-sounding moan, he gazed into my eyes and mumbled in a nervous tone, "I slid down a hole, but it ain't as deep as you might think it is."

"Odell, people can say a lot of things about me. One thing they can't say is that I'm stupid. You got three kids with that woman! And you got people over in Hartville believing you a traveling salesman."

His lips quivered, and his dark eyes looked like they'd got even darker. "That blabbermouth husband of yours didn't leave no stone unturned!" he blasted.

"You could say that. But he took me over to Po' Sister's Kitchen in Hartville, where he seen y'all. One of the waitresses backed up everything he had already told me."

Odell's eyes got so big, you would have thought a ghost had just flew in. "Y'all been talking to people over there about me and Betty Jean?"

"Yup."

CHAPTER 39
YVONNE

"WHAT KIND OF MESS YOU TRYING TO STIR UP?" ODELL ASKED, with his voice cracking. "Them suspicious waitresses cut their teeth on scandals!"

"The one I'm talking about didn't get suspicious. Milton played it off like a pro. He asked most of the questions. Besides, she said she wouldn't mention to you that we was ever there. So, you ain't got to worry about her telling Betty Jean or her sister about our visit. I just had to let you know that I know the kind of man you is now."

"Lord have mercy!" Odell pulled a handkerchief out of his pocket and mopped sweat off his face. Then he blew out some air and gave me a hot look. "You being married to a thug like Milton, I had already suspected you was a lowlife. I didn't think you was *below* the lowest level."

The pickaninny insult was still ringing in my ears and had made me mad enough. Being told that I was on a low-life level that didn't even register on the scale made me doubly mad. I was bent on keeping cool until I finished saying all I had to say. "You got some nerve calling *me* a 'lowlife'!"

"If I wasn't a old-fashioned gentleman, I'd call you a few other names, too."

My chest tightened, and I waved both my hands in the air. "I can think of a heap of names to call you, too. I won't, because I'm old-fashioned, too. But I'll say this much. Shame, shame, shame!

You had me and everybody else fooled. And poor Milton. I was always in his face, telling him I wanted him to be more like you!"

"How come he didn't come with you?" It was hard to believe a man like Odell could speak in such a nasty tone like he was doing now. "He off harassing somebody else?"

"My husband is a *real* old-fashioned gentleman. He don't harass nobody, and I know you ain't trying to say that's what I'm doing. I been ladylike since I walked in your office." I had to pause to catch my breath and rub my chest to keep it from getting any tighter. "He think I only came to pick up them blouses you said I could get."

Odell's eyebrows lifted. "You didn't tell him you was coming here to confront me?"

"Goodness gracious, no! I swore to him that I wouldn't tell nobody your secret."

"Is that so? Humph! He swore to me that he wouldn't tell nobody, neither!"

"I ain't going to tell him about this conversation. And I hope you don't."

"Okay. What I need to know is, What do I have to do to keep you quiet?"

"I'm glad you asked that. As you know, me and Milton been having some serious money problems lately." I rolled my eyes up and shook my head. "He can't stop gambling."

"So, you want me to pay you off?"

"You could say that, I guess. And I want you to know up front that I ain't greedy. Other than some free merchandise as we need it, and you letting us slide when we can't pay our credit account on time, all I want is a few dollars."

"You want 'a few dollars' today, but what will you want later?"

"Nothing, I hope. Why?"

"You see here, Yvonne. I ain't going to agree to give you whatever you want today without guidelines for the future. I don't want to end up in the same mess with you that I'm in with Milton."

"Huh? You gave him some money already?"

"He didn't waste no time putting blackmail on the table. I been giving him money every Wednesday since he came to talk to me about this back in July. And I been giving him 'bonus' money almost as regularly as I been giving him what I agreed to."

I couldn't believe my ears. I gazed at Odell for a few moments with a dumbfounded look on my face. "Milton didn't tell me that. All he told me was that he let you know he knew what you was up to, and that he gave you a piece of his mind. And I believed him. I thought that with y'all being such good friends, he wouldn't make a big deal out of it or ask for no hush money."

Odell stared at me like I was speaking a foreign language. "Why would you think he'd confront me if he didn't want something? I can see you don't know your husband at all."

"Just like I don't know you at all."

"Look, you need to get up out of here. I got work to do, and I need to be by myself so I can think about this shit."

"Before I go, I want to know how much Milton get from you every week."

"We agreed on eight dollars."

"That's a odd number," I snickered. "How did you come up with that?"

"I didn't. One of the things he wanted was a part-time job stacking shelves at the store, and I went along with that. But my in-laws blocked that as soon as I brung it up to them. But because I had jumped the gun and told Milton I'd hire him before I checked with Joyce and her folks, he assumed I could afford to pay him. So, he demanded the same amount he would have earned each week if I'd hired him."

"Why Wednesday?"

"Why not? It's as good a day as any."

My mind was reeling so hard, I almost couldn't think straight. Now I was beginning to wish Milton hadn't told me about Odell and Betty Jean. But since he had, I couldn't turn back now. I had to finish what I'd started. All this time he been walking around with extra money that I didn't know nothing about. I never would have thought that Milton would hold out on me.

Maybe he was not the straight-up, righteous Christian I'd always thought he was. I couldn't get too upset about that right now. Especially since I'd broke my promise to him not to let Odell know I knew about Betty Jean. And I didn't feel bad about what I'd done. As far as I was concerned, one crook didn't deserve no more respect than the crook he or she was in cahoots with.

"I could wring Milton's neck for not telling me everything!"

"Humph! I won't tell you what I'd like to do to him." Odell lowered his voice. "I'll give you five dollars today. I'm putting out a lot of money already, and it ain't easy. If Joyce's daddy was to change his mind and come back to work, I'll be stocking shelves again. Then I wouldn't be able to give you and Milton a plugged nickel."

"What you doing for that woman and them kids? I hope you ain't letting her folks or the government provide for them."

"That's none of your business!" he barked, wagging his finger in my face. "You know too much already. And I don't want Milton to know what went on here today."

"You ain't got to worry about that. I got morals, see. I know how to keep a secret!"

Odell looked at me with his mouth hanging open. "But your morals ain't stopping you from shaking me down?"

"Huh? Explain what you mean by that."

"Never mind. From that confused look on your face, I know any explanation I give would go right over your head!" he snapped, dismissing me with a heavy-handed wave.

"Anyway, I'm mad at Milton for not telling me you was paying him, but I'll let that slide. He got enough problems already. I guess you heard about his most recent gambling woes."

"I hear a lot of things about Milton these days. And most of it is ugly. People been talking about him all over town, especially my customers. A few bootleggers want to run him out of town on a rail. If he don't watch his step, he'll have more enemies than friends."

"Pffft!" I dismissed Odell's warning with a eyeball roll. "We ain't worried about nobody messing with us. Them other jealous, crybaby bootleggers been bad-mouthing us ever since we got in the game. And they ain't chastised us yet. The next time somebody tell you something about Milton, or me, you can tell them I said to go jack off."

"That's a real blasé attitude to have about something that could cause you and Milton a heap of grief."

"I have to get back to work. Can I have my money now?"

As soon as Odell gave me my money—with one of the nastiest looks on his face I ever seen—I bolted. I ignored the nosy expressions on Buddy's and Sadie's faces as I walked real fast past them and on out the door. I cringed when I tried to imagine what was on their minds.

CHAPTER 40

MILTON

*Y*VONNE GOT BACK FROM HER LUNCH HOUR FIFTEEN MINUTES LATE.

"It took you long enough. Did Odell have to pull out a sewing machine and stitch up them blouses from scratch?" I asked when she pranced into the kitchen and showed off them tops she went to get.

Flowers and ruffles? Holy moly!

"Nope. He was busy talking to a vendor when I got there, and I had to wait for them to finish," she claimed, standing at the sink, washing her hands. "Before the first vendor left, another one came in, and I had to wait for him to leave, too. Do you like my new blouses?"

"Them is the most mammy-made pieces I ever laid eyes on," I teased. "My blind grandma could have picked out something cuter."

"Stop making a fuss," she whined. "I'm only going to wear them to church."

I glanced toward the door and around the kitchen. The other cook working today was busy at the grill, and the dishwasher was scrubbing plates. Before I could say another word, Mr. Cunningham came out of nowhere.

"Yvonne, Rolene can't wait on all them hungry folks by herself. And Dotty got sick and had to go home, so you need to shake a leg," he said in his gravelly voice.

"Yes, sir." Yvonne snatched a towel off the counter, dried off her hands, and stuffed her blouses back in the bag. "As soon as I put my stuff away, I'll get on it. And I'm sorry I got back from lunch late. I'll take a shorter break tomorrow to make up for it."

"Don't worry about that," Mr. Cunningham told her. "I didn't even notice what time you got back, nohow."

Yvonne dipped her head and mumbled, "Thank you, sir. It won't happen again." She skittered to the back of the room, to a long table where all the employees kept their personal items, and dropped off her bag.

I waited until our boss was out of earshot before I said anything else. "You didn't say nothing to Odell about you know what, did you? Him and Betty Jean?" I asked in a whisper as she hurried toward the door with me on her heels.

She whirled around, with her eyes as big as pinecones. "Naw!" she blurted out so hard and fast, spit flew out of her mouth. "Now, you better get back to work before you get us both in trouble."

"You sure you didn't say nothing to Odell? If you did, he'll know I was the one that let the cat out the bag. And I . . . um . . . I don't want to upset him."

"Why would you be worried about him being upset? He is the one in the hot seat. We just the witnesses."

"Just be careful when you alone with Joyce. I know how you women like to run off at the mouth. Don't let the wrong thing slide out, the way she do every time she open hers."

Yvonne looked fretful and peevish, but that didn't faze me, because I felt the same way. "Why would I tell Joyce about Odell's other family? What would be in that for me? You seen them blouses he let me take for free. And what about all the other stuff he give us from the store, not to mention all the things we swipe? Why would I risk losing that?"

"Okay, I believe you won't tell Joyce. But I don't *never* want you to let Odell know you know the scoop on him."

"Honest to God, I won't," Yvonne said, crossing her heart.

"I don't want him to think I can't keep a secret," I went on.

"You *can't* keep a secret!" she hooted. "Yeah, you busted Odell, but you didn't have to blab to me."

"You ain't got to rub it in. Anyway, I was drunk, and you was torturing me by praising him. So it's part your fault my lips got loose."

Yvonne sucked in her breath and looked at me like she wanted to slap me. "Excuse me. I got customers to wait on!" she snapped as she rushed out the door.

The rest of the day went by fast. Yvonne was busy, but each time she came into the kitchen, she gave me the fish eye.

Finally, she came up to me and cooed, "Don't forget Joyce and Odell is coming to supper this evening. I know we'll have a lot to laugh about after they leave."

"I know. But I probably won't make it home in time."

"Oh, Milton. And you the one got them all worked up about them pig ears in the first place."

"I know, and I'm sorry. But there is someplace else I got to go."

"Where?"

"Uh, you know Mickey Reese? That husky railroad worker?"

"Yeah. He eat at the grill several times a week. What about him?"

"He done set up some crapshoots for this evening behind the railroad station. I want to be there. I'll eat pig ears with Joyce and Odell some other evening. I'll even cook them myself, and I'll use your recipe."

Yvonne did a eyeball and a neck roll at the same time. "Don't you have enough bad luck playing cards?"

"Yeah. That's why I might only play craps for a while, before I start back up with them card games."

"You lose when you play craps, too."

I chuckled and tickled Yvonne's chin. "Come on now, sugar. I work hard day and night. Don't you want me to have no fun?"

"You don't have fun with me?"

"You'll see when I get you in that bed tonight," I laughed.

"Don't stay out too long. What you want me to tell Joyce and Odell?"

"Tell them my cousin Columbus been having nightmares about getting trampled by them cows. He had a relapse, and I went to see how he doing."

I didn't win but a couple of dollars at Mickey's place, but I still went back again the next night. Within an hour after I got there, I had lost big time.

"Y'all, I got to get up out of here before I get a serious case of the vapors. I'm so disgusted, I'm already feeling light-headed," I whined to Mickey and the other two men still squatting down on his kitchen floor, tossing dice like they was shooting marbles. I wobbled up off the hardwood floor and looked from one face to another. "Can somebody give me a ride to town?"

"What's wrong with you?" Mickey asked. "We just getting heated up."

"I don't want to walk all the way home!" I hollered.

"Well, if you can't wait for us to finish, that's exactly what you going to do," Mickey snapped.

I wasn't about to argue with him, and since I didn't want to hang around to watch them play, I left. I was lucky. After I'd walked half a mile, a farmer who was a regular guest at our house came by on his mule wagon. He rode me all the way to my street.

When I got off at the corner of the block, I was even madder about losing so much money. I cussed under my breath as I walked down the sidewalk. I was too preoccupied to notice I was being followed. By the time I did, it was too late.

I had just made it to the front of Odell's house when a man roared, "Bootlegger!"

Before I could turn around, somebody went upside the back of my head with something hard. The next thing I knew, they clobbered me again even harder, and I hit the ground. My guardian angel must have been with me, because I managed to get up and haul ass. Since I was closer to Odell's house than to

mine, I flung open his gate and ran toward his porch. My at-
tacker was right behind me.

"How you like that, motherfucker?" a voice different from the
first one boomed.

I made it to the steps and went down face-first. Feet started
stomping me all over, and then everything went black.

CHAPTER 41
MILTON

"ARGHH! ARGHH! ARGHH!"

At first, I thought it was me making them bloodcurdling screams. Then I realized it was a woman. What came out of her mouth next almost made me scream sure enough.

"Oh, Lord! They done killed my husband!" That was Yvonne's voice!

I was dead? *Shoot! Oh well.* I guessed I shouldn't have been surprised. When I was eight, one of my uncles warned me that the men on my daddy's side didn't live long. He died of a stroke a week later, at the age of thirty-four, the age I was now. And on that side of the family, I didn't have no men kinfolks left who were over forty-five.

I hoped that all my praying and Bible reading over the years had earned me enough points so my spirit would end up with God, and not with *that other fellow.* If this wasn't a good reason for me to be able to cry, I didn't know what was. But I couldn't cry, talk, or do nothing else with nary part of my body—if I was still in it. I could hear people moving across the floor, cussing and praying, so I knew I was in a heap of trouble.

"He ain't dead. They just knocked him out." That was Odell's voice.

I smelled blood, and I couldn't tell where it was coming from. But some of it was on my lips. I finally opened my eyes. "What the hell happened?" I asked. Somehow, I was able to talk, even though my lips felt like they was twice their normal size.

I could feel my body now, and it was in serious pain. I managed to sit up, anyway, and was happy to see I was on my own living-room couch. Yvonne and Odell was hovering over me. Her eyes was red, and her nose was snotty. Tears was sliding down the sides of her face. I suddenly remembered running toward Odell's house when I realized somebody was attacking me.

"What the hell happened?" I asked again.

"You got jumped," Odell told me in a gruff tone. "I found you on my porch."

"How long was I on your porch?"

"I don't know. I found you twenty minutes ago."

I glanced toward the window and seen it was pitch black outside. I was surprised that Odell had just found me twenty minutes ago. "It was still daylight when I got to our street. That was *hours* ago! Odell, do you mean to tell me I laid on your porch all that time? You didn't hear no commotion before then?"

"I didn't hear nothing, except the usual Halloween whooping and hollering them neighborhood kids make. I figured it was them teenage scalawags that live in the next block. They love to pull pranks. Joyce went to visit a coworker that just had a new baby, so I'd stretched out on the couch to take a nap. When I woke up, I cracked open my front door and seen what I thought was a scarecrow on my porch. That's how them pranksters spooked a few neighbors last Halloween. I didn't realize what I was looking at until you started moaning. It scared me to death."

"I didn't hear nothing, neither. Odell picked you up and carried you home," Yvonne told me.

My eyes stung as I blinked and scanned the room. I was surprised I didn't see nobody else. "Where is everybody at? We usually have at least a dozen folks up in here this time of night."

"A bunch came by. As bad as we need the money, I told them that we wouldn't be entertaining tonight," Yvonne explained.

There was a gauzy-feeling bandage wrapped around my head, covering a throbbing knot on the back that felt like it was the size of a walnut. I had a small Band-Aid on one of my jaws, and another one by the side of my left eye. When I slid my tongue across my bottom lip, I could feel the split in my skin. "I feel like shit," I complained, giving Yvonne a hopeless look. "Woman, go get me something for my head!"

She sprinted toward the kitchen, and Odell sat down on the footstool, facing me. "You lost a heap of blood. Mostly from your nose and lip," he told me. "Yvonne wouldn't let me take you to the hospital. But we cleaned you off, slathered iodine on your wounds, and bandaged you up good enough. Did you see who done this to you?"

"Naw. They got me from behind." I swallowed a big lump in my throat. I wasn't just in physical pain; my feelings was hurt. "Them devils was trying to kill me! Why would anybody want to kill *me*?" I wailed, looking in Odell's eyes.

He rattled off the last thing I expected to hear. "Well, as Shakespeare wrote in one of his plays, hell is empty and all the devils is here . . ."

"So, you a Shakespeare fan?"

"Naw. That's something one of my white bosses shared with me when I was still doing farmwork."

Yvonne rushed back into the room with a jar of water and handed it to me.

"Woman, what's wrong with you?" I yelled, glaring at the glass like it was full of piss. "You know I need something stronger than water. And bring me a straw."

"I'm sorry, sugar. I'll go get you some white lightning." She twirled around and rushed back to the kitchen.

I swung my feet to the floor and looked up at Odell. "The way I been putting the screws to you lately, I'm surprised you bothered to help me get home," I whispered. "Thanks, man." I was going to give him points for being a caring soul, until I heard what he said next.

"I couldn't let you bleed to death on my porch. I wouldn't stand by and let that happen to a snake I don't like."

Even with my face feeling like it was on fire, I was still able to blow out a sharp laugh. Odell was as grim-faced as a pallbearer, so I cleared my throat and got serious. "If I had gone to meet my Maker, at least you'd be off the hook."

"What hook?" Yvonne asked, walking back into the room. She handed me a pint-size jar of white lightning with a long straw in it.

"Huh? Oh, I was just telling Odell about a ornery catfish I caught when me and Willie Frank went fishing last week. That sucker wiggled until he was off the hook."

"Mister, you can forget about fishing again anytime soon," Yvonne snapped, shaking her fist at me. "Odell, you want something to drink?"

"Why not? I need to calm my nerves. Anything strong will do." He sighed and wrung his hands.

"I'll fix you up right away," Yvonne said, rushing back to the kitchen.

Even after two drinks, Odell was still acting kind of agitated. And he was saying things I didn't want to hear. "I hope none of our other neighbors seen what happened. They look up to me and Joyce. I'd hate for them to think we done got ourselves involved in a scandal," he grumbled.

"I wouldn't be too concerned about that, Odell. Y'all ain't involved. Milton was the one that got beat down," Yvonne pointed out. She was sitting on the arm of the couch, rubbing my shoulder.

"Yeah, but he ended up on our property, so we involved," Odell went on, talking out the side of his mouth. "Joyce is going to have a conniption fit when she see all the blood she got to sop up off that porch floor, which she just scrubbed last week."

"Tell Joyce I'll send Yvonne over with a bucket, some lye soap, and a sponge to help her. Next time somebody come after me, I'll run faster, and maybe they won't get me until I'm on my own property."

"You might not make it nowhere the next time," Odell predicted in a hollow tone.

CHAPTER 42
MILTON

A HALF HOUR AFTER ODELL LEFT, SOMEBODY ELSE KNOCKED.

"That's got to be Willie Frank," I said with hope.

Yvonne ran to the window and peeped out. "Uh-uh, Milton. It's Odell and Joyce. Can they come in?"

Since I was going to need Odell's help more than ever now, I didn't waste no time answering Yvonne's question. "Yup. Open the door and act normal."

She had her hand on the doorknob, but she didn't open the door right away. "Meaning what?"

"Don't get emotional and let something suspicious slip out. We don't want Joyce to start asking questions."

"Shhh!" Yvonne put her fingers up to her lips. "Don't talk so loud," she whispered. "If you talking about me letting something slip out about Odell and Betty Jean, why you bringing that up now? You almost got beat to death tonight! This ain't the time to be talking about that subject!"

"You in a weak state, and the wrong words might slip out. Now you open that door! We done kept them folks waiting long enough."

Yvonne gave me a impatient look before she flung the door open. "Good evening, y'all." She grinned, waving Joyce and Odell in. "Sorry it took so long for me to answer."

"We was beginning to think y'all was trying to avoid us," Joyce complained, looking around the room.

"I was using the toilet, and Milton is in too much pain to get up," Yvonne explained.

"Oh, Milton, bless your soul! Odell told me what happened," Joyce wailed, gawking at me like I'd been laid out for my wake. She sat down on the arm of the couch. "We would have come sooner, but Reverend Jessup called to update us about the upcoming Thanksgiving program. Y'all know how long winded he is."

Odell stood by the door, with his hands in his pockets and a stupid look on his face.

"How are you feeling, Milton?" Joyce asked.

"I'm . . . all . . . right," I replied, with a moan in between each word. "I appreciate you asking."

"You poor thing, you. I declare, Halloween brings out the worst in some people. Did you see who jumped you?"

"Joyce, I already told you he was attacked from behind," Odell tossed in. "And I don't think it had nothing to do with Halloween." Then he peered at me with that smug look on his face, which I seen too often. "Milton, I hope whoever done it ain't somebody you disrespected or . . . stole nothing from. I advise you to watch your step from now on. God got his eye on you, and we all know He don't like ugly."

Odell's earlier comment about all the devils being here was still ringing in my ears. If I hadn't heard what he said this time, I wouldn't have believed it. I looked at him with my mouth hanging open. This sucker had a lot of nerve preaching to me—especially after Reverend Jessup had dressed me and Yvonne down at church last Sunday. Some of the muscles in my body tensed up. I had to press my lips together to keep the wrong words from spurting out. Odell had been a little more sympathetic when he brung me home and helped Yvonne patch me up. Now here he was, showing off for Joyce. He was pushing all my buttons, but I was not about to let him get under my skin.

I kept my tone calm. "You right about God having his eye on me. But you should have said, 'He got his eye on *all of us*.'"

That comment made him flinch.

I went on. "I ain't never disrespected nobody, and I ain't never stole nothing from nobody."

"Somebody had to have a reason to attack you," Odell insisted.

"They might have got him mixed up with somebody else," Yvonne suggested.

"Or they might have been jealous," Joyce added.

Blaming alcohol to justify something stupid I'd done had worked before. I decided to get some mileage out of that. "Whatever I done to make somebody mad enough to jump me, I must have been so drunk, I didn't know what I was doing . . ."

"I figured that. If that's true, you weren't responsible for your actions. Just don't drink too much the next time," Joyce advised, giving me a stern look.

"Speaking of drinks, I sure need one," Yvonne admitted. Her eyes shifted from me to Joyce. "Joyce, Odell, y'all want something to drink?"

"Nothing for me tonight. We're going out for a late snack when we leave here," Joyce said.

"I don't want nothing, neither," Odell muttered.

"Milton, did they rob you?" Joyce asked.

"I don't know what they done after I blacked out. If it was robbery they was up to, they picked the wrong man, because my wallet was at home. The cash I had on me was in the bottom of my shoe. Robbers is too dumb to search there." I snorted and rubbed my nose. "Now that you brung up robbery, I remember something. I seen two rough-looking jokers lurking around when the farmer that gave me a ride home dropped me off at the corner. They must have recognized me and suspected I had a pocket full of money, so they followed me," I blurted out real quick. It could have been a robbery attempt, but it could have been another reason, too. By now almost every other colored bootlegger in town had a ax to grind with me and Yvonne. Especially them ones that used to entertain Lyla and Emmalou. "At least they didn't hurt me no worse. But in the shape I'm in, I don't know when I'll be able to go back to work. I declare, this is going to put a financial burden on me and Yvonne . . ."

I cut my eyes in Odell's direction. The expression on his face was so miserable, I thought he was going to puke. I didn't have to be a mind reader to know what he was thinking. He thought I was going to hit him up for even more cash. He was right.

"And I might have to stay home and take care of him," Yvonne threw in with a loud sigh.

Bless her.

"Sweet Jesus!" Joyce yelped. "I hope y'all don't have to take off work for too long. It would be hard on anybody to miss too many days off work with no pay." Her eyes suddenly got big. "I know what we can do to help." She gave Odell a anxious look. He looked as confused as I was. "I'm going to call up Reverend Jessup and have him get a prayer chain going. Last year, when Sister Foster lost her job cleaning house for Mayor Wilcox, we prayed nonstop for several days in a row for her to get an even better job. By the end of that week, the mayor begged her to come back. And he upped her salary by five percent."

A *prayer chain?* This husky heifer had to be kidding! By the time I got through with Odell, they would need a prayer chain a whole lot more than we did!

"How do you think a prayer chain is going to help us? If we don't work, we don't get paid, and Mr. Cunningham ain't never made no exceptions," Yvonne threw in.

"We'll pray that y'all won't have to be off work too many days," Joyce replied with a cheesy grin.

CHAPTER 43
YVONNE

EVERY TIME ODELL'S EYES MET MINE, HE TURNED HIS HEAD. AFTER my tense meeting with him yesterday afternoon, there was just no telling how he felt about me now. He didn't know how lucky he was, though, because I was letting him off easy. I didn't have no plans to shake him down for a payment every week like Milton. The money he already gave me, and a little something extra now and then, would suit me just fine. But with Milton having to miss work, his next paycheck would be skimpy, so I needed a few more bucks right away to fall back on. I had no choice but to plan another visit to Odell, and it had to be soon.

Joyce interrupted my thoughts. "Milton, if I didn't know what happened, I'd swear you'd been fighting with a bear. Thank the good Lord you're not any worse."

"He couldn't get no worse!" I yelled.

Joyce gave me a worrisome look. "Yes he could. He could be dead," she pointed out.

"Yeah, but with God's help, he won't die for a real long time," I sighed.

"And, with God's help, he'll be good as new in no time," Joyce added. "That's why I'm going to get in touch with Reverend Jessup tomorrow about that prayer chain."

All this gloomy talk was wearing me out. "If y'all don't mind, let's lighten up this dreary conversation," I suggested.

"I feel the same way." Joyce exhaled and turned to Odell,

looking and sounding less gloomy. "Sugar, we best be going now if we want to go to Mosella's for coffee and cake before they close." Then she looked at me. "Y'all need any pills, some iodine, or more bandages? We don't have much at the house. But I can have Odell open the store on our way home. We'll pick up whatever y'all need and drop it off when we get back. We can even sit awhile if y'all want us to."

Odell couldn't have looked more impatient if he tried when he tapped Joyce on her shoulder. "Baby, we told your folks we'd stop by after we leave Mosella's. It'll be way too late for us to come back over here tonight." His tone was as dry as a fish bone.

Joyce snapped her fingers, and her eyes rolled up in her head. "Oh, that's right. My daddy is a little under the weather. I told him we'd check on him tonight."

"We got plenty bandages and iodine. And Yvonne just opened a new bottle of aspirin," Milton muttered. "Thanks for being so considerate and generous, Joyce. You and Odell is the salt of the earth, and such a godsend to me and Yvonne. I hope your daddy don't get too sick." I noticed a devilish sparkle in his eyes as he went on. "Uh, Odell, speaking of daddies, how is yours getting along? You didn't go see him last weekend. I don't remember the last time you didn't go visit Lonnie on the Sabbath." It took me a few seconds to realize he was hinting at Odell's bogus weekend visits to his daddy.

"Huh? Uh, he doing about the same. I didn't go see him last Sunday, because I didn't want to miss Reverend Jessup's anniversary celebration, remember? Besides that, Daddy and Ellamae was visiting her folks out of town." Odell blinked hard and scratched the side of his face.

"Oh, yeah, I remember." Milton rubbed his head and moaned. "I declare, I'm aching in places where I ain't never ached before. I hope I'm up and about by tomorrow." When he stopped talking, he all of a sudden looked puzzled. "Hmmm. Time sure flies. I just realized tomorrow is *Wednesday*. Odell, if you ain't got nothing to do tomorrow after work, I sure would appreciate you coming by to check up on me. You, too, Joyce. I know I won't feel like hosting a bunch of drunks tomorrow night. But y'all's presence would do me a world of good."

"We'll come back tomorrow evening," Odell mumbled, with a tight look on his face.

"If we can get away from Daddy before it's too late, we'll be back tonight. And we'll come as often as we can until you get back on your feet." Joyce sounded truly concerned. Even with her and Odell's snooty ways and the fact that they said some stupid shit to us, their hearts was in the right place. The only problem was, theirs wasn't as big and good as mine and Milton's.

"I'd like that," Milton said with a smile. And that made me smile, too.

"We hate to run, but we can't stay another minute longer," Odell blurted out. Before anybody could say anything else, he took Joyce by the hand and they rushed out like somebody was chasing them.

I locked the door and turned to Milton and wagged my finger at him. "Shame on you!"

His eyes got big, and his mouth dropped open. "Huh?"

"Was it necessary to make that comment about Odell not visiting his daddy last Sunday? That was a underhanded insinuation about him spending so many of his weekends with the Betty Jean woman."

"I just need to make sure the secret between me and him stay fresh on his mind. If he get too lax, he might slip up and let Joyce catch him on her own," Milton said with a pout.

I cackled like a setting hen.

"What you laughing about, Yvonne?"

"It stopped being a secret between you and him when you told me. And why would you think something so scandalous ain't always fresh on his mind, anyway? Another thing, I thought you wanted us to avoid this subject."

"Never mind about that."

"Never mind, my ass. And what was up about that 'Wednesday' crack to Odell?" I was tempted to tell Milton I knew about his weekly "payday."

He ignored my question, and I wasn't going to harp on it. I didn't want to make this issue no bigger than it already was. And I didn't want him to trick me into telling him that I'd confronted Odell and shook him down for some hush money myself.

Milton coughed and moaned for a few seconds before he spoke again. "We need to talk about something a little more important. Like us having to miss work."

"We'll see how you feel in the next day or so. If you don't need me, I'll go in. I'll tell Mr. Cunningham and everybody else you fell off a truck."

"Okay, baby. Ask him to let you use his phone so you can get in touch with Willie Frank to let him know I got jumped. Be careful, and don't let nobody overhear you talking. Now help me to the bedroom."

Milton went to sleep right away after I put him to bed. I stayed awake for three more hours, thinking about what had happened and wondering if something even worse was coming our way.

I was sleepy and exhausted when I woke up Wednesday morning, a few minutes before seven. Milton was still asleep. When he felt me moving around, he opened his eyes and sat up.

"How you feeling, baby?" I asked.

He let out a weak moan. "Better than I felt last night." He had dark circles around his bloodshot eyes, and his voice was hoarse. I caressed his chin, and I was glad he didn't have no bruises there. But since he claimed he was feeling better, I did, too.

"Do you feel good enough to be by yourself so I can go to work today?"

"I believe I do," he answered. His voice was already sounding stronger. "Ain't no sense in us both missing work without pay if it ain't necessary."

After I washed Milton off, put more iodine on his wounds, and changed his bandages, I put him in fresh underwear, and he got back on the couch.

"I don't want you to be up stirring around, so I'll leave some sandwiches, aspirin, and a pitcher of water on the coffee table,"

I told him. "In case you decide you want to get buzzed, I'll set a jug of moonshine and a jar on the table, too. That way you can stay off your feet. And you better have your tail on this couch when I come home this evening! Do you hear me?"

"Yeah, I hear you," he whimpered. "What about when I need to use the toilet?"

"I'll set the slop jar close by. We out of toilet paper, so I'll leave some old newspapers for you to wipe yourself off with."

"Damn. I don't know how I'm going to get through today." Milton gave me a hopeless look.

"You ain't got no choice. And it might be more than one day."

"Shoot! That's going to be a heap of money for us to lose out on," he griped.

"Um, I'm going to leave right after I make them sandwiches and get everything else situated."

Milton glanced at the clock on the wall behind me. "You leaving this early?"

"Yeah. My monthly started early, and I just put on my last Kotex pad. I'm going to swing by next door on my way to the bus stop and see if I can borrow some from Joyce. She'll probably hold me hostage for a while. If you don't want me to go now, I'll have to rip up one of your white shirts and use makeshift pads until I can get to the store and buy some more."

"I ain't got but a few white shirts left! You better go get some of them yucky things from Joyce."

I didn't need no pads. I wasn't even on my period. It was the best excuse I could come up with to go next door. What I wanted to do was get a few bucks from Odell so I wouldn't have to pay him a visit at the store today. If Joyce was in the way and I couldn't talk to him, I'd tell her I'd come to borrow some pads.

I walked out the door fifteen minutes later and shot out our gate like a bronco at a rodeo. When I got to Odell's porch, I was surprised and pleased to see that Milton's blood was gone. I was also pleased that Odell answered when I knocked. He didn't look happy to see me as he motioned for me to come in.

Instead of saying hello, he asked in a gruff tone, "Is Milton doing worse?"

"No, he's doing a lot better. I'm making him stay home today. I see y'all mopped up the blood."

"Yeah. Joyce took care of it before we went to bed last night. She didn't want nobody to see it, and she didn't want it to get too dry and be harder to clean up."

"Oh. Well, if she had waited until this evening, I would have helped her. I cleaned up a lot of dried blood when I was in prison." I could hear Joyce humming in the background.

"Is there something you need this morning?" Odell asked with a raised eyebrow.

I leaned closer to him and whispered, "Can me and you go somewhere private?"

His eyes got wide, and he looked over his shoulder before he answered. "Again? What the hell for this time?" he whispered back.

"I need to talk to you about a financial matter."

"Shit! God damn!" He held up his hand. "Look, I ain't about to let you come up in my house with this 'financial matter' bull-shit."

Before I could go on, Joyce came prancing into the room, wiping her hands on a crisp pink apron.

"Good morning, Joyce. I was just telling Odell I needed to talk to you for a minute."

"Sure. I'm sorry we didn't come back last night. After we checked on Daddy, we ran into Buddy and his lady friend. His old jalopy had run out of gas, and we had to give them a ride home. What do you need to talk to me about?"

From the pinched look on Odell's face, I knew he wasn't going to leave the room until I left, so I said, "My menstruation snuck up on me a week early this month, and I just put on my last Kotex pad. Do you have a few I can borrow?" From the cor-ner of my eye, I seen Odell grimace and shudder.

"I got plenty. Come on to the bedroom."

She gave me a whole box. When we got back to the living room,

Odell was nowhere in sight. I could hear water running in the bathroom, so I assumed he was taking a bath.

"I don't mean to rush off, but the lady I ride to work with will be picking me up in a few minutes," Joyce said, walking me to the door. I had no choice but to leave. "We'll see y'all this evening. Now, you have a blessed day."

"Thanks, Joyce. You have a blessed day, too."

I was going to have to visit Odell at the store today, after all.

CHAPTER 44
MILTON

*Y*VONNE DIDN'T LIKE BEING ALONE IN A HOUSE. THE REASON WAS that the relatives that had raised her used to leave her on her own a lot. She said being alone made her think about her unhappy childhood. But her situation was not as serious as mine. I didn't like being in a house by myself day or night. And I was scared to death of the dark. Like most of the folks I knew, I was superstitious and believed in haints. Every time I heard a suspicious noise, or if our windows rattled when the wind wasn't blowing, my heart did push-ups.

When I was single, I went out of my way to get my lady friends to spend the night. Even when they did, I always slept with the lights on. When Yvonne came into my life, I became a changed man in a lot of ways. Within days after the night we first met, she brung out things in me I didn't know I had. I already had a lot of confidence, but she helped me finally feel handsome and smart. My fears didn't bother me as much no more. I didn't even need to leave the lights on when I turned in for the night with her.

Even though I was in my own house now, with all the windows and doors locked, I was still a little paranoid. Them devils that had followed me yesterday knew where I lived. If they was brazen enough to attack me on the street in broad daylight, what would stop them from busting into my house to finish me off?

Around 9:00 a.m. I heard what sounded like somebody scratching on my front door. I panicked. Yvonne had made me get rid of my knife because she didn't want me to cut nobody and go back to jail. If somebody busted in, I didn't have nothing to defend myself with but my fists. But they was so bruised and sore from my beating, they would be useless. I grabbed the butter knife I had used to cut my sandwiches with off the coffee table and scrambled up off the couch. I crept over to the window and peeped out. I was relieved when I didn't see nobody.

I cracked open the door and seen one of the cats that belonged to Janey Hemphill, the bug-eyed retired beautician that lived directly across the street. It stood in front of our threshold, meowing and sniffing my feet. The next thing I knew, the Hemphill woman came out her door in her bathrobe, with a frantic look on her face. She darted across the street and through our gate and didn't stop until she got up on our porch.

"Hello, Milton," she greeted, huffing and puffing like she'd just run a country mile. She scooped up her cat and cradled him in her arms like a baby. "I'm sorry—" She stopped talking, and her eyes bulged out more than usual. "What happened to you? Was you in a accident?"

"Yes, ma'am. I fell off the back of a truck."

"You must have fell in a right clumsy position to get them bruises on your face and have to wrap on a bandage like a headband."

"The truck I was riding on got too close to a cow-pasture fence, and I landed on my head smack-dab in the middle of some barbed wire."

"Goodness gracious. You better be more careful the next time. My nephew fell off a truck last year, and he wasn't as lucky as you. He hit his head on a big rock and died on the spot."

"I guess it wasn't my time to go, praise the Lord."

"I'm sorry Moses is bothering you again," she apologized, nuzzling the top of her pesky cat's head. "I can't keep this little booger from trespassing to save my soul."

"It ain't no big deal. That's what we get for forgetting to close our fence gate so much."

"This fussy little rascal took off when I tried to give him a bath."

"Moses must be looking for some more of them pigtails I gave him and his kin kitties last week." I laughed.

"I'm pleased you didn't give him none today. So long as you keep feeding my cats, they'll continue to pester you and Yvonne." She stared at me. "You don't look too good, so I won't keep you. Take care of yourself, now."

After the cat lady left, I got back on the couch, made myself comfortable, and dozed off.

When somebody stomped up on the porch at a few minutes before 10:00 a.m., I got up again. Before I could see who it was, Willie Frank unlocked the door and shot into the room like a cannonball. When he seen the mess I was, he done a double take.

"Great balls of fire!" He cussed under his breath and ran up to me. "I would have been here sooner, but my brother had my truck." He wrapped his arm around my shoulder and steered me back to the couch. I dropped down on it like a lead foot. "My God, buddy. You look like you been mauled by a mountain lion!" he yelled, plopping down next to me.

"I feel like it, too."

"Who done it?"

"There ain't no telling. They jumped me from behind. I couldn't even tell how many it was. Them low-down dogs," I griped.

"Aw, shuck it. I hope you'll be up and about by the time my birthday rolls around next Tuesday. Yvonne promised me a shindig better than the one y'all gave me last year."

"I'm pretty sure I'll be healed up enough by then. As long as I don't get another beating."

"Well, I'm surprised it took this long for you to get jumped. I'm grateful they didn't do nothing more serious. Like blowed your head off."

"I don't know nobody bold enough to go that far. Ain't a colored man alive want to end up in no prison."

It done me good to see so much compassion in Willie Frank's eyes. I knew he was going to help me and Yvonne get through this mess without us going crazy.

"That's a fact." He nodded and gave me a thoughtful look. "And the same holds true for a white man. Now look-a-here, since you don't know who done it, you can't even give the cops a description."

"Police? Pffft! I'd rather take another beating before I get involved with them scoundrels. For all we know, they could be the culprits that jumped me."

We laughed.

"You could be right. Well, is there anything I can do for you? Anything you want me to go get?"

"Naw. Yvonne made me some sandwiches. But before you leave, I'd appreciate it if you'd empty the slop jar, put some fresh water in the pitcher, and fetch me some more liquor."

Willie Frank stayed two hours and probably would have stayed longer if I hadn't kept dozing off. Them pills Yvonne had made me take last night and again this morning made me drowsy.

By the middle of the afternoon, I was wide awake. All kinds of thoughts was bouncing against the walls inside my head. My legs and feet felt crampy one minute and numb the next. It wasn't so bad after I got up and paced around the floor for about ten minutes. That helped get my blood back circulating the way it was supposed to.

I did my best thinking laying down. I stretched back out on the couch and started planning my next move. I was going to have to put the squeeze on Odell even tighter.

CHAPTER 45
YVONNE

I KNEW ME AND MILTON HAD A LOT OF ENEMIES NOW, BUT WE STILL had a lot of friends, too. I got a lot of sympathy from our coworkers and regular customers when I told them about his "accident." I even got bigger tips than I usually got. A bunch of folks wanted to know if they could visit Milton, but I told them to wait a day or two.

"Yvonne, you want me to come to the house tonight to help you serve drinks so Milton can stay off his feet?" Talking to me was Marvin Kelly, one of our best customers and a good friend. He let me and Milton borrow his truck every now and then.

"Thanks for the offer, Marvin. But that won't be necessary. Willie Frank will be there to take up the slack. I'll tell Milton what you said, and I promise you the next time you come to the house, you can drink for free." I didn't care how corrupt me and Milton was, we still knew when to show some compassion.

Mr. Cunningham was real concerned when I told him Milton had got hurt. He was such a sweetheart about it. "Yvonne, tell Milton I'm going to pray for him. He can stay home as many days as he need to. It won't be easy, but we can make do without him."

"Well, we can't afford for him to stay off too many days." I sounded as pitiful as I could.

It helped, because Mr. Cunningham said something that made

my heart sing. "Tell Milton he ain't got to worry." He folded his arms and gave me a warm smile. "I'm going to pay him half his salary for every day he take off. But only up to five."

"Thank you!" The smile on my face stretched so fast and wide, my lips ached. "He'll be so pleased when I tell him."

"It'll probably be the first and last time I can do something like this for y'all. So he better be more careful riding them trucks from now on."

"I'm sure he will be."

We was in the kitchen alone, but Mr. Cunningham glanced around and started talking in a low tone. He unfolded his arms and gave me a pat on my shoulder. "I wouldn't do this for no-body else, so don't tell your coworkers. See, you and Milton is two of the best employees I got, and the daughter and son I always wanted. I know it's been a few days since I came out to y'all's house for a few drinks. But my liver can't stand but so much. Me and my wife might come by to see Milton in the next day or so."

I got tears in my eyes and couldn't stop myself from giving Mr. Cunningham a hug. He was one of the few people I didn't like to take advantage of too much. But since he was in such a good mood, I had to milk the cow while the milking was good. "Uh, if you don't mind, I'd like to take a little longer for lunch today. I need to go into town and pick up some bandages and pills for Milton."

"Can't you do that when you get off work?"

"The store I need to go to closes up at the same time I get off," I explained, trying to sound pitiful enough to keep his charitable juices flowing. "I asked Marvin and a couple of other folks if I could use their trucks, but they have to get back to work. I'll have to take the bus, so it'll take me quite a while . . ."

"Hmmm. That's a damn shame." Mr. Cunningham scratched his chin and gave me a thoughtful look. "Well, you welcome to use my truck again if you want to. It's just sitting out there in the parking lot."

"Bless your heart!" I squealed. I hugged him again.

* * *

When I walked through the door at MacPherson's, I smelled all kinds of nice aromas coming from the food section. I was tempted to ask for a complimentary pig foot to gnaw on, but they was usually passed out only to folks who had a lot of shopping to do.

"I heard Milton fell off a truck," Sadie began, looking at me with the same sneer on her face she always had when I approached her. I knew she and Buddy was itching to drill me like a oil well.

I gasped and stopped. "How did you hear that so fast? You must have some good connections." Them was the kind of lines that made her and Buddy rejoice and puff out their chests.

"That's true," she agreed.

"So do I," Buddy gushed.

"We got spies everywhere," Sadie added with a smirk.

"I bet he was drunk," Buddy threw in.

"He was. I fussed up a storm, so I know it'll be a while before he do something that stupid again. Um, I hate to run off, but I need to go ask Odell a question. We'll continue this conversation next time I come in, if y'all ain't too busy."

I started walking toward Odell's office. When I reached it, he was already standing in the doorway, with his hands on his hips. Words could not describe the expression on his face as he waved me into his office and shut the door.

"I thought I heard your voice," he snapped. "This got anything to do with your visit to my house this morning?"

"Uh-huh. Because of what happened to Milton, I need more money."

"I figured one of y'all would be asking for more money again real soon."

"You figured right."

"How is he doing?" Odell blew out a loud breath, sat down at his desk, and tapped his fingertips on the desktop, looking at me like I was something he'd spit out.

"Real good. I doubt if he'll be off work more than a few days."

I moved closer to the front of the desk and cleared my throat. "I borrowed Mr. Cunningham's truck, so I can't stay long."

"Okay. So how much do you need now?"

"I need a few more dollars."

"How few?"

"Whatever you can spare."

"Look, Yvonne. I feel for you and Milton, but even the deepest well will run dry if you draw water from it too often. Now, tell me exactly how much you need."

"I told you. Just a few dollars."

"A few like two, three, or more?"

I shook my head. "More like ten."

Odell's eyes almost popped out of his head. "What's wrong with you, girl? I'm just a working man, not a millionaire!"

"If you can afford to support two women and three kids, you can afford to give me ten more dollars."

With a huff and a frown, he pulled out his wallet and handed me a ten-dollar bill. I snatched it like it was a brass ring. "How many more times are you going to come at me for money?"

"I told you the first time we discussed this that I'd only want a little something every now and then. I should have included unexpected emergencies, so I'm telling you that now. I wouldn't be here if Milton hadn't got beat up."

"I hope you don't have another emergency again for a while. I'll be coming over to give Milton his payment this evening, and something tells me he'll ask for a 'few dollars' on top of that to cover his time off work." For such a strapping man, I couldn't believe how weary Odell was starting to look and sound. "You ain't told him about our arrangement, I hope."

"Nope. And I don't plan on telling him. It's bad enough he started getting money from you and didn't tell me. It serves him right not to know I got a thing going with you, too."

He exhaled and stared at me with a stern look on his face. "Before you go, we need to get something straight."

"What?" I asked, stuffing the money inside my brassiere.

"You know how folks in this town like to spread gossip and

start rumors. You done been here twice this week to meet with me behind closed doors. That must look mighty suspicious to Buddy and Sadie. I don't want them, or nobody else, to get it in their heads that me and you got something going. That's a story Joyce don't never need to hear."

"Or the one about Betty Jean," I taunted as I backed out the door.

CHAPTER 46
MILTON

I WAS STILL STRETCHED OUT ON THE COUCH WHEN YVONNE GOT home from work this evening. Willie Frank had changed my bandages and poured me another drink before he left. The cat lady had come back and brung me a bowl of homemade chicken soup. I must have been in pretty good shape to begin with, because I was already feeling almost like my old self. But I liked being pampered and having folks feel sorry for me.

"How you feeling, sugar?" Yvonne asked. She set her purse on the coffee table and squatted down next to the couch.

"I'm doing better," I whimpered with a grimace. "What did Mr. Cunningham say when you told him I fell off a truck and had to take a few days off?"

"He was as sorry as he could be," she told me, massaging my shoulder. "He even let me borrow his truck to go get you some more pills."

"Oh? That was mighty generous of him. But we still got plenty pills left. What kind did you get?"

"Huh? Oh! I wanted to get something stronger than plain aspirin. MacPherson's was out of the kind we usually buy, so I didn't get nothing."

I narrowed my eyes. "MacPherson's? So you seen Odell today, huh?"

Yvonne tried to make out like it wasn't no big deal. "Just for a hot minute. I ducked into his office to say hi."

I stared at her for a long time. "How was he acting?"

"Like always. He'll be coming over this evening. Joyce will, too, I think."

"Good. When he get here, offer to make him some of them butter-flavored hush puppies he so crazy about. It'll make him feel appreciated. With his big-ass ego, it's important for us to keep him feeling like somebody special in case I have to keep, uh, borrowing a few dollars from him when we need it."

Yvonne stopped massaging my shoulder. "You sure you feel up to having guests tonight?" she asked with a puzzled look on her face.

"Uh-huh. The more the merrier. Willie Frank didn't stay long this morning, and it was lonesome laying here by myself most of the day, sweating, aching, and passing gas. I'm feeling and smelling mighty ripe. Go fill up the foot tub with water and soap so I can de-funk myself before folks start coming. I sure hope Lyla and Emmalou come tonight. We can always count on them for a few extra bucks. I didn't know they was so generous."

Yvonne shot me a hot look. "Milton, please don't start borrowing money from Lyla and Emmalou."

With my condition being what it was, I figured a little whining would be justified. I showed her my best puppy-dog face before I spoke again. "I ain't said nothing about borrowing no money from them. Even though we sure could use a little extra since Mr. Cunningham won't be paying me while I'm off."

"Good news!" Yvonne's eyes got big, and she gave me a wall-to-wall smile. "He is going to pay you half your salary for every day you take off, but only up to five days."

"He is?"

"Yeah. He said we was two of his best workers, and the kids he always wanted."

"Praise the Lord. That's the best news I done heard this year. I'm feeling good enough to go back tomorrow, so he'll just have to pay me for today."

"Milton, maybe you should stay off tomorrow, too. A bunch of them railroad workers came in for lunch today. They gave me some good tips, so we a few dollars ahead."

"I don't like being in the house for hours on end by myself. The sooner I get back in the swing of things, the better I'll feel."

"I hope that 'swing of things' don't include you gambling again anytime soon. You don't know who it was that jumped you, and it might have been some of the same men you been gambling with. You show up at one of their games and they see they didn't do enough damage to you, there ain't no telling what might happen next."

"Listen, any gambling I do until I get whoever jumped me off my case, I'll do at home, or with folks I know I can trust."

I decided to stay home from the grill Thursday, too.

A few minutes after we finished eating the scrumptious supper Yvonne cooked when she got home Thursday evening, folks started knocking on the door. I was thrilled to pieces to see Lyla and Emmalou in the first bunch.

About a hour later, Odell and Joyce strolled in. I could tell from the tight look on his face that he wasn't too excited about being back in my house again so soon. Him and Joyce had come over for a little while last night to see how I was doing, and for him to give me my weekly payment. It had been kind of awkward for him to sneak it to me, with people in the living room and me not able to get up off the couch and take him into the kitchen or the bedroom. I had had to wait until he was about to leave. Joyce had leaned down and held my hand while she prayed for me. When she finished, Odell had done the same thing. That was when he'd pushed eight crumpled-up dollar bills into my hand.

Since Joyce was with him tonight—and claimed she was the one that had been itching to come check on me again—I knew he'd have to stay more than a few minutes. I was feeling good enough to stand and walk longer. So a few minutes after they walked in, I beckoned Odell to follow me to the kitchen. We stopped a few feet in front of the back door.

"It's good to see you doing so much better. I guess this means you'll be going back to work soon, huh?" he asked. He was already acting nervous, scratching his head and blinking.

"Yup. I'm going back in tomorrow. This laying around like a invalid ain't my thing." I held out my hand, palm up and fingers wiggling. From the horrified look on his face, you would have thought he was staring down the barrel of a gun.

"What?" he asked dumbly.

"There was too many folks too close by, so I didn't get a chance to tell you last night. But I need more money to help cover the time I have to take off from the grill." I wasn't fool enough to tell Odell that Mr. Cunningham was going to pay me for some of my time off.

"Shit! I guess I should have seen this coming!" he blasted. "How much?"

Regardless of his harsh tone, I kept mine pleasant. "I declare. I'm so impressed with how easy it is to work with you, I'll go easy on you this time. Just give me another eight dollars."

He mumbled a few cusswords under his breath, pulled out his wallet, and handed me a five and three ones.

"Thank you." I clapped him on the back. Then I stuffed the money in my pocket, where it would stay until I got a chance to hide it from Yvonne. "Um, as you know, I done missed two days' work this week. Next Wednesday, I'll need a double payment. That way I'll have a little leeway—in case I relapse and have to miss more days."

Odell blinked and shook his head and didn't even put up no argument. I realized now just how determined he was to keep me from tattling on him.

"Well, now, let's get out there and have some fun. Have a drink, and tonight you ought to do some dancing," I said.

"I ain't hardly in the mood to be dancing," he said in a sharp tone. "I wouldn't even be here now if it wasn't for Joyce. She and Reverend Jessup got a bunch of folks at the church—including my in-laws—to start a prayer chain for you. But she still want to keep a close eye on you herself."

"Bless her soul." Knowing that so many folks cared about me done a lot for my morale. Maybe that was the reason I was recovering so fast. "Well, I hope you have a good time tonight, anyway. We got some good party people in the house. Business sure picked up since Lyla and Emmalou started coming."

Odell must not have been too anxious to leave. By eleven thirty, him and Joyce was the only guests left.

"I declare, it's way past our bedtime, so we'd better shake a leg," Joyce finally said, getting up off the footstool she'd been sitting on most of the evening. She stretched and glanced from me to Yvonne. "Um, me and Odell have had a few conversations about Lyla and Emmalou lately." She stopped and looked at Odell like she expected him to pick up where she had left off. And he did.

"Do y'all think it's such a good idea to still be entertaining them?" he asked.

"As long as they don't cause no ruckus, why not?" I answered.

"For one thing, they connected to Cap and some of them other rough jook joints and bootleggers," Odell pointed out.

"Lyla and Emmalou could be the reason you got jumped, Milton," Joyce said, giving me a hopeless look. "You notice nobody bothered you before they started coming here."

"Pffft! Business is business. I know y'all noticed how giddy the men was here tonight, when they danced with Lyla and Emmalou," I argued.

"Lyla had a fling with Cap, and he still got the hots for her. If a colored man is crazy enough to risk his life to be with a white woman, there ain't no telling what else he might do to somebody that's taking her attention away from him," Odell warned.

"Milton, don't forget it's against the law in this state for colored men to get too close to white women," Joyce added.

"It's against the law in this state to bootleg, but I ain't going to stop doing it." I laughed and turned to Odell with a self-satisfied smirk on my face. I said the next words real slow and clear so he could know they was meant just for him. "Folks, especially men, will do whatever they want to do as long as they don't get caught."

I liked to mess with him, because it was fun to watch him squirm whenever I threw a Betty Jean hint at him. "Ain't that right, Odell?"

"Right," he mumbled, with his jaw twitching. His contempt for me was so thick, it would take a machete to cut through it.

CHAPTER 47
YVONNE

Milton didn't mind having a few small Band-Aids on his face. But he didn't want to wear that bandage wrapped around his head when he went back to work on Friday. He was too vain to go out in public wearing something like that. He said it made him feel self-conscious. He wore a stocking cap instead.

Mr. Cunningham and all our coworkers was thrilled that Milton was back. We got so busy right away, me and him didn't even take no breaks. That impressed Mr. Cunningham even more. At five minutes to 4:00 p.m. he came up to me in the dining area, grinning from ear to ear.

"Yvonne, go out to the kitchen and tell Milton I said for you and him to go home a hour early. I appreciate how hard y'all worked today. But I don't want him to wear hisself out. He could have been killed falling off that truck. I'm surprised, and pleased, that he didn't take off but two days—and I'll pay him half his salary for both, like I told you I would. Now, y'all skedaddle."

A few minutes after we started walking to the bus stop, a regular customer that had just finished his meal drove up behind us and offered us a ride home.

At 6:00 p.m., Joyce was at our door by herself, holding a handkerchief. Without saying nothing, she brushed past me and dropped down so hard on the couch, her legs went up in the air and one of her shoes flew off.

"Where is Odell?" I asked.

"Today's Friday, remember?" she said in a weak voice, sliding her foot back into her shoe. Then she hawked into the handkerchief. "He didn't even come home for supper. Right after he closed up, he went straight to go check on his daddy. He won't be back home until Sunday night." She put the handkerchief in her purse and looked toward the back of the room. "Anybody else here yet?"

"Naw. Besides you, me and Milton is the only ones in the house so far. Folks usually start trailing in around seven on Friday nights."

"Good. I don't want anybody else to hear me so they can go out and start a rumor," she said.

My ears perked up so quick, I heard a ringing noise. "Start a rumor about what? Is that why you seem distressed?"

She bobbed her head. "Yvonne, I think something is going on with Odell. Something worrisome."

"Like what?" Milton asked, walking into the room with a look on his face like he was about to laugh.

He still had the Band-Aids on his face but nothing on his head. There was a jar of moonshine in his hand. When he handed it to Joyce, she took such a long pull, I thought she was going to empty the jar in one gulp. I sat down at the other end of the couch, and Milton stood leaning up against the wall facing us, with his arms folded.

"You want to tell us why you think something is going on with Odell?" he said.

Before she answered, she drunk some more. "Lately, he hasn't been eating much. When we went to bed last night, he tossed and turned off and on for hours. And he's been looking worried for the past few days." Joyce let out a hiccup and wiped her lips with the back of her hand.

"Did you mention it to him?" I asked.

"I tried more than once. But he claims he's fine. Y'all know how happy-go-lucky Odell is all the time. Since the day I met him, I've never known him to be depressed." Joyce stopped long enough to blow out a loud breath. From the dreamy-eyed look that suddenly popped up on her face, I had a feeling she was going to say something that would make me roll my eyes. She did. And her eyes was smack-dab on Milton when she said it. "I bet every colored man in town wish they were *half* as smart, successful, dapper, handsome, and humble as Odell." Joyce was so blind in love with Odell, she didn't even notice how Milton's jaws started twitching. I didn't know if she meant to or not, but she had just low-rated my husband *again*.

"Oh, I wouldn't worry about Odell. If something is bothering him, he would have let you know by now," I insisted.

"Me and him done got closer since we met. If he got a problem he scared to tell you about, I'm sure he would have told me by now," Milton said.

Joyce looked at Milton like he had turned into a toad. "*You?* I don't care how close you and Odell are, you're probably the last person in the world he'd tell something before he told me!" she shot back.

The wounded look on Milton's face was so extreme, it made me cringe. I didn't know how many more of her and Odell's put-downs we could stand. When Milton had let me know how painful being put down was to him, I'd promised myself that I'd never low-rate him in favor of Odell again myself. I had to press my lips together and keep them that way for a few seconds to keep from saying something I'd probably regret. It was a good thing I could control my rage, and in this case, it was a smart move. Each day, our vested interest in Joyce and Odell increased. I didn't want to do nothing to derail the gravy train me and Milton was already on.

"I bet it's his daddy," she went on. "Lonnie's probably dying, and Odell doesn't want to upset me. That's the only thing I can think of that would have him so down in the dumps."

"Well, Lonnie is in bad health. And I hate to say this, but we all got to go sometime. And ain't too many folks in this town done lived as long as your daddy," I said, sounding as sympathetic as I could. And I really was.

"My daddy is even older than Odell's, and he's still kicking," Joyce said, sounding much stronger and not as worried now.

"If it ain't his daddy he so worried about, can you think of anything else it might be?" Milton asked, looking at her from the corner of his eye.

Joyce came up with the stupidest thing I expected to hear. "You mean like him having a health issue that he doesn't want me to find out about yet?"

"Uh-huh. That would be my guess," Milton said.

She had a deadpan expression on her face for a few moments. "No, I don't think that's it. Odell is as fit as a fiddle." Then she gasped. "Lord, I hope he's not foolish enough to be involved with cards and dice, like some men! Gambling is one of the worst sins." That was *another* jab at Milton.

"I don't think he'd be that foolish, neither. Not with a woman like you behind him." Milton was being sarcastic, but it went right over Joyce's head.

"Well, I'm going to keep a close eye on him these next few days. If his mood gets any more serious, I'll make him tell me what's going on!" Joyce vowed, with her tongue snapping over every single word.

"If I was in your shoes, that's exactly what I'd do," I told her.

CHAPTER 48

MILTON

BY 10:00 P.M., THE HOUSE WAS JUMPING. THE LIVING ROOM WAS packed to the gills, and folks was still coming. I was glad Joyce was in a better mood. She had even danced a few times. And she hadn't said nothing else stupid enough to make my chest tighten up.

The only thing I was concerned about was the way Aunt Mattie kept shooting mean looks at Lyla and Emmalou because of all the attention they was getting. Since they'd walked in the door around nine, most of the men had stopped dancing and chatting with the colored women and had got all over them. When Lyla and Emmalou sat down on the couch, Aunt Mattie got up and headed to the kitchen. I waited a few minutes and followed her. She was sitting at the table, leafing through the latest Sears and Roebuck catalog.

"Aunt Mattie, you all right?"

"I done had better days," she snarled, giving me the evil eye. "I know you and Yvonne like the fact that them peckerwood hussies is good for y'all's business. But they bad for mine. I brung Tiny, Sweet Sue, and Dee Dee with me tonight because this is payday for most of the men here."

"Lyla and Emmalou ain't here to make money. They just come to have a good time, like everybody else."

"How come they stopped going to 'have a good time' at them jook joints and the other bootleggers' houses?"

I scratched my neck and snickered. "Well, for the same reasons a lot of other folks stopped going. We got good entertainment, complimentary snacks, and some of the best and cheapest
drinks available. But one of the main reasons is, we live in a quiet,
safe neighborhood—nowhere near them swamps and woods, like
them other places. Our guests ain't got to worry about getting
robbed, falling into quicksand, getting bit by snakes or mauled
by bobcats. Besides that, the fossils running them other places is
so old, they done forgot how to be fun hosts. We make our
guests feel more alive, carefree, and young."

"Well, this 'fossil' don't feel 'alive, carefree, and young' when
somebody interferes with my income. Shoot. I got bills to pay.
Ain't nary one of them black-ass suckers here tonight going to
make no dates with my girls while them white women hogging
all their attention."

"That ain't our problem. You do your business whichever way
you want, but not in our house. Now, if you got a problem with
who me and Yvonne entertain, you can drink at home or at another house. Shoot. You, of all people, should know that when
it come to business, we all do what we have to do to make our
money."

I didn't like to sass elderly people, especially Aunt Mattie. She
was a good friend, and I'd been one of her girls' favorite tricks
for years. On top of that, everybody knew she practiced hoodoo.
She kept a lot of folks in line by threatening to put hexes on
them. I didn't want no witch doctor mad at me, so I decided to
do some backpedaling.

"Um, Aunt Mattie, I been looking up to you since I was a little
boy. You remind me so much of both my grandmothers—may
they rest in peace in heaven until I join them—so I got a whole
lot of love and respect for you. I'm sorry I sassed you. You know
how crazy I get when I'm drinking. I hope I didn't hurt your
feelings." I gave her the most apologetic look I could.

She gazed at me for a few seconds with her eyes narrowed before she gave me a smile. "Aw, shuck it, Milton. I'm just a business-
woman always looking for more money. I guess I done got too
greedy in my old age. Don't pay me no mind."

"Whew! Praise God you ain't mad at me." I lowered my voice. "I been romping with your girls since I was in my teens, and I sure don't want to make you mad enough to blow the whistle on me. Yvonne would kill me dead."

"You ain't got to worry about me or my girls telling. If it wasn't for married men, every sporting house in America would go out of business. We ain't tattled to the wives on nary one of the husbands yet. Since most of our tricks—colored and white—is married, we do most of our work at the house during the day hours, when they can sneak away from work on their lunch breaks. That's why I come over here with some of my girls at night two or three nights a week, hoping we can drum up a few more tricks." Aunt Mattie glanced at the door. Then she whispered, "You just make sure you keep paying your tab—which is behind again."

"Don't worry. I'll catch it up directly. Now, listen, I want you and some of your girls to come next Tuesday night to help us celebrate Willie Frank's thirty-fifth birthday. There'll be a heap of horny men here who your girls can make dates with."

"Oh, we'll be here with bells on."

"Make sure you bring that Sweet Sue. She is Willie Frank's favorite these days. I'll be coming to your house to check her out myself real soon."

"Good! Bless your heart, Milton." Aunt Mattie teetered up out of her chair, and I took her arm and escorted her back to the living room.

Business was pretty good Saturday night. But Sunday was slow. We didn't have but ten guests, so I entertained in my bathrobe and bare feet. After everybody left around 11:00 p.m., I put my shoes on.

"Where you going?" Yvonne asked, walking into the living room in her nightgown.

"I'm going outside for a few minutes to get some fresh air and smoke me some rabbit tobacco. And my legs just started cramping, so I might walk to the end of the block to get the blood flowing right."

"Okay, sugar. If I wasn't so sleepy, I'd walk with you. You should take a stick or my rolling pin with you in case you get jumped again."

I brushed her off with a wave. "I doubt if anybody is lurking around this neighborhood, looking to do me harm this time of night."

The lights was still on next door, so I knew Joyce and Odell hadn't gone to bed yet. He answered the door when I knocked.

"Milton! You know how late it is?" he hissed, wincing like something was caught in his eye. I figured by now I had become a thorn in his side the size of a watermelon.

"I ain't going to stay but a minute. Can I come in?"

He glanced over his shoulder and then back at me with a nervous look on his face. "I'd rather talk right here at the door," he whispered in that snippy tone he'd been using with me lately. "What is it now?"

"Believe it or not, I didn't come to ask for money. Unless you want to give—"

He cut me off by holding his hand up to my face. "Don't talk so loud. Joyce is in the bathroom, but she got big ears." He glanced over his shoulder again and shifted his weight from one foot to the other. His jaws was twitching, and his eyes was blinking. "Milton, if you didn't come for money, what did you come for?"

He was still whispering, so I started whispering, too. "I just wanted to let you know Joyce is getting suspicious."

His jaw dropped, and his eyes got big. "Why do you say that?"

"When she came to the house Friday night, she told us you ain't been eating or sleeping right, and you been looking worried. All that's worrying her."

"What did y'all say to her?" Even in the cool night air, sweat popped up on Odell's face. I couldn't believe how a man who got distressed enough to start sweating at the drop of a hat could be involved in such scandalous activity.

"We didn't say nothing you need to be concerned about." I looked him straight in the eyes and said, "Not this time . . ."

He lowered his voice even more. "Look, I'm paying you good money to keep your mouth shut."

"As long as you keep doing that, I will keep my mouth shut."

"Is that what you came to tell me?"

"Yeah, but now that I'm here, I need to ask a favor."

Odell narrowed his eyes and glared at me. "Can you move this along?"

"Okay. You know me and Yvonne is planning a shindig for Willie Frank's birthday. I need a few items from the store, and I don't want to use my credit account or spend what little bit of money I got."

Odell looked relieved, and he finally stopped whispering. "Come by the store, and I'll let you get whatever you need. Now, if you don't mind, I need to get back to Joyce."

"One more thing." I wagged my finger in his face. "I don't think it's safe for me to be out walking too far and too often these days."

"Then don't," he snapped, giving me a impatient look. "If you afraid of getting jumped again, keep taking the bus and ride with Willie Frank more often."

"That won't solve the problem. The bus only run certain hours, and Willie Frank's truck ain't always available when we need to use it. Us getting around is getting tiresome."

Odell closed his eyes and massaged the back of his neck. When he opened his eyes, they was glaring at me three times as hard as they usually did. "If you expect me to provide transportation for you to get around town, you can forget it. I'm a busy man!"

"Tell me about it. You must be the busiest man I know. By the way, how is that other lady doing these days?" I snickered.

"Shhh! Keep your voice down. Uh, 'that other lady' is doing fine. Now, will you leave so I can get to bed? My wife is waiting for me."

"I bet she is." I chuckled. "And I hope you give her enough of your roaming *tallywacker* to keep her happy until the next time she have to spend a couple of days by herself." I let out a deep sigh and looked at Odell like I was in awe—and I was. "Tell me something, my man. You go do Betty Jean once or twice during the week, and you spend whole weekends with her. Then you come home and lay some loving on Joyce. Man, I wish you could bottle and sell whatever you—"

Odell held his hands up in my face and cut me off again. "Milton, I don't want to hear another word from you tonight."

"All right, I'm leaving. We can discuss the car you going to help me get later."

He gulped so hard, his eyes crossed. "What car?"

"I can see you can't take a hint. That's what I been trying to tell you. We can discuss it on Wednesday, when you come to the house with my money."

"You think I'm going to get you a car?"

"Why not? I need one, and you can get it for me."

"The hell I will!"

"The hell you won't."

CHAPTER 49
YVONNE

*I*T HAD BEEN ALMOST A WEEK SINCE I'D VISITED ODELL AT HIS OF-
fice and got them ten dollars. Him and Joyce had been to our
house a few times since then, but he'd avoided me like I had a
deadly contagious disease. With Milton's paycheck being short,
and us having a couple of slow nights at the house, our money
was real tight now, and I was going to do something about it.

On top of our regular expenses, I got a letter from Aunt Nadine last week telling me she'd lost her wallet. It had all the
money she had to her name in it, so she and my uncle needed
some financial help from me this month. They had never asked
me to help support my kids and had refused the many times I'd
offered them money. There was no way I wouldn't come
through for them now.

It was time for me to pay Odell another visit. Today was as
good a day as any, so I planned to go back to his office on my
lunch break. Mr. Cunningham had already told me I could use
his truck again so I could go into town and pick up a birthday
present for Willie Frank.

I didn't say nothing to Milton about it until a few minutes before I left. He was tending to some steaks he had just put on the
grill when I went up to him. Before either one of us could say
anything, I hauled off and gave him a peck on his mouth to
soften him up. That put a smile on his face.

"You want to eat lunch in the kitchen today or outside, under one of the pecan trees?" he asked. "I can't leave until I finish this order, though. Give me another fifteen minutes."

"Um, don't worry about it. I have to make a run into town, and I have to use Mr. Cunningham's truck now because he needs to go somewhere in a hour."

Milton gave me a curious look. "What you need to go to town for?"

"To get a present for Willie Frank."

"Why come? We already got him a new belt and a month's worth of chewing tobacco."

"I know. But he is so helpful to us. I want to do something extra special for him this year," I insisted. "I was thinking about getting him a necktie."

Milton couldn't have looked more amused if a dancing bear had just shimmied into the kitchen. He threw his head back and laughed. "A *necktie?* Willie Frank ain't no Clark Gable. That old, mangy hound dog he got would wear a tie before he would."

"You don't know that. Just because we ain't never seen him wear one don't mean he wouldn't wear one if he had it. If it wasn't for his snaggletoothed grin, he could look as dapper as you do when you wear one of your pin-striped suits."

"Humph. *Neckties* and *dapper* is words that don't cross my mind when I think about hillbillies. Go on and get him one if that's what you want to do. But if I was going to get him something else, it would be a pair of suspenders or some long johns." Milton laughed again and returned his attention to the steaks, and I took off.

When I got to the street MacPherson's was on, I stopped at the end of the block and got out. I didn't want to park in front of the store, where Buddy and Sadie could see me through the window and be waiting to bombard me with a bucketload of new gossip and nosy questions when I walked through the door. I was going to rush in and rush out.

Halfway down the block, a older man with reddish-brown skin and thick, unkempt gray hair crossed the street and came straight

up to me. It was Delroy Crutchfield, one of the jealous bootleggers that had been running all over town, bad-mouthing me and
Milton. This devil was the same one that had let us get married
in his living room. He blocked my path, so I didn't have no
choice but to stop.

"Hello, Yvonne. Bless my soul! I ain't seen you in a coon's age.
Since you and Milton live on the upper south side now, I hope
you ain't too siddity to speak to me."

"Hi, Delroy. It's been so long, I almost didn't recognize you."

He grunted and looked me up and down. "Well, I'd recognize
a sweet-looking redbone like you even with my eyes closed." He
leered at me with his lips parted and the tip of his tongue stick-
ing out. "Milton was in the right place at the right time when
you showed up at my place that night y'all first met."

"Sure enough. I'm still thanking the Lord for sending me
over there."

"Well, I hope He send you to my house again. Maybe I'll get
lucky like Milton done, huh?" He laughed.

"If you do, it won't be with me. Now that I'm married, I ain't
got no use for another man."

"Oh well. That's life." Delroy pursed his lips and shrugged.
"Anyway, I hear you and your husband is planning to throw a big
birthday bash tomorrow night for y'all's pet peckerwood."

"If you mean Willie Frank, *our best friend*, you heard right," I
hissed. "I'm on my way to MacPherson's to pick up a present
for him."

"Well, do say. Nary one of my women never gave me no presents. Maybe I should get me a generous, considerate woman
like you, huh?"

"Maybe you should."

"Oh, by the way, I heard Milton got hurt falling off the back of
Willie Frank's truck. Humph. I guess Willie Frank don't think
much of him if he don't allow him to ride in the cab with him.
That's a peckerwood for you. It ain't bad enough they want us to
ride in the back of the bus. They want us to ride in the back of
the truck, too."

"It wasn't Willie Frank's truck he fell off. For your informa-tion, whenever me and Milton ride with Willie Frank, we always sit in the cab with him."

"Humph. I ain't surprised. *Uncle Toms* always get treated bet-ter by the man. Is Milton doing all right?"

I was already mad and itching to be on my way, so I was going to let that Uncle Tom remark slide. But I had to answer his last question. "Milton is doing just fine and is back to work at the grill already."

"That's good. Lucky for him, he didn't get busted up too bad."

"I'll tell him you said that."

I started walking away, and Delroy moved right along with me. I had heard that his business had gone deep south. The soles of his scruffy shoes flapped with each step he took, and half the buttons on his green flannel shirt was missing. I almost felt sorry for him, because he used to dress up in suits and spats and keep his hair neat and trimmed.

"Tell him I hope he don't fall off another truck . . ." Delroy slapped the side of his thigh and laughed like a hyena.

"I will. Now, you have a blessed day. Bye." I started stepping as fast as I could and didn't look back. But I could still hear Delroy laughing.

Before I reached MacPherson's front door, another devil came around the corner. He stopped right in front of me. It was Lester Fullbright, the used-to-be I thought I'd marry, until I found out he was fooling around with my best friend. I already had a heap of worries waiting in line, and I wasn't in the mood to add another—especially one I thought I had put behind me.

"Well, do say!" Lester boomed. "This is a mighty big surprise." Except for a few strands of gray hair, he hadn't changed.

"Hello, Lester. How you been?"

"Doing fine. And you?"

"I'm doing fine, too."

The way he was smiling and looking at me with such a gleam in his eyes reminded me of the old Lester, the sweet man I'd been in love with before that car wreck messed up his brain. I was touched by how pleasant he seemed, and was tempted to give him a hug and maybe even forgive him for cheating on me. But before I could let myself go that far, his smile turned into a frown.

"I had nightmares for days after you almost de-balled me and bashed my head with that skillet!" he hollered.

"Well, you shouldn't have messed with me!" I hollered back.

"What did you expect me to do when I found out you stole my money!"

"I didn't take your money, Lester." I stomped my foot so hard, a pain shot from the sole all the way up to my knee. "Now, if you don't mind, I need to go take care of some business."

"Speaking of business, I heard that you and that pig meat you left me for done become big-time bootleggers, living like kings on the upper south side, in a fancy house with a picket fence. Got doctors and white women drinking with y'all. I'm impressed!"

"Everything you heard is true."

"Even the part about them white women?"

"Everything you heard is true," I repeated with my teeth clenched. I was running out of patience, and I let him know that by giving him a death stare. It must have done the job, because he flinched like I had slapped him.

He kept talking, anyway. "I don't like to come back to Branson too often. One of these days when I'm in town, I might pay y'all a visit. Folks claim y'all serve some world-beating drinks."

"If you do come, we'll treat you like we do all our other guests— as long as you behave."

"Humph! I know how to behave. You the one I'm worried about. Ain't you going to ask me what I been up to?"

"Nope. It ain't none of my business."

"I'll tell you, anyway." Lester shifted his weight from one foot to the other, like he was trying to get more comfortable. It didn't matter, because I was going to haul ass in the next few seconds, whether he was through running his mouth or not. "Five months after me and Katy moved in with my mama, I had to dump her because I caught her with one of my friends."

"Is that right? Now you know how I felt when you done it to me."

He rolled his eyes, which was not nearly as bright as they used to be. "Katy hurt me. But what hurt me more was you stealing my money and beating me down like a dog. I ain't never going to forgive you for that!" Spit was flying out both sides of Lester's mouth as he spoke, so I took a few steps back. "I advise you to start sleeping with one eye open and that monkey—"

I couldn't cut him off fast enough. "Get away from me before I holler for somebody to call the police!" I threatened.

I didn't wait to hear what else he had to say. I shot past him and hurried into MacPherson's, with my heart beating like a drum. Now that I knew Lester still had a grudge against me, I was going to stay on guard forever. I hoped that if he came after me, I'd be prepared.

Odell was walking up the canned goods aisle when I got in-side. Buddy and Sadie had several customers at their counters, so I didn't have to worry about them. When Odell spotted me, he headed in my direction, smiling and beaming like he was ap-proaching a friend he hadn't seen in a long time. I knew the only reason he was doing it was to show off for his cashiers and customers.

"Hello, Yvonne." His cheerful attitude surprised me.

"Hi, Odell. I came to pick out a necktie for Willie Frank to give him at his birthday party tomorrow night."

"Good news! We just got in a shipment this morning."

"That's nice. I guess I came at the right time. Um, how you doing today, Odell?"

"Blessed!"

"That's good."

"Uh-uh. That's Jesus!" He motioned me to follow him to the back of the store, where the men's items was.

I was so surprised he was being so nice, I almost tripped over my feet. As soon as we stopped in front of the necktie display, I leaned toward him and said in a low voice, "I need some more money."

"I figured that. How much?" He was still smiling.

"My aunt lost her wallet with all her money in it. I need to send her something to help feed my kids." Before I even told Odell how much I wanted, a sympathetic look crossed his face.

"We can't let them kids starve. I'll do what I can."

"I need twenty dollars." I held my breath and waited for him to fly off the handle because I'd asked for so much.

Odell surprised me again, because he said something that made my jaw drop. "Will that be enough?" He didn't waste no time pulling his wallet out of his pocket. Something was fishy. Either he had cracked up, somebody had put a hoodoo hex on him, or my eyes and ears was playing tricks on me.

When I seen how thick his wallet was with dollar bills, my greed snuck up on me. "How much can you spare? I would like to swing by Mosella's on my way back to work and get something to nibble on. So a little extra would be appreciated."

"If all you want is enough extra to get a snack, you can grab a pig foot or some peanut brittle here and not have to give none of your money to Mosella. She don't need it." Odell laughed and handed me a ten and two fives.

"Okay. I don't need nothing extra, then." I cleared my throat and put the money in my brassiere. "I'd better get that necktie and be on my way. I have to get Mr. Cunningham's truck back to him by one o'clock." I randomly grabbed the first necktie on the rack. It was a loud orange with different colored zigzags. If Willie Frank didn't like it, I'd keep it and use it as a pot holder.

"Do you want it gift wrapped?" Odell was *still* smiling.

"No, I'll do that when I get home." His behavior was so odd, I was too scared to stick around much longer. But I was so curious, I wanted to know why he wasn't talking mean. So I asked. "Odell, do you feel all right? You seem, uh, almost delirious."

He scrunched up his mouth and snorted. "I am a little under the weather. I was feeling kind of poorly when I got up this morning, so Joyce gave me some of them painkiller pills she take for her monthly female discomforts. They made me a little drowsy and confused. I ain't been myself since."

"Hmmm. Is that why you ain't fussing up a storm at me today?"

He laughed and waved his hand. "Even if I hadn't took them pills, I wouldn't be fussing at you. I realize now that life is too short. Wallowing in contempt is a waste of time. Having a positive attitude don't use up half as much energy as being negative. I'm going to try to be in a good mood every day from now on."

"Well! I do declare, I'm pleased to hear that." I had to admire him for looking at things from a more pleasant point of view, especially since it wasn't a normal thing for a man who was being blackmailed to do.

"Let me get a bag for Willie Frank's necktie. Then I'll have Sadie take you to the meat counter and let you pick out a pig foot."

"Thanks, Odell. I hope you feel better by tomorrow so you can come to the party."

"I hope I do, too."

I had a little time left, so I sat in Mr. Cunningham's truck and started gnawing on the pig foot Sadie had wrapped in a napkin. Before I could finish, I seen one of the other bootleggers that had a beef with us. Cleotis Bates was strutting down the street like he owned it. He had the nerve to be wearing a white linen suit just like the one Milton wore the night I met him. There was a scowl on his wide, homely face that made him look scary enough to haunt a house. Out of all our rivals, he was probably the one we needed to be concerned about the most. He was in his late fifties and had been at the top of the bootlegging game for more than twenty years. He'd beat up, shot at, stabbed, and terrorized anybody that made him mad as far back as I could remember. I knew that if he seen me, he would come up and talk trash. I didn't want to hear nothing he had to say, so I cranked up the truck and sped off like a bat out of hell.

I did a lot of thinking on the way back to the grill. I didn't know what to make of Odell's oddball behavior. He was playing his wife and her parents for fools to the hilt. There was no telling how many bald-faced lies he'd made up to keep Betty

Jean under control. Now he was making philosophical comments to me, a woman who was blackmailing him—and who was the wife of the man who had blowed the whistle on him. I hoped he really was going to be in a good mood every day now. If he was, I'd be duty bound to visit him at his office a lot more often.

CHAPTER 50

MILTON

I WAS SITTING AT THE WORKTABLE IN THE GRILL'S KITCHEN, PEELING potatoes, when Yvonne pranced in and showed me one of the most outlandish neckties I ever seen. I laughed. She gently mauled my head with her fist before she dragged up a chair and sat next to me. I laughed some more when she told me what Delroy had said and how she had ducked Cleotis after she picked up the tie and got back in the truck. I had more important things on my mind, so I wasn't about to let them jackasses' foolishness faze me.

"Where did you get that sissified necktie? That novelty shop on Tanglewood Avenue?" I asked.

"Uh-uh. Odell let me have it."

I stopped peeling potatoes and gave her a "You got to be kidding" look. "I wish you wouldn't go to MacPherson's unless I'm with you."

"Why? And you better have a good reason."

I had stopped wearing Band-Aids on my face, but the scabs I had still itched when I got nervous, like I was now. "It's too dangerous," I said, scratching one of the scabs.

"Dangerous how? If you still scared I might say something to Odell for him to figure out I know about Betty Jean, you don't need to keep worrying about that. I done almost forgot what you told me."

"That's good to hear."

I believed Yvonne. But accidents happened every day. I knew

that if somebody got drunk enough, there was no telling what they would say or do. If I hadn't been so drunk the night she got nosy and pestered me, I would never have told her about Odell. Well, that and the fact that I had got tired of her telling me to be more like him. I didn't like this conversation, so I decided to take a slight detour.

"Did you remind Prince Charming about the party tomorrow night?"

"Yeah. I doubt if he'll make it, though. He wasn't feeling too good. Something about being under the weather. Joyce gave him some pills this morning, which he probably shouldn't have took at all."

"What kind of pills?"

"The same ones I take when I get my monthly cramps."

I gave Yvonne a disgusted look and started peeling potatoes again. "Do you mean to tell me that a man getting so many dibs on booty take the same medicine used for female issues when he get sick?"

"Maybe them was the only pills they had in the house. Anyway, the whole time I was in the store, he was kind of light-headed and woozy, and talking out of his head."

I tensed up. One of my worst nightmares was that Odell would have a breakdown and blab to Yvonne about the financial arrangement I had with him. "Oh? What was he saying 'out of his head' today?"

"Nothing to be concerned about. He was acting nicer than he acts when he ain't on medication. That's all."

"Hmmm. Well, medication can do that. Sometimes I get giddy when I take pills. Oh well. If he don't make it to the party, I'll pay him a visit on Wednesday to see how he doing."

Yvonne's face suddenly went blank. A little voice in my head told me she had something else to tell me. And since she was holding back on it, it had to be something I didn't want to hear.

"All right. What else?"

She took her time answering my question. "I didn't want to tell you, but I ran into Lester, too."

"Your used-to-be?"

She nodded. "That low-down, funky black dog is still mad as a hornet about what happened."

"Humph! I'm still mad about what happened, too. The nerve of that spook coming up in my house, behaving the way he done. What did he have to say this time?"

"Somebody told him we was bootlegging and doing good. He said he might pay us a visit someday."

"Good!" I said with a nonchalant shrug. "More guests, more money. So long as he don't start no mess won't be no mess."

"I hope he don't come, because he said he's going to get back at me for stealing his money and beating up on him."

I gave Yvonne a concerned look and set the knife and the last potato on the table. "In that case, he better not come to our house. Do you know where I can find him at? I'll straighten him out once and for all."

"I don't know where to find him at."

"Ain't Katy got a cousin on Reed Street? Maybe they staying with her."

"Uh-uh. They had moved in with his mama in Tuscaloosa. He caught Katy with another man, and he broke up with her."

"Good! If he's in Branson, I'll find him and lay him out!" Basically, I was a nonviolent man. I'd had a few scrapes here and there, but only when I hadn't had no choice. I was ready, willing, and able to beat some sense into Lester's bone head.

Yvonne grabbed my arm and shook her head. "Let it go. Lester was just bluffing. He don't want another beatdown. Now, let's forget about him and get back to work. We got to go home this evening and start getting the house ready for Willie Frank's party tomorrow night. We can't let Lester get us all riled up and put us in a foul mood."

"You right, sugar," I agreed.

I was so excited when I got up Tuesday morning, you would have thought it was Christmas. Mr. Cunningham let me and Yvonne off early so we could go home and finish getting things ready. Him and his recovering wife and all our coworkers was coming to the party.

A few minutes after we got home, the cat lady from across the street came over with a dishpan full of potato chips. "Milton, I won't be able to come back until after my Bible class ends at eight," she explained, setting the chips on the coffee table.

"Don't worry about coming late, Sister Hemphill. We liable to party the whole night."

By 7:00 p.m., we had more than two dozen folks in the house. Lyla and Emmalou had brung a bunch of deviled duck eggs, a neck-bone casserole, and a bowl of potato salad. Aunt Mattie had baked a huge sheet cake for Willie Frank. Her birthday present to him was a free session with his favorite booty babe, Sweet Sue. I set the cake on the coffee table, and the goodies Lyla and Emmalou had brung on top of the ironing board, which I had put up against the wall. A few seconds later, Yvonne came in from the kitchen with a humongous platter that was loaded from side to side with hush puppies, chicken wings, frog legs, meatballs, and fried green tomatoes. She put the platter on the ironing board. Folks was gobbling, drinking, and dancing up a storm. With all the energy in the room, I had a feeling this would be one of the most unforgettable nights we'd ever had.

"Where is our boy Willie Frank?" Aunt Mattie asked, looking around the room. She had been in the house only thirty minutes and was already as drunk as a skunk. She staggered to the couch and dropped down like a bale of hay and undid the three top buttons on her purple and gold brocade frock. "Don't tell me he ain't going to show up for his own birthday party."

"He told me he was going to be late. He got to round up his kinfolks that wanted to come and haul them over here. The way them rednecks is scattered all over the hills, that could take some time," I replied.

Aunt Mattie looked toward the door. "What about Joyce and Odell?"

"Odell ain't feeling too good," Yvonne told her. "Joyce came over a little while ago. She said he too sick to come out or be left alone. She cooked him a pot of chicken soup and made him stretch out on the couch."

Lyla, who was sitting on the couch next to Aunt Mattie,

started laughing. "I ain't never seen a woman as devoted to a man as Joyce is to Odell. I was almost the same way with my husband." She stopped talking, and a sad look spread across her face like a veil. "All the time I was a lovestruck fool, that *beast* I married was playing footsie with his coworker."

"Well, that ain't likely to happen in Odell's case," I said. Everybody laughed with me. "His female coworker is old enough to be his mama, and she look like a swamp frog."

I excused myself and went to the kitchen to get another platter of snacks. Before I could get back, somebody in the living room hollered, "The police just pulled up!"

My heart sunk, and my chest tightened. "Oh, holy shit," I mouthed. I didn't know what to do next, so I just stood stock-still, rooted in my spot like a tree.

Within seconds, people stampeded into the kitchen and bolted out the back door. Aunt Mattie was stumbling and wheezing like a mule. She held her bamboo purse close to her bosom when she ducked into the broom closet and slammed the door. There was such a ruckus, with so many folks trying to get out the door at the same time, one of our coworkers opened a window and leaped out like a frog.

By the time I was able to move and make my way back to the living room, the only person in there was Yvonne. We looked at one another and froze. Before either one of us could say anything, somebody kicked open the door. Four of the meanest-looking cracker cops stormed in, waving shotguns and nightsticks.

CHAPTER 51
YVONNE

"CUFF THEM NIGGERS UP! CUFF THEM REAL GOOD! FRISK EACH one to make sure they ain't got no weapons!" Hollering at the top of his lungs was a tall, lanky white policeman with a shotgun in one hand and a nightstick in the other.

"What's the problem, Officers?" Milton asked in a calm tone. With all the chaos going on, I couldn't believe that he was still able to behave like the upstanding Christian gentleman he was.

One of the cops handcuffed Milton with his arms behind his back, and two others started beating him about his head and face with the sticks and the butts of their shotguns. So much blood was spurting off him, I couldn't tell which wounds it was coming from, the old ones from his other beating that hadn't fully healed or the new ones. The cop that cuffed me gripped my arm so tight, he almost cut off my blood circulation.

"What's this about?" Milton whimpered, spitting out blood. "We ain't did nothing but have a party."

The lanky cop, who seemed to be the ringleader, glanced around the room. "Y'all in a heap of trouble!"

It was hard to believe that as long as folks had been bootlegging in Branson, we was the first ones to go down for it. That was what I assumed our crime was until I heard what the cop said next.

"Where that white girl at?"

"What white girl?" me and Milton screeched at the same time.

"The one y'all lured over here and had a bunch of wild niggers rape!" The lanky cop snapped his fingers at the one that had handcuffed Milton and the man standing in the middle of the floor, with a dazed expression on his face. "Moe, you and Joe Bob go check them other rooms. Shake a leg!"

The two men took off running toward different rooms, waving their shotguns.

Then the lanky cop swiveled his head in my direction and yelled at the one that had cuffed me and was still holding my arm. "Boot, hold on tight to that wench. She look mighty dangerous to me."

I was so scared and mad I could barely see straight. But I could see that Milton was in no shape to make much sense. He was moaning and groaning the same way he had when he got attacked that other time. "Y'all must be at the wrong house. We don't know nothing about no white girl getting raped!" I yelled.

"Uh-huh! That ain't what we was told!" the man holding my arm boomed.

"Who told you that?" I croaked.

Having my hands cuffed behind my back was bad enough. But I was trembling so hard, I could barely stay up on my feet. What was happening didn't even seem real. So many thoughts that didn't make a lick of sense was bouncing around inside my head so fast, I couldn't tell where one ended and another one started.

"Officers, will y'all please tell us what's going on?" I yelled. "We just hardworking, God-fearing colored folks that ain't never gone against the Jim Crow law and done nothing illegal to a white person, especially a female."

The main cop gave me a look that was so mean, it sent shivers up my spine. "Lies, lies, lies! Hush up before I slap a muzzle on you, gal!" Then he kicked over the coffee table, knocking Willie Frank's birthday cake on the floor.

I pressed my lips together so tight, it felt like I had glued them shut. The cop glared at me until the other two who were searching the house ran back into the living room. Them idiots stepped in the cake, laughing all the while.

"All clear, Sheriff Potts. Ain't another soul in the house," one of them said.

"Let's not worry about them for now. We got the main culprits. We'll get the names of them rapists out of these two if we have to pull that information out of their mouths with a pair of pliers." Sheriff Potts looked from me to Milton. Then he shouted, "Milton and Yvonne Hamilton, y'all both under arrest!"

"Sir, no white girl got raped in this house tonight or no other night," I insisted, choking on a sob.

"So you say. I got a call from somebody who claimed he was a eyewitness."

"That's a damn lie!" I shot back.

"It was reported that y'all had a young blonde with blue eyes up in here, making a sport of her. From what I was told, niggers ravaged her until she passed out. And before y'all set them savages on her . . ." He paused and looked from me to Milton. "You two buggers got her nice and drunk first. If she ain't laying dead in a swamp, her life is still ruined—same as y'all!"

"We innocent!" Milton insisted. His voice was so weak and low now, I could barely hear him. "You . . . you must be crazy."

Sheriff Potts stomped his foot and poked Milton's chest with the butt of his shotgun. "Boy, where do you get off sassing me? Where is your manners at? How much did y'all charge them niggers to take advantage of that young girl?"

"Officer, I don't believe nobody told you nothing!" I blasted.

"You calling me a liar?"

"Yes!" That was the wrong thing to say. The sheriff's bony hand slapped me across the face so hard, I seen stars of every color in the rainbow.

"Get these monkeys on the truck!" the sheriff yelled.

We was immediately herded out the door and marched to a pickup truck that was double-parked in the middle of the street in front of our house. A dusty police car was parked behind it. The cat lady across the street rushed out to her porch, with all eight of her cats trailing behind her. She had a coal-oil lamp in her hand and a horrified expression on her face. I didn't think her eyes could get no bigger; she had them stretched open so wide now, they looked as big as hen eggs.

The folks that had come in cars and trucks had left them behind. We'd had such a crowd, vehicles was lined up for several blocks on our street, on both sides. Just when one of the cops started to hoist me up into the bed of the police pickup truck, Willie Frank finally drove up. He slowed down to a crawl, but he didn't stop. Mama and Papa Perdue was sitting in the cab with him. One of his nephews, his oldest brother and his wife, and the paraplegic grandfather they hauled around in a wheelbarrow occupied the bed of the truck. They all gawked, with their eyes bugged out and their mouths hanging open, but they didn't react. It was a blessing they didn't. I didn't want them to get caught up in a mess we didn't know who had caused. Willie Frank made a U-turn and drove off.

As the police truck was pulling away, a few of our neighbors' porch lights came on. Some of the others rubbernecked from their windows and front porches. Joyce and Odell's lights didn't come on, so they must have been sleeping real hard. It was a good thing they hadn't come to the party, after all. They might not have been lucky enough to get away like everybody else.

Branson's jailhouse and teeny-weeny post office was in the same shabby building in the middle of a block in our business district. The jail had only three cells. Like everything else, they was segregated. But only by race. They put me and Milton in the same cell. The prison where I had done time was bad, but the hellhole I was in now was even worse. So many plump roaches was crawling around our feet, it looked like the floor was moving. A bat almost the size of a hoot owl was perched on the windowsill outside, peeping through the bars.

"Baby, don't worry. When they find out they been duped, they'll straighten out this mess," Milton assured me as we huddled on the floor, shaking like leaves. There was a set of bunk beds with scuzzy gray blankets on the flat, piss-stained mattresses, no sheets. The toilet was a metal bucket in a corner, half filled with foul-smelling, murky water, and there was no toilet paper in sight.

"Somebody set us up," I said through clenched teeth.

"That's a fact. But there ain't a lick of proof that we had no white girl raped, so we ain't got nothing to worry about. God got our backs."

We joined hands, bowed our heads, and prayed in low voices for five minutes. After that, we seethed with anger for almost a hour, before we was finally able to go to sleep on the floor.

Not long after that, I heard the cell door open. Milton was still asleep, and I was still in his arms. Before I knew what was happening, two of the same cops that had come to the house tiptoed in.

"Come here, gal," one ordered, pulling me up by my arm. With his other hand, he unzipped his pants. "Well, I do declare. This one is as soft as hog fat, and I bet as sweet as a berry."

"Well, Moe, they say the blacker the berry, the sweeter the juice," the other man snickered, groping me with both hands.

"Turn me loose, motherfucker!" I screamed. When the man that had pulled me up gripped my head and tried to kiss me, I hawked a big wad of spit smack-dab between his eyes.

"You black bitch!" he blasted, slapping both sides of my face.

He was way stronger than me, so there was no way I could fight him off. But I screamed loud enough to wake up the dead. It woke Milton up, but he couldn't do me no good. While the first man wrestled me to the lower bunk and climbed on top of me, the other one sat on Milton's back and kept him pinned down.

CHAPTER 52
MILTON

I WAS RELIEVED YVONNE HAD PASSED OUT WHILE SHE WAS BEING raped. A few minutes after them rapist cops rushed out of the cell, she came to and started moaning. I crawled over to the bunk and grabbed her hand and dragged her down into my arms. Before either one of us could speak, I heard the cell door being unlocked again. One of my eyes was swole shut, and the only light was from a naked bulb dangling from a string in the hallway, so I could barely see. Before I could focus, I heard the one voice that gave me some hope: Willie Frank's.

"Thanks, Deputy," he said.

"Don't get too comfortable in there, boy! I can't let you stay but a few minutes," the deputy barked. He slammed the door shut and left, cussing under his breath.

Willie Frank rushed over and squatted down on the floor next to us. I started babbling gibberish, and tears was flowing out of Yvonne's eyes like a waterfall.

"Y'all get a grip and talk normal so I can understand you. I had to bribe them deputies so they'd let me in." The way Willie Frank's voice was cracking, I thought he was going to start crying, too.

Yvonne abruptly stopped crying. When Willie Frank seen how bloody my face and clothes was, he shook his head and wiped my face off with the tail of his shirt. Then he wiped off Yvonne's.

"Did you find out what the hell is going on?" I asked him.

He scrunched up his face and took a long deep breath. "Well, according to Sheriff Potts, some anonymous person called him and claimed y'all had a pretty little white teenage girl in the house, being raped."

If this situation hadn't been so serious, I would have laughed. "The only white females in the house last night was Lyla and Emmalou!" I screeched. "Nobody would mistake them wrinkled-up hags for pretty little teenagers! They'll jump in the bed with a colored man at the drop of a hat, so ain't nobody got to rape them!"

"I know this is a setup!" Willie Frank boomed. "Did y'all short-change or insult anybody last night? Maybe somebody found out about the recycled booze."

"We didn't insult nobody, and we the only three that know about us recycling our liquor. If we shortchanged somebody, it was a honest mistake, and I know they would have said something. But they was all regulars, and none of them had no reason to finger us for rape," I said. "It had to be somebody that want to bring us down. But who?"

We looked like idiots, sitting in the middle of the floor. I was in too much pain to stand up, and I knew Yvonne was hurting just as much. She sighed and glanced from me to Willie Frank.

"Maybe it was Delroy Crutchfield. He got a big beef with us. He was right nasty and hostile when he stopped me on my way to MacPherson's yesterday! I—I bet he made the call!" she choked out.

"Hold on now. It could have been him, and it could have been somebody else. We still don't know who it was that beat Milton up. And there is probably folks on the warpath y'all don't even know about."

Yvonne suddenly sat up ramrod straight and gasped. "Oh my God! It was Lester!" she shrieked. "He said he was going to get back at me!"

"Lester who?" Willie Frank wanted to know.

"Yvonne's used-to-be. We had a serious run-in with him the day Yvonne left him for me," I explained.

"Hmmm." Willie Frank caressed his chin. Then he flopped and waved his hand. "This Lester sounds like a good prospect, I guess." And then his dark mood got even darker. Them sky-blue eyes of his looked almost black. "I believe in fighting fire with fire. Tell me where I can find that asshole, and I'll give him a dose of his own medicine. I'll sic the police on him for a bogus rap. I'll get one of the gals in my family to say *he* raped her. This is right up my cousin Peggy Louise's alley. All we'd have to give her is a jug of white lightning and a dollar. And . . . and I'll swear on a stack of Bibles that I seen the whole crime!" I had never seen Willie Frank so fired up, not even in prison, when he was kicking another inmate's ass.

I raised my hand. "No, no, no. Don't do that. Let's not get too close to the deep end. We don't know who is behind this mess, and we might never know. What we need to concentrate on now is getting out," I said gently.

I didn't need no mirror to show me that I looked right pitiful. I didn't care about that, though. But to see a woman as pretty as Yvonne looking like she'd been beat with a ugly stick just about broke my heart clean in two. That bastard had slapped her so hard, he'd left his handprint on her jaw. She had a black eye and a busted lip. I couldn't imagine what the rest of her body looked like after she'd been raped by them two sex fiends.

"Don't worry about the house. When I seen that truck pulling away with y'all in the back, I drove around the block so them cops wouldn't see me. When they turned the corner and sped off, with the siren going, me and my folks waited a little while before we doubled back to check on the house. I found Aunt Mattie in the kitchen broom closet and Sweet Sue up in a tree in the backyard, but everybody else got away. All the cars and trucks that had been parked out front was gone."

"Shoot! I didn't even have time to count the money we'd made so far tonight!" I complained. "And we was making money faster than ever before."

"Tonight's profits was the first thing I looked for when I got inside. The cash was in the shoebox under the kitchen sink, where you always put it until the night is over."

"Bless you, Willie Frank. That's a relief," I told him. "Take it to your house and hold it until we know what's going to happen."

Willie Frank stared at Yvonne. When he seen that her blouse had been ripped down the front, he shook his head. "Yvonne, did they put their hands on you?"

She nodded and let out a dry laugh. "This is a fucked-up world we live in. The cops came looking for a raped white girl to rescue, and then they commit the same crime on me."

"What we need to be concerned about now is getting to the bottom of this mess," Willie Frank advised. "And hope the cops don't drag nobody else into it. Was Joyce and Odell at the house?"

"Uh-uh. He wasn't feeling good, and she had to stay home to take care of him," I answered.

"I guess they heard the commotion, because when I first pulled up, I seen their bedroom curtains moving. And when I came back, their lights was on," Willie Frank said.

"I'm glad they didn't come outside and get involved. Knowing them cops, they might have cuffed them up, too." I had to stop talking and cough. When I did that, more blood dribbled out of my mouth.

"Hallelujah! Unworldly, straitlaced folks like Odell and Joyce wouldn't last a minute in a cell," Willie Frank commented. Right after he stopped talking, one of the deputies came back and told him his time was up. Willie Frank gave me a thumbs-up. "Y'all stay strong. Whoever made that call might not be done yet. For all we know, they could be plotting to have somebody steal everything in the house!"

"Willie Frank, there is some presents for you on the dresser in our bedroom. Go back to the house and get them before somebody else do," Yvonne said. "Me and Milton got you something real nice. I hope you'll like it."

"I'm sure I will. Thanks. And don't worry. I'll lock up the house when I leave." Willie Frank looked from Yvonne and back. Regardless of the thumbs-up he'd just gave me, I couldn't ignore the weary look on his face. "Naw, naw. I can do better than that. I'll get my brothers and some of my crazy cousins to go there with me. We'll guard it until we know for sure there ain't going to be no looting."

"And one more thing. Swing by Odell and Joyce's house and let them know what's going on." I had to pause and cough some more. I was glad blood had finally stopped oozing from my mouth. "Tell them what happened."

"I'll tell them all I know. For the time being, y'all get some rest, and don't do or say nothing that'll make things worse. Me and my kinfolks will do all we can to help y'all get through this mess. I'm going to go up to Uncle Lamar as soon as I can."

"All I want to know is *who* made that damn call! I declare, if I find out, their butt is mine!" I yelled, almost spitting out the words. "Raping a white woman is the worst crime a colored man can go down for. It's a miracle they ain't lynched me already by now!"

"Milton, they didn't say you raped nobody. They claimed we set it up!" Yvonne reminded.

"You think that'll make a difference with them racist jackasses running this town? I bet they out there right now, trying to round up as many other colored men they think might have been involved." I was talking so fast, I choked on some air. I cleared my throat and went on. "I already done time for another crime I didn't do. Now I got to deal with *another* one?"

"You hold on there, buddy. Let's wait and see what's going to happen next," Willie Frank insisted. "They ain't even done no paperwork yet, so let's not get ahead of ourselves. Time is on our side."

"No it ain't. Eight of them nine colored boys in that Scottsboro mess back in thirty-one was all sentenced to die, and one was sentenced to life because two hobo white girls claimed they raped them. There wasn't no proof, and one of them heifers eventually admitted they'd lied on them boys. But they went to trial *twelve days* after they got arrested," I reminded. "So don't tell me nothing about time being on our side."

"You got a point there," Willie Frank admitted in a tired tone.

We stood up and group hugged until the deputy came back and told Willie Frank to leave again.

"I'll be back as soon as I can!" he boomed as he stomped out.

I kept my arms around Yvonne, and we crumpled back down to the floor. She was quiet, but when I started crying, she gasped and passed out. And I knew why: She realized, as well as I did, that we had come to the end of the road. Because the *only* time my body allowed me to cry was when somebody I loved was dying or had already died.

CHAPTER 53
MILTON

As hungry as we was, we didn't touch the grits and biscuits on a tray that one of the deputies had set on the floor in front of us the next morning. There was no telling how much spit, piss, or other nasty mess he had added so we wasn't going to eat none of that shit.

One of the other deputies came back a few hours later and dropped off a bucket with some murky water and a sliver of lye soap for us to bathe. When he seen we hadn't ate nothing, he got mad. "You crazy niggers must not be too hungry! But we ain't bringing no more food in here until y'all eat this first meal!" he barked before he kicked the tray across the floor and stormed back out.

We was funky as hell and our clothes was stiff from our dried blood, but we didn't touch that bucket of water, neither. Eating and scrubbing off was the least of our worries.

Wednesday was one of the longest days of my life. That morning and afternoon, we got up off the floor to stretch and look out the window a few times. But we spent the rest of the hours hugged up on the floor, praying and declaring our love for each other.

We slept on the floor again that night. Because of the hellish thoughts bouncing around in my head, I dozed off only a few minutes at a time. The fact that I had actually cried the night they brought us in was a bad omen I couldn't ignore. When the story of our arrest hit the newspaper, every lynch mob in the county would come out of hibernation. We probably wouldn't live long enough to be transported to the county jail or make it to court. The last colored man they arrested in Branson for fooling around with a white woman got shot to death when he tried to "escape" the day after he got locked up.

The sheriff had told us that we couldn't enter our plea until Judge Tucker returned to his office the day after tomorrow. He only came in three days a week. I didn't care what them white devils said or thought, we was pleading innocent.

When daylight broke Thursday morning, I had been wide awake for a long time. My stomach knotted up when I heard heavy footsteps clomping in our direction. I tightened my grip around Yvonne's shoulder and held my breath as the steps got closer. It was one of the deputies and Willie Frank. He let Willie Frank into the cell and hurried back down the musty smelling hallway, cussing under his breath.

"How y'all doing?" Willie Frank asked in a gentle tone, wringing his hands as he rushed over to us. My poor buddy looked so tired and distressed, you would have thought he'd been arrested, too.

"We still alive," I said, shaking Yvonne. She opened her eyes right away and we stood up at the same time. She was so wobbly I had to keep my arm around her shoulder so she wouldn't fall.

"I got to talk fast," Willie Frank said, his tone sounding encouraging. That gave me hope. "I got some good news and some bad news."

"Tell us the good news first," Yvonne croaked. I had never heard her sound so bad before.

"Y'all getting released in a few minutes," Willie Frank blurted out.

What he'd just said worked on me like a tonic. Yvonne gasped and almost collapsed. Both my jaws dropped. "Say what?" I asked. "W-what—"

Willie Frank held up his hand and cut me off. "Y'all remember me telling how my uncle Lamar pulled a few strings and got me a reduced sentence when I cut that man over a woman? If it hadn't been for him and his connections, I'd still be behind bars."

Me and Yvonne nodded. "Is he going to help us?" she asked.

"Yup. They finished up the paperwork and he's outside talking to Sheriff Potts right now. Getting y'all sprung wasn't easy. We paid a visit to the sheriff's house last night and done some serious talking. The deal is, y'all getting off on account of lack of evidence. I'd like to see the look on that asshole's face that set y'all up when he hears his plan didn't work."

"Me, too! Hallelujah! That is good news." I was jubilant, but only for a couple of seconds. "What's the bad news?" Before Willie Frank could answer, I started to cringe and shake so hard it felt like my legs was going to buckle. My heart started to beat so hard and fast, I was scared it was going turn upside down.

Willie Frank blinked and cleared his throat. "It cost a pretty penny. Sheriff Potts wanted two hundred bucks to drop the charges," he told us with his voice cracking. "Uncle Lamar brung the money to him this morning."

Yvonne smiled for the first time since we got arrested. "Your uncle done that for us? Bless his heart," she said, choking on a sob.

Willie Frank bobbed his head. The distressed look was back on his face, so that told me we wasn't going to like what he said next. "The bad news is, he wants his money paid back in full by the end of this month. I promised him y'all would come through."

Me and Yvonne gasped at the same time. "What's wrong with you, Willie Frank? You know we ain't got that kind of money!" I hollered.

Before either one of us could speak again, the deputy came back. "Get going!" he hollered, stamping his foot and motioning for us to leave the cell. "And be quick about it before we find something else to charge y'all with!"

We scurried out like scared mice. "We'll finish talking outside," Willie Frank mumbled as we skittered down the hall and on out the front door.

When we got outside, Sheriff Potts was standing on the sidewalk talking to a roly-poly, elderly, silver-haired white man in a beige suit and a wide-brimmed black hat. I had met him before, so I knew he was Lamar Perdue, Willie Frank's uncle. He was a shady landowner with some deep pockets and a niece married to the district attorney, so he had a lot of pull in Branson. Him and the sheriff glanced at us, but they kept talking. We stumbled over to Willie Frank's truck parked on the street in front of Lamar's shiny black LaSalle.

"Willie Frank, where we going to get two hundred dollars by the end of this month?" I asked with my lips quivering.

"We'll figure out something. I—" Willie Frank stopped talking when Sheriff Potts clapped Lamar on the back. The sheriff was smiling until he looked in our direction. The expression on his face turned so mean it made me shudder. Then that low-down, greedy, hateful dog threw up his hands, shook his head, and went back inside.

"Well now," Lamar started as he waddled up to us with his hands on his hips. "Y'all dodged a real big bullet!" he growled with a dead-pan expression on his pie-shaped face. "I declare, I straightened things out . . . this time." He paused and hawked a huge gob of spit on the ground and sucked in a deep breath. "Milton, I know you ain't no bad egg. Otherwise, I wouldn't have stuck my neck out this far for no coloreds."

"Thank you," was all I could think to say. I reached my hand out to shake his, but he acted like he didn't see it. Instead, he just looked at me for a few seconds with that dead-pan expression still on his face. But when he turned to gawk at Yvonne, he smiled. Even as scruffy and musty as she was, she was still a desirable woman. Lamar's gaze stayed on her so long, I got nervous. Now I had something else to worry about. What if he wanted to pleasure hisself with her, too? I put that nasty thought out of my mind real fast and prayed it wouldn't come back.

"Sir, we didn't do none of the stuff somebody said we done," she blurted out.

Lamar shook his head and spoke to her in a gentle tone. "It don't matter if you did or not. There ain't no evidence and I got the sheriff to realize that. Me and him go way back so my word is good. He wanted to by-pass a trial, hang y'all out to dry, and ride y'all out of town on a rail. Y'all wouldn't have had a chance."

"We . . . we would have if we had hired us a lawyer," Yvonne mumbled.

Lamar's mouth dropped open and he looked at Yvonne like she had lost her mind. "Lawyer? Pffft!" He lifted his hat and scratched his head. His bloated jaws was twitching. "You people typically don't come to court with lawyers."

"That's why we people typically get convicted," I threw in. I wasn't trying to be funny, but Lamar and Willie Frank snickered.

"Well, just go home and get on about your business. Lay this little mishap to rest. Enjoy life while you still can," Lamar advised.

"Um, Mr. Lamar, you ain't got to worry. We'll do whatever we have to do to scrape up the money so we can pay you your two hundred dollars back by the end of the month," I said with a nod.

Lamar heaved out a mighty belch and grunted, "*Three* hundred!"

"Huh? Willie Frank said you paid Sheriff Potts two hundred!" Yvonne pointed out.

"Yup. That's what I paid." Lamar looked from me to Yvonne. He let out a strange laugh before he went on. "I know y'all didn't think I was doing this unless there was something in it for me!" He laughed again. "I figured a hundred would be a real sweet treat for me. Keep in mind, I could have asked for more. And it's a good thing I got to the sheriff before he put this incident in the newspaper and the Klan got wind of it. He was fixing to turn in the report today. God couldn't have saved y'all then."

"Oh. Well, honest to God, we will get you your money back on time," I promised.

"Good, good. Now I got to haul ass. Y'all have a blessed rest of the day and keep your noses clean!" Lamar gave us a tight smile and tipped his hat before he whirled around and trotted toward his fancy car.

Just as Lamar was driving off, the sheriff and one of his deputies came outside and stood in front of the building, giving us more mean looks. We scrambled into Willie Frank's truck lickety-split.

Nobody said nothing all the way to our house. As soon as we got inside, we flopped down on the couch with Yvonne in the middle. I was pleased to see how good Willie Frank had cleaned up the mess the cops had made when they knocked over the food we had set out in the living room. But there was still a few bits and pieces of the birthday cake on the coffee table. "Willie Frank, I'm sorry we didn't get to celebrate your birthday," I said, trying to get my mind off our real troubles.

"Don't worry about it. We can celebrate later. But I did take them gifts y'all got for me. A man can never have too much chewing tobacco. I needed a new belt and that tie was right on time!" Willie Frank gushed. "My cousin Fanny June is having a church wedding next month and it's going to be right formal. She told me I had to wear a tie and now I ain't got to go hunting for one."

Yvonne jabbed me in my side with her elbow. "You said a tie was a bad gift for Willie Frank."

I wasn't in no mood to be talking about a tie when we had a three-hundred-dollar debt to a white man hanging over our heads. It wouldn't take long for it to turn into a noose if we didn't pay it back this month.

Willie Frank must have read my mind. "Look, I don't want y'all to fret none. With God's help, we'll get that money somehow. Even if it means we have to rob Peter to pay Paul."

"Pffft! We'll have to rob a bunch of Peters to come up with three hundred dollars!" I snapped.

"Hold on now. It ain't as bad as you think it is. Y'all still got a lot of friends in this town. I swung by Aunt Mattie's place after me and Uncle Lamar left Sheriff Potts' house last night. That sweet old woman feels so bad about this mess. She said she's going to do a hoodoo that'll help y'all stay strong and also calm down them lynch mobs. If she is that sympathetic and concerned, I'm sure she'd be good for at least a fifty buck loan, maybe even a hundred."

Since I was always late paying my poontang tab with Aunt Mattie, I didn't think she'd be willing to lend me no fifty dollars, let alone a hundred. "Shoot!" I hissed, shaking my head. "I can't tune up my mouth to ask that woman for such big money! Especially since she usually turn me down when I try to hit her up for just a dollar or two."

"Look-a-here, buddy. I'm ahead of you. I already considered that. I'll borrow it from her and lend it to you. You can pay me back whenever you can, no matter how long it takes. After all, she is the one that loaned me the down payment I needed to buy my truck so I know she can be right generous. The only thing is, she always makes me pay her a twenty percent interest fee every time I borrow from her."

"Willie Frank, if you borrow money from Aunt Mattie and don't pay her back on time, she might put a hoodoo hex on you," Yvonne warned. "Don't go to her unless we can't get it from nobody else. And if you do get a hundred from her, what about the other two hundred we need—not to mention her 'interest' fee?"

"Well, Mr. Cunningham might help. And what about that nice Dr. Patterson that invited y'all to have Thanksgiving dinner with him and his family?" Willie Frank added. "Between the three of them, y'all shouldn't have no problem."

"We'll see about that." Yvonne let out a loud sigh and stood up, waving her hands in the air. "We still got that other thing to worry about. When whoever it was that set us up—and gave Milton that beating—find out their plan didn't put us out of commission, they might try something else," she whimpered.

I was just as worried as she was about "that other thing," but I didn't want her to know it. "Baby, we need to set that aside for now and focus on getting the money to pay Lamar back," I replied. "That's way more serious."

"Milton is sure enough right," Willie Frank agreed.

"Sweet Jesus!" Yvonne waved her hands again. "I can't talk about all this no more today. I'm going to go wash up, fix me a mighty big drink and a baloney sandwich, and crawl into bed with my Bible."

"You go right ahead, sugar. I'm going to do that same thing myself. Don't you worry your pretty little head too much. Me and Willie Frank will come up with something to help us straighten out this mess," I told her.

Yvonne blew out a loud breath before she stumbled out of the room. I exhaled and gave Willie Frank a serious look. "Ain't no telling how long it's going to take to get our business back to where our regulars will feel comfortable enough to start visiting again. So our money is going to be real tight for a while. Aunt Mattie will probably give you whatever you ask for, but I doubt if Mr. Cunningham will pay me and Yvonne for missing work yesterday and today. And, I don't know Dr. Patterson too good. He might be the type that don't lend money to nobody."

"Don't throw in the towel just yet. I know of other sources," Willie Frank tossed in with a wink. I was pleased to see him looking more hopeful. "Me and my brothers done hit a few big houses in Mobile. We swiped a heap of stuff that made us some serious money—jewelry, silverware, and even cash left out in the open. We even took the tires off some fat cat's brand-new Ford. Other than heists like that, there ain't too many other choices." Willie Frank's face suddenly froze. His eyes got big and he snapped his fingers. "What about Joyce's daddy? Mac is kind of aloof, but he is one of the richest colored men in town!"

"And the last one we should approach. He done made it clear he ain't got no affection for bootleggers, so I know he wouldn't give us a plugged nickel!"

"Then get it from Odell," Willie Frank suggested.

I done such a hard double-take, my neck felt like it was going to twist up in a knot. I stared at Willie Frank for a couple of seconds with my mouth hanging open. *Get it from Odell?* I asked dumbly.

"Sure enough. Mac would probably lend it to him and never have to know he was borrowing it to lend to y'all." I couldn't believe how excited Willie Frank was now. I had to play this just right so he didn't get suspicious.

Not only could I hit Odell up for three hundred dollars, *I wouldn't have to pay him back!* I didn't want Willie Frank to know that so I said, "I doubt if that would work. Mac and Millie pay Odell to run the store, and I know they ain't paying him no chump change. Joyce got a good paying job so Odell ain't got no excuse to be borrowing money from her folks."

Willie Frank's tone dropped so low I could barely hear him. "Oh. You got a point there, I guess. I hadn't thought about that."

We didn't say nothing else for a couple of seconds. I knew Willie Frank was disappointed, but the thoughts in my head were spinning like a loose wheel. Now I was the one that was excited. It was so hard to sit still I had to cross my legs to keep myself from jumping up and dancing a jig. We could still try to get some money from Aunt Mattie, Mr. Cunningham, and Dr. Patterson, though. I'd pay them debts back with the money I got from Odell. Not only that, I'd demand a *extra* hundred smackaroos from him so I'd have a little breathing room, and some play money to have some fun with. I'd even use part of it to take Yvonne on a buggy ride to celebrate our freedom. I wouldn't tell her or Willie Frank about the money I got from Odell because I didn't want them to think I was too big of a trickster.

Odell was going to shit a brick when I went up to him and told him I needed four hundred dollars by the end of the month. He could shit all the bricks he wanted so long as he gave me that money. I had all the leverage and he had showed me that he was a push-over, so it didn't seem like it would be too much trouble getting him to come through. Besides, he had already proved that me keeping his second life with Betty Jean a secret meant way more to him than money. I didn't think he would get no madder and fuss no more than he did when I put the bite on him for only a few extra dollars all them other times. Shoot!

Willie Frank waved his hand in front of my face and nudged my shoulder. "You still with me? You look like you in a daze."

"Huh? Oh!" I shook my head, cleared my throat, and grinned.

"Um, I was just thinking about how happy I am to be home, and how grateful I am you got your uncle to go to bat for us."

"Well, I'm glad things worked out the way they did." Willie Frank stood up and stretched. "I been real busy these past couple of days. I need to get back to my business before I'll need to scrounge up some money for myself," he snickered. "I got several orders I'm late delivering. I'll come back tomorrow evening and we can discuss everything some more."

"I need one more favor. Can you swing by the grill and let Mr. Cunningham know we out of jail and will be back to work tomorrow? If any of our regulars is up in there, let them know we'll be back in business as of tonight."

"Sure enough. After I do that, I'll make some pit stops at a few other places where some of the other regulars hang out and let them know, too."

I got up and walked Willie Frank out to the porch, patting his shoulder all the way. The sun was shining so bright but it felt a little irritating beating down on my battered face. That didn't stop the wall-to-wall smile from spreading across my face, though. I wrapped my arms around Willie Frank and gave him a bear hug. "Thanks, buddy. I don't know what we'd do without you."

"Well, I only do what a real friend is supposed to do."

"And you better believe we ain't going to forget it!" I declared. I sucked in some air and shifted my weight from one foot to the other. My bruises and body stink didn't even faze me no more. But I was still going to wash myself up as soon as Yvonne finished her bath. Then I was going to put on some clean clothes, eat a decent meal, get drunk, and read my Bible. "Um . . . by the way, you talked to Odell since we got arrested?"

"Nope. When I came over here to clean up yesterday, it was during the day while him and Joyce was still at work. Why?"

"Oh, nothing. I was just wondering."

"Odell is a good old soul. Christian to the bone. I enjoy his company as much as you do. I know he's been as worried about y'all as the rest of us. He'll be pleased as punch to know y'all got out of jail and them charges didn't stick." Willie Frank smiled and gave me a thoughtful look. "I hope he comes back over here to socialize again real soon. Joyce, too."

"So do I." I glanced over at the spot where Odell always parked his car in front of his house. "I'll pay him a visit as soon as he come home from work this evening and let him know it's business as usual."

OVER THE FENCE

Mary Monroe

ABOUT THIS GUIDE

The suggested questions that follow are included to enhance your group's reading of this book.

DISCUSSION QUESTIONS

1. Some criminals blame their misdeeds on bad breaks and miserable childhoods. Yvonne and Milton were raised by wholesome family members and still made bad choices that landed them in prison. Do you think they were born to be bad?

2. Yvonne attempted to walk the straight and narrow after she got released from prison. If Lester Fullbright had not cheated on her with her best friend, Katy, do you think she still would have been attracted to a hustler like Milton?

3. Did Yvonne go too far when she punished Lester and Katy? Did she not go far enough?

4. Even with all their scheming, Yvonne and Milton were still not financially secure. They were greedy and unrealistic. They wanted things they couldn't afford, and they were determined to have them no matter what they had to do. Do you know people like Yvonne and Milton? If so, do you avoid them or cater to their demands?

5. Do you think Yvonne would have been much better off with a man like Odell? If so, why?

6 Yvonne and Milton truly loved each other. But do you think they were bad for each other?

7. According to Proverbs 21:10–11, there is no honor among thieves. Yvonne didn't know Milton was blackmailing Odell until Odell told her. Therefore, was she justified in not telling Milton that she was blackmailing Odell, too?

8. Joyce and Odell were basically nice people, but they were insensitive—and didn't even know it. Their callous remarks caused Yvonne and Milton a lot of anguish. Do you think that if Yvonne and Milton had not spent time in prison and had not come from the "wrong side of town," Joyce and Odell would have treated them as equals?

9. Milton didn't have any qualms about blackmailing Odell. He blamed Odell for his own "downfall" by being stupid enough to flaunt his mistress and their children in public. Do you think if Odell knew about Milton's numerous trysts with prostitutes, he would have used this information as leverage to make him back off?

10. Odell was unscrupulous to the bone. But he was so good at being manipulative and charming, Yvonne eventually started looking at him from a more positive point of view. She still despised his bragging and snooty demeanor, but she admired his good looks and charisma, and she wanted Milton to be more like him. Do you think Milton was justified in feeling slighted and getting angry each time she compared him to Odell?

11. Yvonne and Milton racked up a long list of enemies, so things were bound to boil over sooner or later. Did you think Milton's beating would be the worst thing they had to face?

12. Did you predict that things would get much worse for Yvonne and Milton?

13. Who do you think set up the phony rape charge against Yvonne and Milton?

Don't miss the first book in the Neighbors series

One House Over

A solid marriage, a thriving business, and the esteem of their close-knit Alabama community—Joyce and Odell Watson have every reason to count their blessings. Their marriage has given well-off Joyce a chance at the family she's always wanted, and it has granted Odell a once-in-a-lifetime shot to escape grinding poverty. But all that respectability and status comes at a cost. Just once, Joyce and Odell want to break loose and taste life's wild side, without consequences . . .

Available wherever books and ebooks are sold.

Enjoy the following excerpt from *One House Over* . . .

CHAPTER 1

JOYCE

June 1934

O THER THAN MY PARENTS, I WAS THE ONLY OTHER PERSON AT THE supper table Sunday evening. But there was enough food for twice as many people. We'd spent the first five minutes raving about Mama's fried chicken, how much we had enjoyed Reverend Jessup's sermon a few hours ago, and other mundane things. When Daddy cleared his throat and looked at me with his jaw twitching, I knew the conversation was about to turn toward my spinsterhood.

"I hired a new stock boy the other day and I told him all about you. He is just itching to get acquainted. This one is a real nice, young, single man," Daddy said, looking at me from the corner of his eye.

I froze because I knew where this conversation was going: my "old maid" status. The last "real nice, young, single man" Daddy had hired to work in our store and tried to dump off on me was a fifty-five-year-old, tobacco-chewing, widowed grandfather named Buddy Armstrong. There had been several others before him. Each one had grandkids and health problems. Daddy was eighty-two, so to him anybody under sixty was "young." He and Mama had tried to have children for thirty years before she gave birth to me thirty years ago, when she was forty-eight. But I hadn't waited this long to settle for a husband who'd probably become disabled or die of old age before he could give me the children I desperately wanted.

I was tempted to stay quiet and keep my eyes on the ads for scarves in the new Sears and Roebuck catalog that I had set next to my plate. But I knew that if I didn't say something on the subject within the next few seconds, Daddy would harp on it until I did. Mama would join in, and they wouldn't stop until they'd run out of things to say. And then they would start all over again. I took a deep breath and braced myself. "Daddy, I work as a teacher's aide. What do I have in common with a *stock boy*?"

Daddy raised both of his thick gray eyebrows and looked at me like I was speaking a foreign language. "Humph! Y'all both single! That's what y'all got in common!" he growled.

"I can find somebody on my own!" I boomed. I never raised my voice unless I was really upset, like I was now.

Daddy shook his head. "Since you thirty now and still ain't got no husband—or even a boyfriend—it don't look like you having much luck finding somebody on your own, girl."

"Mac is right, Joyce. It's high time for you to start socializing again. It's a shame the way you letting life pass you by," Mama threw in. They were both looking at me so hard, it made me more uncomfortable than I already was. I squirmed in my seat and cleared my throat.

"Anyway, he said he can't wait to meet you. He is so worldly and sharp, he'll be a good person for you to conversate with."

"I hope you didn't say 'conversate' in front of this new guy. That's a word somebody made up," I scolded. "The correct word is *converse*."

Daddy gave me a pensive look and scratched his neck. "Hmmm. Well, *somebody* 'made up' all the words in every language, eh?"

"Well, yeah, but—"

"What difference do it make which one I used as long as he knew what I meant?"

"Yes, but—"

"Then I'll say conversate if I want to, and you can say converse. It's still English, and this is the only language I know—

and it's too complicated for me to be trying to speak it correct this late in the game. Shoot." My Daddy. He was a real piece of work. He winked at me before he bit off a huge chunk of corn-bread and started chewing so hard his ears wiggled. He swal-lowed and started talking again with his eyes narrowed. "I got a notion to invite him to eat supper with us one evening. He is a strapping man, so he'd appreciate a good home-cooked meal. I even told him how good you can cook, Joyce. . . ."

My parents had become obsessed with helping me find a hus-band. My love life—or lack of a love life—was a frequent subject in our house. One night I dreamed that they'd lined up men in our front yard and made me parade back and forth in front of them so they could inspect me. But even in a dream nobody wanted to marry me.

"What's wrong with this one? Other than him being just a stock boy?" I mumbled as I rolled my eyes.

"Why come you think something is wrong with him?" Daddy laughed but so far, nobody had said something funny enough to make me laugh. If anything, I wanted to cry.

"Because he wants to meet *me*," I said with my voice cracking. My self-esteem had sunk so low, and I felt so unworthy, I didn't know if I'd want a man who would settle for me. "He's probably homelier and sicklier than Buddy Armstrong." I did laugh this time.

"I met him and I sure didn't see nothing wrong with him," Mama piped in. She drank some lemonade and let out a mild burp before she continued. "He ain't nowhere near homely."

"Or sickly," Daddy added with a snort.

"And he's right sporty and handsome!" Mama sounded like a giddy schoolgirl. I was surprised to see such a hopeful look on her face. Despite all the wrinkles, liver spots, and about fifty pounds of extra weight, she was still attractive. She had big brown eyes and a smile that made her moon face look years younger. Unlike Daddy, who had only half of his teeth left, she still had all of hers. They were so nice and white, people often asked if they were real. She was the same pecan shade of brown as me and Daddy. But I had his small, sad black eyes and narrow face. He'd been completely bald since he was fifty and last week on my thirtieth birthday he'd predicted that if I had any hair left by the time I turned forty, it would probably all be gray. I'd found my first few strands of gray hair the next morning. "I know you'll like this one," Mama assured me with a wink. She reared back in her wobbly chair and raked her thick fingers through her thin gray hair. "You ain't getting no younger, so you ain't got much time left," she reminded.

"So you keep telling me," I snapped.

Mama sucked on her teeth and gave me a dismissive wave. "He got slaphappy when we told him about you. I bet he been beating the women off with a stick all his life."

Mama's taste in potential husbands for me was just as pathetic as Daddy's. But her last comment really got my attention because it sounded like a contradiction. "Why would a 'sporty and handsome' man get 'slaphappy' about meeting a new woman— especially if he's already beating them off with a stick?" I wanted to know.

Daddy gave me an annoyed look. "Don't worry about a little detail like that. And don't look a gift horse in the mouth. You ain't been out on a date since last year, and I know that must be painful. Shoot. When I was young, and before I married your mama, I never went longer than a week without courting somebody. At the rate you going, you ain't never going to get married."

I'd celebrated my thirtieth birthday eight days ago, but I felt more like a woman three times my age. Most of the adult females I knew were already married. My twenty-five-year-old cousin Louise had been married and divorced twice and was already engaged again. "I guess marriage wasn't meant for me," I whined. I suddenly lost my appetite, so I pushed my plate to the side.

"You ain't even touched them pinto beans on your plate, and you ate only half of your supper yesterday," Mama complained. "How do you expect to get a man if you ain't got enough meat on your bones? You already look like a lamppost, and you know colored men like thick women. Besides, a gal six feet tall like you need to eat twice as much as a shorter woman so there's enough food to fill out all your places."

"It ain't about how much I weigh," I said defensively. "Last year I weighed twenty pounds more than I do now, and it didn't make a difference. But . . . I wish I could shrink down to a normal height." I laughed, but I was serious. For a colored woman, being too tall was almost as bad as being too dark and homely. I wasn't as dark or homely as some of the women I knew, but I was the tallest and the only one my age still single.

"Well, look at it this way, baby girl. You ain't no Kewpie doll and you may be too lanky for anybody to want to marry you, but at least you got your health. A lot of women don't even have that." Daddy squeezed my hand and smiled. "And you real smart."

I was thankful that I was healthy and smart, but those things didn't do a damn thing for my overactive sex drive. If a man didn't make love to me soon, I was going to go crazy. And the way I'd been fantasizing about going up to a stranger in a beer garden or on the street and asking him to go to bed with me, maybe I had already lost my mind. "Can I be excused? I have a headache," I muttered, rubbing the back of my head.

"You said the same thing when we was having supper yesterday," Mama reminded.

"I had a headache then, too," I moaned. I rose up out of my chair so fast, I almost knocked it over. With my head hanging low, I shuffled around the corner and down the hall to my bedroom. I'd been born in the same room, and the way my life was going, I had a feeling I'd die in it too.

Branson was a typical small town in the southern part of Alabama. It was known for its cotton and sugarcane fields and beautiful scenery. Fruit and pecan trees, and flowers of every type and color decorated most of the residents' front and back yards. But things were just as gloomy here as the rest of the South.

Our little city had only about twenty thousand people and

most of them were white. Two of our four banks had crashed right after the Great Depression started almost five years ago. But a few people had been smart enough to pull their money out just in time. Our post office shared the same building with the police department across the street from our segregated cemetery.

Jim Crow, the rigid system that the white folks had created to establish a different set of rules for them and us, was strictly enforced. Basically, what it meant was that white people could do whatever they wanted, and we couldn't eat where they ate, sleep or socialize with them, or even sass them. Anybody crazy enough to violate the rules could expect anything from a severe beating to dying at the hands of a lynch mob. A lot of our neighbors and friends worked for wealthy white folks in the best neighborhoods, but all of the colored residents lived on the south side. And it was segregated too. The poor people lived in the lower section near the swamps and the dirt roads. The ones with decent incomes, like my family, lived in the upper section.

The quiet, well-tended street we lived on was lined with magnolia and dogwood trees on both sides. Each house had a neat lawn, and some had picket fences. The brown-shingled house with tar paper roofing and a wraparound front porch we owned had three bedrooms. The walls were thin, so when Mama and Daddy started talking again after I'd bolted from the supper table, I could hear them. And, I didn't like what they were saying.

"Poor Joyce. I just ball up inside when I think about how fast our baby is going to waste. I'm going to keep praying for her to find somebody before it's too late," Mama grumbled. "With her strong back she'd be a good workhorse and keep a clean house and do whatever else she'll need to do to keep a husband happy. And I'd hate to see them breeding hips she got on her never turn out no babies." Mama let out a loud, painful-sounding groan. "What's even worse is, I would hate to leave this world knowing she was going to grow old alone."

"I'm going to keep praying for her to get married too. But that might be asking for too much. I done almost put a notion like that out of my mind. This late in the game, the most we can expect is to fix her up with somebody who'll court her for a while, so she can have a little fun before she get too much older," Daddy grunted. "Maybe we ain't been praying hard enough, huh?"

"We been praying hard enough, but that ain't the problem," Mama snapped.

"Oh? Then what is it?"

"The problem is this girl is too doggone picky!" Mama shouted.

"Sure enough," Daddy agreed.

I couldn't believe my ears! My parents were trying to fix me up with a stock boy, not a businessman, and they thought I was being too picky. I wanted to laugh and cry at the same time. A lot of ridiculous things had been said to and about me. Being "too picky" was one of the worst because it couldn't have been further from the truth.

I had no idea how my folks had come to such an off-the-wall conclusion. I couldn't imagine what made them think I was too picky. I'd given up my virginity when I was fourteen to Marvin Galardy, the homeliest boy in the neighborhood. And that was only because he was the only one interested in having sex with me at the time.

I was so deep in thought, I didn't hear Daddy knocking on my door, so he let himself in. "You done gone deaf, too?" he grumbled.

"I didn't hear you," I mumbled, sitting up on my bed.

"You going to the evening church service with us? We'll be leaving in a few minutes."

"Not this time, Daddy. My head is still aching, so I think I just need to lie here and take it easy." I rubbed the side of my head.

"And it's going to keep on hurting if you don't take some pills."

"I'll take some before I go to sleep."

Daddy turned to leave, and then he snapped his fingers. "I forgot the real reason I came in here. Mother's going to Mobile tomorrow morning with Maxine Fisher to do some shopping and she'll be gone most of the day. If you ain't got no plans for lunch tomorrow and that headache is gone, I'll swing by the school around noon to pick you up and we can go to Mosella's. Monday is the only day peach cobbler is on the menu, and I been dying for some."

"You don't have to drive all the way from the store to pick me up. That's out of your way. One of the other aides has an appointment with her doctor in the same block, so I can ride with her and have her drop me off at the store. I need to pick up a few items anyway."

"That'll work," Daddy said, rubbing his chest. "I'll see you around noon then?"

"Okay, Daddy."

It was still light outside, but I went to bed anyway. Each day I slept more than I needed and wished I could sleep even more. At least then I wouldn't have to talk to people and walk around with a fake smile on my face.

Chapter 2

Odell

I WAS SO ANXIOUS TO GET BACK TO WORK, I COULDN'T WAIT FOR TO-morrow to come. I'd only been on my new job at MacPherson's for a week. It was a dyed-in-the-wool country convenience store with benches inside for people to sit on when they needed to take a break from their shopping. Regular customers could expect a complimentary pig foot or some lip-smacking pork rinds on certain days. I could already tell that this was the best job I ever had. It was a nice family-friendly business, and I was really looking forward to the experience, especially since I'd be working for colored folks. Mr. MacPherson didn't pay me that much to start, but as long as it covered my rent I didn't care. I was a born hustler, so I knew I'd find ways to cover my other expenses once I got a toe-hold on my new situation. Stocking shelves was much better than dragging along on farms and other odd jobs I'd done all my life. The small building where MacPherson's was located sat on a corner next to a bait shop. There was a sign printed in all capital letters in the front window that said: WE SELL EVERYTHING FROM APRONS TO MENS' PINSTRIPE SUITS. But they never had more than six or seven of each item in stock at a time. When inventory got low, the MacPhersons immediately replenished everything and gave their customers discounts when they had to wait on a certain item. The customers were happy because this kind of service kept them from having to make the eight-mile trip to nearby Butler where there was a Piggly Wiggly market and much bigger department stores.

People kept complaining about the Great Depression we was going through, but it didn't even faze me. Like almost every other colored person, I couldn't tell the difference because we'd been going through a "depression" all our lives. Some of the white folks who used to have enough money to shop at the better stores started shopping at MacPherson's. On my first day, me and Mr. MacPherson had to help a nervous blond woman haul a box of canned goods, some cleaning products, produce, toys, and even a few clothes to her car. The whole time she'd belly-ached to him about what a disgrace it was to her family that they had to shop where all the colored people shopped, something she'd never done before. In the next breath, she complimented him on how "happy-go-lucky" he was for a colored man, and be-cause of that he was "a credit to his race."

One of the things I noticed right away was how loosey-goosey the MacPhersons ran their business. Like a lot of folks, they didn't trust banks, especially since so many people had lost every cent and all the property they owned when the banks failed. One of the richest white families I used to pick cotton for had ended up flat broke and had to move to a tent city campground with other displaced families.

Preston "Mac" MacPherson and his wife, Millie, only kept enough in their checking account to cover their employees' checks and to pay their business expenses. I'd found that out from Buddy Arm-strong, the tubby, fish-eyed head cashier and the nosiest, grumpiest, and biggest blabbermouth elderly man I'd ever met. The other cashier, a pint-sized, plain-featured, widowed great-grandmother named Sadie Mae Glutz was almost as bad as Buddy.

On my first day, they'd started running off at the mouth be-fore the first morning break, telling me all kinds of personal things about people I had never met. Buddy and Sadie was good entertainment, so I pretended to be interested in their gossip and even egged them on. The MacPhersons were their favorite target. Even though it was supposed to be a company "secret," they wasted no time telling me that Mr. MacPherson kept most of his money locked up in his house. At the end of each day he'd pluck all the cash out of the two cash registers and stuff it into a brown paper bag.

"I hope that information don't get to the wrong person. I'd hate to hear about some joker busting into that house robbing such a nice elderly couple," I said.

"You ain't got to worry about nothing like that. Mac keeps a shotgun in the house," Buddy assured me.

"I hope he never has to use it," I chuckled.

"He done already done that," Sadie added. Before I could ask when and why, she continued. "A couple of years ago, some fool tried to steal Mac's car out of his driveway. Mac ran out just in time to stop that jackass."

"Did he kill him?" I asked, looking from Sadie to Buddy.

"Naw. He shot at him, but he missed," Buddy answered. "And that sucker took off in such a hurry, he ran clean out of his shoes. Then he had the nerve to try to steal another man's car in the same neighborhood. He wasn't so lucky that time. I was one of the pallbearers at his funeral."

"I'm glad Mr. MacPherson didn't kill that thief. He is such a nice man, I'd hate for him to get involved with the law," I stated.

"Thank you. Him and Millie got enough problems already. Especially trying to marry off that gal of theirs." Sadie shook her head and clucked her thick tongue. "She grown and still living at home. And she look like the kind of woman no man in his right mind would tangle with. She a whole head taller than me and probably twice as strong. If I seen her fighting a bear, I'd help the bear. Wouldn't you do the same thing, Buddy?"

"Sure enough." Buddy chuckled for a few seconds, and then he started yip-yapping about Joyce some more. "And she got the nerve to flirt with me almost every time I see her, with her *mugly* self."

"'Mugly'? What's that?" I asked.

"Oh, that's just a nicer way of calling somebody ugly. Anyway, she been messing with me ever since I started working here last September, grinning and sashaying in front of me like a shake dancer. But I would never get involved with a woman with feet bigger than mine. First time I make her mad, she'd stomp a hole in me."

This was the first time I'd heard about Joyce, and it wouldn't be the last. Every time things got slow on my first day, Buddy and Sadie would wander over to where I was stacking or reorganizing merchandise and start conversating and laughing about the MacPhersons' pitiful daughter.

"Y'all got me so curious now, I can't wait to meet this beast," I admitted, laughing along with them.

"You'll see exactly what we mean when you do meet her," Sadie told me.

"Why don't y'all like her? Is she mean-spirited, too?"

Buddy and Sadie gasped at the same time. "No, she ain't no mean person at all, and we do like her," Sadie claimed. "We talk about all the folks we know like this. But Joyce is such an oddball; we talk about her a little more than we do everybody else."

"I hope you'll like her too," Buddy threw in. "She ain't got many friends, so she need all the ones she can get."

By the end of the day, I had heard so many unflattering things about the MacPhersons' big-boned "old maid" daughter, it seemed like I'd known her for years. I felt so sorry for her. The next day when Mr. MacPherson bragged about how smart and nice and caring his only child was and how much he loved her, I told him I couldn't wait to meet her. I'd only said it to make him feel good, because I wanted to make sure I did everything possible for him to keep me on the payroll. I had heard that the stock boys before me had never lasted more than a few weeks. A couple had just up and quit, but the MacPhersons had fired all the others. I hoped that I'd get to stay a lot longer, or at least until I found a better job.

I had just enough money to last until I got my first paycheck. Mr. MacPherson had promised that if he was pleased with my work and I got to work on time, he'd eventually give me more responsibilities and more money. He really liked me and even told me I reminded him of himself when he was my age. I told him that if I looked half as good as he did when I got to be his age, I'd be happy. That made him blush and grin, and it made me realize that complimenting a man like him could win me a lot of points. It was true that I had a lot going for me in the looks department. But I never took it for granted. People had been telling me I was cute since I was a baby. My curly black hair, smooth Brazil nut brown skin, slanted black eyes, and juicy lips got me a lot of attention. One of the main things the women liked about me and complimented me on all the time was my height, which was six feet four.

Some women believed that old wives' tale that tall men had long sticks between their legs. I couldn't speak for other tall men, but I had enough manly meat between my thighs to keep the women I went to bed with sure enough happy. I wasn't just tall; I had a body like a prizefighter. Years of backbreaking farm labor had rewarded me with some muscles that wouldn't quit. Women couldn't keep their hands off me. When I was younger, I used to have to sneak out back doors in bars just to throw them off my trail. I was thirty-one now, so I still had a few good years left to find a wife and have children before my jism got too weak. I was between ladies now, and because my last two breakups had been so bad, I was in no hurry to get involved with another woman anytime soon. I changed my tune Monday afternoon when I met Mr. MacPherson's daughter.